THE HABITATION
OF THE BLESSED

A DIRGE FOR PRESTER JOHN VOLUME ONE

OTHER BOOKS BY CATHERYNNE M. VALENTE

*The Girl Who Circumnavigated Fairyland
    In A Ship Of Her Own Making*
Palimpsest
The Orphan's Tales: In the Night Garden
The Orphan's Tales: In the Cities of Coin and Spice
Under In The Mere
The Grass-Cutting Sword
Yume No Hon: The Book of Dreams
The Labyrinth

CRITICAL ACCLAIM FOR
CATHERYNNE M. VALENTE

"Catherynne M. Valente just knocks me flat with her use of language: rich, cool, opiated language, language for stories of strange love and hallucinated cities of the mind."
— Warren Ellis, author of *Transmetropolitan*

"Valente is writing the smartest, gentlest, deepest work in the field, and she's good enough to do it. I remain in awe."
— Daniel Abraham, author of The Long Price Quartet

"It's never enough to merely read a book like *Palimpsest,* it has to be imbibed, and it's sensuality fully savored."
— Nick Bantock, author of The Griffin and Sabine Trilogy

"There is something lyrical, something evocative and sinuous, about Valente's writing which manages to capture the magic of listening to someone speaking a story amidst the quiet and calm of a snatched moment. [...] Catherynne M. Valente enchants and enlightens in equal measure. She's the real McCoy, kids."
— *Strange Horizons*

"For everyone falling over themselves to find 'The next' who-the-heck-ever, forget that quest and hope that there's someone else out there as good as Valente, who sculpts bizarre, beautiful, ornate dreams into shimmering little jewel-like stories."
— *The Agony Column*

"Valente is a modern-day Scheherezade."
— *SFSite*

"In a genre where transparent prose is king, Valente's opaque approach is both refreshing and confrontational, challenging the genre to wonder when it became so afraid of words."
— *The Guardian*

"Catherynne M. Valente's first three novels earned her a reputation as a bold, skillful writer. Her latest, *The Orphan's Tales*, reaffirms that early acclaim... These are fairy tales that bite and bleed. Every moment of lyricism is countered by one of clear-eyed honesty, and sometimes the moments combine... Now we wait for Valente to bend her knee again and make more myths."
— *The Washington Post*

"The earlier novels and poetry collections have established her as a distinctive presence in contemporary fantasy's landscape, but *The Orphan's Tales* still might make her seem like a spontaneous mountain."
— *Bookslut*

"In short, *In the Night Garden* is downright folk-funky, with DJ Cat V scratching and mixing myth and lore with an original blend given previously untold life by a writer who ultimately made me ponder the question of what happens when a never-ending story ends, while almost making me forget to ask about the power in the name of the teller. *The Orphan's Tales* is the poet, short fiction writer, and novelist maximizing her entire skill set in an offering that caters to the sensibilities of the fan of all forms."
— *Fantasy Book Spot*

"We all have our individual ideas about Sappho, but my vision of her, reincarnated into the American 21st century, is Catherynne M. Valente."
— Diane Wakoski, author of *The Motorcycle Betrayal Poems*

"Catherynne Valente's ambitious, impassioned poems plunge with headlong energy through Western legend and Japanese fairytale, myth and madness, sin and suffering, the alphabet and the biblical apocrypha, never flinching at rage, violence, desire, or dread. As its name suggests, *Apocrypha* is a book of wonders."
— Sandra M. Gilbert, Professor Emerita of English
at the University of California, Davis

"She writes with a casual and ruthless grace, like a lioness or the sea. Calling her work simply delicate does it an injustice. Delicacy implies frailty, and her work is powerful. The precision of her words is not done in brushstrokes but in engraving: the line may be fine and is certainly fair, but it bites deep. Her voice is not dewy cobwebs, but stars and steel."
— *The Green Man Review*

"Astonishing work! Valente's endless invention and mythic range are breathtaking. It's as if she's gone night-wandering, and plucked a hundred distant cultures out of the air to deliver their stories to us."
— Ellen Kushner, author of *The Privilege of the Sword*

THE HABITATION
OF THE BLESSED

A DIRGE FOR PRESTER JOHN VOLUME ONE

CATHERYNNE M. VALENTE

NIGHT SHADE BOOKS
SAN FRANCISCO

First Edition

ISBN: 978-1-59780-199-7

Printed in Canada

Night Shade Books
http://www.nightshadebooks.com

For my tribe, the motley, beautiful lot of you.
Where we are together, there is a blessed land.

Lake of Feathers

Simurgh

Baka
(City of the Cranes)

Gog and Magog

Azenach

Gates of
Alisaunder

The Rimal

Ecbatana
Segunda

PRESBITERI
JOHANNIS, SI
VE, ABISSO
RVM IMPERII
DESCRIPTIO

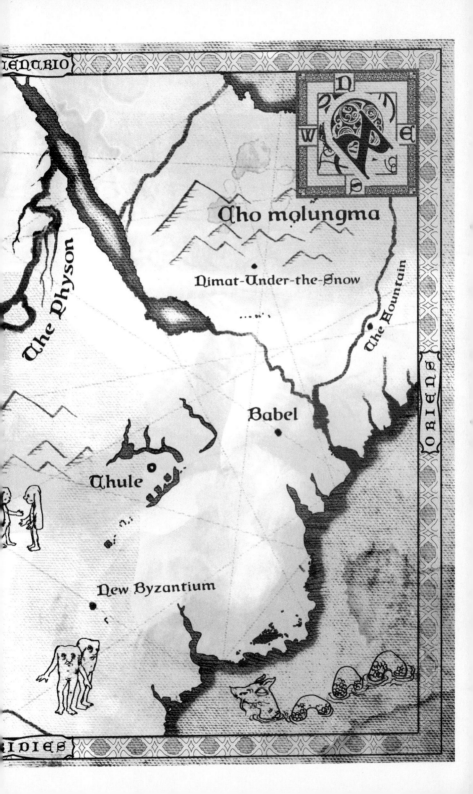

J ohn, priest by the almighty power of God and the might of our Lord Jesus Christ, king of kings and Lord of Lords, to his friend Emanuel, Prince of Constantinople: Greetings, wishing him health, prosperity, and the continuance of divine favor.

Our Majesty has been informed that you hold our Excellency in love and that the report of our greatness has reached you. Moreover, we have heard through our treasurer that you have been pleased to send to us some objects of art and interest that our Exaltedness might be gratified thereby. I have received it in good part, and we have ordered our treasurer to send you some of our articles in return...

Should you desire to learn the greatness and Excellency of our Exaltedness and of the land subject to our scepter, then hear and believe: I, Presbyter Johannes, the Lord of Lords, surpass all under heaven in virtue, in riches, and in power; seventy-two kings pay us tribute... In the three Indies our Magnificence rules, and our land extends beyond India, where rests the body of the holy apostle Thomas. It reaches towards the sunrise over the wastes, and it trends toward deserted Babylon near the Tower of Babel. Seventy-two provinces, of which only a few are Christian, serve us. Each has its own king, but all are tributary to us.

—The Letter of Prester John,
Delivered to Emperor Emanuel Comnenus
Constantinople, 1165
Author Unknown

We who were Westerners find ourselves transformed into Orientals. The man who had been an Italian or a Frenchman, transplanted here, has become a Galilean or a Palestinian. A man from Rheims or Chartres has turned into a citizen of Tyre or Antioch. We have already forgotten our native lands. To most of us they have become territories unknown.

—The Chronicle of Fulcher of Chartres
Jerusalem, 1106

THE FIRST
MOVEABLE SPHERE

There is also in our territory a sandy sea without water. For the sand moves and swells into waves like the sea and is never still. It is not possible to navigate this sea or cross it by any means, and what sort of country lies beyond is unknown... three days' journey from this sea there are mountains from which descends a waterless river of stones, which flows through our country to the sandy sea. Three days in the week it flows and casts up stones both great and small, and carries with it also wood to the sandy sea. When the river reaches the sea the stones and wood disappear and are not seen again. While the sea is in motion it is impossible to cross it. On the other four days it can be crossed.

Between the sandy sea and the mountains we have mentioned a desert...

—The Letter of Prester John, 1165

THE CONFESSIONS OF
HIOB VON LUZERN, 1699

I am a very bad historian. But I am a very good miserable old man. I sit at the end of the world, close enough to see my shriveled old legs hang over the bony ridge of it. I came so far for gold and light and a story the size of the sky. But I have managed to gather for myself only a basket of ash and a kind of empty sorrow, that the world is not how I wished it to be. The death of faith is tasteless, like dust. Such dust I have unearthed by Your direction, Lord, such emerald dust and ruby sand that I fear one day I shall wake and my vision will be clouded in green and scarlet, and I shall never more see the world but through that veil of jewels. I say I have unearthed this tale—I mean I have taken it from the earth; I have made it no longer *of* the earth. I have made the tale an indentured slave, prostrate beneath air and rain and heaven, and tasked it to burrow under the great mountains and back to the table at which I supped as a boy, to sit instead among barrels of beer and wheels of cheese, and stare at the monks who raised me with such eyes as have pierced me these many weeks. They sent me here, which is to say You sent me here, my God, and I do not yet have it in me to forgive either of you.

But I plead forgiveness for myself. I am a hypocrite—but You knew that. I desire clemency for the tale I send back over the desert. It is not the tale I wished to tell—but that is not the fault of the tale. If a peasant loathes his son for failing to become king, blame must cleave to *him*, and not to his poor child. Absolve this tale, Lord. Make it pure and good again. Do not let it suffer

5

because your Hiob is a poor storyteller, and struck that peasant child for lack of a crown. The tale is not weak, yet I am. But in Truth is the Light of Our Lord, though the beacons and blazes of centuries gone have grown diffident and pale of late, still I have never lied. I could sell my soul to the demons of historiography and change this tale to suit my dreams. I could do it and no one would think less of me. It has been done before, after all. But before my Lord I lay the pain and anguish of the truth, and ask only to be done with it all.

Our troupe arrived in the provinces of Lavapuri in the Year of Our Lord 1699, in search of the Source of the Indus River. Officially, we had been charged to shine a light in a dark place, to fold up the Dove of Christ into our saddlebags and bear Him unto the poor roughened souls of the Orient. Of course You know better, Lord. You saw us back home, huddled together and dreaming of gryphons and basilisks. And in the crush of our present heat and dry wind I well recalled those frigid, thrilling nights at home, crouched in the refectory, when a man was compelled to break the ice on his milk before he could drink. In the cold lamplight we whispered brother to brother. We hoped to find so much in the East, hoped to find a palace of amethyst, a fountain of unblemished water, a gate of ivory. Brushing the frost from our bread, we dreamed, as all monks had since the wonderful Letter appeared, of a king in the East called Prester John, who bore a golden cross on his breast. We whispered and gossiped about him like old women. We told each other that he was as strong as a hundred men, that he drank from the Fountain of Youth, that his scepter held as jewels the petrified eyes of St. Thomas.

Bring word of him, the Novices said to me. *Tell us how the voice of Prester John sounds in your ears.*

Bring gifts to him, my Brothers said to me. *Tell us how the hand of Prester John weighs on your shoulder.*

Bring oaths to us, the Abbot said to me. *Tell me how he will deliver us from the Unfaithful. Also in your travels, if the chance presents itself without too much trial, endeavor to spread the Name of Christ into such lands as you may.*

Yes, they did tell me to convert and enlighten the savages.

But my Brothers' mouths were so full of golden crosses and the names of kings. I could hardly hear them.

The Indus seeped green as a weeping eye, and our horses' delicate ankles did not love it well. The dust of the mountains was red beneath grey, and to me it seemed as if the stones bled. The younger Brothers quarreled among themselves as to who should have the delight of hunting the shaggy, truculent sheep of these parts, and who should have the trial of staying with old Hiob in case he needed a less wizened mind to recall scripture and blessings, should we ever meet a soul in need of scouring in these crags of the dead. Two of our number had died already: Brother Uriel fell from a stone jut to his death, and Brother Gundolfus perished of an insect bite which grew to the size of an apple before he showed it to us. I am ashamed to say I was overcome by thirst, and Brother Alaric was compelled to administer their Rites. We buried them both beside the pilgrim road.

But I do not wish to furnish You with a litany of the sufferings of my small band—You know where we failed, where we starved. You know how many had gone to Your same cruel river. Truly, only You know the exact number of fools who came strident and arrogant, making the same demands of the locals: that they must lead them to the cathedral-palace of Prester John on the double, and do not forget to point out the Fountain of Youth along the way! You know how the mountain-folk laughed at them, or called them mad, or flayed them and gave those pilgrims over to the Indus to decide their fates. Uriel and Gundolfus were good men, and at least they died still hoping to see the Priest-king one day; their goodness has been faithfully recorded, and Christ alone knows their sins.

The sky bolstered a spiteful sun, whose dull, thirsty light was scarcely enough to lift our eyes to heaven. Yet the river was true, and cold, and we drank often. Sharp, spicy leaves were all we found to eat for many days—all the squabbling over who was the greater hunter meant little when the sheep were cleverer than the monks. It was not until the thirteenth day—unlucky, yes, but Hiob cannot be blamed for happenstance!—since we had entered the coriander-strewn provinces of Lavapuri that we came upon a village, and a woman, and a word.

The village was mean: twelve small huts and a larger house, some local fiefdom. The village, too, glowered grey and dull in our sight, as though it had burned once, so fast that the ash remained in the shapes of daub and stick huts, in the shape of scraggle-haired goats, in the shape of sharp-ribbed children. The sun lies too close to the earth in this place.

The woman was tall, her clay-colored skin dark and sun-burned beneath smudges of charcoal and dust. She wore a yellow robe, wet at the hem where she had been in the river, pulling reeds into her basket to wrap the evening's rooster, which she carried by the broken neck in one slim hand. And so she seemed to me a candle in the grey mere, a benevolent Virgin in gold, her arms all full of green. Her eyes unsettled me, being a shade of dusty gold like an illuminated page, and tired, greatly grieved. Thin, white hair prickled on her arms and shoulders, not unpleasant to look at, though I am not ac-customed to marking a woman's bodily hair, and felt a dim flame in my cheeks even then, noticing how her silky down fairly glowed against her dark skin. I went to her, with three of my novices clutching crosses to their young and rampant breasts. I stumbled in my eagerness—I beg forgiveness for that indignity.

"Lady," I said to her in the liquid syllables of her own Mu-ghal dialect, for in Your kindness You graced me with a love for foreign tongues, and an ease in their learning. "Tell me!" I said to her, as every fool priest must have done to every poor unbaptized goat-wife since this whole business began. "Where is the great king Prester John?"

She blinked at me, no doubt surprised to hear her own ululating dialect spill from the mouth of a foreigner, and then bent her head as if in prayer, as if in acknowledgment of some old sorrow long past its sting, and her scalp gleamed dully in the slant-light. When she raised her head, she looked down the long scrub-specked plain from whence she had come and sighed through her nose, her lips clamped tight against speech, her reeds already wilting.

Then she spoke her word. Everything that followed was born in that moment, from her mouth, in the dusk and the dust and all of us waiting on her like suitors on a princess.

The word was: *Gone.*

How can such a man be gone? The Letter tells us he has clapped up the Cup of Life within his treasure-house, that the Fountain of Youth bubbles in his courtyard like a pretty Italian marble. Surely his heart swells still; five hundred years is but a cough in the long breath of such a potentate. We were not the first to come with a vision of him blazing like the Sacred Heart in our bones—but none yet had reported him dead, or even reduced in splendor. Yet the woman in yellow shook her head and would not say his name or her own. She took us instead up the small path to the low-roofed house of her Lord, who was called Abbas and presided grandly over a field of rice, fourteen sheep, and a healthy family of breeding goats. The villagers lounged in his hall, laughingly gulped his fermented milk, lustily ate his rice, kicked his one-eared dog and called him the son of a second wife while he smiled ruefully at me, as if to say: *What may a Lord do on this earth but love the roughest of men and care for them as children?*

Our yellow-eyed guide knelt at a fire set into the floor of the Lord's house, and put her reed-wrapped rooster under the embers. Its scent broke the air into savory sighs, and Abbas kissed her brow as though she were a favored sister, or a daughter whose mother had gone before her. He cupped her face in his brown hand, and it was *he* who fed *her* when the chicken had done! She knelt before him, though I did not see in her the submissive aspect of a demure and humble woman. It seemed only that she felt it most comfortable to kneel while Abbas placed each golden slice of roasted flesh carefully on her tongue with his own fingers, as if she were the queen and he a slave bound to her ankle. The hall was quiet during this strange rite; the shabby courtiers did not speak nor drink nor torment hounds, and in the corner of the hall, a man wept softly.

By the time she had finished her meal, the sky had cooled, a flush of pink rising in the east, as if the deeds of men embarrassed the heavens. Slowly, conversation took hold of the room once more. A pleasant sort of flute and drum struck up, played by two children, twins most likely, with our guide's same downy white hair on their bony shoulders. The tune felt sad against my ears, and against those of Brother Alaric and the others as well, if my guess is correct. When the men had returned to gossiping about whose daughter had snuck about with whose son, the woman in yellow left her Lord and took up my hand in hers. The eyes of Abbas followed us as we withdrew from the hall, and those of all the village, too.

She would take only myself: the novices Abbas bade to stay, plying them with goat-liver and chickpea-mash—for once I was not sorry to miss a meal. Young men are often satiated by a little rich food and strong drink, but at my age my liver cannot bear very much of anyone else's. In the red shadows of those toothed mountains my silent Virgil took me through that long plain of garlic-flowers and withered plants, a field agued and sallow. Beneath my feet, O Lord, Your earth sagged in its dying. There are places older than Avignon, older than Rome, and the world there is so tired it cannot rouse itself, even for the sake of guests.

We reached the edge of the plain, where it shed all growing things and began a sheer rise into blue stone and thirst. There she knelt as Eve beside a tree, and beside that tree I laid too all my faith and learning, all that which is Hiob and not another man, and nevermore from that spot would my soul move.

This tree bore neither apples nor plums, but books where fruit should sprout. The bark of its great trunk shone the color of parchment, its leaves a glossy, vibrant red, as if it had drunk up all the colors of the long plain through its roots. In clusters and alone books of all shapes hung among the pointed leaves, their covers obscenely bright and shining, swollen as peaches, gold and green and cerulean, their pages thick as though with juice, their silver ribbonmarks fluttering in the spiced wind.

I leapt like a boy to catch them up in my hands—the boughs arched thick and high, higher than any chestnut in our cloister orchards, knottier than the hoary pines which cling to the sea-stone with roots like arms. In Eden no such tree would have dared to grow so high and embarrass the Lord on his Chair. But in that place I felt with a shudder and chill that You had turned Your Eye away, and many breeds of strangeness might be permitted in Its absence.

I managed to snatch but one sweet fruit between my fingertips—a little brown hymnal that had been a fair feast for worms and parrots. I opened its sleek pages—a waft of perfume assailed my senses. Oh! They smelled like crisp apples soaked in brandy! The worms had had the best of the thing, but there on the frontispiece, I saw a lovely script, elegant and sure, and in a language I could read only with difficulty, a tongue half-infidel and half-angelic, I read:

Physikai Akroaskeos, or,
The Book of Things Made and Things Born
Authored by the Anti-Aristotle of Chandrakant on the Occasion of his Wife's Death
in the Seventeenth Year of Queen Abir
Translated and Transcribed by Hagia of the Blemmyae
during several Very Pleasant Afternoons during
the Lenten Fast, commonly Called the Weeks of Eating in
Secret, in New Byzantium, Under an Ink-Nut Tree.

Only two pages remained intact, the others ruined, a rich feast for some craven bird—and in my heart I cursed the far raven in whose belly my lost pages whispered to its black gizzard. You see? I already thought of them as mine. I touched the lonely, clinging page with a finger, and it seemed to brown like the flesh of a pear beneath my skin:

As an indication of this, take the well-known Antinoë's Experiment: if you plant a bed and the rotting wood and the worm-bitten sheets in the deep earth, it will certainly and with the hesitation of no more than a season, which is to say no more than an ear of corn or a stalk of barley, send up shoots. A bed-tree will come up out of the fertile land, its fruit four-postered, and its leaves will unfurl as green pillows, and its stalk will be a deep cushion on which any hermit might rest. Every child knows this. It is art that changes, that evolves, and nature that is stationary.

However, since this experiment may be repeated with bamboo or gryphon or meta-collinarum or trilobite, perhaps it is fairer to say that animals and their parts, plants and simple bodies are artifice, brother to the bed and the coat, and that nature is constituted only in the substance in which these things may be buried—that is to say, soil and water, and no more.

A fat orange worm squirmed out of the *o* in Antinoë, and I flung the hymnal away in disgust. Immediately I flushed with shame and crawled for it, clutched it back, worm and all. A book is worth a worm or two, even vermin so fat and gorged as the one which even then oozed around the spine unconcernedly. I should have honored all Thy creatures, my Lord, and bowed to the worm, who after all, came first to this feast. I seized the last page, which tore free in my hand with a sound like a child's cry. It read:

That which is beloved is the whole of creation.
Yet there must be an essential affinity, a thing which might be called the blood of the spheres, which exists between and among that which we have determined is artifice and that which we have determined is natural, e.g. Pentexore and all it contains and the soil and water which produce Pentexore and what folk call "creation." For if it is created, it cannot be natural!

In my heart I see all things connected by diamond threads, and those threads I call the stuff of affinity. But I am an old man, and my son makes the palm-wine far too strong these days, and the sun burns my pate.

It is with these thoughts in my heart that I go to bury you, my sweet Pythias, in the black field where you planted sugar cane last spring, beside your orange bride's veil, whose gauzy flowers still blow in the salt-wind off of the Rimal. It is with these thoughts that I will water the bed of veils and cane all winter long, and hope to see your face swell like fruit from some future hanging bough.

"Is there no more?" I cried.

The woman in yellow shrugged her downy shoulders. Finally, she spoke, a full sentence, falling reluctantly from her mouth like a costly jewel.

"Birds and beasts must feast as men do. I do not deny them their sustenance."

In a madness I turned from her, and in a madness I clambered up into the scarlet tree as no man my age should do, reaching for the book-fruit, stretching out my veiny fingers to them. They glittered and swung away from my grip in the hot breezes, the green and the gold fluttering, the covers stamped with serpents, with crosses, with curved swords, with a girl whose right arm was a long wing.

Below me, my guide made a sign with her long fingers. *Three*, her hand said. *Three alone.*

Of course, it must forever and always be three. Three is Thy number, O Lord, of Thy Son and Thy Spirit. How wicked of me, no better than a worm or a raven, to strip the tree for my own gorging. I breathed to calm my heart and reached out again, to the brambled deeps of the tree. I sought out the most complete volumes, in the nests of branches where no hoopoe crept, and this time my grip fell firmly on them, cool and firm as apples.

I drew forth first: a golden book bearing a three-barred cross on its cover. Second: a green antiphonal with a wax seal over its pages that showed a strange, elongated ear. Lastly I strained to pluck, furthest from my reach, a book as scarlet as the leaves of the great tree. A pair of staring eyes embossed on its cover seemed to rifle my soul for riches, finding less than they hoped for. Cradled in the fork of the tree, I opened the pages of my last ripe fruit, my prize, and on the page was the same certain hand as had recorded the strange science of Anti-Aristotle. But it was not the same book—the paper shone a pale, fresh green, and small paintings grinned and gamboled at the edges. Perhaps the same scribe had copied both—to be sure many books in our Library bear my own hand.

I bent my face close to the script, squinting—and onto that page my heart fell out, for the sweet-smelling book promised no hope.

We carried the body of my husband down to the river, he who was once called king, called Father, called, in the most distant of days, Prester John.

The river churned: basalt, granite, marble, quartz—sandstone, limestone, soapstone. Alabaster against obsidian, flint against agate. Eddies of jasper slipped by, swirls of schist, carbuncle and chrysolite, slate, beryl, and a sound like shoulders breaking.

Fortunatus the Gryphon carried the body which had been called John on his broad and fur-fringed back—how his wings were up-raised like banners, gold and red and bright! Behind his snapping tail followed the wailing lamia twelve by twelve, molting their iridescent skins in grief.

Behind them came shrieking hyena and crocodiles with their great black eyes streaming tears of milk and blood.

Even still behind these came lowing tigers, their colors banked, and in their ranks sciopods wrapped in high black stockings, carrying birch-bark cages filled with green-thoraxed crickets singing out their dirges.

The panotii came behind them, their great and silken ears drawn over their bodies like mourning veils.

The astomii followed, their mouthless faces wretched, their great noses sniffing at the tear-stitched air. At their heels walked the amyctryae, their mouths pulled up over their heads as if to hide from grief.

The red and the white lions dragged their manes in the dust; centaurs buried their faces in blue-veined hands.

The meta-collinara passed, their feet clung with hill-dust, clutching their women's breasts while their swan-heads bobbed in time to some unheard dirge of their own.

The peacocks closed the blue-green eyes of their tails.

The tensevetes came, ice glittering in their elbows, the corners of their eyelids, the webbing of their fingers, the points of their terrible teeth. And from all these places they melted, woeful water dripping into the dusty day.

The soft-nosed mules threw up their heads in broken-throated braying.

The panthers stumbled to their black and muscled knees, licking the soil from their tears.

The blue cranes shrieked and snapped their sail-like wings sorrow-ward.

On spotted camels rode the cyclops, holding out into the night lanterns which hung like rolling, bloodshot eyes, and farther in the procession came white bears, elephants, satyrs playing mourn-slashed pipes, pygmies beating ape-skin drums, giants whose staves drew great furrows in the road, and the dervish-spinning cannibal choir, their pale teeth gleaming.

Behind these flew low the four flame-winged phoenix, last of their race.

Emeralds rolled behind like great wheels, grinding out their threnodies against the banks.

And after all of these, feet bare on the sand, skirts banded thick and blue about her waist, eyes cast downward, bearing her widow's candle in both hands, walked Hagia of the Blemmyae, who tells this tale.

I sat in the house of Abbas, my habit and hood full of fruit. The book-plums left a sticky honey on my hands, and they tasted, oh, I can remember it still—of milk and fig and a basket of African coconuts Brother Gregor once brought home to the refectory from sojourns south. I stared at my precious three books with the eyes of a starving child—could I not somehow devour them all at once and know their contents entire? Unfair books. You require so much time! Such a meal of the mind is a long, arduous feast indeed. And then I was seized with terror: What if they rotted as fruit will do? What if time and air could steal from me words, passages, whole chapters? I could not choose; I could not *bear* to choose, and the liver-scented snoring of my novices rose up to the rafters.

I decided to make a liturgy of my reading. I would fashion my work in the image of Thy Holy Church. I would read and copy for an hour from each book, so that they would all rot—and I too, in my slower way—at the same pace, and no book should feel slighted by preference for another. All those fleshy, apple-sweet riches I meant to bear home intact to my Brothers in the cold of Luzerne.

I could choose no other than the book with the golden cross

on its cover to begin: I am ever and always the man that I am, a man of God and the Cross, and that cannot be altered. I believe now that You put these books in my path, O Lord, with Your mark upon them so that I should know that You moved on the face of my fate as once on the deep waters of the unmade world.

I reached for salvation, and opened its boards like curtains.

THE WORD IN THE QUINCE
an Account of My Coming to the Brink of the World,
and What I Found There.
As told by John of Constantinople
Committed to Eternity by his Wife,
Hagia, who was afterward called Theotokos

Chapter the First, in which a Man is delivered into *India
Ultima* by means of a Most Unusual Sea, and thereby
forgets the names of the Churches of Constantinople.

S alt and sand sprayed against the hull, which the roasting
wind had peeled of scarlet paint and bared of gilt. The
horizon was a golden margin, the sea a spectral page. Caps
of dusty foam tipped the waves of depthless sand, swelling and
sinking, little siroccos opening their dry and desultory mouths.
Whirlpools of dead branches snapped and lashed the bulging
sides of the listing *qarib*; sand scoured her planks, grinding
off crenellations and erasing the faces of a row of bronze lions
meant to spray fire into the sails of enemies. The name of the
ship was once *Christotokos*, but the all-effacing golden waves
had scraped it to *Tokos*, and thus new-baptized, the little ship
crested and fell with the whim of the inland sea.

I huddled against the wretched mast. A few days previously, a
night-storm had visited this poor vessel, and its boiling clouds
littered the deck of the ship with small dun mice. They tasted
the mast, found it good, and stripped it to a spindly stick. In
the morning, they leapt overboard as one creature, and I, lone
inhabitant of the wretched *Tokos,* watched as they bounded
away on the surface of the sand, buffeted by little licking waves,
unconcerned, their bellies full of mast. I captained this thin
remnant of naval prowess as best I could: shuddering, blister-
lipped, no sailor, no oarsman, not even a particularly strong
swimmer. My teeth hurt in my jaw, and my hands would not

17

stop shaking—the true captain had leapt overboard in despair—a month past, now? Two?—and the navigator followed, then the cook, and finally the oarsmen. One by one as the sand snapped off their instruments they leapt overboard into the dust like mast-fed mice. But the sea did not bear them up, and they drowned screaming. They each watched the others sink into the glitter and grime, but believed in their final wild moments that theirs would be that lucky leap that found solid land. That they would be blessed above the others. Each by each, I watched the sand fill up their surprised and gaping mouths.

I ate the sail one night and dreamed of honey. The stars overhead hissed at me like cats.

Every morning, I prayed against the wheel of the ship, knees aching against the boards, the *Ave Maria* knotted like a gag in my mouth, peeling my lips open against those blasting hot winds that always smelled of red rock and bone-meal. But Mary did not come for me, no blue-veiled mother balancing on the shattered oars, torso roped with light. Still, I counted the beads of an invisible rosary, my body wind-dry of tears. The dawns were identical and crystalline, and the sand kept its own counsel, carrying the ship where it willed, with no oar or sail to defy its will.

Some days, I seemed to recall that my name was John. Searching my memory, I found Constantinople lying open as a psalter, the glittering quays blue and green and full of splashing mackerels, the trees dripping with green peacocks and pomegranates—and the walls so high! *And I,* I thought, *I myself sat upon those walls.* I remembered the city's name, but not my own. A scribe with kind eyes sat at my side, and drank quince-wine with me as the sun spent itself gaudily over golden domes behind us. Mosaics glowed in my heart, dim as a dream, removed pebble by pebble and replaced and removed again as the whims of Patriarchs and Empresses decreed—until like my ship no gilt remained, and seabirds began to make off with the cobalt-stained eyes of Christ and Evangelist alike, according to whatever laws concerning icons seagulls and pelicans possessed.

With sand in my ears I remembered, with difficulty, pressing my cheek against the cool little stones, against the face of God, half in darkness beneath a towering window. Then, my feet knew the way to the tomb of Nestorius, to the hard, cold shadows there, the font with its porphyry rim. It all swam in my head, sloshing like a tide, as if I were full of the water that had abandoned this place. I remembered horses racing in the Hippodrome dust, an Empress's hair plaited in gold.

But if I am honest, most days, I couldn't even remember the taste of that quince-wine. I lay on the deck and tried to die. Perhaps God had simply taken pity on me, and erased quince from the face of the world, so that it could not hurt me to know how far I had strayed from any branch heavy with rough-skinned fruit.

Thus I lived on the sea of sand, in fear of storms and more mice. I ate my monk's habit, too, after the sail was gone. It tasted only of myself, my own sweat and sickness, and I was wracked with it for days. But the bone-bare ocean was not entirely without pity. After some indeterminate number of days and leagues, the waves began to spit spectacular fish up onto the decks at dusk, sinuous beasts with long, twisted horns and scales of sapphire and gold that I had to chip from their skin with the chisel of the poor, dirt-drowned carpenter. The fish-skins clattered to the decks with tinny, tinkling sounds, and all the corners of the *qarib* glittered with piscine corpses. I gouged out their wet golden innards, soft as water. Under the scales and gleaming livers I found the sweetest possible flesh, delicate and translucent as moonlight. I drank the blood of the sand-fish through tortured lips, slurping the cool, raw meat from their knobby bones.

Not long after the advent of the fish, the ship learned to speak.

The Flesh may die, but never the Word, not even the Word in the Flesh, whispered the mouse-hewn holes in the mast. The sun blazed through those holes like a seraph's many faces, and I listened obediently to all their sermons. After all, the ship spoke words I knew so well, somewhere deep in my desiccated stomach: the holy writ of Nestorius, condemning the Catholic heresy that Christ was one, indivisible entity, an ugly idea, both preposterous and obscene.

When I was a young man in Constantinople—was I a young man in Constantinople? Was I ever a young man? In my mind, the summers there stained thousands of blue silk beds black with sweat, and I cooled myself in the halls of the order of Nestorius. The incense made me giddy, the incense and the droning voice of the *diakonos* wobbling around my ears like a bee flexing his wings. The mosaic floated above me, the pebbled veil of Mary in her floating mandorla like a sea-ray, alien and gorgeous. Her rough mouth seemed to twist in the smoke and show blackness beneath, blackness to the depths of her, where there had never been light, only a child, his umbilicus fat and veined.

The Flesh may die, but never the Word, not even the Word in the Flesh, came the phlegmatic voice of the *diakonos*. Mary's lips contorted above, wide as a fist. She seemed to speak only to me, into the bowl of my heart: *The Logos is perfect, light made manifest. It is the Word of God. You must see it in your mind suspended upon the Body of Christ, a lamprey affixed to the flank of a shark.* I laughed at the image then, my voice high and ridiculous under the dome, and Mary clamped her mouth shut.

I had a son, Mary seemed to whisper tightly, warped by the summer heat and the scented smoke pressing her cracked stone cheeks like bellows. I felt dizzy. *I had a son like any other son. Is it my fault the Logos loved him? That the lamprey held him tight?*

They took that mosaic down in the winter, when the new Patriarch took his mitre and announced that icons were the work of demons tempting us to worship stone and paint and gold instead of the ineffable substance of Our Lord. I remember the smells of the new image-less world as if they were paintings—winter lemons washing the air with their peppery rinds, the sea crusting the streets with salt. I wept, in private, for the loss of my Mary—but they brought her back just before I took my vows, when the old Patriarch died and the new one changed the game once more. Seagulls cried out above bloody Basilicas as the icon-breakers were shown the error of their doctrine, and everyone was free to make wretched, lopsided paintings of God again. It was exhausting. But Mary's black eyes burned at my back as I repeated my holy vows. She said nothing, her stone lips pursed and thin.

The Flesh may die, but never the Word, not even the Word in the Flesh. The mast whistled in the wind, and its voice was not the voice of the old *diakonos*, nor Mary, but something else, raspy and pale and harsh. I snarled at it, shaking, fresh sand spattering my beard, but the dome of the sky was unmoved. I begged it to be silent, and it laughed, a shower of sunbeams scattering over the deck.

In this way did I keep myself from the despair of the sailors who bore me to this waste: I tended to Mary-in-the-Mast like a fresh-shaved novice. I ministered my parish of golden fishes. John, salt-spackled and wind-mad, kept his church. I cried to the sands and promised the life within that I would not falter, would not forget, and perish quince, Mary, Constantinople, forever from the Earth. The sea did not answer, but I feared that soon the fish would begin to speak as well, and their voices would be like horses snorting and thundering in the Hippodrome, scrabbling hooves rounding bronze tripods as they draw so close to the end.

It became my habit to fashion a blue cross each morning from the horns of the sapphire-fish, lashed together with their ropy, golden intestines. The sea of sand was unwilling to tolerate this new divinity, to allow its lone mendicant friar to consort with any other deity but itself. When the moon clattered like alms in the cup of the sky, the waves tore down my poor, wet cross and were satisfied. In the mornings, I set it up again, and said my prayers. But as the suns and moons rode their tracks, I began to lengthen my salutations, so that in addition to my phantom rosary, I would recite the names of all the churches of Byzantium I could remember. For if God could remove quince from the cosmos for the sake of His lost servant, what might He do to that half-imagined painted city of domes and mackerel? With my hair knotted back and my red skin bleeding, I called out to the whistling mast: *Holy Apostles! Sergius and Bacchus! Theotokos Panachrantos! Christ Pantokrator! John the Baptist!*

Theodoroi! Theodosia! Euphemia! John of Studius! The Myre-laion! And Hagia Sophia, oh, the Sophia!

In time this seemed not quite enough to keep God from cupping His Hand over Constantinople and raising it out of the Bosphorus of my heart like a dripping fish-heart plucked from the world. The streets and alleys and grocers faded from my mind, scratched out by sand. So I began to add the names of all the people I had known, the presbyters and *diakonoi*, the scribes and fishermen, the dancers and date-sellers. *Damaskenos with your damned bee-voice, Hieronymos whose hand was so tight and clear on the vellum, Isidora with your sweet kisses, Alki of harbor-side, your swordfish blue as death! Niko who sold artichokes with tight green leaves armoring their hearts, Tychon who drank fennel-liquor until he vomited after evening services! Pelagios with such a voice, Basileus the eunuch, Clio with her belts of coins, Cyprios with his seven daughters! Phocas made beer and Symeon was a calligrapher, but his wife could not read. Iasitas was the man to get your lettuce from, and old Euphrosyne sold linen that would make you cry to touch it. And Kostas, Kostas, with your black hair shining, you sat on the wall with me, and the quince was sweet.*

Soon my devotions spanned sunrise and sunset like a bridge. I held to my fish-cross at night, and the sand threw itself upon my helpless flesh instead. I wept against the hard horn cross-beams, but the desert tide had wracked my eyes of all moisture. I sobbed empty and hoarse against the waves, and began again my litany of churches and apricot-sellers.

But each time the moon went dark, I lost one of them; a Basilica with tripartite windows snuffed out within me, a distiller of lime-liquor scooped up and away. I thought in those days that the sand would never cease, that in this world there were seas that had no end.

The flotsam of jeweled fish crammed the decks of the *Tokos*, scales spilling out onto the salt-surf. Rheumatic Euphrosyne and the emerald reliquaries of the Myrelaion had gasped their last and dissolved from my desiccated mind. It seemed to me then that there had never been a soul aboard but my own and those tiny, squeaking spirits of the storm-brought mice. I had not been able to close my eyes for days. Sand filled all the creases and ducts. I wept sand; I breathed it. *Had* there been a captain, I wondered, before me? Had there been a man with a green belt and a young wife in Cappadocia, whose hair was a most extraordinary yellow? Had he known a song about St. Thomas? Had he knelt in horror at the feet of the navigator when the blue and cheerful sea turned to sand? I could not tell, I could not tell.

Folly, I assured myself. No man knew this ship before me, it was impossible—yet I seemed to remember a green belt drifting on the golden eddies. I could not be sure.

The Word Dwells in All Things, whispered the mast, *the Word in the Quince, the Word in the Mouse. The Logos of the Sand. Mary-in-the-Mast, John-in-the-Ship—the Word in the Flesh.*

"Leave me alone," I said. I could not close my mouth, with the sand so hot in my jaw.

Listen, John-my-Grist: Christ, the Shark, and the Logos, the Lamprey, hummed the lacerated pillar. *Go into the Sea, Trust to the Sea, Breathe the Gold of the Earth and Fear Not. In the Depths, the Lamprey will Find you, and you will know It by Its Teeth in your Side.*

"I am afraid," I said, clutching my blue-horned cross before me.

I will take the Sophia from you, hissed the mast, *with its great bronze dome. I will take your Purpose, what you came for, to find the Tomb of St. Thomas and glory for your Master. And I will take Kostas on the wall. Be my Shark, John, and I will be your Star-of-the-Sea, your Star-of-the-Sand.*

"No," I whispered. My hands shook terribly. "I need them."

Be my Shark, be my Endless Swimming.

I clutched my cross to me, glancing back fearfully at the stern mast, its mouse-mouths grinning. The sun seemed so bright, bright as the sugary wine in my friend's brown hand as we sat on the wall and discoursed as the fishing boats came in, his gentle voice chiding: *John, surely the nature of Christ is vast enough to encompass all of these things, the Logos and the poor lost boy and the Dove moving in His breast. Surely we are all vast, and He, the greatest of us, cannot be less than you or I, who are made of light, and still suffer in our flesh.* I clung to his voice, receding down the darknesses inside me, the memory of Kostas, ever wiser, ever more gentle, growing weak and dim, his echo coming before his words, dissipating along the rim of my heart until only fragments of his whispers floated unmoored in me: *vast, vast, vast.*

I could not even close my eyes to leap; the sand had wedged them open with fire and pain. But leap I did, and the wind made no sound when I landed—hard—on a solid spit of sand. I stood shakily, my eyes scalded, my cross bent irreparably.

The mast laughed with all its hundred broken mouths, and the *Tokos* rode on in the glare, across liquid dunes, unmoved by the loss of her last man.

I, John, lately of Constantinople, began to walk East, as though a star ever rose in another direction.

THE CONFESSIONS OF
HIOB VON LUZERN, 1699

y candle-of-the-hours had dripped its way down. The nail I had set between the seventh and eighth marker clattered onto its tin dish, and I started from—dare I say such a thing?—John's chronicle, John's book, his own hand and thoughts. I could not help but believe it genuine. This was certainly bad scholarship, but faith and hope are inarguable virtues. I believed it; it was so. Where my unworthy fingers had pressed the corners of the pages, brown blemishes rose up, as on the flesh of a pear left out too long. I trembled, with that unnamable emotion that only those men devoted to books and letters know—to come so intimately close to that which I had studied so long, with passion and sleeplessness and cramped hands.

I set aside the golden book, my back stiff and aching with the effort of copying. Such work I had not done since I was a youth, struggling with my *rosa-rosae-rosam* and my tripartite God and my lust for certain city girls who, even if my mother had not promised her sons to the Church, would have been far out of my reach, their round, milk-colored bodies swaying down other roads, toward other men. I have boys to scribe for me now—for I have often and in secret thought that it is boys' work, to copy and not to compose, to parrot, and not to proclaim. Out here on the edge of the world I feel it safe to confess, my Lord: I once wished, and still do, on some idle occasions, that there had been wealth enough in my family to give me a poet's leisure, to fill my days with wine and quills and all those women with their braids bound up so tightly, so terribly tight I thought it must hurt them so, and how much more lovely they were to me then, suffering the passion of their beauty. Young Hiob, in his garret, with his sonnets whirling like starved angels in the snow-motes of some sweet Alpine November—he would have entertained a cheese-merchant's daughter on each arm, and with his toes scratched out such verses as to give Chaucer a good thumping.

But that impossible Hiob would not have journeyed so far, to the grey and red and thirsty land of Lavapuri, or seen the lady with the downy arms, or held the book of Prester John in his old, spotted hands that never touched so much as one cowherd's girl. He would have been abandoned of God, and possibly have written verses more concise and less meandering than this old man's babbling. Yet I fancy that the Lord my God is the most elderly grandfather of us all, and is perhaps comforted by hoary chatter and reminiscences—after all, He sometimes longs to share His own.

I found myself disturbed by the strangeness of John's words, so riddled with baleful ghosts of the Nestorian heresy, and darker things still. All men know Christ was one being, united in Word and Flesh, the Divine Man, who walked among us so briefly. I did not like to think of John as a heretic, subscribing to that mad false prophet Nestorius and his confusing philosophies, slicing Christ down the middle like a joint of meat. Word and Flesh, separate, struggling one against the other? It is an ugly thought. It was always an ugly thought. I did not wish to send back word that I had found the great king, only to have him repeat the Devil's own lies. Even less did I enjoy the thought of his friend-ships with half-literate Turkic cobble-rats. I shook my head to clear it in the close, damp cell. *Hiob, you old rooster, have you not yourself been as close as kin to your own scribes and novices? Have you not embraced them with fatherly love, frankly and without judging their poor parentage? If boys came to you uneducated, did you not take it on yourself to do the work of making them wise?* I passed my hand over my eyes. They should have sent a younger man. With less fog in his pate. With more hair on it, too. I called one of those dear and gentle novices to me, and bade him fill me up with bread and that runny cheese they favored here and also something fortifying to drink, even if it be full of spices whose richness endangered both my soul and my digestion.

There, there, belly of mine. Be peaceable. I look after you, don't I?

I took up the scarlet tome, with its embossed eyes staring, staring, pricking up my marrow with their gaze. It possessed a bloody scent, lurid, like a pomegranate, or bubbling sugar, or beer when it is still so sweet, and the yeast bellows up from the barrel, soft and thick as skin.

I reminded myself: when a book lies unopened it might contain anything in the world, anything imaginable. It therefore, in that pregnant moment before opening, contains everything. Every possibility, both perfect and putrid. Surely such mysteries are the most enticing things You grant us in this mortal mere—the fruit in the garden, too, was like this. Unknown, and therefore infinite. Eve and her mate swallowed eternity, every possible thing, and made the world between them.

But oh, those eyes, they did hound me, and I feared them.

THE BOOK OF THE FOUNTAIN
an Account of Her Life
Composed by Hagia of the Blemmyae
Without Other Assistance

When I was born my mother cut off her smallest finger and treated the skin with a parchmenter's oils. She stretched it on a miniature frame of hummingbird bones, making a tiny book in which she recorded one word for each year of my life with her—the tiny pages left room for no more. It was a strange thing, a little horrible, but I often asked her to take it down from the shelf so that I could look inside it. *Hagia*, it said on the first page. *Cry*, on the second. *Lymph*, on the third. *Silence*, the fourth. I did not understand. But I understood the tenth page, which said *Fountain* in Ctiste's tight, angular hand. No child could mistake such a word, written in such a year. I would go to the Fountain, and I would drink.

My mother tied red skirts below my mouth and, though I protested, buried the little book she made me in a patch of wet, cakey soil ringed in henna bushes. I wept and scrabbled at the dirt for my book, but she would not be moved, and she had buried it deep. With red eyes I clung to her as we walked together over the Shirshya fields, past our donkeys and cows, past the skin-trees waving, past the brindles and reds and whites.

As we walked, I considered my life, as solemnly as a child may weigh her slight ten years in the world on each of her small hands. Our family tended groves of vellum-trees, sprouting out of the earth with bark of gold leaf, their boughs bearing strips of pure skin, translucent and wavering in the peppery wind. Each year, when the harvest lay stretched on hoops in the fields, tightening in the sun, we would cut squares of skin from our dumb, mute beasts and bury them in the earth to sleep until spring: donkeys, calves, camels. Up their skin-trees would come when the winter released the soil: white skins for scripture, brindle for scientific treatises, red for poetry, black for medical texts, dun for romances. Spotted for tragedies, striped for ballad-sheets. The skin of each shows differently when it is stretched and treated and cut, and we knew how the infinite gradations of literature may be strained and made more perfect through the skin of a cow.

Despite my muscular memory, which may easily lift both my mother's laugh and my husband's psalms and still have strength for my own long-buried desires and soliloquies, despite the coming darkness and the urgency of my pen, this thing beneath my hand is a difficult book to write. I have been all my life a scribe. I have personally translated and copied the works of the Anti-Aristotle, Artavastus, Catacalon of Silverhair, Stylite the False Lover, Pachymeres-who-spoke-against-Thales, Ghayth Below-the-Wall, Yuliana of Babel, and countless catalogues of poisons, harvests, sexual adventures, and pilgrimages to the Fountain.

It is strange. I have forgotten when we began to call them that—pilgrimages.

I have copied out the great works of our nation in ultramarine, walnut gall, and cuttlefish. Very occasionally, for the most precious volumes, I have crafted my own tincture of zebra-fat and mule-musk, the soot of frankincense and errata pages, and tears. It is this last I use now, though I thought for a long while that something humbler might be best, as I do not consider myself an author, and therefore cannot expect to be allowed to use the finer tools. But in the end, as I attempt, with clumsy but earnest need, to compose and not to copy, perhaps the quality of the ink will stand in my place, and lend some small beauty where I, of necessity, must fail.

As I write, it is morning in New Byzantium. I am comforted, as I have always been, by the scrape of quill against parchment, something like the scratching of chickens in dust—it seems full of tranquil meaning, though the next dancing rooster shall erase the work of all those white and fluttering hens, and the next scribe with her pumice stone will someday take up these pages and make room for a decade's record of the Physon's chalky inundations. I am not entirely at peace with this. But I shall have my comeuppance and must be sanguine in the face of it—for I have scoured my own healthy share of careful calligraphy from donkey-skin. It is the natural life-cycle of literature, whether I like it or not.

I live now in a red minaret whose netted windows let in a kind of glassy light, cut by palm-fronds and the tips of quince-trees into fitful scales of shadow, scattering this stack of neat lion-skin pages. My friend Hadulph cut them for me with much solemnity out of his uncle, who fell into a chasm and spilled out the gift of the Font into the dust. Hadulph's claws were quite sharp enough to the task, but he wept, and the pages are spotted with feline grief. This is not, I think, unapt to my tale. When my pen passes over the stretched and chalk-dulled tracks of my friend's tears, it goes soft and silent, and so must I.

In truth, I do not rightly know where to begin. I want to speak of my childhood; I want to speak of those terrible events that occurred when I was grown. In my head, in my heart, it all happens at once, one moment lying on top of the other, a palimpsest of days. But that is no way to write a book, and if it is a choice between beginning with *him* or beginning with myself, I must turn my back on the shade of the man who was once my husband and abjure his usual assumption that all things in the firmament are primarily concerned with his person. I am sure he will be affronted; I feel the wind off of the persimmon groves chill and bristle.

Quiet, John. Quiet, my love. The world existed before you came. We lived; we ate—we even managed to laugh and have a few children before we knew your name.

Bells ring low and sweet in the al-Qasr. It will be warm today, and the wind will bring roses.

When my mother took me to the Fountain for the first time, when I was ten years of age, I felt nothing in the world could be hard or cold or implacable. These days we would call our long walk a pilgrimage, but I did not know the word *pilgrim* then. No one did. What could such a thing possibly mean? But I knew that my mother was called Ctiste and that she had a waist like a betel-tree and high, small breasts tipped in green eyes like mine—for the blemmyae carry their faces in their chests and have no heads as men do. But we are capable of beauty, whatever you will hear men say. Ctiste was beautiful, and I loved her. I remember her best bent over her parchmenter's work, and so too my father, working the hoops of laurel wood outside our house, fragrant and white, stretching piebald skins over their curvature. My parents set the pegs true under boughs of champaka flowers; pale orange shadows flitted on their long, muscled arms, the mouths in their flat stomachs no more than hard, thin lines.

I held her hand very tightly as we walked from the city—for you must always walk to the Fountain. If your feet are not road-filthy when you arrive, you have not suffered enough to be worthy of the water. My mother was very strict about this, stopping every few miles to rub red, clayey mud onto the soles of my bare feet, in case I was not sufficiently squalid. The Fountain bubbles and flows quite far from what is now Ephesus Segundus—then sweet, gently dilapidated Shirshya, where no one wrote their name without touching my family, our work, our skin.

The Fountain-road astonished me. Such an extraordinary thing for a child to tread. So long, so bright, so loud! Tight as a girl's hair it curled northward from Shirshya, cutting through fields of spiky kusha grass like brown bones. Pink-violet lotus floated on pools of white sand like lakewater, pale green leaves tucked neatly up beneath their petals. Around her ample waist my mother had tied a belt of books for barter; the spines and boards thudded dully against her hips as we walked, and the smell of the dry grass smoked the air. Ctiste wore red, too. We all wear red on the pilgrim road.

A road can be a city, no less than Shirshya, no less than Constantinople. The Fountain-road formed a long, wending capital—we must all walk it, and so it became our own sweet home, no matter where we were born. Every mile was occupied as firmly as war-won territory, by lamia selling venom

and lemon cakes, by fauns selling respite in their arms, by tigers selling tinctures of their claws and eyelashes, by gryphons
selling blank-faced idols of chrysolite and cedar. The turbaned
tensevetes, their flat, frozen faces gleaming, let their cheeks drip
and melt slowly into amethyst vessels, which are then sold to the
peregrinating multitudes as holy and magical draughts. At the
time we thought them charlatans, but now, when my journeys
Fountainward are long done, I think on those cerulean hermits
and suppose they never did lie. They let their bodies flow out
to ease the throats of the faithful, and that is holiness true, even
if it was never more than water. We drank those purple phials;
we paid the sharp-toothed tensevete with a novel about a river
of ice flowing deep within the earth, peopled with the ghosts of
jewel-divers who lived upon the pearls that line the river-floor,
feasting on them in misery. It was written on silvery sealskin,
and clasped to Ctiste's belt with an ivory buckle.

At night, the road stretched on forever, up into the mountains, lit by countless lanterns, a thin, spiraling line of lights,
moving slowly in the mere, buffeted by gentle laughing and
gentler singing. The lotus fields turned to turmeric and coriander, wide and green, and the sharp, fresh scent wound among
our silver lights, wound among the shadows, wound among a
thousand and more arms swinging in time to a thousand and
more steps. Where the land grew rocky, we helped each other
climb—a man with stag's horns and a chest thin as balsam lifted
my mother onto a high ledge dotted with shoe-flowers, glinting
wrinkled and red in the dark, and placed me beside her with a
chaste wink. I carried a bronze-eyed woman's child for several
miles, pulling the girl's braid and telling her stories about headless heroes with stomachs like beaten brass.

When the turmeric died away, and the rocks grudgingly allowed only moss and the occasional lonely pea-plant, we came
upon a cart owned by an astomi, her gigantic nose twitching to
catch the faintest aroma on the wind, her prodigious nostrils
grazing her own breast. Her cart brimmed full of the most extraordinary wares—at least to the eye of a girl who had seen only
parchment-trees and the Shirshyan toymakers' wooden baubles.
The cart-woman's nostrils shone; astomii have no mouths, but

eat scent from the air itself, sniffing apples and turmeric and girlflesh with abandon. Ignoring my impatient mother, as a canny merchant will, she showed me a miniature model of the universe, no bigger than a walnut, impossibly intricate, all in gems dredged from the Physon's glittering inundations.

"The crystalline spheres," the astomi said, her voice coming pinched and nasal from the vast tunnels of her nose. "With Pentexore at the center, bounded by her sea of sand—rendered in topaz—and ringed in jeweled orbits: opal for the Moon's circuit, gold, of course, for the Sun, carbuncle for Mars, emerald for unfeeling Saturn. The cosmos on a chain around your neck—excuse me, charming blemmye, your waist—and, if you'll allow…"

She turned a tiny silver key in the base of the device, and the spheres began to click and whirl slowly around the plain of Pentexore, where I could make out a thin sapphire river and specks of carnelian mountains like pin-heads. Oh, how shamelessly I begged for this thing! How wickedly I wheedled! But Ctiste was merciful, as indulgent as any mother on a holiday. Quiet as ever, and more patient than I deserved, she unhooked a volume from her belt: a dissertation on the matriarchal social structure of the scent-farmers of the plains, bounded in bone boards, and into the bargain the astomi threw a little ring of lapis and opal which my mother slipped over the stump of her severed finger.

I wore the cosmos on a belt around my waist. Even now as I write, it dangles in my lap like a rosary, and the slow clicking of the spheres calms me.

I fear this must be tedious: any child in Pentexore could tell the same story, describe the same road, the same lanterns, the same trinket-bearing nose-maiden. There is comfort, there was always comfort in the uniformity of our experience. *Yes, my child,* says each grandmother, *I walked that road, my blisters pained me just the same as yours. I saw the line of lights; I broke my feet on the same boulders.*

John, too, walked this road, our dilapidated priest—do not believe otherwise, no matter what he assured certain of his own folk. Who does not elide their private matters in the presence of family? But no—no matter how his shade rattles the quince for attention and demands I perform as graceful amanuensis for his gospel, this is not his story. It is mine. He cannot have this, too.

The air of the Fountain howled thin and high, blue as death, giddy. A rock-table wedged itself in the ring of mountains like a gem in a terrible crown, and in the rock-table sunk a well, deep and cold. The table allowed room for only a few folk at once on that narrow summit. Just as well, for each creature's experience of the Fountain remains their own, uninterrupted by the rapture of another. Thick, grassy ropes edged the last stony paths, so that our lives might not be entrusted to disloyal feet. Clutching these, clutching the rocks themselves, we climbed, we climbed so far, by our fingernails, by our teeth, panting in the ragged wind. The silence loomed so great there, so great and vast, wind and breath alone polishing the faces of the mountains. It was hard. Of course it was hard. All pilgrimage is difficult, or what use would it be?

I crawled up into my mother's lap and laid my thin chest between her breasts as we waited for our turn. I felt her lashes on my shoulders; the wind beat at us with both fists, the ropes swinging wildly below. Finally, hand over hand, our red skirts snapping against our legs, we balanced on the thinnest of rock-spindles, our toes sliding off the shale into the ether, and we crossed to the well, to the Fountain.

Apples grew there, withered and brown, branches tangled in the masonry of the well. The stone snarled like ugly, purpled roots chewing their way out of the ground to make a vaguely well-shaped hole. I thought it looked like the mountain's mouth, sneering at me, grimace-twisted. The apples slowly swelled as I watched them, thickening red and fat and glossy, huge as hearts, even budding a glisten of dew. Then they shriveled again, extinguished, sallow and past cider-making. As I ran my fingers over their soft, rotten faces, they began to rouse once more, billowing up hard and scarlet. They stuck through the cracks of the well like tongues. Ctiste ignored them and knelt by the well where the Oinokha sat, a woman in scarlet wool with a swan's head undulating out from her thin and narrow shoulders, her feathers buffeted by the winds.

The Oinokha pulled me forward and fixed my hands to the twisted blue-violet stone of the well. I looked within—and the roots of the mountain twisted in the pool like jealous fingers, still and sharp and violet-grey, pulling the water away from a thirsty wind. The Fountain was a low puddle in a sulking, recalcitrant cistern opened up in the crags by a hand I could not imagine. The water oozed thick and oily, globbed with algae and the eggs of improbable mayflies, one corner wriggling with unseen tadpoles. It glowered, bracken-green with tracks of brown streaked through it, unmoving, putrid, a slick skin of frothy detritus over water which had sat motionless for all time at the bottom of a dank hole.

I had imagined the water would be so clear, clear and clean as a gem. I thought it would be so sweet.

The Oinokha put her hand over mine, the palest hand I have ever seen, as white as if it had been frozen, and her blood turned to frost. Her fingernails shone black.

"Somewhere very far away," she said, her voice playing underneath the wind like a violin bow caught up in a sand-dervish, "a mountain rises out of a long, wide plain and an ocean of olive trees. Clouds as white as my thumb cover its peak. On top of this mountain lives a crone in a pale dress that falls around her body in crisp folds, like marble cut into the shape of a woman. She lives alone among eleven broken columns, and her eyes shine so clear and grey, grey as the tip of her spear, grey as the feathers of the owl that lives in the place where her neck curves into her shoulder, his broad, breathless cheek against hers, talons always gentle on her collarbone. I know her—she likes her olives a little under-ripe, so that they slide hard and oily beneath her tongue. There are people who call this mountain Olympos, but they do not guess that mountains have roots like trees, and the purple stone of Olympos reaches under the earth to join with the gnarled, senescent root-system of volcano and sea-drowned range, foothill and impossible cliff. Under everything, they knot and wind, whispering as old folk will do, chewing darkness like mint-leaf and grumbling about the state of the world. Olympos is far away, my child, but she splays out here, like an oak whose smallest root humps up a mile from any acorn. Sometimes, when I press my head to the stone, I can hear the crone and her owl spitting olive pits at little laughing rills."

The Oinokha gripped the roots with her strong, pale hands, and bent her head into the well. I could not breathe—I had never seen a meta-collinarum before, the swan-maidens who stayed so private and silent when, rarely, so rarely, they graced Shirshya with their swaying steps. Her feathers puffed and separated in the wind as she pecked at the apple-leaves with a flame-bright beak.

"The same people who know the name Olympos," the swan-woman went on, "say that there was once a dark-skinned girl named Leda who loved a swan—and who among us should judge the habits of foreigners? They say she bore two sets of twins, two daughters and two sons who burst out of eggs dripping with yolk like liquid gold, and between the four of them they broke the world on their beauty." The Oinokha smiled, as much as a swan can. "But my friend who piles up olive pits among the columns whispers to me through the mountain-roots that Leda had a fifth child, who did not have the beauty to fill out recruiters' rolls, but the head of a swan and the body of a woman, a poor, lost thing, alone in her egg, without another heartbeat to keep the beast in her at bay. Her sisters loved only each other, and her brothers loved only bronze swords, and so she wandered into the desert, away from her family's burning cities, to the end of the world."

The Oinokha turned her arched neck to me, and a tadpole caught from the masonry wriggled helplessly on her bill before she slurped it back.

"Why is the water like that?" I asked, bashful, trying to retreat behind my mother's skirts.

"What do you expect a mountain's blood to look like?" the swan replied.

My mother laughed gently. She reached just behind her left hip and unbuckled a book—a compendium of the traditional mating ballads of the seabirds who lived on the edge of the Rimal, the dry sea that hurls its sandy waves at their nests on golden cliffs. The Oinokha took it shyly, her eyes glistening. She ran her icy hands over the feather-stalk spine.

"Such riches!" She pressed it to her breast. "It is so tedious here, with nothing to read!" she chuckled, and reached for a stone ladle, stained by countless circuits through the water. And I understood why she had told me about Leda—a trade, a story for a story.

I did not want to drink from the Fountain—it smelled like peat-wine far past wholesomeness, and my throat closed against it. But suddenly white, downy hands pressed my face, and my mother's dark mouth whispered soothingly against my shoulder. I squeezed my eyes and lips shut, but between them they coaxed open my mouth. The Oinokha lifted a brimming ladle and I am ashamed to say that I choked on the sacred waters of the Fountain. My body did not want it; my tongue recoiled at the over-rich taste of earth, thick and dank, and several slippery, too-green lumps of algae like phlegm rolling over my teeth. I choked—it was not at all seemly, and they held me while I spluttered and spilled it onto my pretty red belt. The Oinokha laughed; a tight, fluted sound from her slender neck.

"I choked the first time, too," she said kindly.

There are no more journeys to the Fountain, and the turbaned cart-masters are gone. No more graffiti on the mountain walls extolling the truth of it all: pilgrimage is long and monotonous and we do it because we must, as children wash the sink. If there are ropes still atop that mountain, they wave in the scentless wind and help no one to cross the chasms.

But I drank there, and so too did all the folk of Pentexore until after the war. After John. We drank at ten, at twenty, at thirty, the great pole-marks of our lives, and once we had forced down a third draught of sickly, fetid, fecund water, we aged never after, and never died save by violence or accident; and this is not so terrible a trade for three long walks and three foul swallows.

THE CONFESSIONS OF
HIOB VON LUZERN, 1699

I wonder sometimes what the memory of God looks like. Is it a palace of infinite rooms, a chest of many jeweled objects, a long, lonely landscape where each tree recalls an eon, each pebble the life of a man? Where do I live, in the memory of God? When Your great triple Heart turns to me, where do You look?

Do you remember, Lord, when I was a boy, and my father ordered me to assist with the birth of that calf? How are child's prayers ordered in Your sight?

I did not like the cows. They stank, and nipped at me wickedly as if they sensed and shared my distaste. *What pot*, said my old father, *you like milk and cheese well enough. Nothing you make of your body is half as sweet, yet we turn up no nose at you.*

Truthfully, my contempt for the farm was no fault but his. Since I was a babe my mother had told me I was promised to God, and upon my twelfth would be delivered to You. What should I care for cows, then, knowing the comfort of a monk's bed and the gentle work of paper and ink and prayer and song were to be my vocation? If one morning had risen fresh and pink to reveal all our cows lying dead on the frozen field I would have rejoiced. I have no shame left on it: I was a bad son.

But my father dragged me anyway, out to the stable with the cold cracking like broken bones, and the stars overhead so bright and sharp and white, streaked with milky, diaphanous mist. *Take me now, God*, I prayed silently, sure You would Hearken, as I was Your promised child and so specially loved.

The heifer lay in her straw, mewling pitifully and glaring with spite at myself, a little furry ear sticking out of her rear. But there was much blood, and other fluids besides that I dared not guess at, the secret wetness of women, be they cows or angels. But my father could not content himself to let me watch and learn and quickly forget the whole affair. He got me into the great beast up to my shoulders, hauling at the calf. The hotness of her pressed all around me, the smell buffeting me, barnyard and blood and fear. I could feel the calf in my arms, its complicated bones, its hooves and its ribs, and my skinny arms wrapped around it, pulling, weeping along with the mother as she lowed. Finally the babe came free, and I fell back with a huge lump of cow and blood and white mucus in my arms, so sopping I could not even tell where its eyes might be. My father righted the creature and scooped muck from her eyes with a tender grin such as he never had for me—for it was a heifer, and that meant good milk and breeding with my uncle's brown bulls.

"Life is like this," quoth my father. "Ugly to begin with, ugly to end with, and hard to manage all the way through."

The girl-calf wobbled on her new legs in a way I suppose others might find endearing but I saw only as a clever attempt to curry favor with humans. I refused to love it. The creature plopped herself down in my lap and proceeded to fall asleep while my father tended to the mother, whose privates were torn and miserable. And as I sat there with the calf snoring lightly against my knee, I could not help but think of the Christ child, and His birth in the hay and stink of what was surely not a very clean barn. Was it like this, I thought? Did Joseph or some other poor country midwife struggle against the close hotness of Mary, hear her pain and smell her blood, pull the Divine king from her body like so much cow? Perhaps Joseph did not much care for babies, as I did not, and stared stupefied at the son who was not his son, and wondered how something as big as a man could grow from a wet lump of squalling?

Of course, one ought not to entertain thoughts of the close hotness of Mary, or, for that matter, of the squalling of Christ. Yet I have always considered these practical things, and wished to know not only what is written, but what it was really like, if I could have been there. If You were troubled by human ugliness and the workings of women, I suppose You would have chosen some other way to be born. Yet I wonder if I could have stood by and held Mary's hand in her travail. Would I have been stead-fast? Would I have loved a wet, unhappy child?

I am not too much bothered by cows or blood anymore. And if I could have been there when a priest called John stumbled onto this kingdom, if I could have held Hagia's hand as she drank her strange draughts, I believe I could have been stalwart. I believe I could have stood with them. Though surely it was not *the* Fountain of Youth, not that oozing, disgusting mountain crevice she believed to be the holy Font. The Fountain of Youth is no such miasma—it is crystal and gold, trickling in perfect melodious harmony from dish to dish, a water pale as diamonds and as pure. All men know this to be so. But I allowed it might have been some unloved sibling of that radiant spring that sus-tained John's strange and hideous wife—and oh, how my heart disturbed my chest, to think that our Presbyter, Priest and king, should have sullied himself with a spouse.

Guide me, Lord. Should I have told all to my brothers at home with their frozen feasts and their dreams of righteous rule, or concealed at least the wife, who could not be suffered to exist? Is it the historian's part to include what is right, and excise what is shameful, so that in the future souls may be elevated by our deeds? Or is it his duty to report everything, and leave nothing hidden?

I was all full of disquiet in that long first night, as though I were even still struggling to bring forth some hoofed, toothy thing from black innards.

The last book, the small green antiphonal stamped with the sigil of a single great ear, glinted at me, its sharp, herby scent piercing the air: serrated coriander leaves and lime pulp and bitter, bitter roots. The nail had fallen from the candle. I could not afford idle dreams of cows who were now long dead and all their milk drunk. I prayed for no new surprise to dint further the golden image of the king in the East that hung still within me, like a lamp.

THE SCARLET NURSERY
Told by Imtithal the Panoti
to the Three Children of Queen Abir,
Who Were Lamis the Reticent, Ikram the Intractable,
and Houd, Whom You Might As Well Indulge.

Here I shall set down some few of the things I told to the children of the queen during the long spring of their rearing, when they seemed to my heart like fig blossoms blowing wild in white whorls around me. I shall also speak of my own love and thoughts, for no tale can be believed if the teller is a stranger to the hearer. Let it be known that in that life I was called Imtithal of Nimat-Under-the-Snow, but the children called me *Our Butterfly*, because I slept with my ears wrapped around me like a cocoon, disappointing them when I emerged each morning still their old nurse, without spectacular violet wings or antennae tipped with emeralds. Of course, it is part of the duty of a nurse to disappoint her charges as often as possible. Children must practice disappointment when they are young, so that when they are grown, it will not go so hard with them. It is the hope of this small being that these tales might form a long rope, connecting me to those long-grown children. I loved them, and where they have gone now I cannot say. That is what happens with children—they leave you. It is a kind of heresy to try to pull their little hearts back from the wide world and into my arms again. Thus, I am a heretic. And perhaps those who read this book in some future summer I cannot know will also be as my children: many Lamises, many Ikrams, many Houds. I imagine you all now, and you all will imagine me then, and together all our imagining makes a kind of family of the mind. Perhaps some gentle souls read my little letters even now, already, as I am still writing them. For when a body lives forever, all of time is one thing, a single bauble hanging in the black. Perhaps, when you have finished what I now begin, I might be your butterfly mother, too.

Perhaps I might even, one day far from now, in another place, open the wings of my ears in the morning to reveal something quite other than Imtithal, and everyone who has read this will gather round me to be amazed—and Lamis and Ikram and poor Houd as well, and they will all run to me laughing, as they once did, and so will you, and we will all of us lie in the sun together.

First I shall enumerate the virtues of the most famous of my charges, and afterwards my own.

The royal family in those days were in the main part cametenna, (barring those married into the noisy brawl of them or adopted), whose hands are as huge and deft as the ears of the panotii, which is to say my own ears. One of their palms spread open could hold my whole body, though my ears would drape like silk over their fingers. I spoke softly to them, cross-legged in their great hands, while they leaned their small faces in to hear. Lamis, whose wide eyes shone orange as a tiger's fur; Ikram, who possessed the most beautiful lips ever recorded in Pentexore, as deep a rose as I have ever seen, forever pursed as if she were kissing the very wind; and Houd, who did not love me until I had told him every story I knew. Only when I finished the last of them did he set me down on the ruby floor of the Scarlet Nursery and say: *There, Butterfly. Beginning tomorrow I will love you for all the rest of my life.*

How strange children are. As strange as any story I ever told.

Lamis enjoyed best the tales of how things came to be, for she could never quite believe that she was alive and everything around her was real. This may seem a peculiar attitude for a child to hold, but many think such things, and deeper and more peculiar still, but never tell a soul. How could they bear it if they, tremulous, asked after the solidity of matter over boiled bananas and lamb-hearts one evening, and the terrifying grown folk laughed imperiously and answered: *How can you be so silly? Everyone knows nothing is real.* And so they keep silent and try to discern by listening whether anything that keeps them wakeful and shivering in the night is true. But in time, in the dark close-ness of the nursery, when all the stars have come out and the wind is very sweet, they sometimes confess to their butterfly mother.

Ikram liked best the stories of love, particularly the sort of love that hurts and is never satisfied and comes to no good end. If it had been up to her, no lovers would ever have been at peace, but permanently masked, disguised, betrayed and betraying, stolen and stealing, mistaken at every turn and forever in the dark, reaching out to one another but not touching. She cheered when wicked men with handsome black wings kept maidens from their darlings, when hippopotamus-princesses killed their rivals with vicious tusks and took as many kings for their own as they could manage, the poor males lamenting all the way.

At first, Houd did not want to hear stories at all. So he told me, many times when I arrived to care for him. *Stories are for babies, and other helpless things.* He sat in the corner more often than not, and put his hands over his ears, which meant that his whole body disappeared into his huge, graceful fingers. I do not think he knew how much like me he looked in those moments, hiding inside his own body. But when I spoke of battles, and gentle boys dying, and bad fortune, and young girls with hair like his sisters' losing hope, I heard him weeping from within his cage of knuckles, and saw him peeking out.

For myself I will say that I was born in Nimat, where snow begins. Like all panotii, my eyes gleam white as winter, and my ears flow out like wings from my skull, shot through with the pink of my blood, and whatever you think is silent, beyond si-lent, but incapable of the smallest whisper, that thing I hear as a trumpeting song arcing through space for myself and myself alone. We live in the high places, where snow covers all things and hushes them for our sake, where the air is gentle on our ears. We are listeners, and before the reign of Queen Abir, when the cycles of all of our lives were set by her prodigious hands, I had listened in the yak-huts of Nimat to every soul who would speak to me, every creature who looked up at the peaks of our great mountain and called it the Axle of Heaven, or Chomol-ungma, or Sagarmatha. And I wrapped each sore traveler in my ears and they would lay their heads on my breast and tell me of such grandiose griefs and passions and histories. So I made the acquaintance of Queen Abir, around whom my ears could not fit. She wrapped her hands around me instead; her body overwhelmed me. I could hardly bear to be held when I was accustomed to holding. She kept me warm while the mountain howled and groaned, as it does, as it always has. The world has forgotten how beautiful she was, how orange her bright, bright eyes.

Come with me, she said, *and make my children into good people.*

What would you pay me for such a hard and cruel task?

When it is done I will tell you the story of my life.

So I ate my last meal of the sound of icebeer trickling into a cup and the melody of bone stew boiling. I kissed everyone who would bear kisses. I went with her, seeking that story. I followed her into the warmth of Pentexore and the al-Qasr with its amethyst columns, and that red, red room, with all its silk and garnet toys and wooden scepters banging against bedposts.

This is the first story I told the children, when the heavy summer rains had come and banana leaves clung to the window-papers and they could not be calmed by any song or game. I will tell it to you as I told it to them, and where they would not let me go on until I satisfied their endless, urgent questions, I will not go on until I have answered them. You must know my audience to understand my tales, for as all tellers do, I molded each story to their little hearts, to their savage ears.

I began with a question. This is a very good way to begin a story. The question was: Do you know how the world began?

Lamis, Who Always Answered: Mother made it.

Ikram, Who Always Argued: She did not! Grandmother made *her*, so if anyone made it, Grandmother must have.

Houd, Who Always Frowned: I think the world was baked, like the apricot cake we had for supper, all soaked in wine. The apricots are the stars and the cake is the earth and the wine is… souls, I suppose. Or blood. Not that I care.

And I, Who Was Always Patient: In the beginning were the Spheres and the Spheres were with us and the Spheres were us. Think of the little glass balls Rastno the Phoenix-king brings for you when he visits: all clear and shining and so many colors, and how you love bashing one against the other, even though they never break, for Rastno knows you all too well. They make such a lovely sound, don't they? Well, imagine thousands and thousands of them, all crowded together in a long black void, hanging like lanterns, silver and gold and scarlet and violet. The only sound in the beginning of the world was the Spheres creaking against one another as the lightless wind of the void rustled through.

Ikram, Who Demanded Walnut Milk Before Bed: If it was a void, how could there be wind?

Where the wind came from we cannot know. There has always been wind, because there has always been change, and the wind is the sound that changing makes.

Houd, Who Didn't Care: That's stupid. How could there be change if the world hadn't even begun yet?

I answered the needful, grasping hands of my charges: The world didn't begin only once, dearthumbs. The Spheres, milky and rose, crystal and gold, clanged one against the other in the darkness, for they were as blind as they were bright. Now, you will ask me why they did not go along scraping and knocking as they always had forever, which would have meant no scarlet bedclothes or walnut milk or mother or Lamis or Ikram or even Houd, even though he wouldn't care if they had just kept bumping along forever.

I have no answer, except that nothing can stay as it is forever, no matter how sweet, no matter how bright in the black. No matter how much we might wish that all we love could stop and hold its breath in our arms, things will insist on happening. Catastrophe is natural, my darlings, perhaps the only natural thing. And so, though there can be no reason it occurred at the moment it did and not another moment, or another, one of the Spheres cracked.

It was the Crystalline Heaven who did it, as best folk very much wiser than your Imtithal can measure it. Why the Crystalline Heaven and not the Benevolent Gold of the Sun's Sphere, or the Base Metal of the Leaden Spheres? Lean in, and I will tell you a secret: because the Heaven was lonely, and it had a weakness in its upper hemisphere, due to some trauma in its mysterious infancy. It is important that you know this. That loneliness and weakness were always part of us.

The Sphere of Heaven ground slowly through the windy pitch, and crushed against the Benevolent Silver of the Sphere of the Moon. All along its rose-colored meridians, the orb of Heaven cracked, and splintered, and shivered. Lines of gold like fire appeared in its great face; glass formed and bubbled in long rivers, and in the beginning of everything it cried out as the Sphere of the Moon passed into the Sphere of Heaven. Where the Moon had entered, so the Sun followed, and Mercury Lined with Quicksilver, Jupiter Hot and Moist, and all of the Planetary Spheres and Elemental Spheres, one after the other, like one of Ikram's poor dolls. The Crystalline Heaven swelled with all it contained, and lost all its rosy color, becoming instead the color of black glass. Thus when we look upward in the evening, we see the very furthest rim of Heaven that can be seen from where we stand, on the last and smallest and best of the Spheres, the Habitation of the Blessed, our own dear Earth.

Being lowest, it falls to us to anchor the rest. In a place utterly hidden, somewhere in our gentle world, a pin is fixed that keeps all things turning. The pin is called the Spindle of Necessity, and all the rest whirls around it, bound, tethered by invisible strands. But each of those Spheres is studded with a world like our own, as a ring is studded with a gem, and though we may not go there, we can imagine how, perhaps on furthest silvery Saturn, another Imtithal speaks softly to another Lamis, another Ikram. But not another Houd, for on no heavenly Sphere is there a Houd who likes stories or can keep quiet.

All you see and can be seen is fashioned from the stuff of the

Spheres. The sea is where the Benevolent Silver of the Moon meets Venus, Cold and Moist. The panotii are the children of Saturn, Cold and Dry, and the Fixed and Colorless Stars, who dwell in the deeps. You cametenna carry shards of Jupiter, Hot and Moist, and Mars, Hot and Dry, within you, the Jasper and Ruby Spheres of such hot hearted worlds, born in the strange circling of Spheres within Spheres, that motion which only the panotii can hear.

I can hear it now, ever so softly, the flowing music, like a sea, a tide moving round and round and round us, singing its private songs as it goes. It says: go to bed, little ones, fold your great hands over your small hearts, and listen to your nurse.

Houd, Who Did Not Like Being Teased, Even in a Story: Imtithal, what was there before the Spheres? Did someone make them? Is there someone out there, beyond the Spheres, who made everything, and watches us, and loves us and punishes us?

And I thought on this a long time, for some many folk do think so, and tell such stories: of gods with swords that drip with flowers, of the moon walking upon the earth in a dress of deerskin—but to that child I owed nothing more or less than my whole heart, and all I believed and knew to be true, and this is what I said to him:

No, my golden-eyes. There is only us, making and watching and loving and punishing. Only us, sleeping below the stars.

THE CONFESSIONS OF
HIOB VON LUZERN, 1699

Full of the strength of supper, I sprang from book to book, from Imtithal's odd Sanskrit dialect back to the marvelous clarity of Hagia's charmingly creaky Greek. Excitement flowed in a constant circuit from my left hand turning pages to my hungry eyes to my right hand scratching a translated copy with admirably few mistakes. The work, in those early hours, seemed a pleasure, and I found my rhythm in it, my body remembering old days in the library, adorning manuscripts with golden cameleopards and angels with the heads of lions. Stopping for lunches of a few apples and bits of bread soaked in milk, and then back into the breach, into the sub-clauses and hexameters, into the lions' heads and allegorical bodies. I touched the Word of Christ—Thy Word, O Lord. I put my hands on it and it was as warm as if it lived. I felt so close to the Divine, to You. As close as a calf and its mother. I could not help but touch the pages of John and Hagia's books the same way, with the same thrill of recognition—and these books *did* live, and have scent, and browned slightly beneath my fingers like true fruit. Then, I felt it was all a kind of sanctified play, and that feeling returned in the little hut, surrounded by books reeking of fruit, my candle burning, my ink-cup brimming, and Hiob with a young man's ardor.

Pride has always been my sin. On Your Sea of Glass You must know this, and chuckle at my stating so plainly what should be obvious to the king of All. Indulgently, I hope, as Your servant compares Your Own Writ with the mortal work of these tarnished, motley souls. But at first, I was so happy, just to be in the presence of those volumes, hearing their confessions as though administering, at last, the great rites to their dust.

No longer did I take the time to rest my knuckles and stretch my back and think on how Mary was like a cow and Hagia was like Mary—I leapt like a faun between the tomes, without a break between them, and my pace quickened where I had been certain I would fail. Truly, You were with me then, Lord, and guided my hand and my eye. I dwelt in Grace for a few sweet hours before my doom came on me.

THE WORD IN THE QUINCE:

Chapter the Second, in Which the Borders of a Strange
Country are Explored, the Name of the Country Revealed
to a Stranger by a Bird of Very Great Size, a Peculiar War
Commences, and a Brusque Hospitality Offered.

S and washed up onto sand. Golden skeletons skittered
onto the shore, the points of their ribs finer than needles.
I dreamed, face down on the beach, and while I dreamed
the sun peeled my skin from me, pink, then red, and no wave
came to cool my flesh. I dreamed that I swam in the cisterns
underneath Constantinople, through that underwater city
with columns carved as precisely as if men meant to live there,
frescoes stippled into the wall as if some fish-faced, green-eyed
lady might come to view them. But it was never so—black water
covered all like a drop-cloth. In my dream I swam near the ceiling, in the space between the slow little waves and the roof of the
busy streets, washed in slant-light from bronze grates.

And Kostas was there, by my side, with a spearful of blue
mackerel and a smile. His white teeth hurt my heart. I wanted to
tell him I was sorry I left, that the iconoclasts had returned to the
Patriarch's roost, and they painted over every Christ-face in the
city. I could not stay, not each night filling with the wet sounds
of hooded fools knifing painters of a mild-eyed Christ, not with
the unpaintable Logos so strong at my back, burning into me,
burning me crimson, burning me white. Not when I myself had
painted the Mother of God, and made myself a criminal.

We are heretics now, I whispered to Kostas as we floated on
our backs and looked up through the grates at passing hooves
and cart-wheels. *Or, I should say, we are heretics again. Who can
remember if on Tuesday we are damned and on Thursday we are
saved? My soul is weary of wars of art.*

50

Kostas shrugged and ate a blind cistern-fish raw, the dark entrails wriggling into his brown mouth. He understood. Kostas always understood. He held the dead fish out to me, its pale belly ruptured and torn. In the dream, I wanted to eat it, to take all that Kostas offered, ever offered, and I tried furiously to remember that there was no beauty in a body. Flesh was no more than corrupt, dead meat. The divine self has no hunger for such a thing. Kostas was no more beautiful than the poor fish with its tiny blackish liver splashing into the cistern. I was no better.

Dreams scrape everything up from the underside of the heart. It is rarely lovely, the sludge that comes dripping out. I am a good man. I am a good man.

I dove down beneath the dark dream-water, down through the lightless ripples, past the shadowy columns with their intricate capitals, the frescoes with their leaping dolphins and bared breasts: I saw them, I marked them, and coral quietly covered the faces of dancing nymphs. I dove deeper, until there was no breath in me. In the place of breath, a light grew, pushing my lungs out like hands. Deeper still sun-deprived fish glided by, their tongues glowing ghostly against the walls. In their tongue-light, unwholesome and pale, a mockery of moonlight, I saw the depths of the cisterns and the colossal stone feet of Constantinople herself, still delicate and graceful in their enormity, sandaled demurely, holding up the city. Mussels clustered at her heels; mold greened her nails. I touched the stone of her toes. They prickled like flesh, and I took her warm marble ankle in my pitifully insufficient arms, weeping against the impassive limb. I opened my mouth to call her name, and the cistern flooded through me, black and cold.

I woke at night, my skin hot and tight enough to crack like the shell of an egg. My mouth was full of sand, my chest scoured raw. The sand brought me back to myself, and I was relieved to find I still remembered Kostas and Constantinople, still clutched them in my heart's hands like two tiny marble figures. Much else had spilled out into the sea. My heart was a net of fish torn open. I came for something, didn't I? To find something. Images flickered and died: a tomb, a cross, a face with hollow eyes. I thought that I had a purpose, once.

The moon lay long and silver on the planks of dead ships on the beach-head, masts tangled with golden seaweed. Far off, in the shadows, I thought I saw the broken, useless hulk of a light-house, its thin, fiery beam illuminating only the endless sand. Dark cliffs hunched behind it, circled by silent birds battling the wind through a heaven crowded with unfamiliar stars, a flock without their shepherd, wheeling wide, constellations broken open against a sharp sky. I moved towards the black mountains, my bones weeping in my flesh, begging to be allowed to lie down on the shore of the sand and perish.

In this way shall I grind sin from my soul, I thought then, *for the desert was always the redeemer of folly and flesh. Who under the copper domes will not laugh when I find my way home, and tell them of these far places? The purity blazing from my scalp will blind them! It will force their gaze aside, and crown me in silver! When I crest that range I shall sit upon it as on the wall of the world, and the Logos will sit on my shoulder like a keen-eyed crow. I shall feel its claws in my bones.*

Thus I made my way, babbling to myself, imagining the wonder and envy of distant monks, and found grace for my blistered feet: a smooth rock path through the cliffside, winding thin and reluctant, slowly upward. The sandy sea pounded below, its gold turned to white by the moon gliding through her sphere. Waves sent sprays of glittering mica into the wind. Long cries, like unhurried arrows arced through the sky, low and sweet along the crystal breakers. If not for the sand and my bleeding back, the land would have seemed something like the coast of the Bosphorus in the summer, if lacking a thousand colored tents gleaming in the heat.

Dawn was nearly on me when I saw them—there had not been enough light before, or too much mountain. A line of stone cranes peered down at me from the heights, their long beaks beaten out of the golden cliffside rock, fronds of waving palm crowning their small, curious heads. They were fitted to the crest of the crags like a small fence, and as I squinted it seemed to me that real cranes crept cautiously up between them: scarlet faces and long, lithe bodies all of blue, fine, thin feathers like gold thread spiking from their delicate heads. They frowned grimly, like nothing so much as the front face of a phalanx staring me down, stone pupils and black, wet eyes alternating.

"You're too big!" one cried out, the largest of all, whose cobalt feathers shone even in the thin light of just-before-dawn. "It would be Unfair Advantage!" It snapped its long beak several times, like drum-strikes.

I finally struggled up the last rough stair of stone and stood upon the summit, the sea of sand whirring and heaving far below, my face welted with yesterday's heat, my rags scant comfort against the high winds that tore at me with their bony fingers in place of the moon's flat, hard palm. The great crane stomped in consternation and danced up to me. With its neck fully erect, it nearly rose to my chin.

"No!" It stamped its clawed feet. "Go back down! You're far too big, it is entirely out of the question! The whole affair would fall to the enemy on grounds of unsporting conduct!"

I blinked. In my reasoning, I supposed that if birds could now be expected to talk, it was not too surprising that they talked nonsense.

"I can't go back down," I said slowly, as if to a very dense foreigner, "I've only just come up, and I am lost." I paused, wilting slightly under the accusing stares of two dozen birds. "Lost beyond measure. My name is John; I am a priest."

The crane looked somewhat disappointed. Its fronds drooped. "Then you haven't come for the war?" it sighed.

"I have no hunger for war," I answered the crane. "It's all the fashion in my own country, but unlike fish stew, each nation does not perfect their own recipe. It's much the same everywhere, bland and bloody, and I have no more stomach for it here than I did there."

The crane gave an odd avian snort. "You are foreign, and therefore ignorant. It is forgivable, but not attractive." It cocked its head to one side. "The Rimal is treacherous and deep. You are lucky. Perhaps your survival is an omen. As to where you are, lost creature, well, that is easy. This is Pentexore—but of course, that is like saying 'this is the world, and you are in it.' This is the land of the Gharaniq, the great cranes, and we litter it with our feathers. I am Torghul, I lead the charge this year, and I have come with my crane-knights to survey the higher ground before the enemy arrives."

Torghul stamped the now-sunny ground and screeched; an answering cry ululated from the long throats of the other birds. Their long wheat-stalk legs flushed red in anticipation.

"And who is the enemy?" I asked, if only to be polite.

Torghul blinked slowly, masterfully retaining his calm in the face of such shocking idiocy as mine. "The pygmies, of course! We fight them every year. Miniature men, miniature women, like little dolls—their fingers are so tiny, we might mistake them for worms if we are not careful! They invade our territory in the spring, armored in mint leaves and fossil-filthy amber, waving miniature swords of sharpened antler. They come screaming up over the hill with such a distasteful sound! They say we took a queen of theirs once, and made her a crane—oh, who knows if it ever happened? War cares nothing for factual histories. We beat them back with our wings, our claws, but it is harder and harder, as the years go by, and they grow cleverer while we grow tired. But war gets our blood up, and we cannot help but feel joy when the spring winds blow over the Rimal, bringing the scent of mint with them."

I sighed, and spoke slowly, rasping in my thirst. "In my country, I remember, I seem to remember, there were endless wars over pictures: some thought it was a sin to paint the face of God, others thought it a virtue. And they met, and fought, and died, and met again, and the paintings came up and down, up and down, like leaves changing."

Torghul hooted derisively, but some of the other cranes nodded as though seriously considering the issue of iconography.

"There is no silly aesthetic debate *here*," Torghul answered, tossing his golden fronds into the air. "The pygmy must be fought, or else the Crane would perish! There is no choice. But as I said, you are much too big—if you fought with the pygmy it would be Unfair Advantage, as you are twice the size of their tallest warrior. If you fought with us they would cry foul for the hiring of mercenaries. In either event the whole business would have to be halted on account of the technicality."

My whole flesh shook. I wanted no blood, no talking birds, no arcane military lore—only to rest in a shadow and drink cool water. When I think on it now I flush with embarrassment still, for my body's weakness, then—and later. I said to Torghul: "I do not wish to fight. I did not wish to fight for paintings, I do not wish to fight for birds."

"But we cannot let you go," the crane-general protested. "You might reveal our positions, expose us to despair and defeat, for the sake of a simpering pygmy woman and a bed of mint!"

"I swear I will not. I am chaste; I have taken vows. But give me water and point my feet in the direction of a city, and I will not trouble you."

The cranes conferred, blue heads bobbing up and down. Torghul finally cried out, clapping his beak again—*clack, clack, CLACK*. "We have determined that water is acceptable, if you stay well out of the battle, and we will send you on your way when it is done, but for now, you are a prisoner of war, and will be treated as such! Now go sit under the old fig tree and don't talk—the army will be here soon, and on their heels the pygmies in their preposterous armor."

I sank gratefully down beneath the glossy brown branches of the fig tree. Green fruit hung above me in crowded constellations. Shade closed over my wooly, grown-in tonsure, and I could have wept for its cool hands on my brow. I plucked a fruit and cracked it open, slurping the juice from the seedy pulp. It seemed odd only afterward that each seed was colorfully painted with the tiny image of a woman cradled in the blue shell of a mussel, her head rimmed in silver. My belly would not hear of examining such things when they could be eaten instead, and so I devoured five figs before a crane, smaller than Torghul and more silver than blue, walked gracefully towards me on legs I could scarce believe would hold the weight of the bird, so like were they to stalks of white grass.

The crane gently tapped the lids of her beak together, a much softer and kinder gesture than Torghul's loud clapping. She approached, I realized, as a man would approach a wild lion, with ginger politeness.

"I am Kukyk," she said in a fluted voice, "I have been..." her cheek-feathers flamed orange, "*excused* from the war. I am here to feed and water you."

I tried to smile, though my teeth ached and rattled in my skull like rusted locks. The crane ruffled her feathers in a starry display and then, quick as a pelican collapsing into the sea, wrangled me onto my back and wedged open my jaw with her long, precise beak. I fought her and screamed protest, but she was so strong, stronger than a shipwrecked, starved man like me. So pinioned, I had full view of Kukyk as she closed her eyes and worked her pink throat until her gift came retching out of her: a pale mash of fish and fig and mouse and nameless prism-winged insects. I gargled and thumped the ground uselessly with blistered fists, but my mouth was already full of it, over-sweet and over-salty, porridge-thick and thin as water by turns. I could eat or choke, and so like a baby bird I submitted to the crane's ministrations, and swallowed over and over until she had no more to give. Trickles of the stuff dripped from the corners of my mouth, and my jaw throbbed when she withdrew her beak. I sat up, slightly sick with the indignity—but already stronger, less ravenous and addled beneath the wide fig boughs.

Kukyk sat herself beside me, beaming, quite without any notion of my discomfiture. Without hope of apology, I thanked her; she demurred.

"I am glad that at least you are spared the battle to come," I said, attempting genteel conversation.

The crane deflated. Her shoulders slumped and her wings made disconsolate gestures in the sand. "I am not glad," she said. "I shall have to wait all year now, before I can fight. My heart is ashamed, and lonely for my comrades. But it is not in the smallest part correct to let prisoners starve. I have been assured that I will be in the front line next spring as compensation."

I shook my head. "In my country birds do not battle at all, yet you are so thirsty for it!"

"This is not your country—and anyway, my heart doubts your words. Have you never seen a flock of crows savage a hawk?"

"Certainly."

"Then do not wonder at us. I daresay you do not make a study of the sociology of birds. All Nature wars with itself."

"Well, if I may not rejoice for you, I do rejoice for myself, who might have been drafted but for my height."

Kukyk laughed, a long sound that took a great while to work its way through her sinuous throat. "Would you like to watch the battle at my side, Stranger John? It is certainly an honor, and in this fashion I may not be entirely robbed of the season."

I wished to do no such thing, but I feared to be wrestled to the earth once more, and so I followed the stately crane from the shade of the fig to the rear edge of the golden cliff. The sun hung high in the air, like a bucket in an endless blue well. Kukyk searched us out a squat ink-nut tree and leapt into its branches, waiting for me to follow. We leaned out of the leaves to peer at the valley not far below, filled with two gilt armies standing at the ready.

The cranes needed no armor or banners—their golden fronds bristled in the hot wind, and they puffed out their chests, screeching and stamping. Blue and silver and red their ranks went; as one they clapped their beaks like sergeants rat-a-tatting on a thousand drums. Across from the avian line, the pygmies stood as a mass of bright green and gold, the joints of their amber breastplates bulbous and bubbled, knotted with mint leaves, and those same leaves spiked through their hair. Some rode liquid-eyed fawns, others stood their ground on bare feet. Their swords were dull bone, some antler, some the sharpened ribs of creatures I did not want to see with their skins on. The pygmies threw their heads back and keened, their tongues loose and wild. The sun blazed on them all, and the color rose high in countless cheeks.

Kukyk had begun to breathe heavily, hardly able to contain her excitement.

Without warning the two armies charged at one another, and for a moment the valley was nothing but dust and feathers and terribly bright leaves. Kukyk hooted in solidarity for her brothers and sisters, and flapped her great silver wings, sending a shower of nuts into the sand. When the first flurry of dust settled, I saw that the pygmies and cranes did not often kill each other, but were satisfied at a wound, a simple gash or dent in the bone, a bruise, their opposite numbers winded and gasping. The cranes danced with arresting grace around the pygmies, who for their part vigorously stomped and arched their backs in their own arcane steps. I was relieved, and thought that perhaps I had been wrong to be so intolerant—it was clearly a sportsmanlike, theatrical kind of war, nothing serious, quite provincial and charming, really.

Kukyk began to writhe beside me in the boughs. Her wing-tips brushed my chest, and they grew terribly hot, as if she had fallen into a great fire. I tried not to watch her in her martial ecstasy and squinted, trying to see more clearly into the melee.

My lips drew back in horror.

A crane had leapt upon a prostrate pygmy maiden and thrashed gently on top of her, his great wings enveloping her green-leafed hair tenderly. Her face beneath him was contorted in pleasure, her heels digging into his blue back with delight, and she had her arms thrown wantonly around his feathery white neck. As I watched, I saw that the whole battlefield had degenerated thus: pygmy men, small and fierce, had fallen upon the crane-hens, and their lustful cries were like wolves howling. One maiden had thrown herself over a black crane and was rocking back and forth lasciviously, holding her brown breasts in both hands, her amber armor cast aside. The war-ground had become a rutting field, and the wind was full of gasping. I turned to Kukyk, who was in a frenzy of envy and loneliness, gazing at me with flashing wet eyes.

"What is this?" I cried. "What is this disgusting ritual? What sort of perversion do you practice here at the end of the world?"

I was unkind, then. I would like to say I am kinder now, but no man is a meet judge of his own virtue.

The crane stared at me. "It is our mating dance. Have you never heard how the cranes dance to call their mates?"

"But they are not cranes!"

"Do your women mirror your men in every way? This is our great dance! It is the most magnificent of our behaviors. We battle every year, and every year we mate. If we wound them overmuch, and take the day, the children are cranes, long of neck and wing. If they win, our eggs crack open and out run little pygmies with golden eyes! We are eternal enemies, immortal lovers, it is our way; it is our nature. *Perversion* would be to deny our beloveds, to deny ourselves, and simply look with longing over a wide field, holding ourselves back from the charge."

"It is against the law of God," I insisted. "Nature dictates that like shall go with like."

"What?" Kukyk blinked. She shook her garlanded head. "You are a stranger here, you ought to keep uncharitable thoughts to yourself."

"Please, Kukyk, I cannot bear to witness such debauch. Send me to a city, where men and monks live with whom I might converse, with whom I might hear and see sense, who can find me a map to Byzantium and away from this place."

My cheeks burned, and though my body was weak—cursed flesh, wicked and corruptible!—it was moved by the keening of joy below. I tried to stifle myself, and thought of the cool shadows of the Hagia Sophia, of the mosaic Mary and her small grey mouth. *The Flesh may err, but never the Word*, I whispered to myself. The air around me rippled with sin. I shut my eyes to it. The silver-blue crane was very near; I could hear her breath, smell the figs-and-fish still lingering there. *The Flesh may err*, purred my body, betraying me wholly, allying itself with serpents and goats. *The Flesh may err.*

"Please," I whispered, "I am a good man."

The ink-nuts rattled in the boughs as Kukyk spread her wings wide and drew me inexorably into her embrace. I could not resist her when she fed me of her mouth; I could not resist her when she fed me of her body. I opened my eyes and was full of her, her silvery plumage, her black eyes which lashed at me in frenzy. She bit my shoulder; blood sluiced down my blistered arm. I snarled and tore her feathers from her skin. Perhaps I hoped to find a woman beneath. If so, I was disappointed.

Yes, I did these things. Hagia, my wife, forgive me. I have tried to remember this as beautifully as I can. To give myself good arguments, but not to show the cranes in too poor a light. They believe themselves to have a virtue, too. Do not turn your face away from me, when I tell you what I have done. I did not even know you yet. In that moment, I betrayed only my God and myself.

Kukyk folded me up against her, and I could smell the Rimal, the sand-sea, on her hidden, secret skin. Her heart beat very fast within her feathery breast.

"I am the only one kept from the war, for your sake," she breathed, "I have fed you of my body, no less than your own mother. You must feed me, too; I am so alone, the world has gone to roost and I am bereft!" She wound her neck around mine, and I felt its awful softness against my fever. "You are not so unlike a pygmy," she whispered. "Think of Leda—it will not be so terrible."

THE BOOK OF THE FOUNTAIN:

We find it difficult to demarcate the time, when time is infinite and lovely as polished silver. Even so, Pentexoran engineers once tried to make a Rimal-hourglass from copper and mahogany. The panotii polished it with their long ears until the wood was red as cinnabar paste, the copper as bright as the wet eyes of those shy folk. But when the sands were poured into the glass they stormed and raged so against their prison that the glass was shattered and the angry sand skittered away, refusing to be used so roughly.

Thus ended our clockmaking ventures.

But the panotii are never stymied. They fashioned from the polished shards a far more useful mechanism: a mahogany sphere top-ful of sand, pierced with copper poles, which, when held to the ear, tells us when those four blessed days of the year have arrived, and a bridge forms within the sandy sea, adamant beneath a scalded sky.

John, my priest, my husband, made me a true clock once. It stands near the window as evening descends on our new Constantinople, wheedling through my minaret with blue and diamond fingers. I can hear the night-wine sellers in the Lapis Pavilion; the dueling songs of the prayer-callers in the north and south meeting below my window in a violet puddle of exquisite dissonance. The face of John's clock is warped and bubbled amber, in which is trapped a most peculiar skeleton, the tiniest bird I have yet seen, its neck contorted in death. He fixed golden fish-bones as clock-hands, chiseled gears from the roots of his

Relic-Tree. It was well made, and with love—but I let it wind down years ago.

How I wish I had an imp at my shoulder to dictate each passage to me! I should stretch my feet, drink green wines and read silly poems, while she scribbles away in my place, her claws like a familiar parrot, and how much easier my work would be then! But imps are selfish and conceited creatures, and I would end in cataloguing the fathers of the kingdoms of the goblins and seasonal varieties of maiden and forget my purpose entirely.

I prefer translation infinitely to this gross composition: the lattice-work of another woman's text lying beneath my fingers, glowing white where I ought to choose words of passion, blue for the terminology of sorrow. The original author's intention guides my hands, like the grain in marble that cannot be avoided even by the finest chisel—it *will* be a faun's mouth, or a fish-tail, and no sculptor may defy it. In translation I feel safe. I lie by the side of the dead author, curled into the shape of their salt-sweet body, and together we whisper, and together, hand upon hand, we write. How many lovers have I had in this way! How many lovers wooed and won!

But to have only myself to seduce, only Hagia's story to tell—it is a meager victory.

To write my own words is more kin to reaching out into the darkness and commanding the shadows to coalesce into a marble figure the dimensions of whose face I cannot imagine, even for myself. I lie alone with no friendly ghost-hand on my knuckles, and am buffeted by didacticism, digression, daydreams. I imagine that when I look up from this work at last, there will be nothing left of the world but an old clock long run down, as useless as my old heart.

Time stretches out so far before and behind me. No clock could demarcate a tenth of my memory. Yet in this wasteland of the hours, Time still seeks some hold, and we in Pentexore do know a kind of calendar.

The Great Queen Abir reigned over the Age of Tallow and Tines, in which the Fountain was first discovered and the Oinokha set in her place like a jewel fast in a ring. With her wide hoof Abir marked out the laws which have kept us aright as little ships in a great storm.

I recall once that John asked me if I knew the tale of Eve in Paradise. To which I gave his favorite reply: "I know nothing of this."

He did so love to lecture, and he told me straightaway of the apple and the named animals and the flaming sword set across the gate. In those days it was his theory that we Pentexorans dwelt yet in Eden, no matter how many times the lions showed him the several gates of our country and not a one of them with a sword stuck through the bars.

His allegory spent, I took his head between my breasts, and he clasped his arms about my waist. While the glass bells rang out high as a hummingbird's song in the al-Qasr, I told him the truth of his story. Sometimes I think that was my greatest use to him, to take his ugly tales and teach him the gorgeous truth hidden in them.

I said: "Your Eve was wise, John. She knew that Paradise would make her mad, if she were to live forever with Adam and know no other thing but strawberries and tigers and rivers of milk. She knew they would tire of these things, and each other. They would grow to hate every fruit, every stone, every creature they touched. Yet where could they go to find any new thing? It takes strength to live in Paradise and not collapse under the weight of it. It is every day a trial. And so Eve gave her lover the gift of time, time to the timeless, so that they could grasp at happiness."

John did not think I interpreted the text correctly, and he scribbled for days in the corners of the palace in the strange, patchwork Bible he had compiled from memory, trying to make right his story of Eden. It was some time after this, his memory coming and going like a vicious tide, that he gave in to my theory and presented me with the gift of the clock: time to the timeless.

And this is what Queen Abir gave to us, her apple in the garden, her wisdom—without which we might all have leapt into the Rimal within a century. The rite bears her name still. For she knew the alchemy of demarcation far better than any clock, and decreed that every third century husbands and wives should separate, customs should shift and parchmenters become architects, architects farmers of geese and monkeys. Kings should become fishermen, and fishermen become players of scenes. Mothers and fathers should leave their children and go forth to get other sons and daughters, or to get none if that was their wish. On the roads of Pentexore folk might meet who were once famous lovers, or a mother and child of uncommon devotion—and they would laugh, and remember, but call each other by new names, and begin again as friends, or sisters, or lovers, or enemies. And some time hence all things would be tossed up into the air once more and land in some other pattern. If not for this, how fastened, how frozen we would be, bound to one self, forever a mother, forever a child. We anticipate this refurbishing of the world like children at a holiday. We never know what we will be, who we will love in our new, brave life, how deeply we will wish and yearn and hope for who knows what impossible thing!

Well, we anticipate it. There is fear too, and grief. There is shaking, and a worry deep in the bone.

Only the Oinokha remains herself for all time—that is her sacrifice for us.

There is sadness in all this, of course—and poets with long, elegant noses have sung ballads full of tears that break at one blow the hearts of a flock of passing crows! But even the most ardent lover or doting father has only two hundred years to wait until he may try again at the wheel of the world, and perhaps the wheel will return his wife or his son to him. Perhaps not. Wheels, and worlds, are cruel.

Time to the timeless, apples to those who live without hunger. There is nothing so sweet and so bitter, nothing so fine and so sharp.

My first Abir came for me when I was quite young. I had only sixty years, practically an infant, still full of my third draught of the Fountain. Festival flowers swept scarlet and green through the square of Shirshya, violins of orange-wood and cinnamon played songs both heavy and sweet. My mother and father kissed my eyelids and rubbed the soft, empty space above my collarbone—like a fontanel, it pulsates silkily, a mesh of shadow and meat under the skin, never quite closed. Each blemmye finds their own way with it, protective or permissive. But often others catch us, deep in thought, stroking the place where our head is not. My parents caressed that place quietly, and kissed it, too. They embraced each other with abandoned tears beneath the vellum-trees, and left their parchment fields to the next family, thoughtfully sown and ready for new hands.

The bronze Lottery bell spun in the courtyard; we drew our stones, our old selves vanished.

Ctiste drew a small amethyst, and went north to crush grapes and sell wine on the Fountain-road; my father drew a pearl, and walked west to dive for sapphires in the cold, depthless Physon. They trembled with joy and sorrow, but my stomach was as full of fear as of breakfast, for I was unready to lose them, and it was my first Abir. I did not yet know how to bend with grace beneath it. My mother looked so beautiful, so young, her black skirts flapping, her eyes bright and wet! She already thirsted for swollen purple grapes, for a new man beneath her and new children at her heels. I wept, as the innocent will do, and envied her first new daughter.

I changed too, that day. I drew an amber bead and married an amyctrya named Astolfo, who had bright green eyes and a great huge mouth like an empty barrel, in which he brewed tea and stew and poisons and perfumes, squatting and stirring draughts in his deep jaw with an iron ladle. I married him in a yellow crown, and on that day he became an ink-maker, to brew walnut-leech behind his teeth, and I no longer a child at play but the keeper of all our groves, which stood still and pale and waving, a long and shady library waiting for Astolfo and I to read it all. The Lottery went gentle with me that year. It did not send me far. My heart tore open and was stitched back together in one stroke, and this is the way of the Abir. It has a wisdom we cannot know or guess at.

After the yellow crown was quite ruined in the mud by the laughing, eager thrusting common to all newly married folk, I went walking. My skin flushed with heat and memory, I wound through the groves to find the place where my mother had buried my little book, the one she had made of her smallest finger.

She was no longer my mother, and could say nothing about it. I ate dry and spicy page-berries as I strode, and my shoulders were already red with summer.

I found it, after some searching, between a pomegranate-quill tree, hunched and spiked, and a tall, stately glue-pine. My breath caught, and I clasped my hands to my belly.

It was small, hardly as tall as I, its bark smooth as a front-board, pearlescent as a fingernail. Its leaves drooped, rustling faintly in the lazy wind. It bore few fruit, peeking from the page-leaves: the soft brown hands of my mother, with her long, graceful fingers, the oft-traced lines of her palm. I knelt beneath the little tree, and one of the dear, familiar hands turned slowly on the branch, as an apple will turn in a wavering breeze. It cradled my breast, wiping the tears from the eye at its tip, and another caressed gently the empty space above my collarbone. The hands of the tree held me so tenderly, and later I would swear to Astolfo that I could hear her old humming in the branches.

Cradled so, I looked up into those boughs, clustered with pale pages, and read on each the same word, the single word of my thirty-first year:

Forget.

THE SCARLET NURSERY:

Children wish to know where they come from. It is a burning, terrible question for them, and they will phrase it a hundred ways: Why is the grass green? (Why am I not green?) Why does the wind blow? (Why do I blow and blow and make no storms or snap flowers from the stem?) Why do we live in a city? (Why am I myself and not some other child?)

It was always my part to answer, little by little, the questions they asked and did not ask, until they woke up grown.

One evening, Ikram, who liked the bloody parts best, gathered up all the bones of her supper and brought them into the Scarlet Nursery. I believe she had the entire skeleton of their delicious black swan in her enormous hand. Her fingers had been quite scratched by her brother earlier in the morning over the not-insignificant matter of a toy gryphon and his missing feathers. I myself had dined already, as I am accustomed to do, upon several savory dishes: the sound of their laughing, of the bones rubbing together in Ikram's brown hand like a witch casting her eye, the whispers of the moon moving over the floor of the nursery, the snorting of the camels in the stables, the little harp a queensmaid played that afternoon in a far room of the al-Qasr, plucking to herself a little ballad in which some lover or another suffered calamity. It was a rich meal; I groaned with the weight of it. I sat in the center of the red room, the walls soft and crimson, the pillows of the floor sewn with ruby silk, even the bowls of the lamps lacquered as red as burning hearts.

Everything large, everything strong, everything shaped to their mountainous hands, and meant never to break except on purpose.

I sat while they ate below, opening my ears to their full span, which is to say I filled the room entire, my ears waving softly in the red light like sweet fishes' fins, sampling a few notes of the roof creaking as a dessert. Only in solitude do I eat, and open myself so far, so wide. I have only to listen and I am nourished; my food is the sound of the world.

If I was forced to eat with the children, I chewed demurely upon a flute of bamboo or stick of cinnamon. I never wished to be rude.

That evening, Ikram set out all her supper-bones, according to size. She was an exact child, and very orderly when it came to things like bones and pinching and other things that might result in tears out of her siblings. Lamis watched her carefully, her long fingers twitching as if to help, in secret. Cametenna may have hands like boulders, but their fingers are deft, and Ikram cleaned each bone of meat, washed it, and set it beside its brothers.

Lamis, Who Loathed to Be Left Out: What are you doing?

Ikram, Who Was Proud of Her Bones: Houd broke my gryphon, and since Our Butterfly says I may not break his head, I am building a new toy which only you and I may touch. It is a Houdless Toy.

Houd, Who Hated That Gryphon Anyhow: When I am grown I shall thump you, then everyone. I don't want your horrid old bones!

And then Ikram showed me what she meant with her bones, and I smiled, for she was so very dear and clever. *It is the Ship of Bones,* she said, *and my gryphon's old feathers will serve for the sail that was virgins' hair in the story, and I shall set it sail upon a sea of pillows, and that will be the Rimal, and I shall wiggle my fingers among the pillows and that will represent Octopuses, who are very fearsome, and if I meet one I shall make it throttle Houd, for I am very good with pets.*

I asked if I should not then tell them the tale of the Ship of

Bones, and how Folk came to Pentexore, while Ikram harassed with her waggling fingers the little ship she graciously allowed her sister to pilot over the pillows. Lamis squealed and giggled when the bony boat crashed on the silken red waves. It was not a pretty vessel, but we all forgave its awkward disposition and that it smelled very strongly of roast swan.

Houd, Who Had Been by That Time Much Maligned: I would rather a Moral Tale. One that teaches us something Grown-Up and Important, such as how sisters ought to shut up, and those who are insulted and trod upon shall inherit the Earth.

Ikram left off her worrying of the ship and held out her palm for me. I confess that I loved those girls so when they held out their giantess-hands. It meant they wished to hear a story, they wished to listen, and in that I felt kin. I always wish to listen. That I spoke endlessly to them was my sacrifice for their joy. I settled onto her hand, nestled next to the pad of her thumb, upon which I reclined like a marvelous prince. This is what they heard:

In the old books, the place we came from was called *Ifriqiya*, and also *Afar*. But who is to say whether those are real words and true names? Perhaps there is no more meaning in them than in Lamis calling her toy lion Grof. Sometimes, we cannot remember what a thing is called, but we pretend to, because it is better to know something than to have to admit you have forgotten it. Forgetting is sad, and knowing is sweet. But one thing is certain: all the folk we know now came from Some Other Place, though not all of them rode on the Ship of Bones. The panotii, for example, came from the icy places at the top of the world, and followed the sound of laughing and building and orating down through the many rivers until we came upon the Axle of Heaven, and there we stayed. I believe I have heard it said that the red and white lions came out of the sea, though they do not like to speak of it. And of course, the phoenix come from Heliopolis, the City of the Sun, and they tell no one else how to get there.

But that does not mean we found Pentexore empty! At the

very least, octopi were in abundance.

Ikram, Who Feigned the State of Being an Octopus: And fearsome?

I smiled solemnly and answered her: Very. But do you remember when I spoke of the Spheres, and that Things will insist on Happening, and nothing stays forever? Countries are like that too. Many people come and go from them, and no one can say they were the first, for before them there were at least ants and spiders and wooly beasts, but very probably the sort of beast that writes down their own history and thumps their sisters and wants to learn Grown-Up and Important Things.

Lamis, Who Wanted Very Much to Know Everything in the World: Who was here before us?

The crows say they have always been here. But others, too, who are no longer here to claim it, perhaps lived and died right where we sit.

When the ragged and wretched souls who sailed the Ship of Bones across the Rimal stumbled past the wetlands and the mountain-rills and the long colorless desert, the al-Qasr waited for them, already shining, and empty, with a wind blowing through its halls. The al-Qasr, your very home, your mother's palace, all its amethyst walls, its porphyry columns and hematite staircases, its cypress roof and endless halls. This room, Lamis, was already red. A very famous philosopher called Catacalon, who lives yet in Silverhair and has horns on his head like a ram, wrote that once a race of stone men and women lived here, their faces faceted, their skin every color, and the al-Qasr is a living child of theirs, so old it does not even move any longer, but broods and sinks in the earth and dreams of the old days when every cheek sparkled.

The children breathed, even Houd, looking about at the walls, the floor, the ceiling. They fell very quiet.

But I was speaking of the Ship of Bones, wasn't I? Every sort of Pentexoran claims to have had an aunt or a cousin on it, but Ghayth Below-the-Wall, who was a Peacock and a Historian, tells us that the crew consisted of the sciopods, the cametenna, the astomii, the amyctryae, the meta-collinarum, and the blemmyae. Some few crickets also stowed aboard. Some argue over the list, when they are drunk or grieving or boasting in a strange city or in need of tenure. But if everyone who claimed to have been on the Ship had been, it surely would have sunk under the weight. Why these creatures and not others? It is not for your butterfly to say. Perhaps they were prisoners, set adrift with prayers of drowning, or representatives of some extremely dubious government sent to make a glorious new kingdom, or a persecuted religious sect in search of holy land, or a troupe of actors. They had but bones and hair to build their ship, and so I think they must have come from a war; they must have been so tired, and in such grief, living in some awful place where bones were as plentiful as wood to them, and hair as easy as linen to weave.

Even if the worst of these is true, even if they were prisoners or actors, their lives were hard, so terribly hard. We must never forget, and never forget to pity them. They did not discover the Fountain in their first halting steps into the gold of this country, and so died in their time and speak to us no more, for their children did not know to plant them and have flowering branches bearing their loved ones to converse with, but instead set them in high trees according to some dreadful custom only they know. Even the heart of the roughest beast must pity them for their cold blood, for their hearts of dust.

Houd, Who Was a Rough Beast: I don't.

Whoever they may have been before, they became lost upon the Rimal.

Ikram, Who Loved Tales of Disaster: Mother tells that joke! A blemmye, a red lion, and a centaur became lost on the Rimal—

Everyone tells such jokes. Woe to the man who is not a queen possessed of giggling children, who in his cups leans in to tell his friends of the amusing antics of a trio of mismatched fellows lost on the Rimal, for he will surely be doused in beer and shunned. Of course, our sea of sand is passable but four days a year, when a kind of road forms in the currents, and whisks ships through this golden channel and to the shore. The Rimal is a strange beast, rougher even than Houd and more cunning. It rings the blue, briny seas of other nations in mischievous and insidious ways, sending its yellow tendrils into the water and catching the rudders of foreign ships, hauling them from their familiar waves and snatching them into the sand, where the Octopi and worse have at them.

Ghayth says that the pilot of the Ship of Bones, who was a sciopod, saw a light in the sky that called to him, a violet light so lurid and awful and beautiful the sciopod felt his arch ache and his heart pull apart within his chest. None of the others aboard the Ship believed him, or so the sciopods now say.

Was it a star? his companions said. *No, not a star.*

Was it the moon? his companions pressed. *No, not the moon.*

Was it a thing like us, with eyes and a soul and a hunger for bread?

I do not know, said the sciopod. *It might have been, but I think not.*

Yet he could not unsee it, and he steered the ship towards the violet light in the sky, and sometimes he thought it was a living being like himself, but with wide wings and eyes like wounds, and sometimes he thought it was a great fire in the distance, and that when they reached the shore he would find only charred earth and more bones, more and more. The light tormented the pilot, and even when he shut his eyes, all he could see was the light that was not a star, or a moon.

On the thirteenth night of the pilot's watch, the Ship shuddered and quaked, and the grey-blue arms of an Octopus—

Ikram, Who Had Been Waiting for This: Hooray!

The grey-blue arms of an Octopus—though some say a

Squid—wrapped around the hull, lapping at the rails, sucking at the sails. With great difficulty, the crew struggled to steer, and though one astomi was caught by the nose and died, they rode the Octopus into the beach and stove in his soft head against the rocks. So it was that the first meal eaten in Pentexore by our people was Octopus, raw and dripping under a very cold moon, for they were so ravenous they could not take the time to cook it. This is why we eat Octopus during Midsummer, in remembrance. Perhaps you will not slurp it down so greedily next year.

Houd, Who Was Always Hungry: I shall. And I shall not cook it either! It will be delicious.

Lamis, Who Had a Delicate Stomach: Ugh! It will be slimy!

I have not finished. The sciopod-pilot woke in the night, and he saw again the violet light, brighter and more terrible than it had ever been at sea. He followed it, hopping on his single foot, over the desert hills and the wetlands and the long, long fields of wild pepper, pink and black and green, until he came upon a valley so green it shone white in the dark. There he saw the violet towers of the al-Qasr, gleaming, silent, satisfied, as if the stones themselves had called him from the other side of the world, and now held him fast.

THE WORD IN THE QUINCE:

Chapter the Third, in Which a Certain Morbid Orchard
Entraps a Pilgrim, Whereupon He Devours an Entire Cannon
and Engages in Debate With Several Sheep.

O n the day I discovered the forest, the sun opened sores
like kisses on my head, and I thought of my mother.
Creeping knock-kneed from the satisfied and sleeping
crane in whose softness I shamed myself, I found my thoughts
full of the woman who bore me, far across the stony face of
the world. In the places I walked, veins of red writhed through
golden, half-shattered plinths and cairns—everything rock and
dust, everything hard and dry, and not a little grass feather-
ing up to feed me, not a green bulb that might hide water. I
trembled beneath the weight of the sky, the bloody smear of
sun that seemed to droop too close to the earth, too close, too
close. Only the cairn-shadows offered solace, and that of a grim,
hot sort. The colors of the place blinded me, gold and blue, a
brightness like a blow.

And yet, instead of water, instead of shade, I thought of my
mother. If she had been a man I think she might have been no
less honored than Nestorius himself—but she was not a man,
and she lay her hands not to holy books and relics but to cloth
and to water, to bread and to cheese-straining. Each of these
acts she performed as exquisitely as a priest lifts his chalice,
and I remember her black eyes always through a veil: the steam
of a bath, or of some sweet thing cooking. All the daughters
she bore my father died, and then my father, too, long before
I could remember him. Only I lived, small and coughing, and
every year until I took my orders she told herself to be hard and
strong as bronze and bone, for that year would take me, too.
Because I stood so near to the doors of this world, she fed me of

her breast long past other children, and spoke to me of myrrh and aloe and the kingdom of paradise, where every possible tree grew and would sate me, where angels with wings of fiery violet and black would take me up, and call me good. Those visions filled me, and weighted me toward God.

But she also spoke strangely, as a mystic in the desert might, balanced on his high pale pillar under the infinite stars—if a woman could stand thus, and speak thus, and bear the pain of it—which she could not.

Shame comes upon us like lightning in summer, she whispered once, over the sound of her needle pricking a hem with a tiny pop, *and though the horror of it flashes so fiercely, there is pleasure in it, too, a prickling of the skin, of the stomach. That is the danger. Like the lightning, shame shows the world in terrible colors, so that you might see, if you look closely, not only the stain of your sins as they seep into your soul, but the extent of your act, all its consequences, revealed like a thousand burning reflections, every-thing that was changed by the moment of your fall. Perhaps Eve saw that way, not just the fig in her hand but a hundred thousand figs, shivering forward and backward, sizzling, deadly, in that moment, through all the sorrows to come, and slipping backward through all her innocent days, tainting them even though they had passed.*

Even then I wondered how she could think such thoughts. Even the gossipy market-wives, their strong arms full of honey-soaked cakes and wine-jugs that we could never have hoped to buy, considered my mother pure and kind as a clutch of doves. What did she know of shame? Her heart was unfathomable to me.

And as I walked inland—though I knew nothing of where I meant to go I could not escape the feeling of *inward*, of moving up and in and toward something—I thought constantly of my mother's words, her blasted, weary black eyes, and the lightning of her shame. I felt as though I could almost see that way, some-thing dancing at the corners of my vision, Eve's fig, my crane, moving forward and back, to what end—or beginning—I could not then say.

But it would not be long. Illumination came swiftly in that

place, and with the heaviness of a great stone.

The cranes had hooted vaguely in the direction of the sun, east and north, now a little more east, now a little less north. *Many cities*, they shrugged. *That way, out there, not so far.* Post-coital etiquette occupied them, and I felt desperate to leave, to stop blushing like a child, to forget it all. And so I aimed my broken body, east and north and in and up. After days wandering through the golden stylite-pillars with their pitiless shadows, days under the accusing sun and a moon that burned me no less than her brother, her great single eye like God's own, staring at me with such disappointment, I came upon a kind of forest. My sunken chest heaved, and I wanted to die for the hideousness of it, the kind of ugly madness contained in those trees. I would have died happily, if dying would have recused me from that place, from whatever thing my mother's black-violet angels had planned for me here. But a man cannot die his way out of Hell.

The sky poured the first of its sweet-sour light over a copse of trees, each of them withered and twisted and grotesque in equal parts. Some trunks glowered blackly, slick with grease, and as I came near I saw them to be cannons, worked in fine designs like those of some great Emperor's ship, and among their silvery leaves hung fruit like shot. In the wood of others I perceived arched windows and platforms on which small birds sang and pecked—these trees were fashioned like siege towers, the color of baked mudbrick, shrunken and warped as all living things may be, but nonetheless, arrows that might have flown from their heights thatched themselves into branches, and pitch-berries dripped from their boughs. Worse yet were the horse-trees, whose bark bristled like chestnut pelts, their long, whip-like leaves snapping at passing flies. The devilish fruit grinned at me: horse-heads, in full silver armor and bits, their plates clinking lightly in the wind. One snorted. I stared at the war-garden as it stared back at me, for many of the trees—which I shudder to relate—were soldier-oaks, and knight-elms, swords and helmets crowned with long white plumes sprouting from their foliage, and here and there, here and there I thought myself to see brown eyes and blue peeking among the thick green leaves.

A good man would turn away from such a clearly infernal presence. A good man, on returning home, could say: *though I starved and thirsted I did not so much as look at that serpent's orchard*. A good man would have let the sun hollow his body and think nothing of how if a thing grows it must be possible to eat it, no matter how strange, and given enough days to starve in the desert, he might succumb to that awful, awful fruit.

But the flesh, the flesh may err, and I am not, I am not, I was never a good man.

I dug my nails into the fleshy wood of the cannon-tree; it gave beneath my fingers, slushy, slimed, and beneath the grease I felt hard iron. I reached up and from the harsh boughs, twisted and spiked as all desert trees are, pulled a heavy fruit, round and black and pitted as any cannon-shot I have known. I tested it; it was warm, solid, a little soft. Oh, Mother of Us All, how must you have stood, at that first tree, testing the weight of a fig in your hand, wondering what world might crack open at the meeting of your jaws in that sweet, seedy thing?

I bit. The charcoal skin of it gave, a crackly, papery crust. Within, the meat of it melted into my mouth, powdery, soft, but oh, the spice of it bloomed in my senses, a black pepper snapping on my tongue, an overwhelming, dusky sweetness, worse and better than any plum, and the metal pit tanged the flesh all through. Black juice trickled down my chin, into my beard, staining my teeth. I drank it, slurping, slovenly, and reached for more. I stripped the bark from the cannon-trunk, and this, too, I found good, a kind of coppery cinnamon. I dashed to the siege-engine tree, and chewed with relish the sticky pitch-berries, treacle-thick and bitter, bitter, as bitter as a walnut-skin. I spat. But oh, how much more terrible the weight of all that dark fruit in me. Not a fortnight in a heathen land and already I had soiled my body in several unusual ways.

And hadn't I come for something? Wasn't there a reason that had driven me from olive-shadows of Constantinople and shared mackerel-slurry with Kostas in the market? Didn't I want something, then? Why was I here?

"He who shall eat of such a tree is like to a grave-robber," came a soft, bleating voice from further into the awful forest.

"And a grave-robber is like to a devil, and if the devil had been punished more in his youth, he'd never have come to such an end." Silence, and the sun slashing through the leaves. "Bad!" the voice cried louder, reduced in its rage to a squeal. "Bad man! Stop! Desist! Bad, bad man! That's not yours!"

I peered into the wood and crept forward, afeared to find the voice and yet too curious to leave the place and press on without seeing the source of that reedy bleat. Some ways into the nodding trees I saw it, and for all the cannon-fruit heavy in my stomach and the sun-boils weeping on my skull, I sank to my knees and laughed. A man can only take so much. The grave horror of a siege-engine planted in the earth is one thing—but before me a sweet green tree shaded the cracked earth, broad leaves fluttering over several large sheep-heads, their wooly bodies like stalks of wheat puffing out below their necks before disappearing into the trunk, which seemed to be made of ram-horn. Some of the sheep had black faces, some creamy and pale, drooping lazily, half-asleep or wholly. A few sported their own curling horns and chewed at the wide leaves; the tree fed itself and on itself, round and around. One ram glared at me with a sharp look.

"You haven't the right, sir. Not to eat of us. Or else give me a bit of your blood in exchange—that would be only fair!"

"The fruit of the forest belongs to God, and thus to all men," I said softly, drawing my laughter back in.

"Whose God is that, then?" sneered the sheep.

"Our Lord in Heaven, and Christ at His right hand."

The ram snorted, and a puff of wool drifted off on his breath. "Well, I've never heard of such a creature, neither one of them. The Shear, who is the god of my people, and certainly far more terrifying and important than *yours*, who doesn't even live here but in *hefen*, spake unto the first ewe and the first ram and said: *Let no one enjoy the produce of thy body unless he offers his own in kind.* Which we have always taken to mean: if you and your own want to spin and weave from our fleece, you owe us at the very least a nice soft pen and sweet clover and a bit of cold, clear water. I hardly think it goes differently for cannons!"

"While it is charming that you think thus, there is certainly no God but Christ, and He gave men dominion over the land beneath His feet, the sheep and oxen, and the beasts of the fields."

The ram regarded me stonily. "When I lived I saw my God in his Fearful Aspect come upon the dewy field before dawn. His great black fleece blotted out my sight, and the candles of his eyes dripped tears of tallow. His teeth were gnashing shears, and with them he took up my lambs and chewed them, and I wept, but where his shadow fell clover grew, and new lambs gamboled as if in the sunlight, and I knew I would mate again. In the morning my young had been carved up for winter supper, but the spring brought more, and they grew strong. Can you say the same of your God? Did he come and sit by your bedside and offer you peace when pain came? Did you look into the candles of his eyes, smell the brume of his musk? Or do you make up stories because you are lonely and bray about it all day long?"

"You are a beast, and do not have a soul. Worse, you seem to be a sort of plant as well. What purpose could there be in ministering to you?"

"That's the loser's argument if I ever heard it," smirked the ram, and chewed at a bit of leaf.

I felt it best to inquire after some other subject—I have never been a missionary, or aimed at that golden felicity of tongue that such men possess. When I attempted it, I used too many words or too few, and no one was converted by peals of light exuding from my inspired mouth. In the world I knew, in the world I loved best, the world of Constantinople, painted blue domes and artichokes and quinces and loyal, simple men with God's own devotion in their eyes, everyone knew what God looks like. We may have disagreed on points of scripture, we may even have divided a room and called some heretics and some pure on the basis of a single verb, but no one argued that Christ reigned in Heaven as king, that His Crown was Many-Storied, that Mary was His Mother and He Died to Rise Again. Except the heathen Saracen, or even more perverse Easterner. I often thought in those days that deviance and perversity must increase the further one ventured eastward. But even in the east they admitted that Christ was holy, His Birth miraculous. When the argument centered not on whether Christ lived as one being and one flesh or separate in the Word, His Breath and Spirit, and the Flesh, His Earthly Body, but whether or not a gargantuan sheep had appeared to another sheep in some blasted farmyard, there could be no real discourse.

I tried another tack, less successful even than the first. "You said 'when I lived.' Are you dead, now, then? I confess I would prefer you to say you are, for then the logical conclusion would be that I have died myself and blundered into some heretofore uncharted sphere of Hell, and that would explain much to my heart."

The sheep marveled at me, his yellowish-green eyes wide and rolling. By now the other heads had roused themselves and regarded me with the drowsy interest common to their kind.

"Of course I am dead. What kind of simpleton are you?"

One of the black-faced ewes snapped at the scrap of fleece that ringed the ram's neck like a collar.

"He's a stranger," she bleated. "Can't you smell it on him? It's a wonder you lived as long as you did, old hoof-rot." She turned back to me. "A sheep knows three smells best: master-bearing-food, stranger, and master-bearing-a-blade."

The ram snorted. "I lived to a fat old age with a patch of ewes to my name and more young than I could count. I and the missuses made a good mutton for our master's table, and they buried the bones like sensible farmers. They still come to collect the wool off of the trees, though not so much these days—most humans find this a sad and ugly place, on account of the war."

"I am sorry," I said, shading my eyes from the sun which would not let me be, not for a moment, dazzling my vision and my wits. "But you are a tree, are you not?"

"Certainly," sniffed the ram. His horns gleamed bronze.

The ewe chortled to herself. "I suppose you weren't well brought up? No education to speak of? Never read the *classicks*, I'll warrant. Never learned your letters."

"Not at all," I protested. "I read very well, in four tongues and half a fifth. I have read Scripture and much more, Augustine, even pagan books. I know my Plato and my Aristotle." Forgive my pride, O Lord, but the learning of tongues was hard-won for me, and a man may treasure that which he bled to gain.

The ewe wrinkled her dark, soft muzzle. "But it is Aristotle who teaches: *If you plant a bed and the rotting wood and the worm-bitten sheets in the deep earth, it will certainly and with the hesitation of no more than a season, which is to say no more than an ear of corn or a stalk of barley, send up shoots. A bed-tree will come up out of the fertile land, its fruit four-postered, and its leaves will unfurl as green pillows, and its stalk will be a deep cushion on which any hermit might rest.* I remember the master's daughter reciting that for her lessons while she spun my wool, I do. She said it so many times I can't help but remember, even all these years down the warp."

"But Aristotle didn't say that at all! He said a bed-tree could *never* grow, even if you planted a bed deep in the earth, because a bed is made by man and a seed is grown by nature, and that is how one may tell the difference." I stumbled in my argument. "If I had a place to sleep in the shade and water, I might recall the quotation exactly." I felt myself blushing.

"And yet, we are talking, you and I," the ram opined, cutting the ewe quite out. "So someone here has Aristotle wrong and I rather think it's the one who thinks God isn't a sheep."

My head pounded and ached. "No, I know I have it right, I know it."

"*When you bury a thing, you must tend its tree. You gave it life, and owe it obligation.* Achyut, the Saint Under the Root said that," bleated the ewe, but she was beginning to nod off again. "I know a lot of quotations. The master's daughter was very clever. They buried our bones, and we grew, and we remember being their sheep, but now we drink rain and feel very fat about things generally, as there's no chance of being mutton any longer."

The ram eyed me with suspicion. "We aren't good to eat if you were considering it. Of course, a man who'll eat a cannon-ball…"

"Well, at least I didn't eat the horse-heads!" I pleaded. "And who buried cannons and engines and horses here? What happened that such a vicious orchard was ever planted?"

Behind me, one of those damned horses neighed softly, mournfully, and the wind clanked armor against bough.

"It was before the Wall," the ram whispered, and cast his eyes away. "Gog and Magog walked here, and where they walked fire followed, and towers rose, and there was no sun or moon but the blaze of their hearts, which they wore outside their bones, like jewels on their chests. When it was all done, the earth covered the wreckage, and nature took its course."

My mouth dried and the pulp of the cannon-fruit went sour within me. I could not think where I had beached myself. It was as though every story I had ever heard had broken itself on the shores of this place like blind, brittle whales, and I walked among their shards, that could never be made whole again.

I passed out of that forest with the laughter of sheep following me, and into lands so blasted I thought I walked on ash alone, with no rock to bear me up, only the void opening beneath my blistered feet. I saw the moon both day and night and thirsted so sharply that in the depths of those wastes I opened the vein of my arm and drank my own blood, as the sheep ate the leaves of their own tree. I thought of nothing. Not the wild dreams and visions of the great sand sea, not my mother or her black eyes that are Mary's eyes that are my mother's eyes, nothing at all. My mind became sifting ash, ash upon ash, and where the grit of my intellect fell, there too was ash, and the whole world burned and I burned with it and when I think of it now I see nothing but grey before and behind and beside; grey, and the scalded, terrible face of the moon stripping the life from me.

It seemed to me, near the end, that I smelled costly spices, pepper and myrrh, and I thought: *I am dying and it is as my mother always said, after all. The sanctified dead smell sweet, and on their beloved breasts the living array spice and perfume.*

I cannot say how many days and nights wound their way around this earth before I possessed a calm thought again, or knew my name.

THE BOOK OF THE FOUNTAIN:

The close of day has a kind of music to it. The descending blue, the rising silver stars, the parrots croaking their paeans to their own reflections, the market below my minaret closing up, clapping board to board, the boil of their last huge stew, full of every unsold thing. And my pen, always my pen, scratch-scratching away the last minutes of the world, little clock of my pen. The branches of the quince and the pomegranate began to snake through the upper rooms of my minaret some years back. I find them friendly, and now and again they have fruit for me, red and cracked as a heart, green and new as faith.

The fish-sellers call up to me. *Hagia, come down and try my oysters, they'll turn your guts to pearl!* The artichoke-mongers, too, who know, still, after all these years, to keep the heaviest for John, and now for me. It doesn't matter, him or me. They keep them back out of habit, for someone who loves them best. He loved the fruit because they brought his home back to him. I love it because they bring him back to me.

I recall several lines of Catacalon. Sometimes my brain claps upon some phrase and I cannot shake it loose; it runs the circuit of my body, down to my stomach and my heels and all the way back—a chariot-race, and tonight the old ram of Silverhair whips his beasts on that track. *Maids of amethyst there lived, and youths of jet! Each stone of our palace, not cut but born weeping from the warm womb of some crystal bride. Would but those silent bricks could reveal to me one of their names! What a betrayal is death, in the land of life.*

You betrayed me, John. My love, who chose death over me. In all your world of sins, was it never shameful to reject life and all its works?

I once met the philosopher himself—who during his third Abir lived as a gem-diver in the great caverns. His eyes had grown large and waxen in the lightless caves where the strong plunge into black pools, prying jewels from those secret clefts to bring into the light. I could not bear it, the closeness, the darkness, the cold water—the colder the tide, the brighter the stone, I heard the divers say. But Catacalon said, over a plate of orange cakes, that it suited him. In the dark, he came closer than ever before to the bones of those ancients who lived in this blessed country before us. It is not polite, of course, to make much of who we have been in lives past—more than impolite, it is forbidden. But I am a wicked girl, I have always been so, and loose with my love and my memory. He let me embrace him as he was and in my heart will always be, down there in the black, and I kissed his ram-horns, with orange sugar on my mouth. Sometimes the terrible pleasure of remembering is too much to deny.

Here in the al-Qasr, I almost believe that these stones could live as he said. I almost believe that nothing dies, and I am not a widow, but that someone among us must have been right, and I will see my mate again, in a strong brown tree, or in Heaven, or in a citadel built from his bones.

Oh, how I miss you, John. What a betrayal is death, in the land of life.

But I was speaking of my life with Astolfo, after my first Abir. Simple and sweet as cream we lived. The Lottery had gone easily for me—I kept my parents' orchards of parchment-trees and my name and gained a handsome boy with a mouth like a chalice in the bargain. Not so my husband's lot. Astolfo, as I have said, was of the tribe of amyctryae, whose mouths jut from their skulls and provide a deep bowl in which they brew all manner of things: teas and tinctures and unguents and intoxicants, poisons, even, and brandywine. His previous life had been well suited to him: a vintner, tending the vines grown from full bottles of old, dusty wines, ripened in the sun. Sometimes this viticulture failed him, and the vines would sprout berries of solid glass, or dozens of red wax stoppers. But sometimes the most delicate and marvelous liquors would blossom there, and Astolfo knew all the best coaxing ways—well I knew his coaxing ways! In his vast mouth he sampled and mixed those wines, sometimes vowing silence and shutting his lips for months, just to give them space and shadow to grow. What knowledge had he of the stretching of parchment, the scraping of vellum, the preparations of books for poets, tragedians, record-keepers? What use could his wonderful throat be to me?

I remember our wedding, in the Lapis Pavilion, how the little red bell-shaped flowers garlanded everything, and me in gold like all the other brides, gold and a black veil. The light of the future, and the laying to rest of our old lives. The great communal wedding takes place on the third day of the new Abir. The red lion Hadulph roared his benediction, he who would be my friend one day, against whose flank I would sleep in the pepper fields. We all cheered, and kissed, and there music shone as heavy and bright in the air as food on a table, and we were so fed, so fed by all those fiddles and psalters and drums.

The Fountain is gone now, and I know that should anyone one day read my little hand on this broad page they will be to me as a firefly to a woman—abrupt, here and gone. You must choose your mates so carefully, your pursuits, your kings. In your lives there can be room for but a few, perhaps only one. I have read John's books. They teach the virtue of choosing but one love, one passion, one occupation, perhaps even your father's occupation, so that he might not feel so brief. In the small space you have, to make that singular choice is so momentous that you can feel the grinding of your life as it opens to allow only one thing to enter. For us—perhaps the only new thing John brought us was regret. What need had we for it? If we did not like the mate the Abir brought us, we had but to wait a little while, and she would be gone. Perhaps we would grow to like her. Perhaps we would take lovers and leave her to her own pursuits. Perhaps we held back our mating stone from that Lottery entirely, and let a span pass by alone, in peace, or loneliness, or joy. If we did not wish to be a shepherd and hated the smell of sheep, before we knew it the time came again to stand before the great barrel, turning in the sun, and we would hold our single breath in such excitement, to hear what the world had prepared for us now, and a little unhappiness would have made us lean and sharp, bright and ready.

In your world there are more choices than time. But not for us. Not then. We had time enough to make them all.

So when I say I loved John the Priest, it does not mean I did not love Astolfo, or Hadulph, or Catacalon, or Iqama who came after John. Love is a fish: it grows as large as its vessel, and I—and all of us—were vast.

On the night of our marriage, Astolfo opened his great jaw and showed me what he had brewed there: the secret silver liquor of the wed, the bride-milk meant for me. It tasted like frost on the honeycomb. It tasted like a new life. It flowed between us as we kissed, his face to the mouth of my belly, and when I had taken it all he kissed the place where my head is not and I moved my hands once more in his dark hair. He never spoke much, but from the draughts he mixed in his jaw I took communion, and comfort.

But he did not love my orchard, nor the work of cutting and quartering the pages from the trees. He hated the taste of ink steeping in his mouth, the bitter iron gall, the grease of musk-glands. I showed him the tree of my mother's hands, and he wept bitterly for the loss of his old life, where he knew every step through every row of green and curling vines. This happens sometimes—it is unavoidable. I tried to show him how beautiful a finished book could be. The crispness of the paper, the scent of it, the ghost-patterns of the old hide that had made it, like a story, even before a story had graced the pages. I tried to sweeten the ink with honey and cane. We were very young, both of us, and trying with all our strength to get older as fast as we could.

Hadulph, the red lion who brought me these very pages on which to write the long tale of my life, who cut them from his uncle's hide and wept all the while, met me first in those days, when Astolfo sat sullenly by our hearth, letting the least offensive of my favorite brown inks darken against his teeth.

In those days Hadulph was a satirist—you see how even writing this is a crime, small or great. I betray him with every stroke of the pen, betray all of them, all my friends and even myself: I tell you who we were then, and who we would become, and do not grant any of us the Abir's privacy. Let me be forgiven or despised—I am what I am, and a historian knows no propriety.

Hadulph embraced his profession with typical leonine relish. He savaged our mule-headed king Abibas in sketches and poems, the braying lord of velvet nose and chronic indigestion, all on my paper, in my books. Abibas did not take it personally—everyone must make a living.

Now, among the lions of Pentexore are two tribes: the white and the red. They grow enormous, less like cats and more like horses. Their language rolls and drawls and was easy to learn. Much philosophy separates them: the white lions live in solitude on the slopes of the freezing mountains, often bearing the panotii of those snowy wastes upon their backs through long hunts. They hunt by singing, each to each, like the whales of the sea, and are devoted to the faith of the panotii: a godless cosmos, governed only by their own pale paws and what tenderness they feel in their thundering hearts. The red lions do not allow themselves to be ridden, and worship Yiwa the Nine-Horned Antelope Whose Eyes Weep Milk, the gentlest of all the gods, who allows herself to be continually and eternally devoured to nourish her people.

Once, I remember, I told John of the red lions' god. He expressed amazement that they would worship an antelope, and I said: *They think you childish, that you insist your god looks just like you. That is how a baby thinks, because she has only her parents to protect her, so all the power in the universe bears her own face.*

But red lions are city cats, while their white cousins remain wild highland beasts. They stamped the streets with their scarlet paws, in Shirshya, in Silverhair, in Nural where the al-Qasr shone and stood. Hadulph, with his broad blaze of white on his red chest, had been born of such delight: a red mother, a white father. Some cross-mating between the two tribes does occur. Pentexorans bear children but carefully, for if we did not we would soon be overrun with a million deathless babies. Still, we are flesh and bone, and the forbidden is always alluring. Sometimes I think Queen Abir perforated our lives in her way so that we would know keener pleasures. If nothing is forbidden, nothing can be perverse, and what delight is there in that sort of world?

In his despair, Astolfo did not agree with my generous assessment of the virtue of Queen Abir.

"She was a despot. A tyrant. What right had she to give over our lives to chance?"

"Everyone agreed to it. They voted, with tiny carbuncles for their chits, and into a black basin and a clear one they plinked their stones. You know this. In the end the black basin was empty save one speck of ruby, and the clear basin was full." I let the heaviness of my breasts fall against his shoulder, and blinked my eyelashes there, against his skin, the tiniest of kisses. I believe we both thought on that solitary red gem glinting in a dark bowl at that moment. We did not need to say it; we knew whose stone it had been.

"It's not fair. I wasn't born yet. I had no say." He frowned more deeply, the massive line of his jaw setting into a full grimace. He had no trouble speaking with his mouth full of ink—like pelicans, an amyctrya's throat is deep and two-chambered.

"But if not for the Abir, we would not have each other, Asto," said I, for I was young, and I was in love, and we all say foolish things when the world seems well-ordered. But he relaxed in my arms. I settled into our long bed, and absently he stroked the soft place where my head is not, his fingers on the rough hoop of bones that do not quite meet, as if our bodies meant to have a head, but simply never got around to it.

"How wicked must men have been," my husband marveled, his green eyes shadowed, "if this was the remedy?"

I touched the corner of his mouth with my finger and tasted the ink there. Not ready, too tannic, not nearly ready.

"Did you mother ever read *The Scarlet Nursery* to you, when you were a child?" I whispered. When one lies in bed at such an hour, every word seems a secret.

"Oh, yes," he smiled, his ink-stained lips shining in the dark. "I haven't thought about those stories in years. I think I spent most of my youth in love with Imtithal. In my first Abir, I prayed to be matched with a panoti. I wanted to be wrapped up in those ears, and told tales, and kissed by a cold mouth. I could have killed Houd for his cruelty to her."

I bit him playfully on the hip.

"Think of it, Asto. She lived through the first Abir, when it would have been hardest, most agonizing to endure. When no one knew how to keep from calling out to their former mother in the street or embracing their former husbands at the market. When no one knew how it was done. And she *chose* to live by the queen's law, not to return to the snow and her family, to cast her lot with us." I moved sleepily against my new husband. "We do not think of Imtithal the sherpa, leading pilgrims into the mountain peaks, though we know she lived that way before, or Imtithal the lamplighter, though we know she lived that way after. We love Imtithal the storyteller, and wish she had been our butterfly. But the Lottery chose that for her, chance chose it—and who knows when it may choose a life for us that will lead to glory and love, and tales told over and over by a thousand fires? What if this life holds wonder for you, my love, and you pull blackness over your eyes, down and down until you cannot see it?"

"But the queen cheated," Astolfo countered. "She wanted Imtithal for a nurse for her children, and that's what the barrel chose. How could that have been true chance? No, she rigged it, to have her way."

"You don't know that," I sighed. It was an old debate, even then. "Chance is a kind of god, and what ought to be generally comes to pass. We love her now, so she had to be a nurse then, or we wouldn't be talking about her in our safe, rosy house." I looked out at the warm, orange-gold moon, hung like a gourd drying in the sky. "And what if the old queen did cheat? It was worth it, if our Butterfly came in the bargain."

Oh, my memory. I wish you would soften, I wish I could hang

a veil over those times and remember only whispering and love in the dark. Instead, my own words mock me, and pierce me to the very quick.

And in the morning, Hadulph came for his monthly pamphlets, and nuzzled my shoulder, and asked what sucked my belly thin and turned my eyes red.

"My husband does not love his life," I answered, and that was the first day Hadulph and I went into the pepper fields and I learned how his tangled mane bristled, and how rough his tongue could be, and that some coupling among Pentexoran goes easier than others. Ours was difficult, and brief, and earnest, and fierce. I did not care, I only knew that with the lion I was not alone, I did not have to coax him to love this world. I did not know how much I could come to love that old beast, and how far we would go, he and I. For it would not be the last time. I told Astolfo of it that night. He had no jealousy, only interest in how we managed to contort ourselves enough to accomplish it.

I have told you. An infinity of time crafts a much different soul than a few anxious years. I knew that Astolfo had at least once visited his old vineyards and seduced a panoti girl there among the grapes. He told me how her ears enclosed his whole body, and I marveled, even envied him. Envy and jealousy are sisters, but not twins. Anyway, the first years of a change are hard, and we soon had other griefs than fidelity—for in time my husband grew sick, and though we do not age much past thirty, sickness we do know, even if it is rare, and disease, and plague. His face lost all color, and I drained the ink from his gullet, for he could no longer hold it all in. His weakness sparked such fear in me; I trembled with it, as with a child, knowing that it must sooner or later come to term. He slept often and rarely woke, and my arms ached from the stretching of every parchment alone.

Finally, I lifted him from our bed and strapped him onto Hadulph's broad crimson back. We walked thus, Astolfo as silent in his illness as in death, and the sun overhead dim and diffident. The tall banana trees let us pass, and the mukta flowers, clusters of pearls heavy as peas on their stalks, bent under our feet and shattered, the rain came and just as quickly went. More than once, I fell to the ground weeping, so tired and thirsty and afraid. It was a long road—but like the road to the Fountain, if it were not long it would be worth nothing, and I find it hard to speak of such a private thing as that journey.

As Imtithal said, weakness has always been a part of us, from the beginning. And so the world knows how to answer weakness. There are many secret places in Pentexore, many answers. I knew the place I sought, deep in the forest, a still white pool, like milk but not milk, where two old men stood knee-deep in the chalky water. Cattails of glass would bob and chime there, but no birds. The two old men, whose white mustaches had grown so long that they braided them in huge spirals like wheels of hay, hummed a single note, forever, unbroken unless a broken body came before them. I knew the place, so did Hadulph, though we had no name for it. He bore Astolfo's body stoically, and never once complained.

In that pool, a mussel-shell taller than a camel rested, dark blue, crusted with barnacles like lace. The two men, so old their wrinkles pressed on their eyes until they could not see at all, guarded it and tested the patient. They wore identical gowns of long grass. I propped Astolfo up on his feet; he groaned, his head sagging under the weight of his jaw. I staggered beneath his heavy body, which stank of sickness, sickness I thought bloomed from his despair as a nut from a nut-tree. If he had not despaired he would not be sick now, I was sure.

"Do you wish to be healed?" said the first man. It would be their only question.

Astolfo moaned and struggled to open his eyes in the thin sunlight.

"Do you wish to be healed?" said the other.

If he lied, the water would turn black and nothing the mussel-shell could do would help him. Faced with the gaze of the ancient men, many say no. They realize they want death, rest, not to be well and go on with living. Not everyone wishes to be well, in their hearts. Some wish to vanish. The question is not an empty one, no matter what John said later. Some reach out for darkness instead, and find it.

But Astolfo murmured: "Yes. Please, help me." His body could summon up no further word, not even one.

The men opened the mussel along its edge with their finger-nails, grown long and orange with age. Within, it showed pink-ish-white wetness, like soaked silk, and a kind of pearly sweat seeping from the flesh of the shell. I helped my love forward, my poor creature, my lost one. He stepped into the deep blue mussel; it closed up after him. He did not emerge for four days, and all the while I kept vigil, leaning against Hadulph's flank, watching the stars wheel, warm and certain in their spheres. I tasted the milky water once—it tasted like skin. Once, as we waited and the old men hummed, Hadulph asked me:

"Do you wish the Abir had gone another way? That it had paired you and I, or you and some less delicate soul?"

After a long while I answered: "No. I wish everything to hap-pen exactly as it did, for if it had not, it would not, and what trouble we would be in then. And after all, I have you anyway." And I rubbed his soft muzzle.

When he emerged, Astolfo was whole and flush, and such joy shone from his eyes that I felt it as a blow, heavy and pleasant against my breast.

And from that day, he never spoke again.

The shell takes its trade, always.

THE SCARLET NURSERY:

The summer rain ran rivers around the al-Qasr. Rain is a melancholy animal. It pads after one in the late afternoon, when all is soft and dim, pricking the spirit with silver darts. When I looked out of the nursery window all curtained with thick red and tied back with crimson cord, I always wished it were snow instead. In the wide basin of Nural, the great capital city, the city of sard and onyx, home but not my home, it never snowed.

One morning some years past I woke to find the water in our chapel's lustral basin lightly iced over, the barest whisper of ice, so that one touch of my fingertip shattered it. I was filled with such delight on that day; I walked through every hall and street full-up, as though carrying a wonderful secret. But it was a single crystal bead in an endless strand of hot stones. In Nural, clinging warmth was our constant companion, clinging to papaya leaves and baobabs, milkberry vines and bleeding roses. The great rains circled the summer solstice like a great golden drain, and though every flower opened up on the streets like beggars' hands, I drooped in the warmth. The children could not play outside, and in their thwarted wildness broke a dozen toys and several other objects which were not toys, such as my snowshoes, and all before noon.

This is how it went with us:

Houd, Who Was Mainly To Blame for the Snowshoes: I shan't apologize, either! You oughtn't to have such ugly things! It never snows here!

93

Ikram, Who Broke Three Clay Soldiers Herself: One day she might go home, Houd. Especially since she has to look after beastly things like you.

Lamis, Who Broke Nothing and Was Mild: No, never! Mother would never allow it! You must never go home! You are *our* Butterfly, and no one else's, and I shall thump anyone who says different right in the face!

Children, you must understand, are monsters. They are ravenous, ravening, they lope over the countryside with slavering mouths, seeking love to devour. Even when they find it, even if they roll about in it and gorge themselves, still it will never be enough. Their hunger for it is greater than any heart to satisfy. You mustn't think poorly of them for it—we are all monsters that way, it is only that when we are grown, we learn more subtle methods to snatch it up, and secretly slurp our fingers clean in dark corners, relishing even the last dregs. All children know is a clumsy sort of pouncing after love. They often miss, but that is how they learn.

Their hands are so big, so big, because they need so much. They reach out and out and you could disappear in their grip.

I know all this now, for I am much older. Then, I felt that I might cry, I missed the snow and the ice and the cold so terribly much. I missed my old life, and the girl I had been. I did not want to be shut into that oppressively dark and blood-colored chamber any more than they did. But you cannot show weakness to monsters, even small ones. Still, my snowshoes lay splintered on the floor and all three of the children studiously avoided looking at them. I summoned a deep pool of peace within myself, and iced it over until I could speak to the beasts again. Sweetly, with love, as much love as I had. Sometimes when you are sad all you can do is tell a story about sadness, so that by some obscure law, sorrow will cancel itself out and the rain will clear.

Besides—all royal children should know that they are not the center of the universe, despite all the evidence of their senses.

Darlings, I said to them, do you know that there is a world very far away from our own? With domed cities like herds of jeweled camels and towers so tall you cannot see their tips for all the creamy orange clouds?

Houd, Who Knew Everything: That is a lie. You shouldn't lie.

Ikram, Who Felt Very Poorly About the Soldiers: Says the lyingest liar who ever lied!

Lamis, Who Wanted the World to Be Big: Are there children there, like us? With big hands, and orange eyes?

There are children everywhere. And some of them, logically, must have hands like yours. But you should ask me, instead: How do I know such a world exists if I have never been there nor ever so much as seen a cup made by a man from across the sea?

Houd, Who Would Have Smashed Such a Cup: I don't care.

Lamis and Ikram, Whose Eyes Had Gotten Very Big: How do you know, Butterfly?

The rain said *plink, plink, hush*. I said:

Once, a very long time ago, before your mother was queen and before she pulled a bronze barrel into the Pavilion and spun all our lives inside, a man came to Pentexore from this other world. I was very young, not much older than you are now, and my ears had not yet turned white. When panotii are young our ears are blue—so blue they look black in the moonlight, like water. I lived in Nimat-Under-the-Snow then, and I had two mothers and a lobe-father. Not everyone is like cametenna, with their one greatmother and a dozen mating males, those dear and mute boys, dancing at night under rose-colored tents!

This strange man came into our city, wretched, starving, his toes near black with frostbite. He had not eaten in days, and when we fed him ox-tea he choked on it; he could not get enough. Perhaps I shall make this for you one day. In a cup of white tea, the sort that looks like silver sewing needles before it is picked, you pour ox-blood and honey, and add a lump of ox-butter to melt in the brewing. Nothing is better for starving souls.

Ikram, Who Ate Three Quince-Jellies That Morning and Was a Bit Ill: Ugh! I shall never drink that!

Houd, Who Liked the Sound of the Blood: I shall.

I was the only child in Nimat in those days, for we bear young infrequently, and the mating trio must be chosen from among all the village. In this way, a child is assured the protection of not only their parents but so many souls, and Nimat never grew too crowded nor too lean. Everyone adored me, and I adored everyone. We, all panotii, remember such overwhelming love, and it is from this memory that we draw up our kindness and patience with those who never knew what it was to be cuddled and kissed by every grocer, nursed at the breast of every blacksmith. When we are tried, by lovers or queens or pestering children who break everything in sight, into that full well we must immediately dive to cool our tempers.

Lamis, Who Was the Youngest, and Most Often Forgotten: I should like to be loved like that.

I ran wild, and rolled in the gardens until my blue-black ears got all covered in snowflakes. I sang, and everyone listened, called songs charming and dear. I loved in my turn a little white fox, who ran about my ankles and slept in my lobes. And when the starving man came into Nimat, with his huge dark eyes and his long beard, I went running to him, as I ran to everyone, knowing as any child of Nimat knew that he would catch me up in his arms and kiss me and give me some gimelflowers to suck. My ears flapped in the winter wind and I leapt, so sure I would be caught—and he dropped me. He tried to catch me, he did, but I was heavy, and he was weak.

I sat on the snow. Nothing like this had ever occurred before. I had been *dropped*. I looked up into the man's eyes, and they were strange to me; they had a whiteness circling a deep, dark well, instead of a panoti's total white. It seemed to me that he had an open void in his eyes, I was afraid of another soul for the first time. His cheeks sucked in, so hollow! He stared down at me, a little blue-black creature with great huge ears like an elephant's, her furry clothes all stuck with snow, about to start crying for the clumsiness of a stranger. And the man, with a great effort, picked me up and soothed me. He stroked my ears, which is very pleasant for panoti, and in language prickly and soft all at once, told me all was well. I understood him, though some of the words echoed weird and warped. It was as though we spoke languages that had been siblings, but separated at birth, and left to grow up on their own without knowing that the other had a passion for diphthongs or certain ornate verb tenses.

His name was Didymus Tau'ma, he said, and who was I?

Imt'al, I whispered, now in terror, hardly able to say my own name. He smelled hot, and faraway, like baking sand. *Do you have any gimelflowers?*

He didn't. My mothers and my father made him the ox-tea and listened to his tale: he had come from a place I could not even pronounce, called Yerushalayim, where all the domes were made of gold, and olive trees grew all full of oil and fruit. When he spoke of his city, even though his accent jangled strangely, I sat slack-jawed, as though I could see it before my eyes: dusty streets and palm dates smashed on the earth, evening prayer-songs like swans calling, and a man called Yeshua, who Didymus said was his brother, and Yeshua had died because the governor said he must. But three days later he rose out of his tomb and ate bread and drank wine somewhat gone to vinegar and spoke with all of them. Didymus himself had needed to touch Yeshua's wounds, half-scabbed and half-healed, warped and ropy with scars, before he could call him brother, and believe it true.

You must have planted him deep and well, one of my mothers said, *for him to sprout so quickly*. The foreign man stared at her and she stared at him and even I could see that he did not understand in any part what she meant. But neither asked further, not wishing to be rude.

While Yeshua's friends ate and drank and told old jokes concerning donkeys, Didymus looked toward the sun for a moment, just for a moment, and when he looked back to the table his brother had gone, never more to return to the living. Yeshua had returned to them—and all Didymus had done was doubt and frown. He was ashamed. Didymus Tau'ma dwelt deep in grief, he said. He would never see his brother again, not until he died himself, and perhaps then he would know how to smile.

If you die here, my lobe-father said, putting a slim arm around the stranger's shoulders, *we will see to it that you are buried near your brother's tree, even if we must walk all the way to Yerushalayim.*

Didymus Tau'ma thanked him, but he did not understand. He did not yet know where he was.

Now, as you know, there is a sea that surrounds our country, a sea of sand, and it is called the Rimal, and I know you have drawn pictures of it in your lesson books, and used up all the yellow paint. But four days a year a path forms in the sand, which might lead someone lost at sea to our shores. Such a thing happened when the Ship of Bones beached here. But there is another way, I think, through the mountains, the way my friend Didymus Tau'ma came.

He stayed with us for many years, and came down into Nural to see the al-Qasr, and tell the story of his brother to the king, who was called Kantilal and was one of the astomii, with a nose as big as your hands. Didymus made a house for himself of ox-skin and the great long bones one sometimes uncovers on the slopes of the Axle of Heaven. Every day I went to him, for I was deathly curious about the single soul in all the world who did not love me—though that did not last long. Soon enough I pounced upon him and kissed his face and he scratched my skull where I had begun to molt and show my new snowy coat beneath the blue. When I had grown and another family was busily swelling up with Nimat's next child, my friend often blushed when I greeted him in the fashion of the panotii when among intimate family: wrapping my legs around his waist to sit in his lap, closing him up entirely in the expanse of my pale ears. He whispered to me, in that sacred space my body makes, that it was not right that we should sit so, that it was bold and shameless.

I was confused. *Why should there be any shame within a family? You are Nimat now, and one of mine. It is not my fault your Yeshua had such small ears and could not teach you proper manners or sit in your lap.*

No, he said roughly, *that is not what I mean. A husband and wife might embrace thus, but not an unmarried woman and an old man.*

I did not understand him. He did not understand me. So I did as I liked.

Didymus liked best to tell his stories, of his brother, and their friends, and Yerushalayim in the autumn-time, when they ate goat together around a long table, and talked together about the nature of the world, and the nature of the soul.

What is a soul? I said.

A soul is what makes a man a man, he told me, *and not a beast. It is the immortal substance of a man, that will live forever.*

I will live forever, I said, and leaned my cheek against his.

Didymus did not really believe me. In his world, people live a short time and then die, like the first pioneers who settled the capital of Nural. In his world, when you bury a person in the earth, they stay there, and turn into bones, and do not grow at all.

Lamis, Who Visited Her Grandmother's Tree Every Saturday and Talked to Her About Government and Cream-Making: No! No, Butterfly, say it couldn't be. That's too terrible, to die and stay dead!

Ikram, Who Trembled: Don't cry, Lamis. We don't live in that awful world.

Another time, I asked him: *Do I have a soul?*

Didymus Tau'ma said: *I don't know, Imtithal. I wish my brother were here. He could tell you. But I am only a man, and I do not know what you have, where my soul is.*

And I could feel all his body beneath me rigid and tense, and I wanted him to be at ease, so I warbled a little, my favorite song, and fluttered my eyelids against his cheek, and he began to weep within my ears, because strangers are mystifying and sometimes incomprehensible.

Didymus lived with us for many years, until he was terribly old. We tried to tell him about the Fountain, but he insisted that he was happy to be so near to seeing his brother once more, and did not wish to lengthen their time apart. His hair turned white; his skin withered up like a walnut. He learned to make ox-tea. He built a little chapel where he could worship his god and prepare himself to meet his brother. He asked us to join him, but we did not wish to, taking comfort as we do in the universe as it is: subject only to our own love and seeking after wisdom, and governed by no jealous divinity.

And then, one day, he lay down and did not get up. He called me into his hut and I lay on him, lightly, since he could not move, and covering his face with my ears for the last time. By then, he loved the closing of them around him, the secret space they make. This is what we said to each other:

"Listen to me, Imtithal."

"I listen."

"I have been happy here. It has been a good life. I have known joy."

"This comforts me. I do not want you to die."

"Yet, I must. But before we part, I wish to tell you, and know that you will tell everyone: there are paths from my world to yours. Men will take them. Perhaps not soon, but one day they will."

"I will be so jubilant, to meet others like you."

"They will not be like me, Imtithal. Not all men from my world are kind, nor ever stood in the light of my brother's love. They will come with swords and they will come with many loyalties that you will not understand, nor will they try to make you understand."

"Like Alisaunder, you mean?"

And a look crossed his face as he considered the name. It seemed to sit on his tongue like a brand.

"Do you mean Alexander?"

Our languages clashed often thus—squabbling cousins.

"Alisaunder the Red, who closed the Gates, and trapped the tribes beyond the mountains, and made our land safe. It was a long time ago. Long before me, or even my parents. Before even the sciopods founded their great forest away to the east. Did he come from Yerushalayim, too?"

Didymus Tau'ma shook his head, troubled. I touched his face, grown old, but no less dear.

"They will come," he sighed, "and they will not be called Alexander, nor called Thomas Didymus, and they will not make you safe. You must be wary, and not leap into their arms like you leapt into mine."

"I am not a child anymore. I do not leap so often."

And he laughed a little beneath me.

"I know now," he rasped, "that this is part of God's great scheme, this place. I think perhaps there was never an apple here, nor a snake."

"We have many snakes and apples. And I never liked that story. I don't think it's true at all. Nothing in it is right."

"Not right for you, not here. But the men in my world, they can be so wicked, Imti, so wicked. You will live so much longer than me. They will hurt you, because that story is true for them, and they cannot help the terrible instincts in them, to eat everything, and know everything, and destroy whatever is not like them. If a man should come walking over the sand, treat him carefully. Be wary, like a wolf."

"I will," I promised.

And after we had lain together thus for many hours, I said: "Let me bury you here, Tau'ma. You do not have to go a Heaven for men who are wicked. Let me bury you, so that we need not be apart."

And though he had always refused, in dying he yielded to me. The temptation, when a man from that world stands at the black door, is too great.

"All right, Imtithal. Bury me deep."

Houd, Who Was Also Wicked: And did anyone else come? Did they bring swords?

It has been many centuries since. Perhaps there is no other world, and my friend was only a bit mad. Perhaps he wasn't, but it is just too difficult to get here from there. But it is wonderful to think about, isn't it? Another world, right next to ours, filled with such fantastical things?

THE HABITATION OF THE BLESSED

Our land is the home of elephants, dromedaries, camels, crocodiles, meta-collinarum, cametennus, tensevetes, wild asses, white and red lions, white bears, white merules, crickets, griffins, tigers, lamias, hyenas, wild horses, wild oxen, and wild men—men with horns, one-eyed men, men with eyes before and behind, centaurs, fauns, satyrs, pygmies, forty-ell high giants, cyclops, and similar women. It is the home, too, of the phoenix and of nearly all living animals.

We have some people subject to us who feed on the flesh of men and of prematurely born animals, and who never fear death. When any of these people die, their friends and relations eat him ravenously, for they regard it as a main duty to chew human flesh. Their names are Gog, Magog, Anie, Agit, Azenach, Fommeperi, Befari, Conei-Samante, Agrimandri, Vintefolei, Casbei, and Alanei. These and similar nations were shut in behind lofty mountains by Alexander the Great, towards the north. We lead them at our pleasure against our foes, and neither man nor beast is left undevoured, if our Majesty gives the requisite permission. And when all our foes are eaten, then we return with our hosts home again.

—The Letter of Prester John, 1165

THE CONFESSIONS OF
HIOB VON LUZERN, 1699

The nail in my candle plinked onto the tin plate, and I stirred myself from that terrible tale. I could not believe, not quite believe, that Imtithal's friend had been Saint Thomas lost in India, the answer to a riddle older than Prester John. How many secrets did you hide in one small country, Lord? I did not want to think of him beneath that alien story-teller—bold and shameless it was to touch an animal thus, and it dredged silt from my soul to read of it. It did not seem chaste, even if it did not seem lustful, either. I was disquieted, in my still, dark cell, its earthen walls close and warm.

I rubbed at my eyes. The book before me, Imtithal's book, all scarlet and thick, had gone deep brown at the edges. The smell of it had sweetened as I read, and the creases showed dark, softened. I knew then that I had little more than that night to read and to copy—the books would rot, would die as a body dies, and their words would vanish as the soul. No wonder I could only take three—in one night even I could manage no more, and probably not even this.

I called for Brother Alaric, my closest friend in our troupe. He is old enough to jealously guard his stories of youthful vigor, which is to say he is near enough to forty, and his mind is swift, severe and sharp. He came silently, and his presence comforted. He brought with him a mug of some thick, fortifying tea and something like a yoghurty beer, a rough plate laid with a slice of fowl the woman in yellow had cooked in her lord's hearth, and a clay bowl of flat red leaves.

"She says they are stimulating, and will help you to stay awake. She bade me ignite them, thus," Alaric said, and he took up my candle, holding the flame to the leaves until wax spattered them and finally, they lit, releasing a savory smoke into the room which did indeed rouse me somewhat. I drank the draught and chewed the dark meat gratefully, while Alaric looked over my copying, exclaiming over this and that thing.

"Of course we cannot credit that the Priest-king had a wife!" he marveled. "Nor this nonsense about Thomas Judas and some kind of elephant."

I inhaled the smoke deeply, and took up the role of the worldly advocate, thinking to draw out Alaric's thoughts and to help order my own. "You think so? Many holy soldiers did worse in the Holy Land than taking a lawful wife or making friends with a child."

Alaric touched the browning pages. "It must be a fiction," he said firmly. "You know how writers love to sully the reputations of the saints. It is a fiction written by Abbas the king, or worse, that woman with her awful eyes."

"Perhaps," I said, savoring the last of the beer. "I no longer know what to think. For all we are here seeking a man no one has met, and whose deeds are preserved only in an ancient letter."

"But Brother Hiob, many have met him! Many doctors of learning and soldiers of fortune have returned from the east with tales of Prester John, and stones from his throne, branches from his orchards."

"I have not finished my inquiry, Brother Alaric, I could not possibly say."

And thus settled, we sat for a time, enjoying the scented smoke as I allowed my old eyes to rest.

"As I read, I have been thinking on what has befallen us here, Brother. Do you know, the woman in yellow allowed me only three books from her marvelous tree?"

"Certainly, Brother Hiob," said Alaric dubiously. Do not blame him, Lord. He was not there; he did not see the beautiful tree, overflowing with books. I would not have believed me, either. But my thoughts whirled too quickly, one after the other, making connections and chasing after them. I hurried on, feeling alive as I had not for years.

"Poor man. Incredulity is not a virtue in your line of work. But can you not see what I see? Seth, too, was granted but three grains from the Tree of Knowledge and the Tree of Life entwined in Paradise. He ate them and a bush grew from his mouth, all aflame, and from the wood of that sapling came the wood of the doors of Solomon, and even the Holy Cross that bore our Lord Christ."

Alaric frowned. "Tell me you do not intend to eat these books."

I shrugged, affecting unconcern, embarrassed by my effusion before the younger, stronger man. "No, no. I only find it interesting, to walk in the echoes of the Word of God. One might see it as a sign from Heaven that we have found a true narrative here, for where we repeat the stories of Scripture, surely we walk in virtue."

Alaric sunk his head into his rough cowl as shrinking from a chill that was nowhere to be found.

"Do you believe then, that we are dead, and in Paradise, and that tree you saw and touched was none other than the Tree of Eden, and we poor souls have passed from earth, but not lifted up our glasses to look upon the light?"

I looked up at the rooty mud roof of my chamber. I wanted a cheerful debate—Alaric gave me sepulchral poetry.

"Like Thomas Didymus, I do not know," I sighed. "In all my days I have known nothing stranger nor more unearthly than this place, yet it does not have the tang of Paradise, to me."

"Nor me," breathed my Brother.

"Leave me to my work," I said. "Prester John must soon meet the people of his nation, I feel certain. My pulse quickens each time I reach for his book among the others! Go, and make friendly with our hosts. Perhaps if I press, they will allow me to harvest more fruit from that tree." I felt my excitement growing again, running away with me—for did I not wish to study this mortal trinity of books, to do Your work, Lord, without concern for my own hungering after knowledge, after the Priest-king? But instead of these reasoned thoughts I heard myself barking roughly: "More and more, until I am sated—and God gifted me with a great appetite for books, Brother Alaric!"

My friend adjourned, shaking his head, and I, my fever stoked all the higher, pushed a new nail into the soft tallow.

And I prayed for an improvement in the virtue of Prester John in future pages, for as of yet, I loved him more as a man than a priest.

THE WORD IN THE QUINCE:

Chapter the Fourth, in Which John
Suffers a Troubling Dream

I do not remember being found. I only remember a dreaming like drowning, a heavy weight pressing upon me. No matter how I strained, I could not get free. But at least it was dark and cold in the dream, and I saw neither sun nor moon. I liked the dream better than living, better than wandering in a world of unbaptized sheep. I do not even remember being carried, or cleaned, or laid upon a bed of any kind—though I dreamed so long that all of this must have occurred while I slept. I only remember the dream: I sat in a long field under the cooling evening sky, and all the stars, all the many stars, hung like lanterns, their strands tied to the terrible belly of a golden-rose sphere hanging heavy in the sky. The sphere drooped low, huge, bigger than any sun or moon, as big as the whole sky, pure crystal, the color of candlelight, with veins of blood flicking through it. I felt that if I put up my arms I could hold some tiny portion of its grand belly. The stars hung from it on silken strings, each no bigger than a pearl. And yet, when I looked up at it, I felt deep shame, and wept, though I knew not why. It turned, slowly, in my dreaming sight.

Below this sphere sat a throne of carved black wood, and the posts of that chair had collected a sifting of snow, though no snow now fell. None other than my friend Kostas sat upon the throne, his narrow face regarding me with sorrow. At his feet two hounds crouched, one made of gold and one of bone.

"In the kingdom of memory," Kostas said, "the amnesiac is king." He watched me implacably, the good and measured soul who carried my parchment and ran for wine at dusk with my coin, who remained so perfectly untroubled by the question of whether or not painting the face of God was an act of devilry or divinity, whether Christ was Flesh or Word, or the awful mystery of Word-in-Flesh, who wanted in all the world little more than a few wet dates and a bit of lamb-fat for his bread.

"Kostas," I whispered, and fell before him with my face to the stony earth. "I want to go home. I should not have left. Look at how I am punished the moment I abandon my city."

"What home can there be for heretics like us?" said my friend, and I knew he spoke the truth—at least concerning myself, who had thrown his lot with Nestorius and the Logos.

I looked up at him, throned in glory. "What heresy could you have committed? You are an innocent."

Kostas put his naked brown hand upon the head of the golden hound; the creature arched her head to meet his palm.

"I was an idolater, and you my golden bull. I wished not to be like Christ but to be like you. I worshipped you, and tried to imitate your life, instead of that of a saint who might deliver my soul. I dreamed that one day, if I performed every act perfectly, you might praise me with some small word, and that word I would have folded into a cedar box and preserved forever. That word would have been enough."

Again, shame washed over me like a hot tide. I pressed my face once into the earth, which gave way in the dream, black and soft. Yet upon my pate a new pair of eyes opened, and I saw with them perfectly, and was not spared any sight. I whispered: "I have never heard you speak this way."

"Well," said the dream-image, and he removed his hand from the golden hound to caress her bone sister, who ground her teeth in pleasure. I could see her fangs through the bones of her narrow cheek. "I am not really Kostas. In the kingdom of sleep, the insomniac plays his tricks."

Kostas turned his dear, lovely head full to one side, and when he turned it back towards me, it had become the face of an old man, but one hale of health and rosy of nose, as though he either drank much or spent his days in snowy crevices where the wind bit at his extremities. He possessed a beard, and dark hair not yet yielded up to white. His eyes shone huge and deep, lights in the dark, stars wheeling within him. All this I saw through my dream-eyes, which blinked on my skull. The golden sphere bore down on us.

"Raise your head, my son. Did you not come seeking me?"

I looked through my natural vision, but knew him not.

"I am Didymus Thomas, Thomas the Twin. I am an Apostle of Christ. Child, do you not know me?"

Thomas the Saint smiled with a tenderness so keen and sad I thought I might die there and never wake, but wander in this half-lit place forever, until in waking life my bones shivered into dust and blew down the length of some unnamed valley and out of anyone's memory save a few damned sheep. On his throne beneath the golden sphere, Saint Thomas opened his shirt, not to beckon, but to reveal: he bore a second pair of eyes upon his chest, and a mouth in his navel. Out of this second mouth he whispered:

"Go now, my son. I forgive you all that is to come."

The golden sphere descended, and I felt it press on the bones of my back, crushing me with its impossible weight, its solemn light.

Many years later, in the green-curtained bedroom I shared with my wife, I told her of this dream. She did not care for it. She would have liked to forget those first days. *You were so ugly then*, she said. *You forgive yourself in your dreams. What if I do not forgive you?*

I put my hands to the soft space between her collarbone and her shoulder-blades, where another woman's head might be. I kissed it, and pressed my face to her warm brown shoulder. Outside, the summer rains steamed down from a heavy sky.

If you do not forgive me, I will be lost.

THE BOOK OF THE FOUNTAIN:

When we first found him, he lay face-down in the pepper-fields, his skin blazed to a cracked and blistered scarlet, his hair sparse as thirsty grass. It might have been anyone.

King Abibas had chosen us, a fair sampling of nations, to investigate the thing that had manifested in the farm-speckled suburbs of Nural.

I was two hundred and fifty-eight years old.

I should mention that in those days our king was Abibas, a blue mule. Blue mules are not, of course, truly blue, but more of an ashen color. However, they swear that their primal ancestor, Urytal, could walk unseen through the summer world, for his coat was the color of the sky. Other than this, Urytal's main characteristic was a rampant priapism, and the ability to sire children simply by coughing. When a brace of mules related this tale to John during his mania for origin stories, he told them this was mere wishful thinking and ridiculous, masking their shame at being unable to produce offspring themselves. Abibas bit him. Rather, three of the Abibas-fruits on the funeral tree bit him.

For in the midst of his reign, Abibas died in a duel, which seemed to him the best way to resolve a certain issue of personal honor. Duels do not normally proceed to the death, but mules, after all, do not normally leave well enough alone. He was buried with much pomp, and in due course his tree sprang up and he continued to rule very much as before. And when the stranger arrived, the returned Abibas, his first blossoms just starting to show, chose us as his representatives: Hadulph, myself, and a pair of pygmy twins. He might have chosen anyone, and when I think on it now I wonder, had I not been chosen, if I would have cared even a little what happened to the piece of human flotsam we inherited from the unforgiving Rimal.

I am a Pentexoran. I am a loyal and darling child of luck. I submit to it, like a dog. But it terrifies me, sometimes, how near we come, every moment, to living some other life beyond imagining. In my heart's eye there are two Hagias. One standing above the man I did not yet even know was called John, and one home safe with Astolfo, eating hazelnuts in the orchard, kissing his broad jaw and never once thinking of a city called Constantinople. I feel my entire self separated in that moment, prodding John's body with my foot, the sun burning my shoulders, a kind of tableau we did not know was a tableau, because no one can ever know when the world changes. It just happens—you cannot feel it shift, you are only suddenly unbalanced, tumbling headlong toward something, something new.

The pygmies wanted to eat him.

"He must have been strong to have wandered this far, from whatever strange country," the girl-twin reasoned, tugging her beaded beard. "We should have the right to bisect his liver and take the strength into our tribe."

"Don't be selfish," I said, still watching his motionless form. We had not yet even turned him over.

"Selfish? Us?" the boy-twin scowled, his tiny face bitter. "I have not tasted strength in some time, I'll have you know. There are rules. We are prepared to receive his vitality, and bear it into our family. You don't need it. Let us have it!"

Hadulph nosed the man's maimed feet, and snuffled at his dark clothes.

"He smells of salt water and pressed flour," the red lion announced, "and he who smells of pressed flour knows the taste of baked bread, and he who knows the taste of baked bread is civilized, and we do not eat the civilized, unless they are already dead and related to us, which is a matter of religion and none of anyone's business."

I looked down at the man's shape between the black and red pepper plants, laid in their long rows like a chessboard. It looked like the end of a game to me: I, the broad-shouldered knight standing over the toppled kingpiece. I stroked the fontanel above my collarbone, considering the wreckage that the desert wind had washed onto our beach of black peppercorns. He did not look dangerous at all—soft, and unclawed, and shaped more or less like a very small giant. Perhaps the giants would adopt him as a pet. But I did not say this, nor side with the pygmies. Instead, I chose for all of us, and so, if blame is to be had, I will take it. I said:

"He is wretched, like a baby, wrinkled and prone and motherless. Take him to the al-Qasr, and iron him out until he is smooth," I said quietly, and the pygmies grumbled, gnashing their tattooed teeth.

Hadulph took the stranger on his broad and rosy back, where the fur bristles between his great shoulder blades, and that is how our world ended.

We laid the strange man on one of the fallen pillars in the central hall of the al-Qasr—the smooth tower of violet stone had crashed to the floor one day as the quarter-moon market bustled in the portico. When it fell, tile-shards of gold and splinters of ebony came tumbling after it, and now one could see the stars through the hole it made, like coins dropped into the hand of heaven. I was there that day: A brace of tigers looked up from arguing with a two-faced apothecary about whether she should be allowed to sell the powdered testicles of greater feline castrati as aphrodisiacs; the lamia paused in their venom-dance; I placed an arm beneath my breasts and lifted my eyes from the scribe-work before me to the ceiling. We all looked back and forth from the fallen pillar to the hole in the roof, up and down, up and down: work to sky to ruined architecture.

This is how memory works, when you live forever. You lay a man on a stone, and you see the man and you see the stone but you also see the history of the stone, as you saw it when it was whole and polished, when it was cracked and poorly cared for, when most everyone knew it was going to go, when it stuttered, when it fell. You remember who built the stone pillar, the debate over the color of it, whether or not it was garish. You think of the books you know that deal in pillar-hood, perhaps Yuliana of Babel's architectural poetry. Perhaps the sciopods' ranting about the decline in quality construction. And because you have seen so many patterns shape and ravel and unspool, you also see, flickering just out of reach, the possibilities inherent in a stranger with such small ears, such a small nose, such a tiny jaw. You see, dancing at the edges of his shape, what he might become. What you might become.

On the night the pillar fell, I was busy at my stall, writing for coin. After Astolfo's illness, he had found a kind of grudging love for the groves of parchment-trees and the long hoops for drying skin in the sun. Finally, he ignored me completely, dwelling among them always, happy and silent, in a kind of communion with them of which I had no part. I began to take our vellum and ink to the quarter-moon market, and it began to grow famous and desired, for it was always fine, and I have a good hand. A lovely script makes any paper shine.

Of things that exist, some exist by nature, some from other causes, I had copied out from one greenish sheet of pepper-leaf paper to another. It was a passage from the Anti-Aristotle of Chandrakant, which a widowed gryphon by the name of Fortunatus bade me make into a small book for him. The Anti-Aristotle, you see, was himself famously widowed in his youth, and suffered bitterly, as his wife had drowned, and no body remained to bury. All of the philosopher's passion he poured into his master-work, the *Physikai Akroaskeos,* and when he had finished, he fell into such a grief that no one could come near him without being quite clawed and wet with tears.

The philosopher went to the mussel-shell, and the old men there, but could not tell them he wished to be healed. Words failed him. He walked into the west and did not return.

The night the pillar fell, with the market clamoring all around me, I wrote smoothly: *Animals and their variegated parts exist, and the plants and the simple bodies exist, and we say that these and the like exist by nature.*

The pillar chipped its complex torus, and tottered on the onyx floor. I ignored the sound. Distraction is the enemy of perfection.

All the things mentioned present a feature in which they differ from things which are constituted by art. Each of them has within itself a principle of stationariness (in respect of place, or of growth and decrease, or by way of alteration).

The constellation of Taurus-in-Extremis, the Slaughtered Cow, could be seen winking through the broken wood. Ebony dust drifted down on a soft breeze off of the river.

Even motion can be called a kind of stationariness if it is compulsive and unending, as in the motion of the gryphon's heart or the bamboo's growth. On the other hand, a bed or a coat or anything else of that sort, insofar as it is a product of art, has innate impulses to change.

The stone column crashed down; rich black earth spurted up through the ruptured floor. The pillar's belly shuddered in it, and cracked from side to side, loud and unignorable. But I dutifully finished my line, so as not to lose my place: *as an indication of this, take the well-known Antinoë's Experiment: if you plant a bed and the rotting wood and the worm-bitten sheets in the deep earth, it will certainly and with the hesitation of no more than a season, which is to say no more than an ear of corn or a stalk of barley, send up shoots.*

Past the ruin of the pillar, I could just glimpse the edge of the sardis-snake that guarded the entrance of the al-Qasr, ensuring that no folk who are not lamia and therefore licensed, could never bring poison under its roof. Behind it and far off, the Cricket-star flickered as if in chirruping song.

The quarter-moon market gave a collective shrug and went about itself, stepping over the purple column and leaving it where it had fallen—wasn't it better, the cyclops murmured, to let a little light in, and have a nice place to stretch one's feet? I glanced back at my thrice-copied treatise, tiresome as all secondhand treatises are, and finished the page.

However, since this experiment may be repeated with bamboo or gryphon or meta-collinarum or trilobite, perhaps it is fairer to say that animals and their parts, plants and simple bodies are artifice, brother to the bed and the coat, and that nature is constituted only in the substance in which these things may be buried—that is to say, soil and water, and no more.

I laid a man on a stone and watched a stone fall and there was no separation between the two nights. I did both things, and I thought while the pillar fell over and over in my heart:

He is so unlike us. What does that mean?

By the time we laid the stranger out on the pillar, it had grown over with phlox and kudzu and lavender and pepperwort, and we rested his battered head on a thatch of banana leaves. He moaned and retched like a sailor coughing up the sea, and I held him while he wracked himself clean. I held him like a child, and felt myself drift upward, and backward, through my memory, as his sickness ebbed and flowed. It is tiresome to nurse someone, though no nurse would admit it. Illness has a certain sameness, the cycle of purging, fevering, chilling, purging again. I had had enough of it with my husband. I had no patience left for a stranger's travail—yet I managed to hold him, not very heavy at all, as folk gathered around—Grisalba, a wealthy lamia, shouldered in, and behind her the widowed Fortunatus, and I thought on how his golden fur shone that day when the pillar broke, how red his eyes from weeping. I tried to think of anything but the wet bodily palpitations of that stranger, so helpless in my grasp.

It was some ways past the fishing hour when his eyes slitted open and his moth-voice rasped:

"Thomas…"

"Is that your name, boy?" growled Hadulph, who by dint of his size could call anyone boy.

"Ah," the man coughed, dust and ash spattering my arm. "No, my name… my name is John."

The name should have echoed. We all should have stopped to let it pass between us like a premonition. But we did not. We watered his blistered lips instead, and he had not yet noticed that I held him in my arms, propped against the breasts he would soon enough call demonic and unnatural. But he had not yet called us all demons, succubi, *inferni*—he only asked for bread, and more water.

He had not yet screamed when Hadulph spoke, or trembled when the crickets chirped in iambic rhymes. He had not yet called us all damned, demanded tribute to kings we had never heard of, forbade anyone not made in God's image to touch his flesh.

He had not yet castigated us for our ignorance of the Trinity, or preached the Virgin Birth during our mating season. He had not yet searched the lowlands for a fig tree we ought not to touch, or gibbered in the antechamber, broken by our calm and curious gazes, which we fixed on our pet day and night, waiting for him to perform some new and interesting trick.

He had not yet dried his tears, and seen how the al-Qasr was not unlike a Basilica, and how the giants were not unlike Nephilim, and how Hadulph was not unlike the avatar of St. Mark, and the valley of our nations was not unlike Eden. He had not yet decided that all of the creatures of our world were not unlike holy things—except for the blemmyae, except for me, whose ugliness could not be born by any sacred sight. He had not yet called us his mission, and followed Grisalba the lamia home trying to explain transubstantiation, which she, being the niece-by-marriage of a cannibal-dervish, understood well enough, but pretended to misconstrue so that he would follow her home.

He had not yet called her a whore and tried to make her do penance with a taper in each hand. She had not yet sunk her teeth into his cheek, and sent him purpled and pustulant back to Hadulph.

Hadulph had not yet licked him clean, roughly and patiently, as cats will, and called him his errant cub. He had not yet fallen asleep against the scarlet haunch of the lion.

He had not yet retreated into the al-Qasr to study our natures and embrace humility, ashamed of his pronouncements and his pride. I had not yet brought him barley-bread and black wine, or watched over him through three fevers, or showed him, when he despaired, how my collarbone opens into a sliver of skin like clouds stretched over a loom.

He had not yet come crawling through the dark, shame-scalded, to hear my belly speak, and read to him from the green pepper-papyrus of my daily calligraphy, just to hear the way I said my vowels. He had not yet said that my accent sounded of seraphim.

This is how memory works, when you live forever. You look back from a perch of years and it all seems to happen at once.

"My name is John," he said, "I… I think I have become lost. I know that I came searching for Thomas and his tomb. The Apostle, where is the Apostle? Take me to him, if you are a Christian soul."

Hadulph and I exchanged glances.

"What is an Apostle?" the lion said.

THE SCARLET NURSERY:

In the wake of any visit from the phoenix, the children descended into an orgy of new ambitions and phraseologies and wild dreams, all balanced on the pyramid of toys and baubles Rastno brought them, half of which would be broken inside of a month, the other half ensconced among the most treasured toys of our little creche. I never devised a method of predicting which way any single glass ball or cage or crystal lamia with her tail flaming bright orange and blue would go. He was a great glassblower, Rastno. He reasoned that his glass should be finest of all, since he feared no flame but his own. And true to this he filled the capital with beads and baubles and bowls and chalices, plates and amphorae and children's toys. And mirrors, mirrors of every shape. The children prepared for weeks for his visits. Nevermind that he came to meet their mother, and inform her of much sadness and more fear; for my dears he came only to dazzle them. His scarlet and cream feathers arced and curved in a dance for their delight; the golden plume of his brow bobbed in interest when they shared their small triumphs and betrayals. He was hardly bigger than Lamis, if you excused her hands, but to them he was big as a mountain.

The dead moon slid low in the sky; we had prepared a night-picnic for her rebirth. Ikram had boiled mint and berries all afternoon to make jam—it appealed to her nature, the fire, the bubbling, the pain of scalding her thumbs. Lamis had rolled out little cakes as round as the living moon, the dough eggy and yellow, very quietly and diligently, as if with her own virtue

120

encouraging the new moon to rise. Houd had brewed coffee for all of us in a silver pot, crushing the beans with his prodigious fist, already as strong as a mallet. He peered at it with some excitement: dark, bitter, hot, smelling deeply of cinnamon and earth and even a little of the blue flowers the queen keeps ever at her bedside. All because, as Houd said: *the moon likes these things best.*

And so we sat under the stars, on a hill behind the al-Qasr, just high enough that we could peer over the sardian tips of her towers, and their crowns of bronze stars that silhouetted against the real and blazing ones. The cakes tasted a bit of anise, and I praised Lamis, for she often needed praise, being young and unsure of everything in the world. We waited for the moon to rise. I sang a song about the gentle manners of the cyclops.

Ikram, to Whom Rastno Gave a Glass Horn: Butterfly, why is Rastno the phoenix so sad?

Lamis, to Whom Rastno Gave a Glass Flower: He tries to be sunny for us, but he cries beneath his wing. Even I have seen it.

Houd, to Whom Rastno Gave a Glass Dagger: He is a grown-up. Grown-ups are always sad. It's their hobby.

I bade them come close to me. I let my ears flow around their shoulders. I coaxed them to look down into the valley of Nural—to see the midnight flowers, how black they were, how they fluttered on the long grass like moths. The moon makes that wind, as she gets ready to be born. The trouble was not that Rastno was grown-up. It is true that we pile up sadness in our hearts like treasure—though love and happiness too, I promised them. The heart is greedy and vast. But Rastno's sorrows were also greedy and vast—they sufficed for a whole people. And I asked while the coffee steamed, for I was always a teacher to them: What do you know about phoenix?

Lamis, Who Sang a Song for the Phoenix, When They Were Alone, About Having a Cruel Brother, and Not Being Pretty: They bring presents!

Ikram, Who Danced for the Phoenix, When They Were Alone,

Mad as a Dervish, Spinning Around: They live five hundred years, and then burn themselves to death in a cinnamon nest, and rise up again, a new bird, to live a new life.

Houd, Who Said Nothing to the Phoenix When They Were Alone, But Stared Stonily at Him, and Then Wept: Like the moon. Like us, when the lottery-barrel spins.

Oh, I had such clever children. But I knew something more, and so did Rastno, and this is why he was sad.

Listen to me, now. To listen is to become like the moon, silent and full of light, a witness in the dark.

Once, so many phoenix lived in the cinnamon forests that it all seemed like a long red river. The forests nestled south of the great lake of silver that borders the city of Simurgh far to the north of Pentexore. Not so terribly far from Nimat-Under-the-Snow, but in the warm lowlands, where the great mountains of my heart can be seen bright and bold against the gentle sky. There the trunks of the trees are made of a soft, fragrant amber called frankincense, their leaves ruddy brown, sweet cinnamon flake the color of embers. Those forests once teemed with phoenix-life, and Simurgh was their city. They held autumn balls there, and at the end so much passion and such complex dances had crossed the floor that the whole palace would suddenly go up in flames, and the birds would stand outside in their finest dewcloth and applaud by stamping on the ground and crowing.

When an elderly drake and duchess—for that is how the male and female of the species are properly called—felt her time coming upon her, every soul in Simurgh would bring her gold and cassia, cinnamon and incense, tea-leaves and pepper-root to build her nest, and it would be a festival day, and they would cheer her and praise her long life before she immolated and the sky turned dark with her smoke.

Now, in those days, it was not enough to burn on a soft, sweet-smelling nest. The phoenix who reached the end of his days and wished to resurrect had a long journey ahead of him, as long and arduous as any he might take in life. Before the flame took him, the aging bird would fashion for himself an egg of myrrh, a funeral egg, and into that egg he packed not only his own ashes and charred red bones, but all of his memories and loves, his disappointments and terrors, everything that was the old bird. For days the old matron or master would sit upon the egg as if it might hatch, as if they meant to nurse the ghosts of themselves. Even when the nest burned, the egg remained, unspoiled, not even blackened, and the first task of the new phoenix would be to take the funereal egg in her talons and fly far, far off, to a city called Heliopolis, beyond the Nural, beyond Silverhair, beyond Nimat and the Axle of Heaven. Rastno said it lay beyond even the Rimal—but only they knew the way.

In my heart I suspect Heliopolis dwelt in that world where my friend Didymus was born, but Rastno himself, the *Bazil* of the phoenix, the emperor who makes such beautiful toys, does not know, not anymore. Only the former Bazil knew the place, and when a matron went to her conflagration he would whisper the way into her ear, so she might perish in peace. But this chain of emperors was broken, and the map is lost.

Long ago, you see, Alisaunder the Red came to this country. You remember I spoke of him with Didymus Tau'ma in his hut. Do you know why he was called the Red?

Ikram, Who Sat in Awe of All Warriors, And Longed to Be One, Whispering: Because of the crows.

Because of the white crows, the merules, who can see so many things we cannot. When he first came over the Rimal, which in those most ancient of days was not so forbidding as it is now, not so full of salt and fish with teeth, the merules drew back from him, and whispered that they could see his death hovering over his head, a red splash like a crown. He came with his wife, who was called Roshanak, and his lover, who was called Hefaistes, and four young men with shoulders like stones who carried his palanquin across the sea of sand while he and his beloveds rested on rose- and sky-colored pillows and shared bread and honey together. He exclaimed with delight when a delegation of sciopods greeted him, led by Tarsal, who was their greatest princess. Alisaunder marveled at their ropy, muscled legs, their enormous single knees, their broad, flat feet, and how such a wonder could be. He eagerly asked of Tarsal, whose hair streamed silver: *Is there a sea on the other side of your country? A great sea that spans the world? It is this thing I seek.*

And Tarsal replied: *I do not have time for children's lessons. Take food, if you want it. Take water, and oil for anointing. Take even fresh pallbearers to hoist you back to your own country. For we are at war, and the merules say you are soon to die.*

Alisaunder smiled, for he was a god of war. He knew it better than marriage or eating or sleep. He beamed so broadly that Tarsal was charmed, and her retinue laughed at his childish enthusiasm as he put his hand to her shoulder and pledged: *I can bring ten thousand officers, and as many horses, and each of these mounted nobles have in their service a dozen infantrymen. And each of the infantrymen have a brace of servants, and even the least of these knows how to march in formation, and hold up a shield, and cut down an enemy between two breaths.*

Tarsal, whose foot had broken the necks of many soldiers, was no fool. What would they have to give him for such things? No man makes war for nothing. But Alisaunder the Red said that he asked only to allow some few of his officers to intermarry with us, if they could find willing mates, and to call some small town or hamlet by the name of Alisaundry. He required also that the merules take counsel with him, and speak unto him concerning his death. Tarsal, who had done with marriage after her third husband, to whom the kingdom referred as her Third Irritation, took stock of the tall Roshanak, with her skin like cassia, and the gentle, almond-eyed Hefaistes, both of whom watched the Red with patient love. As long as Tarsal herself would not be compelled to take on a Fourth Irritation, she felt well-satisfied to sound Alisaunder's horn across the sand-road.

But no officers came thundering across the crisp sand. It roiled and crashed in white-gold waves behind him, as the road that had borne Alisaunder's palanquin off the course of his constitutional vanished once more. Alisaunder smiled a second time. *I do not need them,* he laughed. *Only tell me the root and cause of the war at your door and I shall end it.*

And so the sciopods took a knee, and Alisaunder and his family sat in the shade of their silver palanquin and listened closely, not only the Red himself but also his man and his woman, and even his four servants.

Tarsal explained, very gravely. For those were the days of Gog and Magog, and their ravening over our country, their terrible teeth seeking any soft thing to devour, their stride leagues long, their blades so sharp they could cut your breath from your chest and leave you dead without a wound. Tarsal sighed: *They do not want territory or wealth. They love only death, and eat only death, and they are killing us because we live so long that no meal could be sweeter to them. They are the end of things, that is their only purpose.*

Surely that cannot be so, Roshanak protested. Her long black hair was caught up in many lapis beads, and Tarsal found her too beautiful to look upon—even the long scars on her cheeks made her only more severe and lovely. *Everyone wants something. Everyone desires.*

And Tarsal allowed the truth of her words. *In this country,* she said, *which we call Pentexore, we have a philosopher called Artavastus. He lives still, and has a very long coat, for he is a bear of great size, and the color of him is like pearl. He dictated to his amanuensis a long book, which I will summarize for you, for bears have little concept of brevity in literature, as they expect any book worth its weight to last through several hibernations. Artavastus said that the cosmos as we know it is always in a state of decay, hurtling toward dissolution, toward a kind of fire at the end of all things. He thought that we, by which I mean Pentexore itself, presented a kind of pin in the substance of the spheres that kept it all from flying too fast toward that end. And so it is natural that we should claim as our native land the same earth that gave life to our opposite. Gog and Magog, madam, are agents of that fire, that blackness at the end of everything. They work towards it, long for it; it is their mother and their wife and their child.*

Alisaunder beamed with a fullness of pride. *Do you mean to say that your war is against two men alone?*

They are not men, Tarsal snapped. *You do not understand.*

Every field they touch comes to serve them.

Have you seen them? What are they, if not men? This from Hefaistes, who spoke softly, and with much grace.

Tarsal considered for a long while. In the end one of her generals spoke. *No one sees them,* he said. *We only see what they leave behind. And perhaps the wind of their passing as they strike us down.*

Alisaunder took counsel with his own heart as the sun moved across its blue sphere. And just before the evening took sure hold, he asked for three things: a pass in the mountains, high on both sides and very narrow; a great quantity of diamonds, as many as could be gathered from every mine, every secret pool beneath a black rock; and several giants, if they could be had in this country of wonders that produced men with only one leg.

Such a pass Tarsal knew, but on the other side of it lay Simurgh, and many other wonderful cities, all besieged, but holding firm. Yet Alisaunder's terrible plan could be accomplished nowhere else. With the help of the prodigious giants Holbd and Gufdal, long may their names be remembered, and the Great Dive, in which the diving boys and girls of the deep pools held their breath for four days and nights to pry diamonds bigger than camels from the darkest caves, the Gates of Alisaunder were built with a swiftness. This is why you will find any gem in Pentexore but diamonds, for they all went into the Wall, and there they stay. Upon the night the Gates swung shut, closing up not only Gog and Magog, but the beautiful cinnamon forests and Simurgh itself, the greater part of all the phoenix in the world— and perhaps also Heliopolis itself, that secret place. Adamant, as all men, even foreigners like Alisaunder know, repels wickedness as well as magnets and blades and possesses such light as to burn the hearts of the cruel. Gog and Magog remain trapped there, weakened, bitter—and in their frustration and rage they most surely have devoured the phoenix and their city, the grievous sacrifice made so the rest of us might live. But Ghayth, the historian who lived in the shanty-town below the Wall, said he could hear them singing at night a thousand years later. Who knows which of these is so?

Singing, or screaming.

And thus it was the phoenix lost their secret home. Only the Bazil knew it, and the Bazil was trapped behind the Wall with every wicked thing, and the phoenix hate the merest mention of him, for he was arrogant, and did not believe the Wall could keep him—thus he warned no one and told no one the secret paths. But the Wall did keep him, and all others. We cannot know what passed behind the Gates, why no bird can fly over them—surely, we do not want to know. Some few of the phoenix had business outside Simurgh, and remain living. But one by one, they live their five hundred years and burn, only to waste and die, because they cannot bury themselves in the holy city, they cannot preside over their own funeral, and so their soul escapes the egg, and flees. Now only five are left, and Rastno is their Bazil, though he has the diadem and not the secret. They mourn, and can do nothing to stop it.

Afterward, before he returned to the shore of the Rimal with many calculations that would grant him a relatively safe passage, Alisaunder called the white merules to him. They came, like tall jackrabbits, hopping on their black talons.

He asked them: *Will it be a good death? Will it be noble, in battle, victorious, spoken of in song? Will I choke my enemies with my blood?*

The crows looked at each other, and at the red splash only they could see above his head.

No, they said. *It will be a small death, without reason or sense. You have made enemies of those who wish to destroy meaning and order.*

Alisaunder looked out, back toward his home and his life. He could accept that. No war is without casualties.

But will my empire last?

And on the sea of sand the silence of the crows carried long and far.

It will crumble. That will be their revenge on you, they said finally, *those you trapped beyond the Wall.*

THE WORD IN THE QUINCE:

Chapter the Fifth, in Which John Makes a Rather Long Speech About Religion, After Being Frightened Badly and Also Drugged.

E ven when I walked among the cranes, it seemed I both understood their speech and did not. To my ear, the inhabitants of this strange land spoke something like a kind of Greek that had had unmentionable relations with both Persian and Turkic, but also with some strange tongue which seemed to me to be less like a backbed cousin of these dialects than their ultimate mother, full of words I recognized, altered and metamorphosed into a kind of mirror of those that I knew. The only language that seemed to have no part of their speech was Latin, though such an absence might seem incredible. Fortunately, as a man of Constantinople, I was accustomed to hearing a dozen languages before noontime, and could make my way with some facility—until they heard me struggle with one word or another, and universally switched to a rather pleasant, if stilted and old-fashioned Greek. When I inquired after this to Fortunatus the gryphon much later, he laughed in his way, half-clucking, half-roaring.

"Don't all barbarians speak Greek?" he said, and this was the first inkling they gave me that the whole of their nation was quite aware of my world, and simply chose to eschew it. He told me about Alisaunder, and his wonderful method of teaching languages, and how he had taught the giants Holbd and Gufdal, and the giants had taught the rest. I shivered, as any man might. I still, even now, cannot quite believe that the great man could have walked here. And yet I have seen the truth of it with my own eyes.

In my heart I believe that what they speak is the sacred Adamic language, the tongue we all knew before Babel, that perfect language granted to man by God. On the distant day when we came upon the ruins of the monstrous tower I would feel this truth rise in me like love.

But I get ahead of myself, and Hagia is impatient, her breath all dark with figs and her eyes bright and slick in the dim light. We burn our tallow so fiercely—we must finish before my heart or my breath loses the race to fail first.

I chiefly remember the horror of waking on that jeweled pillar. I felt my eyes crack open and thought the light of day might shatter my skull. Sand still seemed to stick in every inch of me. Though some kind soul had scrubbed me clean, I could still feel it scratching at me. Leaning over my poor, wracked body I saw: an eagle's head with a wide beak, a scarlet lion's muzzle, a very beautiful woman's face with long black hair and eyes of a violent coppery shade, with rings of violet chasing each other within them, and a pair of full brown breasts tipped with cool green eyes where the nipples ought to have been. At first I thought I dreamed yet, and St. Thomas stood before me with his mouth in his belly—but my eyes took in the heaviness of her woman's breasts, and a fiery dread filled me, a panic like the tremors of death.

Forgive me, wife. I was so young, then.

I gulped for air, I tried to ask after Thomas the Saint and to tell them my name all at once, but it came out on top of itself, backwards, and they did not seem to mark me well. My weakened body betrayed me and I shrank back on the stone with that monster over me, her lash-fringed eyes huge, interested and amused, and somehow their amusement enraged me. I saw, more clearly, that she had no head, but carried her whole face on her torso, and it was intolerable. I could not look her in the eye without witnessing the shame of her nakedness. She wore wide black silken trousers with a thick band of blue at the waist, but her navel was a red mouth and her breasts, her breasts tortured me already, and I could not look at her, but I could not look away.

The other woman, with a serpent's many-colored eyes, laughed at my discomfort and moved in, her motion too smooth and easy—I glanced down and groaned, for the lady possessed nothing like legs. From her waist she was a serpent, the copper and pinkish-green patterns of her tail coiling and uncoiling. An awful bustle echoed around me, as of many souls in transit, and after so long alone it assailed my ears, my heart, and I prayed fervently to be delivered from this new hell.

"Does it do anything interesting?" said the snake-woman.

"It said: 'My name is John,'" mused the eagle—which I saw now had long, feathered ears shaped like a horse's, the long golden body of a lion, and deep black-violet wings folded neatly onto his back. "That's interesting enough. I don't know anyone named John."

"It wants something called an Ap-oss-el," piped the red lion, whose voiced seemed unusually high and gentle for such an enormous beast.

"Oooh!" exclaimed the serpent. "Is that a machine or a vegetable?" She moved her massive, heavy hair back from her face. Her torso shone, clad in coins that jangled when she moved.

"I think it is a person," the horror of horrors said thoughtfully. "It called him Thomas. It mentioned a tomb."

"I'll wager it's a 'he,'" the snake-creature smirked, and pawed at my clothes. I shrieked a little, and immediately felt ridiculous.

"Don't make assumptions, Grisalba," the red lion scolded her. "We know nothing about its people. It could be female, or hermaphrodite, like the tensevetes. If it wants to tell us, it will. Until then, use your manners, and the neuter pronoun."

"Who will look after it?" said the gryphon—for my sodden brain could at least recall that, swirling with old pictures drawn in delicate detail in margins, wings of gold paint, eyes of red. "Someone has to claim it."

I tried to slow my breath, but my body pounded and shuddered horribly. I needn't have worried. No one spoke up for me.

"It will have to be me then," the gryphon sighed with a pert nod of his great head. "I claim this lost beast as my foster until such time as it can take care of its own damned affairs. Witnessed?"

The others acclaimed, and it was done. I belonged to a gryphon.

"Thomas," I whispered. It was all I could hold onto, the terrible vision of him beneath the sphere. "Take me to St. Thomas, I know he is here! Leave me be, demons, I want no traffic with you!"

The snake, whom the others called Grisalba, sidled up to me and draped the tip of her tail over my waist, easing lower, as her wanton nature dictated, for I could already tell she had an irredeemably lascivious aspect. She lifted her finger and I watched as a drop of liquid formed on it, like a raindrop. It glistened green, then gold, then rosy as it shifted through the rainbow, searching for the right shade. The succubus looked thoughtful, as if it cost her great effort. Then she seized my mouth as if I were a babe refusing to take his medicine and thrust her finger into it. The liquid coursed into me and I groaned—the pleasure of its taste took me fiercely, and I could not help but suckle greedily at her, ashamed, but overwhelmed by the thickness of it, the milky richness. *This is my body*, I thought wildly, *this is my blood*.

And then the drug struck my brain like a fist wrapped in rose petals and I knew no more. Her laughter chased me down the black stair of sleep.

I woke in a warm darkness, with savory smells around me. As my eyes crinkled open, I saw that I lay on a long plinth within a cavern whose ceiling soared up into the distance. Some clever mason had carved shelves and alcoves all through the cave, up to its highest cranny, and many surfaces were laid about with rich furs and piles of scrolls and books. As my vision cleared I gasped, for the walls of the cave were all of gold, and the sheer wealth of those humble steps could have purchased a papacy. Over a pleasant fire the hulking gryphon stood sentinel, stirring a pot with an iron spoon clapped in his beak. I smelt onions and wild beets, harsh, bitter herbs, and even pepper—priceless pepper, for an invalid's supper! Dimly, I remembered collapsing into fields of the precious stuff, but then I had been too sun-

...ldened to marvel.

"I can't hold your head and let you sip it like a baby," the gryphon growled. "Anatomy is unkind. You will have to feed yourself."

And so I did, ravenous, desperate. The beast directed me, still shaky, to a pot of yoghurty beerish stuff, and my gratitude swelled so great I could not give it voice. He introduced himself as Fortunatus, and the name seemed to me Latin and home enough to bring tears to my eyes. I ventured some words:

"We have tales of creatures like you, where I come from."

His barrel chest lifted a bit in leonine pride. "Is that so? Well, I *am* a fascinating individual. I suppose that is understandable. What do they say?"

I considered. My duty to minister and witness warred with my desire for more soup, and shelter against the demon with eyes on her breasts. I felt stronger already, and the nightmare of the sandy sea receded in the face of my own name, my own self returning.

"We say that you are like Our Lord Jesus Christ, part strong earthly lion, which is like the flesh, part soaring eagle, which is the divine soul. You are a symbol of the mystery of God."

The gryphon blinked at me, his limpid golden eyes gleaming with concern in the firelight. "I am Fortunatus. I am not a symbol of anything."

"No, what I mean to say is, God's wisdom dwells in every living thing, and in your people He has chosen to illustrate His Divine Nature."

"My people are gryphons. Not illustrations or symbols. It is not a simple thing to be a gryphon, but you are over-complicating it."

I held up my hands. "Let me begin again. In the beginning was the Word and the Word was with God and the Word was God." Fortunatus settled himself by the fire, kneading the fur rugs on the floor and after a long feline stretch, dropping his hindquarters abruptly down.

"Which word?" the gryphon purred pleasantly.

"What do you mean?"

"Well, there are many words. Which one is God? Love? Joy?

Quince? Sandal? Blue? This is very interesting!"

"Christ is the Word of God, but Christ is God, and God is Christ. But Christ was also a man."

"Like you?"

"Not like me. Christ was the Son of God. God incarnate, born of a virgin, died of crucifixion, ransoming us all from death."

Fortunatus bent his feathered head. "Forgive me, John. I do not quite see how death can ransom death."

"Your questions make me tell it all backwards! Before Christ comes Eden and Eve and the serpent, and Abraham and Sarah and Isaiah and many other very important things. The whole history of the world."

"Please tell me about it, John. I enjoy stories."

I sweated in the cave. I was not meant for such practice. Books and quiet prayer, study, reflection. I have never seen conversion come from words alone, and I have not the heart for those other tools. "God... God dwelt in the Void, until he made all the beasts of the field and the fruits of the earth, and he caused the water to be separate from the land, and great mountains to rise, and oceans to swell, and set the stars in their firmament."

"Why?" The beast had a heart like a child, never able to let a sentence lie unworried.

"What?"

"Why did God make the... *beasts*," the word seemed bitter in Fortunatus' mouth. "In your opinion. Why did he make the water and the mountains? Why did he do it then and not at another time? Was the Void unsatisfactory in some way?"

"I... I could not say. I could not possibly say." I was accustomed to wrangling my faith with men who all knew the same things I did, who shared a kind of tribal knowledge, a common table, and no one of them would have asked if the Void was not good enough for God. Yet he required an answer, and no older priest would appear and save me. "Perhaps He was lonely."

For a moment I could not continue—a dreadful sorrow came over me, in this place, this golden hovel, without a friend or a face anything like my own. When I continued on, I felt the roughness of my voice in my throat. "Finally, He created Man, in his own image, and called him Adam, and this was the greatest of His endeavors. He breathed the living soul of His Divine Love into Adam, and set him in a wonderful garden full of every good thing, every green and growing plant, every proud and noble beast, and gave him dominion over all of them, and made his son to name each flower and beast according to their nature. This place He called Eden. Out of Adam's rib He fashioned Woman, and called her Eve, and bade them eat and drink and enjoy every thing in the garden, save one tree, which was the Tree of Knowledge, and that God said was His and His alone."

"What kind of tree was it?"

"Some say apple; some say fig. It isn't important."

"I'm sorry, but I must disagree. The Tree of Knowledge sounds like an astonishing thing. I would give very much to know its botanical properties. Did it speak? What sort of knowledge did it own? Was it a book that gave it life, a stone, a corpse? Was it perhaps some earlier attempt of your God's to incarnate, and upon his death, did he become the tree you speak of? Or perhaps one of his lieutenants—I assume your God has them?"

"Angels," I said numbly. "Like men, but pure, sexless, winged."

Fortunatus furrowed his owlish brows. "I think you must meet my friend Qaspiel. It is also sexless and winged."

I admit it, I snorted in disbelief. The spices of the soup pricked my nose.

Fortunatus hurried on, warming to his topic. "Perhaps one of these angels perished and from its body a tree of perfect, sexless apples grew, garlanded with wings and leaves, the most beautiful tree!"

I thought of the sheep-tree, the siege-elms. "Fortunatus, I am afraid that where I come from, a dead thing planted remains dead. There are no living trees like the ones you speak."

"Oh, your pardon, John. I did not mean to be prideful or boast of my land over yours. But you cannot deny the tragedy of your home. I must take you to see my wife's tree, and my daughter's. Then you would know how death may be ransomed."

Not knowing how to reply to this madness, I continued my scripture as though he had not interrupted me. "But Eve was a woman and therefore possessed within her the seed of wickedness, and the serpent, who was Satan, also dwelt in the Garden, came to her and tempted her to eat of the forbidden tree. Because of her weakness, she did so, and with her skills of seduction convinced Adam to eat as well."

Fortunatus worried at his feathers in distress, his beak clicking. "What ugly things you think," he whispered. "How sorry I feel for you."

I cleared my throat. My hands shook slightly. "God cast them out in punishment, and made them ashamed of their nakedness, and thrust a flaming sword in the gates of Eden, so that they could never return. Thus sin entered the world, and this trespass is the reason for all terrible things we must endure, for we live in the fallen lands that were the punishment of Adam and Eve, and outside the kingdom of God there can be no perfect peace." I coughed and reached for more of the milky, acidic beer. "But the Lord Our God did not abandon His people."

"It rather seems he did. Why did he not forgive them? A parent who does not forgive a child's first offense is a tyrant. If I did not clap up my girl and cuddle her the first time—or even the seventh!—she pulled my tail or ate my portion of cameltail soup as well as her own, what sort of father would I be? If she spoiled her coat with mud and instead of dropping her in a clear pool and laughing while she splashed I cast her out of my house and called her… all those things you called Eve that I am too polite a beast to repeat? How could I forgive myself? And if she suffered, out there, because I did not yield, how could I live?"

"God's ways are not the ways of mortals," I said weakly. The great gryphon started some other protest, but I held up my hands; I prayed for the space to finish. I felt it best to skip over the many generations of Israel, since the Creation found so little audience with him.

"Much later, He sent to us His Son, whose very existence is a mystery no human can fathom. The Child's being was part Flesh of his Holy Virgin Mother, and part Divinity, the Word of God. God walked among us, incarnated." I smiled ruefully. "Where I come from we do little but argue about that last. I came here fleeing a war over it, seeking something holier, more direct, than scriptural debate on the point of a sword." I shook my head, trying to get back on course. "Our Lord, who was called the Christ, had twelve disciples, who were great men, but not divine. But the earthly powers did not understand Him, and what they did not understand, they feared. He was crucified, and died in agony for all of us. In His death He redeemed us from the sin of Eve, and three days later He rose again, to break bread and promise the coming of the end of earthly life and the beginning of the kingdom of Heaven. He purchased for us Paradise and life everlasting at the right hand of God." My heart quieted, as it had in the chapel when I first took my vows. As I finished my witness, I felt the long shadows of those summer windows grow within me, and a gentle calm. "Perhaps God could not forgive Himself," I said softly, "and suffered for His own sins as well." This was heresy, no doubt and no argument, but I was moved to utter it.

Fortunatus said nothing. He flicked his tail back and forth.

I pressed forward. "It is the tomb of one of those twelve disciples I seek. Thomas the Doubter, Thomas the Twin."

The gryphon frowned deeply. His pelt quivered. "John, I do not wish to offend you. I have little experience with foreigners, nor their religions. But you are wrong."

I laughed. Never had a heathen presented me such a firm and simple rejection. Fortunatus laughed a little himself, a throaty, purring thing.

I felt my balance return to me. "Christ did not come among you, and that makes things difficult. That is the nature of faith, to believe what you did not directly experience."

"Oh, no, that's not what I mean. I believe you, about Christ and his twelve brothers, and crucifixion and all that. But I already possess life everlasting."

"Impossible. You spoke of a dead wife."

The gryphon shrugged, a rippling of his broad muscles. He cocked his head as a bird will do, and thought for a moment. "Come with me," he said abruptly, and snatched my collar, tossing me onto his broad back like a doll. I held onto his coarse bristles, and he left his cave, stepping into starlight and leaping up into the air. I squeezed my eyes shut; I could not breathe. I could not look down. It was not a long flight, but I felt I might

THE HABITATION OF THE BLESSED • 1

vomit my heart onto the gryphon's back. I shook when he
me on the ground again, my whole self trembling, trying to fold
into my heart the singular experience of flight.

A tree stood stately and tall before us. It possessed a thick
black trunk, twisted and looped, and many fringed, furry leaves
of some indeterminate color—starlight turns all things silver.
Among the leaves, dozens upon dozens of golden eyes opened
and blinked like fireflies, some small, some large and clear.

"This is my wife," said Fortunatus thickly. He nuzzled the tree
with his feathery forehead. The eyes closed in warm recognition.
"I hoped for a face, a mouth to speak to me and give me comfort. But sometimes the world treats us without grace. Certainly
death may occur, if one is uncareful, or fate unkind. But it is
easily gotten over, and so long as I am lucky enough not to crack
my skull, I will live forever. So can you, if you stay here, without any recourse to your Christ. I think that more or less spoils
your whole story, and in truth I am not sorry, for it had rough
and ungenerous aspects." He stretched his paws and regarded
them with interest, avoiding my shocked gaze. His voice grew
infinitely gentle. "John, you must see that there is no place for
me in your story. At best, I would be a beast of the field, would I
not? And never given a choice to obey or defy? Never presented
with temptation, only part of a dominion. And so I know you
think you speak the truth, but it *cannot* be so. I refute it with my
very being. I breathe, I speak, I think, I dream. I grieve, and love.
And I live forever. My mate, who was my body and self, died in a
storm that ripped whole forests into dust, and I will never cease
mourning her until the end of everything that is me, nor for our
cub who died with her. Am I less than you, who you say stand
master over me?"

My mind raced itself and got nowhere. I could not stop looking at the tree of eyes, the evidence of a life far beyond my com-
prehension. Now, I can admit it: I was looking for the trick, the
mechanism by which the beast had fooled me. I could believe in
a gryphon, but not in this tree, not in life everlasting on earth,
without God.

"I... I cannot say. I did not know such things as you lived, before now. Am truly I to believe there is no death here, or simply

that demons will lie, after their nature?"

"I am not a demon. We love our religions, John, just as you do, and it is such a pleasure to convert a friend to one's own faith, isn't it? But I think you will find few buyers here, when your story needs such work, being ignorant of more or less everything important in the history of the world."

It came clear to me in that moment, like a seed of light sending out leaves within me. I was not lost. God had sent me here, to complete the work of his saints, and show these marvelous creatures the glory of God, to lead them to salvation and joy. I nearly gasped with the strength of my revelation. The beer came up in my throat, in such turmoil dwelt my flesh. I would simply have to rise up, become the missionary I had never been, find somewhere in this kingdom so full of miracles the golden tongue I never possessed. I would learn their ways and fit them into Scripture. Like Paul, I would interpret the Word for them, so that they could come to God.

You may smile at me now, you who read this, who know how it all came out. Who know what a fool I was.

I began, as my Greek teachers would have, questioning and learning, learning so as to teach: "You tell me, then, how was the world made?"

Fortunatus rolled his tongue in his beak and clacked it twice.

"A gryphon's heart beats at the center of the world..."

THE CONFESSIONS OF
HIOB VON LUZERN, 1699:

I cried out in protest, in agony; the sound ripped from me. *No, no, no!*

The page below the gryphon's last words had gone brown and soggy, all its text rotted away. My fingers came away stained with the mush of the book, rich-smelling and soft. Lord, why would you punish me so? Why did you give me these riches and snatch them away so cruelly? What did I do to offend You? I admit, I am old; I am not fast enough, I cannot outrun putrefaction. But have I not been a good man, Your servant?

If what John recorded was so, and this strange country possessed all things without corruption and in their fullness, it certainly did no longer, for the rot veined through Hagia's beautiful letters even as I watched.

It would have been heresy. Of course. How could it be anything else, the foundational myth of a gryphon? But I felt a hole form in my heart where that tale might have been. Did I believe that Prester John had held discourse with a gryphon? I could not say. I certainly countenanced that such beasts might exist, or have existed, though it is preposterous to think they possessed human reason, any more than the pigs of the yard. It was not impossible that allegory ruled the text, and that dialogue passed between John and a foreign man with great personal strength and some brand of spiritual wisdom, after his way and not being a Christian, and John chose to represent him with the symbol of the gryphon. Perhaps some further key to the metaphor lay in that ruined page, but I would never find it, or know.

I cursed my meal with Alaric, which had stolen precious time from these books. I was a wolf, a dragon, snapping over my treasure, unwilling to share. But I could no longer hoard the privilege of this fruit. I summoned Alaric to my side once more—I chose him specially for this journey, for I had known him since he was a boy, delicate of face, almost punishably gentle of heart, good for nothing but books. I had taken him under my wing and taught him his Greek, but also Aramaic, the ululating tongue of Araby, the slushing envowelation of the Rus, and the more piquant dialects I knew: Phoenician, Aethiop, Welsh. With his Latin and our local French and German, Alaric had become nearly my equal in translation. He took the same deep, thorny pleasure in the puzzle of it. His favorite was always Aristotle, a pagan, yes, but hardly a man alive has constructed more maddening sentences. I recall so many days when we pledged to make certain the other ate and drank throughout his work, since we were wont to forget the needs of the flesh. We were so alike—and I argued strongly for his inclusion in our delegation, despite his inexperience with and total disinterest in missionary work.

Once, on the long road to this blasted wasteland of dust and roosters and its bruised sun, Alaric and I ate a clutch of wild eggs together we had found in foraging. A small sin: we did not share with the others, but instead squatted beneath a gnarled, many-rooted baobab and spoke in our favorite fashion: switching, sentence by sentence, between the tongues we knew. The game went thusly: I would begin in Greek, and shift to Latin, then to Egyptian, Alaric would then begin in Egyptian, nimbly moving into French, and so on. If we felt particularly clever, we would begin to trade dialects of a single language.

"Brother Hiob," he began in Hebrew. "Do you believe the world is infinite?"

"Nothing is infinite but God," I answered in Latin.

"The universe is infinite in space but not in time," Alaric whispered in English, the one language he knew that I did not. But that line I recognized. "Of course," he re-asserted himself, side-stepping into Greek, "but by extension, could not all God's works be called infinite? How can finitude proceed from an infinite source?"

"What are you getting at, Brother Alaric?" I asked in old French, sucking down a golden yolk.

"Nothing. I only wonder if the world itself, not the universe, but *this* world, is infinite, infinite enough to contain what we seek. Abyssinia is conquered, the New World found and no dragons there, vanilla and saffron in the East but no wonderful king. I wonder if the world is not very much poorer than we hoped, and smaller. There are so few places left to look where anything might be kept secret. Unless it is infinite, and the further we sail the more and more New Worlds we will discover, each full of pumpkins and chocolate and potatoes and slaves. What a beautiful solution that would be, a world without end, a reversal of those awful words of the heathen philosopher—a world where everything is true and everything is permitted." This impressive speech, conducted in Spanish, Amharic, Aramaic, and finally Arabic, to quote the old assassin Hassan-i Sabbah, seemed to take the wind from my young friend. "That is the kind of world I would like to believe I live in," he finished in our own honest Swiss-German. "And I think the only sort of world in which we could find Prester John."

I considered the mess of a sunset, lurid and orange, light sifting through the ashy dust. "Infinity, I think, is not a matter of outward space, but inward depth. We all of us spiral in and in and in, towards the spark of divinity buried at our core, and this slow spiral has no end. I think the world is like that—bounded, but deeper still than death." I chose Akkadian for that last, and felt well-satisfied at having check-mated such an extraordinarily difficult tongue. "How very fond I am of you, Brother," I said in Sindhi, one of the local dialects we had been practicing. "Have the last egg."

He demurred, and that is the way between friends. I could have borne no other hand touching the books of that tree of awe I saw waving in the wind. I shuddered to even think of those red leaves. I shuddered to think of another reading my books—yet it had to be done.

As Alaric entered, head bent, humble before his elder, I saw the blue-yellow creep of dawn behind his cowled head. I showed the novice the ruined pages—they were several, but not the whole book. Between us we could do our work faster, and I gave him materials to do as I did, and we used palm-needles to lift the remaining pages of the tomes, so that the oils of our hands would not hasten their moldering. We gently cut away the ruined pages, scooped their mush into a small clay cup and set them aside, holy, full of regret. I began again in Hagia's recount, which reeked of oversweet wine, the mealy pages now streaked with long strips of red. My heart hurt: already I could not read her flowing hand in places.

Alaric took up John's narrative. It was my gift to him, to surrender John's book. The last egg.

But after a moment I could not bear it. I apologized profusely, and took it back, helplessly stroking the cover as if it were a sweet little hound that could love me back. I am jealous. God on High, if You Yourself admit to that sin, I cannot be blamed that I was not more virtuous than You.

THE BOOK OF THE FOUNTAIN:

I held back from him. The newcomer disquieted me. Most everyone else, it seemed, considered him a marvelous new toy: it talked and walked and made such charming noises when proven wrong. Imagine! The poor thing did not know about trees or the Fountain, did not know about the mussel-shell or even what an astomi was! It became a popular pastime to drag some specimen before the priest that would shock him—the greater John's shock the more puffed-up the exhibitor would get. He seemed to dislike the tensevetes the most, their huge icy faces brushing the soil like shields, their silent regard of him unsettling. I cannot blame him. They are peculiar, even to me.

I remember when Fortunatus brought his friend Qaspiel to the al-Qasr to meet John. Since our king Abibas had been planted primly in the center of the Lapis Pavilion and no longer required a royal palace, the al-Qasr was now open to everyone, the curtains thrown wide, the rooms made bright for any soul who needed it. In the scarlet nursery of fable, a perfumer plied his trade, and every pillow smelled of crocus. In the throne room children's games ran wild round the great chairs.

Qaspiel and I knew each other well and dearly—I met it on my final sojourn to the Fountain, which I undertook by myself, a grown woman, solitary and serious—so I fancied myself. I first saw Qaspiel buying long sleeves for its wings so that the heights of the mountain would not freeze them. We spoke of little things, as pilgrims do, even when they are not called pilgrims yet. It looked forward to having a twin, for anthropteron do not give birth, rather, they manufacture a substance in a certain gland when in heat, something like royal jelly. They remove this stuff, colored like snow, and apply it to the space between their wings. In due course a growth begins there, and the poor anthropteron must eat vast quantities to sustain it. Qaspiel said it already felt a strong desire for coconuts. Finally, the growth completes, and another creature, whole and adult, steps away from its parent and twin, and immediately tends to the wound of separation that the parent-sibling suffers. Each heals the other, of loneliness, of pain.

Qaspiel worked then as a vanilla-farmer, and it smelled rich with spice. I held it while it drank; it held me. When we returned home it lifted me up in its arms and we flew over all the towns I knew, spinning and spinning like an arrow in the air, and its pale body was the whole of my vision. The thick, green water of the Fountain soared in me, and we soared together, the first day of our infinite lives.

And so with the joy of recognition of an old friend I greeted Qaspiel as the gryphon brought him before John. Its delicate feet hardly left depressions in the thick black soil of Nural, not unlike the fine, moist sand of vanilla deep within the pod. It had shorn its hair since I had seen it last, and strewn its short locks with little beads of hematite for the occasion. Its dress gleamed nearly colorless, a cobweb that would flatten and spread out in flight—and its wings, taller than itself, were a deep sort of cobalt that played tricks with the eye. I went to embrace my friend, but before I could hold out my arms, John fell to his knees between us. I stared at him as he wept, his jaw slack, his body shaking in a kind of rapture.

[Here corruption had eaten up three passages, a fuzzy deep red kind of mold that devoured text and left no small word for me. Nothing of it remained legible except for a few spare lines which none could help but recognize, in the second passage: *And Jacob was left alone; and there wrestled an angel with him until the breaking of the day. And when he saw that he prevailed not against him, he touched the hollow of his thigh; and the hollow of Jacob's thigh was out of joint, as he wrestled with him. And he said: Let me go, for the day breaketh.*

The text became clearer some pages thereafter, and I could not find more concerning John's words with his angel. The text began again thusly:]

Behind the ivory-and-amethyst pillars of the al-Qasr, which so much later John would insist we rename the Basilica of St. Thomas, I sat with my hands demurely in my lap, fingering Hadulph's flame-colored tail on the one side, Astolfo silent and still on the other. We sat in rows like children—the pygmies picked at their ears, a phoenix ran sticks of cinnamon through her beak, the sciopods relaxed on their backs, wide feet thrust overhead, each toe ringed with silver and emerald. Grisalba combed her long black hair, looking bored.

John the Priest tried not to look at me. His hair had grown back, but it was white, whiter than a man his age should own.

I told him once, many years later while he ran his tongue over the small of my back, that the sun had taken all his blood, and left him with nothing in his veins but light.

Ever the good teacher, John tried to meet each of our eyes in turn, but he could not look at mine, he could not look down to the full curve of my high, brown breasts, and the green eyes that stared calmly from their tips under a thick fringe of lashes. He always tried to avoid looking at me, or any of the other female blemmyae. But something about me in particular seemed to shame him. Perhaps because I had found him, seen him weak, nursed him. He blushed like a child when he accidentally looked me in the eye. Later I teased him about it, but he did not laugh. *Of course I could not look at you. You were naked.*

But I did not understand his morality. Even when I did understand it I looked on it much as a dead thing whose stench I had to endure. I was shamed, to be singled out so, to be ignored. I blinked often, to interrupt his droning, to draw his gaze, but he tried to look only at where my head might be if I were a woman.

A-ve.

He repeated these words as if they had any meaning for us, sounding each syllable. We did not like Latin. It sat on our tongues like an old orange, sweet-sour and rind-ridden.

A. Ve.

A-ve Ma-ri-a.

A. Ve. Mari. A.

Grisalba yawned and picked at her tail, lazily slapping its tip against the chalcedony floor. Hadulph chuckled and bit into the consonants like elbow joints. In the front row, a little panoti with her ears drawn in listened intently, with her whole being. But then, that is how panotii listen. I could see the bluish blood pulsing in the delicate skin of her lobes.

A-ve Ma-ri-a gra-ti-a ple-na. Ti like she. Ple like play. She plays, gratia plena, Maria plays, Ave Maria gratia plena.

A. Ve. Mari. A. Gra. Tea. A. Plea. Na.

"I wonder what his sweat tastes like?" Grisalba murmured beside me. I grinned, but the priest could not chide me, for that would mean glancing down past my nipple-eyes to the mouth-that-is-a-navel, and he would not risk it. I wondered too. I wondered what his stranger's kiss would be like. But it was an idle thought, a summer's cloudy dreaming.

No, no. She plays. She; play. Shall we try the Pater Noster instead then?

Pa. Tear. No. Star.

[Another slab of fungus and putridity stole the blemmye's words from me. That time it swallowed up a whole page, of which all I could rescue was a measly exchange already turning purple in the lines of the characters. The M of Maria was blackened with rot:

I understood that this Maria business vaguely referred to a virgin who had had a child. I did not think this particularly impressive. Qaspiel, after all, had managed it. "Virginity confers strength," John said during one of his lectures. "It is the pearl that purchases paradise." None of us understood this.

"What paradise do you mean?" said Grisalba angrily, when he tried to explain the necessity of chastity. "What pleasure there can be bought with misery here? John, look around you! What do you need that the paradise of our home, which we so generously share with you, does not amply give?"

He looked at me as he answered: "Virtue."]

Did I want him because he hated me? I do not like to think so. I want to believe better of myself than that. But perhaps it is true after all. The priest loved to walk with Qaspiel and speak with it, even to hear its voice, which was always musical, kind, fluid. Qaspiel did not even know what John meant by the word *angel*, but he allowed that if it pleased the stranger, he might call it one. He broke bread with Fortunatus and sipped the juice of the blackbulb fruit, which he liked specially. I like it, too. The fruit is small and soft, the flesh deep purple, the pit like a single pearl. Children love it specially, and must be kept away, for it brings rich and terrifying dreams. I marveled that Fortunatus let him indulge so often. I thought perhaps the gryphon had a more decadent heart than I had guessed, but when I asked him, he said only: "He is not my child and I will not scold him."

Even in Grisalba he found a sort of friend. She let him believe her a convert for a while, because it amused her. She even wore a veil, when he asked her to. She prayed with him on the Sabbath, with one eye open. She even filled several goblets with the poisons and drugs her body could produce, so that he might know her better. She had seven in all, and was very proud of their colors. She showed him everything about her people, with pride, with grace and eloquence. But one evening, when he was instructing her in eschatology, she leaned forward and kissed him. When she told me about it, she said he kissed her back, even after she had eaten her dinner in front of him, which I cannot imagine he took with aplomb, as her nature was unavoidably serpentine. Thus she would have been compelled to dislodge her jaw to take her meal whole and alive. Lamia kiss in much the same way. She twined her tail around him, squeezing his skinny frame, her teeth on his lips, a hungry kiss and he all hers. But John pushed her away, and his eyes filled up with tears, and he called her a whore and clawed at her tail like a wild thing. She shouted at him that he was useless, a eunuch, a dog, and bit his cheek savagely—even to the day he died he bore a pale violet scar there, almost as though the kiss never left him.

He fled from her passion to the al-Qasr, where more or less

all of Nural sprawled in the late summer heat, the drowsy slow sweetness of it, with the fountains trickling thin and quiet. Hadulph tended to the priest, and John was much mocked by several monkeys hanging from a six-armed statue of some forgotten god. Finally, when the day had got on in hours, Grisalba came looking for him, her cheeks flared green, anger decking her like gems. She snarled at him in full view of the better part of our nation.

"I am a serpent, and I do not care what you think. Yes, I have a great hunger for mating, and for many other things besides. Yes, I drink blood—not because I am wicked but because my body is made in its every part to want blood, to digest it, to take life from it. You cannot help that you take life from cakes and stews and roasts. You drink your God's blood! What right have you to judge my lunch? Try living on wood and then tell me my habits are filthy and sinful. And yes, I devour my own eggs. There's nothing wrong with it; it's part of our most private rites. The child finishes its growth within me. The egg begets the snake half, the womb the human half, and I really think a little less queasiness about the biology of your betters would look good on you. I live after my nature, and if your God made everything then he made me and you shouldn't be such a baby about a little kiss." She sat down, her coppery tail curled around her. "Now, if you want me to say a rosary, I will. But that will be the last I ever say to your God, because it seems to me he is a very specific God, and has nothing to do with anyone but you. If you want to stay a virgin and turn up your nose, that's your business, but don't ever call me a whore again, just for doing what is right and good and natural. It's bad manners."

Thus Grisalba, nominally, remained John's one convert, for he never made her say that final prayer. From then on they were easy together, and he blessed her eggs when they came, after she had found a more suitable lover, who brought her turmeric flowers to decorate his own clean, sweet flesh.

John even loved the little panoti I saw at his lesson. She followed him everywhere, and learned Latin so well that they conversed together, a secret language, and I could not help it—I felt envy. My husband could not speak to me, and everyone had gone so mad for that useless stranger, and I was lonely. But I alone he would not tolerate, would not even acknowledge. I once saw him play with a little blemmye child. Her name was Oro; I knew her, a little prodigy of mathematics, and a great pride to us. John tickled her, and they both laughed, and I felt the sting of it, that he could look at her, her skinny, undeveloped chest with bright brown eyes blinking up at him, her navel with its pretty mouth, but not at me. She recited theorems to impress him and he behaved exactly as though she had babbled an infant's nothings. He smiled in a fatherly way and patted her shoulder. I cast down my eyes and suffered such shame.

One day I happened upon John's own lessons at Fortunatus' paw, in the long, shaded library of the al-Qasr, the scrolls in their alcoves like long clusters of citron.

The gryphon read aloud: "'The long bones are found in the limbs, and each consists of a body or shaft and two extremities. The body, or diaphysis, is cylindrical, with a central cavity termed the medullary canal.'"

The presbyter cloistered with his companion: cross-sections of satyr and blemmye inked in delicate, costly brown inks lay spread out on a low desk of sethym wood, the male blemmye with limbs outstretched, encircled with diagrammatic symbols as though pinioned to a wheel, showing the compact perfection of his four extremities, which correspond to the elements. The satyr was bent double, clutching her hooves, a goat-haired ouroboros.

"Please concentrate, John," begged Fortunatus, his conscripted tutor, "if you do not learn our anatomies how will you live among us? How will you help portion the harvest if you do not know that the phoenix require cassia and cardamom for their nests, while the satyr cannot eat the pepper plants that the rest of us prize? How will you build, brick upon brick, if you do not know that the blemmyae orient their houses in clusters of four, facing outward, while the sciopods have no houses at all, but lie beneath their own feet, like mice beneath toadstools? How will you sell your goods at the quarter-moon market if you do not know that the lamia especially love honeycomb still clung with lethargic bees, while the dervishes eat nothing but their dead?"

"Where I come from, all men have the same shape," grumbled the priest, his eyes bloodshot from reading, unwilling to acknowledge me, who all in secret had become the best of his own students—his *discipuli*. I had done my scribe's work and translated each of those illuminated anatomicals into Latin so that John would believe them true—for he told us that Latin was the language of truth, and the vulgar tongues are the dialects of lies. Still he would not thank me for it.

"That is a sad country, and you should give thanks to your God that you need not return there, where every face is another's twin," the gryphon said with a long sigh.

"All the same I long for it, and wish myself there, where nothing is strange," John murmured to himself, and stared past me. I made myself appear busy, copying out my own scroll concerning the accounting rituals of centaurs, under the long, candle-thin windows. But out of one eye I watched him. His hair still showed scalp in patches, but the scalp itself not so scorched and peeling as it has been. And I thought: *Yes, he must be homesick. He must be sad. He must wish to not be a stranger somewhere. He must still long for his Ap-oss-el.* John shook himself and concentrated again on the wheels of flesh before him.

"I do not understand the blemmyae," he announced, without turning his head to me, as though I were not even in the room. "They carry their faces in their chests and have no head—I suppose the brain is just behind the heart then, in the chest cavity—but how," the Priest blushed, and shifted in his seat so that it was clear that he did not address the indecorous question to me, "how would she nurse a child, Fortunatus?"

The gryphon twitched his dark wings—once, twice.

"Why, she would but weep."

At home, Astolfo was lost in his own dreams and thoughts, his eyes often glazed and happy over some distant thing I knew nothing of. He prayed often to Vishuddha, the eleven-mouthed god of his people. He carved an altar in eleven stones and spent much of his love there. Vishuddha's worship, so full of harmonic chanting and poems in eleven parts, always made my head spin.

I attended the amyctryae's holiday services politely, for Astolfo's sake, but could never quite embrace it. I learned the antiphonals and agons but I could not find the faith. I suppose that is something of a habit with me.

My husband could not speak to me, only to his god and his trees. I ate my soup in the silence that had become our third mate.

[Long fingers of scarlet obliterated any further mention of the husband, or John's wonderful conversion of the lamia, or even a further discussion of anatomy—You see how I dreamed what might have been on those pages, how I guessed that it *must* have been wonderful, because it was invisible to me? The text turned liquid, and when it cleared again, the whole city had gathered to cast judgment on the priest.]

Fortunatus clawed the sand of our crumbling amphitheater, where the nations of our nation gathered—as much as the nations are inclined to gather, which is to say lazily and without much intent of discussing anything. The gryphon was nervous; the color in his tail low and banked, his throat dry. The hulking beast did not love speaking, and he loved less that his size bought him respect he did not feel he had earned. So everyone listened, and he hated them for listening.

"I think," he began, his beak glittering gold in the glare of the sun, "that we ought to let him cast his chit in the Abir with us."

"Why?" shouted Grisalba, trying to wrangle a slab of honeycomb from her sister, who had thought she was invited to a festival, and not a makeshift parliament. "He has not asked to."

"And what if he drew the monarch's piece?" said Hadulph, his red muzzle lifting in concern. "He would rule us. I cannot think that would go well."

Fortunatus frowned, and the glare went out of his gold. "What if he did? Would it be worse than any of us? If Oro drew it, or Qaspiel? The Priest, at least, would not be partial—there are no other creatures like him among us, no faction for him to favor." The gryphon cast his yellow eyes to the sand, speaking softly, "And he must be lonely. There is no one here for him, no one of his kind who understands his passion for the Ap-oss-el, no one to speak his trilled language and look him in the eye without reflecting their own strangeness back to him. A king has a thousand friends; he cannot be excluded from social events or sniffed at in disdain. I pity him—do you not?"

"If he stays, he will make us convert!" cried the sciopods, snapping their stockings in consternation. "He wants to make the al-Qasr into a church and we will all crawl around begging forgiveness for who knows what!"

Fortunatus shrugged his great, shaggy shoulders. "And when Gamaliel the Phoenix was queen, she called the al-Qasr an aerie, and set it aflame every hundred years. We rebuilt it, and called it what we pleased. This is the way of government. That is the way of the governed. How could John ask for more than Gamaliel did? Besides, the Lottery is a strange god, and he will likely end up a shoemaker or a lettuce-grocer. You cannot deny a man for what he *might* do, in circumstances that will almost certainly never occur."

I held a long green canopy over my torso with both hands to keep out the sun; a pair of rooks alighted on it, and their weight dragged the warm cloth to my shoulders. I said nothing, but scowled and practiced my verbs silently.

Regno, regnas, regnat. Regnamus, regnatis, regnant.

I reign, you reign, he or she reigns over.

"He cannot take part in the Abir because he has not drunk from the Fountain," I said loudly and clearly. *Ignore me now*, I thought, looking at his patchy, wretched head down there on the lower benches. *Ignore* that.

A murmur rippled among our folk, and Fortunatus appeared to honestly never have considered that point. He turned to John, who really needed new clothes; his habit looked worse than a cobweb.

"Are you willing to make the journey?" the gryphon said, his voice clarion in the amphitheater. "You would call it a sacra-ment. If you drink from the Fountain you would be wholly one of us, bound to our fortunes. You say life in your world is brief—would you reject eternity?"

John said nothing. Finally: "Life everlasting can come only

through God. There is no life but in Christ. I cannot, Fortunatus. I can never repay your kindness to me, but that is too much. My God could never forgive me."

"Then it's settled," I said, not bothering to hide the blade in my voice. "He will die in forty years or so. No need for an Abir."

Fortunatus had no answer to that, but looked at me with grave, sorry eyes. We were not close in those days, not like Hadulph and I, or even Qaspiel. He thought me bitter and vicious, and perhaps I was.

Forgive me, husband. I love you now, but then you were so cruel to me.

"Wait," called John, and held up his hands, still scarred and pink from the desert. Grisalba chewed a vanilla bean, bored. It jutted smartly out of her mouth. "Wait," he said again. "I came here seeking the tomb of St. Thomas, and I have not found it. My memory is still sore, but I remember that. I wish to go out into the wilds of Pentexore and find it still—I cannot truly answer any question put to me until I am satisfied that it is or is not here. Let me go, give me a sack of food, a wineskin of water, perhaps even a companion or two, and when I return ask me again. Too much newness makes a man dizzy. I cannot think."

Qaspiel folded and unfolded its long bluish hands in distress. Its wing-tips flicked back and forth.

"How will you find it, John?" The anthropteron said. Its voice quivered with such intense desire, a desire I knew so well: to give no offense. This is one of our chief motivations, and I realized then that John did not at all understand why we behaved in such unfailingly kind fashion toward him, no matter what bizarre rituals he encouraged us to practice. Among the immortal, good manners are as important as bread and water. When we cannot forget anything, courtesy behooves us all.

"The Lord will guide me, Qaspiel. He will show me the way through the mountains, through the desert, through any trial."

A murmur passed through the throng. It was all well and good to learn Latin, but to trust one's precious body to those mountains, those deserts, with only John's alien God who very manifestly did not speak or appear or do much of anything? I am not faithless. My mother taught me the secret hymns of the

Navel of Heaven, which connects us all. I believe, on good days when it does not rain or freeze, that in my very need that connection will shine, and preserve me. But I also believe in maps, and cartography, and magnetic north, and a good, not too ornery, camel to carry me along. John stood firm, but we saw for the first time that he might not have come from the Rimal unscathed, that his mind might be bruised, half-jellied. The priest could not go alone. He would be killed, immediately.

Hadulph yawned. Fortunatus held still, a rictus of concentration. Grisalba belched. And I saw my chance. I would not be left out again. He could not ignore me anymore.

I stood up, so there could be no mistake, and called out clear as prayer: "I will go with you, John. I will protect you and keep you living on this road." And I will bring a map, I added silently.

The priest scowled, and I had won. He could not reject me in front of everyone—how small and mean he would look! But Astolfo beside me, my husband of the voiceless love and jaw like a barrel, looked up at me, his eyes filled with loss. "I will come back for you," I said softly, and brushed the hair from my love's brow. But we had learned too well to converse in silence. He would not hold me to it.

Hadulph, in the end, agreed to go as well, and of course Fortunatus. Qaspiel, too, and the little panoti, though many protested that she would be no help and should stay where she could be loved and cared for. She hissed through her perfect, tiny teeth. I looked at Grisalba, but she brayed in laughter. "Not on your life, my decapitated love," she said, shaking her head.

All our talk done, the sun threw its golden arms up and surrendered behind the far hills, where we would go, all of us, together, and return nothing like ourselves.

THE SCARLET NURSERY:

O nce, Lamis came to me when the night rung like an old, empty jar, almost dry of dregs. She held out her huge hand, her lip trembling, wanting closeness, afraid to ask, as she was not supposed to be awake, not supposed to trouble her Butterfly when the stars were tucking themselves into bed.

Lamis, Who Was Only Lonely: Tell me a story, Butterfly. One only for me. Tell me where you come from.

You ought to be asleep, my lambfleece love.

Lamis, Who Wanted Something Her Siblings Did Not Have, Something All Her Own: If you tell me, I shall fall asleep.

A child in need is the worst trap the world can lay.

Well, I began, here is the truth of it: I am not like you. I was made of other things than street-dust and spices, other things than cities can forge in their endless and wending hearts. My people did not come with the rest upon the Ship of Bones. We dwelt here in the years before bread and salt, dwelt in honey-combed snow, frozen bees crawling in the rafters of the world. You are all foreigners here, even your mother, even those stone men Catacalon dreamed of, but this is my home.

I am not like you. I sleep curled on the floor of the nursery. I hear the sounds of the palace moving all around me, every one of them: onions chopping in the kitchens, and limes, too, crocus-hearts drying into orange saffron in the scullery. I hear your fathers, all twelve of them, dreaming and snoring. I hear lovemaking above me, the body of the queen moving in the dark. I hear the stones of the walls breathing, the wind slowly wearing them to dust, too slowly to ever see, but I hear it. I hear the lamps being snuffed out, for dawn is coming, and I hear the sound of dawn coming too. It's like a bell ringing, very long and very low. I know everything that happens in this valley, because I hear it, all the time, every night, every day.

Listen to me, now. The panotii learned to listen; it is this gift we brought to the city. My sacrifice for those children, the sign of how dearly I loved them and their mother, too—was that all those evenings, all those days, I spoke more than I listened.

Close your eyes. I can make you like me.

Once a child was lost in the crags of the mountain which was once called the Axle of Heaven, and also Chomolungma, and also Sagarmatha. She had grey hair though she was a child, not the grey of age but the grey of stone, and her eyes were colorless, prismed like hard crystal. Her name is recorded, and though all things written down are flawed, we believe this: the child without pigment in her eyes was called Panya. Her family loved her, we think. We hope that she was loved, that she slept near a warm yellow horse with a soft nose that nuzzled her when she dreamt of fire. It is pleasant to think so.

But the snow took her mother and the ice took her father and the child clutched the stones with blue fingernails, her milk-teeth chattering, her lips wracked white. And yet she climbed upward, for the child listened, and in listening she heard a music the color of bridal flowers—the closer you get to the heavens, the more jumbled are all things of earth. Music has color, stones have voices, smells have weight and taste. Having no one to scold her and tell her to come down like a good girl, Panya clawed from crag to crag. The music played to her, and only to her, who could listen so well in the white shadows cast by death.

By the time she finally reached the lip of the world and the peak of the great mountain, Panya had grown up. But she had eaten only twelve frozen rice stalks in all her years of growing, so only her eyes had grown large. She was pale as a diamond worm, and wound her arms around the stone spires of that place that are not unlike the copper spires of this place—and she found there the source of the music, still fainter than whispering, and it covered her with love the color of a horse in the darkness.

Panya had found a Stair.

The Stair was neither violet nor golden, neither green nor black. It yawned up, taller than she could ever hope to reach, carved for a giant's stride, and clouds clung to the top. The Stair wound out from the mountain's peak in a long spiral, and if she squinted in the terrible, freezing sun, she could see the next Stair beginning. At the foot of the Stair Panya stayed, and listened to its music until it filled her up. In time, she gave birth to a son whose eyes had no color, and a daughter, and a son again, until the village of her children dwelt at the base of the Stair, and ate the frozen milk of her body, and listened.

They listened for so long that their ears grew wide and flowing as sails to catch the quiet, reluctant music of the Stair, and they wrapped themselves in those ears to keep warm, but also to listen to their own hearts. They began to learn, and in learning they began to understand that the Stair is the place where the First Moveable Sphere of the heavens touches the Sphere of Gross Earth. Where the two join nestles our village, which is truly a monastery, and all of us who are brothers and sisters listen there, to the music of that meeting, and to each other, and to ourselves.

I was born there, in the village of Nimat, which contains the Stair as some villages contain a lovely little square with a statue or two, and I supped at the sound of snow falling.

And as she fell down into sleep I told Lamis, the smallest of them, that in the morning I would wake her and her siblings and give them bread brushed with cream and yellow fruit because Lamis liked yellow best, even though Houd preferred violet. I would light the red tapers in the evening, and set out roasted meat and celery-leaves and salty soup, so that they would grow strong and clever. And I would tell them all the things I knew, so that they would learn to listen like Panya, like me. We lived in a city full of spangles and distractions. I opened their ears and curled into your palms.

I sang the story of myself, which is also their story. *Listen*, I whispered to her. *Become like the panotii, who alone have heard the evening ablutions of the stars.*

Lamis, Who Was Nearly Sleeping: You are so light, Butterfly. I can hardly feel you on my hand. It's like you're made of wind.

THE WORD IN THE QUINCE:

Chapter the Sixth: in Which Three Tales Are Told
Concerning the Nature of Love, and a
Very Lovely Country Is Crossed.

A parade of well-wishers followed us onto the long, thin road out of Nural, tossing tortoise-flowers and guava-seeds and wet green rice over our heads in blessing, ringing copper bells, stamping hooves and hands and feet and singing traveling songs, lascivious songs, any song of which they all knew the chorus. Once a throng of jangling dervishes spun so fast their bells flew off like sparkling blossoms. They sang my name: *John, John, John.* It sounded foreign and lovely in their mouths. Finally, all had gone still and they all stood, simply waving goodbye until we vanished over the rills.

We avoided the pilgrim-road to the Fountain. I had no wish to go near that devilish place; the source of all their strength could not be the source of mine. The little panoti, who called herself Hajji, insisted that she knew where to take us, if not to find the saint's tomb, at least to discover where it might be. But she would not say where she aimed, and when I tried to ask her about her name, which I could not help but recognize, having heard it from the mouths of many Saracen pilgrims streaming into the Holy Land, she narrowed her clear white eyes and refused to speak at all.

"Are you a pilgrim, then?" I tried to say, and she rebuffed me, her small, snow-colored back turning away, her bare, rough feet scrambling up the stony road like the inscrutable goat who nursed the baby Zeus.

Pentexore brings to mind every old story. I took them out like laundry, to hold them up to this new sun, and see if they

159

looked threadbare, or whole. As we journeyed out from Nural, three tales were told—one in sleep, one in waking, and one in love. I wish to record them here. I remember them like reliefs in crystal, so strongly they struck me, then and now.

On our first night we decamped beneath the curling, arching roots of a great banyan tree, each knurled, woody tentacle a torture of bumps and crevices. The roots soared so high we passed beneath them and craned our necks to see their apexes. I thought some sweet, thin mist coalesced there on the heights, as on the tips of some hills. The braided, woven canopy of roots the color of baked bread could have sheltered a city entire—

"And does it not?" said Hadulph the great red lion, whose muzzle and golden whiskers loomed larger than my head and the better part of my shoulders. "The ants have nations, too, and also the worms their empire. The moths rule over a vast collective, greatly concerned with the accumulation of light. Even the asparagus shoots we shall roast for our supper, and the amla fruits with their green rind, even they are dukes and viscounts in a potent vegetable court, whose customs we cannot know. Woe betide those who by ignorance or malice cross the laws of the tulip bulbs they suck for sweet syrup."

"Are you being quite serious?" With these folk it is impossible to tell, and worse if they have any cat about them, as in the tufted tails of Fortunatus and Hadulph.

Hadulph shrugged—and I had already learned that this shrug, rippling down from his broad shoulders and across his colossal back, was his primary expression of any sort of emotion. "When you lived in your Konstantinii," the lion habitually blundered the ending of *Constantinople*, "with all your domes and mackerels and crosses, did you think that if you took the wrong turn on the Bosphorus that there might be a place where sheep trees grow and lions talk? Well, that is how we stand to the cities of the banyan. *We* do not have the luxury of believing ourselves the only world in the world. Perhaps if you and your own had better senses of direction, we could wallow in solipsism as you do."

"Do you not like me, Hadulph?"

"I neither like you nor dislike you, John. Fortunatus tells me your God says we live under your dominion already, by nature and fate, so it doesn't matter what I think, does it?"

"Then why did you volunteer yourself? Surely you had better things to do."

"I came for Hagia," he growled simply, and I fell silent. I had not yet spoken to the monstrous woman, nor even, truly, glanced her way.

No, I should not lie. I glanced at her, and more, when she could not see my gaze drift. If she turned her back she could almost be human, her broad brown muscles working, her strong arms, her thick waist. If I did not look up to her shoulders—ah, but I always did, and always shuddered. If she turned toward me, the horror of her breasts and her belly hit me like a blow, and I could not bear it. She wore nothing above the waist, could wear nothing, or else be blinded, but still the indecency of it shocked me, how brazenly she wore her nakedness, the *bigness* of her—for she stood a head and a half taller than I, and no farm-horse could have been stronger. In all her body and soul dwelled not a drop of shame. I could not look on her; I could not look away. She wore a beautiful belt, dark goat-leather all studded with opaque gems: agate, carnelian, obsidian, malachite, in patterns like constellations, and from it hung an ornament like an orrery in miniature, turning and clicking as she walked. When—terrible moment!—she caught me staring at her, I took shelter in pretense, and studied her belt intently.

Did I want her then, already? No, of course not. I was still a priest. I was a good man.

I always wanted her. I was a fool.

While Qaspiel prepared us the promised roast salad of young asparagus, amla fruit, tulip bulbs, and salted yak we had brought from Nural's endless stores, Hadulph settled down in the grass, like a gargantuan ruby statue, roots thatching and crossing behind him. We all ate; Hagia laughed and joked with Qaspiel, to whom it—ah, how difficult it was for me to use the neuter, as they all gently reminded me to do! I wanted to say *him*, when Qaspiel looked fierce and brutal, in the manner of angels, *her* when Qaspiel looked gentle and loving, as it did that night, singing a song to Hagia to make her smile, a song about fairies that plagued the vanilla harvest, stealing the beans to make their long lyres. I know Qaspiel said it was not an angel, did not even know the word. And yet I could help but tremble in my bones when it sang.

Night drew on, and I took comfort in knowing some few of the spangled stars overhead, the whole sky like a jewel-box spilled out on a black cloth. Qaspiel slept on the high roots, its wings closed over its face like a bat. Fortunatus slept close to the fire, snoring a strange hooting, chirping snore. Hajji, the panoti, kept her own counsel and put a peach to her lips, listening to some hymn I could not hear. Hagia concealed herself in the shadows and I knew not where she lay. But the red lion sat impassively where he had settled, and sleepless, restless, I turned toward him, only to see that his eyes remained open, glittering white as stones in the dark, though a deep, rumbling snore bubbled up from his chest, escaped, and boiled up again.

"Do you wake or do you sleep, lion?" I whispered, but he did not answer. I crawled closer, between his huge paws, and repeated my question.

Baroom, his snore answered. *Buroom*.

Bats squeaked overhead, flitting over the hot stars.

"How can he be one of us?" the lion said, his voice so much deeper than usual. I could not tell if he spoke in his sleep or knew I stood there listening. "He has never loved anyone but God. What kind of man is that?"

"I did, though," I whispered, in the truth-trance that deep night brings. "I loved a boy named Kostas, and he loved me. I should not call him a boy. But his face was so narrow and youthful I could never think of him as quite grown. In the end I suppose he was only a few years younger than I. It was simple—love is service, and he served me. Love is nourishment—and I fed him. Love is knowledge—we taught each other. I gave him his letters, he gave me all the secret places of his city."

"Love is love," hummed the great lion, and as he spoke his voice went lower and lower, and his language became the language of dreaming, more and more like that of a child. "That's all. I love Hagia; she loves me. I don't have to love her forever. I love her now. I love many others, too. My mother was so good at loving that other cats would come to her and beg her to teach them her devotions, the rituals and practice of her loving, so that they could become magi. Her eyes shone golden and spun like mandalas as she told them what she knew. She said: *Love is hungry and severe. Love is not unselfish or bashful or servile or gentle. Love demands everything. Love is not serene, and it keeps no records. Love sometimes gives up, loses faith, even hope, and it cannot endure everything. Love, sometimes, ends. But its memory lasts forever, and forever it may come again. Love is not a mountain, it is a wheel. No harsher praxis exists in this world. There are three things that will beggar the heart and make it crawl—faith, hope, and love—and the cruelest of these is love."*

I blinked, recognizing a bizarre inversion of psalms I knew by heart. The lion went on, as though speaking to someone else in his dreaming, someone he trusted, someone he loved. "At my mother's breast I learned best of all. I was still a cub when a tensevete came to her, and his name went: *Tajala.* The cub that was me was afraid of his icy face, like a crag chipped off a mountain, flat and violet like frostbite, and his whole head bigger than his chest. Tajala wept; his lover didn't want him anymore. When he loved her, they melted together until they became a lavender pool under the moon, and there was no ending to them. I shuddered, hearing this private thing. The Abir came, and his lover drew an emerald with a red flaw out of the bronze barrel, and that meant: *Go to the plains of Aamra and cultivate the green mango, learn the significance of its five-petalled blossom, of its leaves changing from rosy to red to green, of its hairy, hidden seed. Take ecstasy in weeping onto their roots, so that they may be watered. Do this with Rasaala, not Tajala, and be happy. Bedeck yourself in mango blossoms, count your wealth in pits sticky with rind.* I felt glad for her, since I loved mangoes. Tajala drew a black stone with no flaw, and this meant: *Go to the Axle of Heaven, and spin wool from the fur of the very stubborn musk-ox who love to munch the blue poppies there. Do this with no mate, learn the psalms of solitude.* I was glad also for him, as musk-oxen are funny, and make us laugh.

Tajala said: *She will not look at me as if she knows me. She melts* with Rasaala now. *She could leave him and we could be lovers in our new lives, I could spin covers for her trees to keep the frost off, but she won't. I want to die.*

Mother said: *The Abir is difficult.*

Tajala said: *I want to die.*

Mother said: *Do not die. Instead, love me.*

And she licked him like a cub, like me. She licked him all over, all his cheeks (and they were very big) and his eyelids and his forehead and his ears (and they were very long) and all the time Tajala cried and all the time Mother purred, and then Tajala was a pool below her, lavender. Mother stepped into the pool and it covered up her whole head (and Mother is the biggest thing there is) and I was afraid again. At night Mother came out and shook her fur and the pool froze again and Tajala was there and he was not well but he was better.

Mother said: *Love, sometimes, ends.*

For the third time her cub was afraid."

In the morning I asked Hadulph to explain further about his mother and the grieving tensevete. He claimed to have told me no such thing and was very abrupt with me throughout the day, though the sky swelled terribly hot and I would very much have liked to ride instead of walk, as Hagia sometimes did, but Hagia had privileges I did not, and God in His Heaven knows how she earned them.

At noon the sparrows descended.

[If this war between my eyes and the page continued much longer I felt I would scream. I could not read any faster, yet the rot battled me for sovereignty over the page. My eyes raced my brain and both of them panted, exhausted. Fat globs of soft, furry mold swarmed up and took a great swath of words, and I felt tears prick my heart. When the text picked up again, Qaspiel was already telling its tale, squatting by the fire, I imagine, those long dark wings brushing the red earth, long yellow beans in a clay pot, all of them chewing tea leaves to make the evening pleasant.]

"…so the man Herododos, whose beard was so black it shone blue, but whose head was entirely bald, and who liked tamarind beans specially, and who told excellent jokes about elephants, had a pet bird, which some say was a mynah and some say was a parrot. In either event it could speak, and in either event Herododos also had brought with him a half-wife, as he called her, from a place called Lydia, and her hair shone blue, too, and her name was Sapham. The blemmyae put passion-flowers into her braids, because the red petals looked so radiant against her hair, and she sang them a song about a man who knew everything in the world, but told it more beautiful than it really was, so that a poor Lydian maid became a queen, and marmots became giant, noble ants with souls of incorruptible gold. Everyone gave the wise man food, and everyone loved him, even if they knew he would leave them behind when he returned home to his whole-wife, no matter how many clever songs his half-wife sang. Sapham winked while she sang, but she also wept. The blemmyae took her knuckles in their mouths, for this is an affectionate gesture among them," and there Qaspiel paused and extended its own knuckle to Hagia, who bit it gently and smiled, if you could call it a smile. "The blemmyae loved her, because she knew a very large number of clever songs, and some of them were lascivious, and those are the best kind. The mynah-or-parrot began to sing duets with her, and the blemmyae called the bird Pham, because it echoed her, and fed it plum-seeds so it would keep making its pretty harmonies." Qaspiel spoke as though it could not bear to end a sentence, each one going on and on. It used the word *and* like a desperate hand, reaching back to haul its words forward.

"But one day Sapham grew sick, and no custard-apples could rouse her to her old songs, and no knuckle-chewing could delight her, and no sight of Herododos herding the cameleopards could amuse her, and her face swelled up red and sweating, and her hair fell out, and when her half-husband took her to the mussel-shell, which had only just sprung up out of the white pool, so the old twins who guard it were then young, she said she did not want to be healed, but to stay here where the blemmyae loved her and put passion-flowers in her hair, and not go back to Lydia where she would be left, lonely, while her half-husband went back to his whole-wife and had a brace of children who looked nothing like her. She made all of this into a song, as was her habit, and the twins on either side of the mussel-shell marveled, and begged her to come in and be healed, but she would not.

Sapham died, and everyone was very sorry because this does not happen much and they had all told Herododos how no one died here and there was much embarrassment. Around this time the mynah-or-parrot Pham also grew sick and the day they buried Sapham, Pham fell dead after her, echoing her to the very last, and they were closed up in the earth together, Sapham with passion-flowers in her hair and Pham with black feathers shining blue, clutched to her breast.

After a year, a tree began to grow where Sapham had been buried, and it had a kind of heavy, dark, furry fruit. Everyone waited expectantly to see what would come of it, even though Herododos had already gone home past Lydia to wherever he lived and loved his whole-wife, as foreigners seem to have trouble believing about the trees. A second year passed before the fruit split open, and I came out, and several siblings, with hair like Sapham and wings like Pham, and we have no gender because we are not animals but fruit and we like to sing, too, and we like to fly, and we like to be loyal, and we like to love. The tree opened up and flew away and when it was done only twigs and a few blue leaves remained, and then they blew away, too, and we were all born, and ready to live." Qaspiel twisted its long fingers together, upset, I think, if I could begin to interpret. "A hundred years later the tree fruited again and we were so happy, so excited, so ready to love our new family! But Gog and Magog first appeared in those days, and their monstrous stride shadowed the plains, and the fluid of their boiling faces, their tears and saliva and snot and sweat, fell on the tree and blighted it and we thought there would never be any more of us, ever, but then the first parent, Irial, began to secrete, and we learned that we were not all fruit, but a little animal, too, and we were happy, but the tree was still dead, and no one can make songs as clever as Sapham could, and we wish we could have known her."

I chewed a piece of salted yak and considered it all. A bit of stringy fat caught between my teeth.

"Who will tell the next tale?" I asked. I looked for the ghostly slip of the panoti, in the shadows. "Hajji?"

She pulled another fruit up close to her ear, this time a plum. "I don't tell stories," she said quietly.

I looked down at the last crust of yak, chagrined. When the rest of them mocked me, I could bear it. When Hajji rebuffed me, misery settled on me like a coat.

"Bury it," Qaspiel said. "So that the next traveler will have a fine salted yak-tree to feast from."

I dug in the soil with my fingers—I wanted Hajji to smile at me, to be charmed at my pliability. But more, I wanted not to be a stranger anymore, to look upon that miraculous soil as they did, as something usual, every day. I wanted to do something as a native soul would do it. And perhaps that was my first acceptance of the magic that lives in this place, the first time I really believed a tree would grow where I dropped the rind of my supper.

"I know you believe what you have told me to be true, Qaspiel," I said gently, still hoping to pull some parable out of the evening, or an allegory. I confess I was not wholly sure of the difference. "But if you would do me the courtesy, I would tell you what an angel is, and perhaps you might draw some illumination from it."

"I am not an angel."

But in those days I was as full of my own notions of the world as a jar of oil, so eager to pour it out all over everyone that I did not care even a little what Qaspiel thought it was. "The angels dwelt with God in the beginning of the world, when all the stars of the morning sang out together and rejoiced—"

Qaspiel held out its long-fingered hand, and made its palm flat. Out of the flesh a single, stark red passion-flower sprang up, its petals ruffling slightly in the night breeze.

My words died in me. Hagia laughed cruelly, and the passion-flower began to—

[Here the mold had so corrupted the text that it hurt my eyes—the brilliant colors of it, no longer like an apple going brown, but bright gold with fuzzy growths of violet and green, like flames shooting up through the letters, devouring, conflagrating, tipped in bitter, black degeneration. *The colors, Lord, the colors!* The volume voluminated with scarlet and orange, with deep magenta, with tiny fungal fronds, disturbed by his breath, a fine cloud of spore tufting up and settling on the rough table. It was getting very bad now, and I feared that the third tale of love would drop into a puddle of muck and slime and escape us forever.

From six or seven broken words (*ash-basket, bitter-gourd stew, bombax, moths, stars*) I surmise they made their next night-camp in an open field of red-silk cotton flowers teeming with moths, under a wheeling, starry sky, and Hagia telling the last tale.]

"John, listen to me. Look at me. No one else is awake. No one will know you acknowledged that I live."

I suppose Saint Thomas might have looked on her without fear or shame. I could barely turn myself halfway toward her, barely place an ear in the path of her voice.

"*Why* won't you look at me?" Her voice pleaded; my resolve stammered in my breast.

"You are naked," I whispered. And those were the first words I spoke to my wife. In shame, my soul aflame.

She fell silent. "I have seen you discourse with other blemmyae. With Oro."

I felt myself blushing furiously then, and gave thanks for the dark of night, and the flutter of moths on orange flowers, that hid me. "Oro is... unformed yet. She is innocent. And the males of your kind... they are not voluptuous. A man's naked breast is made in the image of God. A woman..."

I knew she would not like such an argument, but I could not help but make it. What should I have said? *It is only you I cannot bear, and I cannot yet face the reasons why? I wonder if you have any kind of mind or soul, when you have no head, the seat of reason? I fear you have only a ferocious heart, and that it, like your belly, has teeth.*

Through clenched teeth she answered me, cold and hard: "I cannot help how I am made, John. I do not ask you to put your face away before I can summon up the strength to speak to you. I do not ask you to go blind for my comfort. A body is just a body, and all bodies are naked before God—how could any God count as shameful her own creations?"

"God is not a *her*."

"So you say. Neither are you—I cannot think this is a coincidence."

Hagia moved swiftly across the gap between us—despite her size, she moved so quickly, like the turtle who sees the spider, suddenly, and dashes. She seized me by the shoulders and then the cheeks and dragged my eyes to her breasts, her full and heavy breasts, and the eyes at their tips, black in the dim starlight, fringed with long lashes, and her lips below them, the mouth in her flat belly, and oh, I tried to look at her belt, and I feel such shame now at my shame then, when I prayed fervently in my heart that God should preserve me and pluck out my eyes to spare my soul one glance at her.

"John, look at me, look at me. I am not ugly, I am not a demon, I am Hagia, just Hagia. I copy manuscripts and I know how to take care of trees and I've read everything you can even think of. I am no different than a woman of your kind. I wear cucumber flowers around my waist sometimes, because I like the smell of them, and how they are just a little green, as though they know what they will become. I loved my mother and my father, just as you did, and I came with you, *I* came, first of anyone, to help you find your saint, to find your way. Qaspiel itself, whom you revere, has flown with me in its arms and you will not even look at me, please John, look at me."

I looked. I believe God has forgiven me for it. She looked back, her eyes wide and clear. I let my eyes move over her, taking in everything I had refused to see. Her muscled shoulders, her arms and her hands stronger than my own. A place where her head might have been, (and I wondered then what she might have looked like with a face like mine—would she have been beautiful, plain?), where some shadow moved beneath her skin, a fluttering. Her powerful legs crouched near me, sheathed in their flowing black trousers, her jeweled belt. And her mouth, frank and friendly, her body warm and smelling of something odd and soft, cucumber blossoms perhaps, and ash from the dinner-fire. The night moved over us, and I was moved.

She took my hands and I tried to hold them back from her, but not much, I confess it, not much. She held my palms to the round undersides of her breasts, and their weight was not so much, not so.

"Just flesh," she said. "It cannot hurt you."

"Oh, of course it can," I laughed a little. "It can obliterate me."

And yet I could not take back my hands. She began to speak slowly.

THE CONFESSIONS OF
HIOB VON LUZERN, 1699

A nd there a gentle flush of amber stained the page, erasing whatever Hagia might have said to him, whatever tale she might have told. Small veins of silver shot through it, and in my hands it had the feel of wet ash. And yet, that loss alone of this whole sad affair did not grieve me. It was a private thing which passed between them, whatever Hagia might have said that changed everything, whatever secret she might have given him like a gift—I have never had a wife, but even I know that a curtain must sometimes draw over that moment when some interior door opens and the world between bodies is no longer innocent, no longer empty and without need.

An amber curtain, shot through with silver.

I hoped she said something beautiful—I knew she did. Maybe something about her mother's tree, and what word it bore for that year of her life. Maybe something about her husband. Maybe something totally unknowable, a fable of the pygmies or lament for the soul of an ant-lion. There is nothing I would not believe concealed beneath that suffusion of amber. And perhaps it was only because I could not see it that I believed it so fiercely to be perfect, to be the incandescent syllables of love that would move even me, that mysterious key which would induce any priest to rescind his vows. It could not have been less, to court Prester John. It could not have been less than the most splendid and piercing of pleas, of arguments for the world, for the body, for life.

And nothing perfect can be seen.

Alaric looked up from his book. "Are you well?"

I will never be well again, I thought.

You know what she said, my God. That is enough.

How do I know that she seduced him, somewhere beneath that amber moss of decay and sweet, fading fruit? Because as the chapter ended in a mass of gold, only this remained, slowly disappearing, seeping into the mold:

And I lay in the silk-flowers with her weight above me, and I kissed her mouth, and felt her lashes on my face, and I thought of the cranes, and we both wept.

"Say it, Hagia," I whispered, and her voice floated quiet and warm, up to the stars:

"Ave Maria," she said, stroking my face, and she said it perfectly, without hesitation. "Gratia plena, Dominus tecum. Benedicta tu in mulieribus…"

Dawn came full and bestial. I sunk my face in my hands. Only Imtithal's neat green book remained untouched by the corruption of the air. Its sharp herbal scent had dimmed, perhaps, grown less piquant, less eye-wateringly fresh. Its pages still gleamed pale gold-white, its letters still stood prim and brown against the flesh of the fruit. Like the third portion of the Trinity, it was immaculate, incorruptible. Small favors, and thanks be unto You, O Lord. The others were not destroyed yet, but stood at the brink.

I should have given thanks to You as well for the blessings of those pages I had left, those that stayed unmarred; here and there a word or three had rotted through, but I had not spent half my life bent over desks in inadequate candle-light without picking up the tricks of the scribe. I needed only half a sentence to make a whole—or I had, when I did not care whether my Cicero were perfectly accurate. But John's words inspired more care than old Marcus Tullius. Yet my heart was hungry—yes, hungry and severe, like a lion's love, and the streak of golden corruption obliterating everything dredged up only rage that I had *this much,* and yet no more, that each page brought me closer to the last, and yet I could not even reach the end for the poisonous, invisible air. Alaric tried to calm me, and I began to hate him a little for it, the young man with his carefully patient voice, raised up a register and sweetened, cultivated to calm the elderly, like talking to an irascible child.

That was unworthy. I could scratch it out, but You would not be fooled, and John's honesty provoked an equal virtue in me.

I have failed, I thought, and then said: *It is over. Who cares for children's tales?* But Alaric, having not lost a night's sleep to this, being younger and less prone to the rage or despair that plagues the old, we who dwell so near to the end of all striving's worth, possessed a clearer head and heart. He left me and the puddled waxen ruin of our candle-clock, and went into the village. Some time later, as I was finishing the copy of Imtithal's curious origin story, he returned with the woman in yellow, with her strange downy skin and topaz eyes. She regarded me calmly. I did not think that woman had ever parted with calm in all her days. She inquired as to the trouble. Speechless, I indicated the miasma of rotted fruit before me. She took in the sight.

"You should have worked faster," she sighed finally, and left us alone.

"A callous thing," remarked Alaric.

"Who knows what they fashion hearts out of in this country," I sniffed. "Pure red rock, no doubt."

"She fascinates me, I confess it," my Brother said. "She speaks almost never, and yet when she does, I feel in my stomach as though a nail pierced me, and with much rust. It is disquieting."

"I am sure that our Brothers in Luzerne would prefer you not indulge your nail ideations," I said wryly, turning back to the books to make the best of it.

"I do not speak of love," Alaric snapped in Aramaic. "I do not want her. You know I have never given thought to women."

"Then what?"

"When she speaks, I suffer," he said simply, and would not say more.

To my surprise she returned to us, a basket in her arms. Her yellow dress caught on the dry reeds of the weave. She had filled it with boiled bluish eggs, strips of dried bird-flesh, and several flowers which I understood she meant us to eat.

"It's not breakfast that grieves me," I protested, but my stomach disagreed. We fell to, and as we did the woman in yellow drew out of the feast a few slices of some golden substance—ginger, by the smell of it, though terribly sharper than the ginger I had known, which, fairly speaking, was never much. At Luzerne, our Abbot never considered pungent spices as virtuous fare.

I watched as, with infinite delicacy, the woman picked up our books and rubbed their remaining fragile pages with the golden root, barely touching them, yet coating them in heady trails of oil. She scooped away the worst of it and added it to our cup of mash, and after much silence, much eating, and much application of her cure, gave the books back over to our care.

"It will not stop the rot," she said. "But it will slow. Perhaps you will even finish."

Alaric looked up at her through his hair, grown too long on the road.

"Tell us your name," he said softly.

"It is not important," she answered.

"Please."

"My name is my own. You have not earned the right to hear it."

And she left us, the pads of her feet flashing clean and lovely as she moved.

I cleared my throat. "I loved a girl when I was young, Alaric," I said when I had swallowed my egg and wiped my chin. "She made the sweetest cheese you ever tasted, and her hair smelled like thyme. She had never read a book in her life, and only knew half the Lord's Prayer. I thought she was as perfect a creature as the world might own. Here at the end of the world I will even confess to you, my dear friend, that I broke my vows and made love to her one summer among her cows, with the bright cold stars overhead and the lowing of the spotted beasts in our ears. She kissed me—well, like a lamia. I felt her tail all squeezing me in and her soul in my mouth and I loved her like fire, Alaric, I loved her like a gospel. But when the morning came and I woke with her sleeping in the grass beside me, she wasn't a lamia or a gospel, but a simple girl with pretty skin and a good head of hair, nothing more. Nothing worth my fall. I renewed myself to God. What I mean to say is that love has natural defenses and offenses, strategies. Love wants to win, to make children, to further the world. It is nobler to stand above it. To choose to be better than a beast. To choose knowledge instead of a barrel of children and very sweet cheese. But if you break your troth with that woman, I will not betray you—it happens to us all. I am confident you will see the wisdom of my words when you have done with her. I think there is little danger of you taking up yak husbandry in this village of ash."

Alaric listened stonily and finally uncreased his mouth to speak. I felt a lightening of my soul, having purged that long-lost girl from it, and was reminded how great a gift Thy sacrament, confession, may be to the burdened.

"Hiob, let us not waste breath on this. I did not mean to say I felt a yearning for her. It was only that when I hear her voice, it seems as alien and far to me as if an angel spoke from Saturn, and my bones quake with trepidation. That is not love, or its defense. Let us return to the books. We have so little time, and the light is full, and we need no candles now."

The lurid scarlet mold that cut into Hagia's neat hand retreated under the woman in yellow's ministrations. Alaric showed me: they had drawn back, into the margins, glowing there like marginalia, like an illumination, wine-stain colors, claret and grape, and gold strands like harpstrings. It made abstract patterns—if we had less reason to hurry, I think we could both have been happy simply peering into the slowly seeping decomposition, finding shapes there, like children find in clouds. *There, it is a dragon. There, it is a cart full of tinker's scissors.*

I could still see the strokes the woman in yellow had made with her odd sponge of a plant, and now it seemed to me another author had entered our three sacred books, that the woman in yellow dwelt there in the pages, too, leaving her mark, her signature, in the sweeping brush of her sure hand, showing white, healthy fruit where the rot had all but taken it. Despite

Alaric's fascination with her, I prayed for her in my heart, asked for blessings for her, her soul, her roosters, her sharp-smelling ginger and her boiled eggs, even her bright yellow dress. We returned to the books with a ravenous delight, starving sailors having found an unexpected port, safe and tidy.

THE BOOK OF THE FOUNTAIN:

On the eighth day, Fortunatus dropped back with me, his beak glinting glaringly in the sun. He spoke solicitously; we were nearly strangers then. "Where did you get your map?" he asked, carefully measuring his tone so as to imply no disparagement, only a professional curiosity.

"I know a tree in one of the southern districts of Nural. Some poor cartographer buried her toenail clippings there, and the resulting teak is enormous, its trunk deep brown and stamped with directionals, its leaves all parchment-piebald and soft. When we get home, I think I will barter for a sapling, and take it as an apology to Astolfo—my husband. Before we left, when the tigers were still dancing their prayers for our good fortune, I spent hours climbing in the branches of the map-tree, looking for something we could use. The boughs sprout scrolls, but you know how unpredictable trees can be. Some of the maps lead around the whole world and back to the tree, some of them show details of Nimat before the mountain sprang up, some of them show the path to enlightenment, some show a land across the sea bigger than Pentexore, full of strange creatures. Some show a single heart or soul, diagrammed until it can be perfectly understood. I only hoped I could find our map among the harvest."

"Does the map show the tomb of the Ap-oss-el that John seeks?"

I had to admit it did not. But it showed something, a long road, and portents, and menaces—the sort of thing a map is

177

supposed to illuminate—and at the end something that looked to me like a grave, and I thought that might… be enough. For him. Any grave. We have so few, any single one might belong to anybody. "Besides," I sighed, "I barely use it—Hajji leads the way. Where she rests, we rest. She is quiet and subtle, but surely you notice that she seems to know where we aim?" Fortunatus looked troubled, his brow-feathers furrowing—but he nodded.

In truth I barely understood the map I carried. Delicately drawn, veined as a leaf, the mountains were tipped in silver ink and the names of the cities we meant to pass through drawn in a rich cuttlefish tincture. When I picked it from the branch, I ran my hand over the stiff parchment—almost, but not quite, as stiff as a toenail—wondering where, in the alchemy of the earth, the slant of the penmanship on this map was decided. *Babel*, it looped. *Ultima Thule*. And more mysterious still, it showed the banyan tree, and the field of red-silk cotton flowers, and small figures whose shapes I did not want to guess at.

"Do you love the priest, even though he wants to convert you?" I asked. I did not know if I sought the gryphon's answer or my own.

"I pity him. Pity is a cousin to love. When he forgets himself, he can be dear, like a baby. He made me soup one afternoon, all onions and no meat, because, he said, he did not know what could be killed for meat here, as according to his God I am a beast, but at least he knows that I should not be eaten. It was not a good soup, but it was meant well, and I think that is John in sum."

We walked in companionable silence, and after a while, Fortunatus picked me up by my belt and hauled me onto his back. I smiled—gryphons are not vocal with their affection, but you can't miss it, when you're ankle deep in golden fur. Nor are they so sensitive about being ridden as red lions.

Not long after that, we came to a high cliff, which dropped away below us into a hazy mist, and a soft rushing sound. Trees jutted from the rock, twisting up to get at the thin light that filtered down. We all peered over the edge. Hajji, to whom I had not yet said a word and would not until she spoke to me, tossed a chip of rock down. It tumbled end over end in the air until it sank into the mist—where it hung, stuck, suspended in the cool fog. It still descended, but so slowly we could barely see it move.

"Thule," sighed Hajji, and rolled over onto her back, her ears stretching out on the weedy grass. "A friend with very steady eyes once told me about the place. There is no longer any land or air or sea, but a mixture of all of these, which is in consistency like the body of a jellyfish, and holds all of Thule together. Something happened here, to mix up the world this way. Thule is reachable, findable: but once found, it is impossible to move, to step further than a few stumbling feet onto the glassy shore. It is impossible to penetrate the heart of Thule, impossible to progress, pilgrim or no, impossible to leave. At least, I have heard it is impossible. I do not know everything under the sun."

I knew of it, dimly. I wanted to know more, to beg Hajji to tell us everything, to tell us about the smallest soul who lived down there, or her friend with steady eyes. Anything. But I kept quiet. It is only manners, and manners are all we have. Still, it was the most I had ever heard her say.

"Perhaps if we flew in very fast," Fortunatus mused. "A well might open up—all air possesses patterns, currents, even this gluey fog, and certainly at some time or another the aether must billow aside, must part, and allow some leaf or nut to drift down onto some parapets—rounded, I should think, and bulbous, palaces built to bear the weight of the miasma. I could fly; I could spy out a bubble that might carry us down, to see what is there—" he paused and remembered his friend John, who had little interest in new and exciting locales of which one could tell wonderful tales of back home. "To see if they know anything of the Ap-oss-el, if anyone is living at all down there. At any rate, going through is always faster than around—this chasm cracks for miles."

"You might also get stuck like that pebble, and then we should all laugh at you, and spend a month tying up a rope to drag you back up," remarked Hadulph.

"I, too, could fly," said Qaspiel. "We are both very quick. Fortunatus could take John on his back, and I have flown Hagia before. Perhaps even Hajji could ride behind John? I'm afraid I don't know how to get you across, my leonine friend."

Hadulph wrinkled his muzzle. "I expect we could manage it, if anyone meant to get *across*. But look at all those eyes shining to get *down*, get *in*, get *to*. I believe I will take the lion's lot, which is to say the practical route, and walk the chasm until I find a way around, or a bridge. I shall see you all on the other side if you don't dash your brains out or get stuck in an eternal mist."

Hajji said nothing, but scrambled nimbly up the lion's crimson haunch, and though he growled protest—but the white lion in his nature took rough pleasure in a panoti on his back. The pair began their quieter journey, the panoti flopped on his enormous back, looking up at the clouds.

Qaspiel took me in his arms and lifted me up, safely over the mist, into the fresh, biting air. For a long, spiraling, wind-ragged moment, I didn't think about John at all, and felt some small peace in me, like a pebble suspended in mist.

Just as the sun slipped past noon and into the falling golden hours of afternoon, Qaspiel did spy a bubble below us, or at least a hole in the mist. It whooped with success and several unseen parrots echoed it back to Qaspiel with an extra harmonic scale of irritation. Through the gap, the four of us saw little—darkness, maybe, but it might have been shadows. Rooftops, perhaps, but perhaps only more mist. A road? A statue? I was certain I saw a garden all full of silver champak flowers and heavy iron pomegranates, their dew frozen, their leaves edged in ice. I saw it so clearly for a moment, and then I could not be sure. But John cried out, and the parrots shouted him down.

"A church!" he shouted over the rushing wind between us. "I see a church there, in the mist! I'm certain of it! A cross all of silver and opals, frozen in ice! A chapel! We must go down, whatever the risk. A church, Hagia!" He met my eyes and I saw a pleading, a silent barter, that if there was a church, not to tell its priest nor any other Christian soul what had passed between us. I set my mouth, and my heart beat angrily. I would not be ashamed, not of the sweetness of those flowers against his skin, of any small shiver that might have moved between our bodies, one to the other, like a secret, or a promise. That was his world.

I did not want to talk about it with anyone, truthfully. I had not yet decided where to place it within myself, in the heart or in the gut, as Hadulph might have said. What you put in your heart remains. What you put in your gut is digested and forgotten. It adds its energy to the whole, but vanishes in the process. Where to hide the smell of those flowers, and how I did, finally, speak his Latin out loud, speak it into his skin and his mouth? Presently I was keeping it somewhere dark and safe, for later brooding. Did I even want him? I didn't know. I wanted—yes, I wanted to show him his wrongness, my beauty, even to corrupt him, as he claimed, but not in a wicked way. In the way that says: *this world will swallow you, and I am first in line.* Everyone else was fascinated, but *I* broke him. The one he hated; the one he would not see. That reasoning suffices for one night, but for more? I could not say. And that red field was behind me—before me lay Thule, something new and thrilling—we might even be in danger. I snuggled into Qaspiel's cool grip. All of us felt it, except perhaps John, little more than forty and still a baby. Who knew if he felt anything, if he had the capacity to sense the friction of a story approaching, one of our very own, one we might be able to tell and re-tell and exaggerate and demure for at least a century. *Oh, you don't want to hear that old thing again! Well, if you insist.*

The man was digging.

"Oh, la!" he sang, and dug further, his bronze shovel rising from the smooth, featureless street laden with piles of diaphanous, milky mist, which he piled up beside him in a sagging pile, like old snow. "Oh, la, the world is made of sugar—see? And I am a cup of tea. Oh, la, oh, la, the world is made of cobwebs—aye, and I am a little black fly."

He had a pleasant, high voice, especially given the difficulty of a goat's head and long tongue. His horns whorled impressively, his grey fur curling in the damp. His legs were human, but covered in goat-hair trousers that matched his waist-up pelt. Only his large, flat, man's feet and his thick fingers revealed any ungoaty nature. His big arms had found a kind of halfway point, covered in sparse, coarse fur that showed through to brown skin beneath. His body stretched and bunched with labor, altogether shaggy and impressive. I didn't think he meant to sing out loud, but the tune bubbled up out of him, the sort of nonsense song that served to pass interminable work.

We called out to him; he greeted us with glad hands and a goaty, frank smile.

"Oh, hello, hello! Oh, la, I didn't hear you come down! If I'd known company was coming, I'd have shoveled faster—oh, but it is good to see a soul!" He embraced us all, kissing faces, paws, hands, his humor high, his name Knyz, his profession digging, his home this very city.

"But where is everyone?" I said—we could see only ourselves, and Knyz with his shovel, its pearly handle wet with condensation. The rest faded into fog and cold, a few rounded lumps, shapeless shadows. We heard no sound but the amiable scrape of the spade.

"You're in my bubble," bleated Knyz. "It's terribly hard work to keep it going—stuff just slides back in. Thule abhors a void, you know." He indicated one of the huge, fog-shrouded humps behind him. "Someday I'll reach the palace. There are probably others, too, with bubbles. Though no more than two or three, or we would have met by now—at first I thought you all were Thulites and we'd finally managed to thwack into one another! But alas—no shovels."

"I saw a church," John said breathlessly, and I rolled my eyes. He couldn't even see the wonder of it, stuck in his longing for home and God. I felt an embarrassment for him, the priest being too dense to feel it himself.

But Knyz nodded, his horns spattering dew. "Near the palace, where it won't hurt anyone. And if there are tunnels in Thule like mine, they all went towards the palace. Like blind worms we nose toward our sightless queen, oh, la. And if along the way little airy mineshafts collapse, and the bodies of old sciopods drop down out of the mist, dazed, if travelers drift in, well, then, hurrah. But I don't stop digging. The chief industry of Thule is digging, digging toward the queen. And perhaps the queen has a black spade in her own hands, too, but sits still by the window in the heavy air, barely able to dig out her own front door. It's like when it used to snow, and you couldn't open a gate for the slush of it."

"What happened?" Qaspiel asked, running its hands over and through the jellied fog.

"Oh, la," grinned Knyz sheepishly. "Gog and Magog, I suppose. They bled here, on their way back beyond the Gate. No one meant it, but they'd got wounded and a few drops fell—caught us all by surprise, and everything coalesced like cream in a bucket, and here we are. I don't blame anyone, though. Times give and times take."

"Even their blood is so caustic?" Fortunatus clucked. "Even their blood."

"Oh, no," Knyz said, "you don't understand. They can't help it. Just like you can't help those big long feathers there. Someone made them that way, and set them going, and they just keep being that way, just like I keep digging. You'd be surprised how digging makes a soul sanguine about such matters." This chilled me, for it was my own argument thrown back at me.

"They destroyed your city!" John interrupted.

"Oh, la, cities come and go. You're too young to grasp the situation. Gog and Magog don't destroy things, they change them. Thule is still here, it's just different now. And the fog—well, we're not stopped, just slow. They say stopped; they mean slow. They say impossible; they mean no one has. Everyone is so imprecise. When you live slow as slinking, you have so few words to call your own—you learn to be precise. Precise or pretty—you must at least choose one. Preferably both. You know, twenty years ago I broke through to a little kissing bridge over a spit of river, and two children had been caught there plaiting flowers. They'd managed six whole blooms in a thousand years! Not so quick as in the old days, but progress! And good for them, I say. They loved those flowers so. Because they spent so long plaiting them, they knew every single thing about each blossom, the smallest blemish on a petal. And when my bubble wrapped them up, they could even kiss, before the fog slid back in. Not so bad, to be able to concentrate on a kiss that way, for a thousand more years. Them on loving, me on digging. The queen on whatever queens do, which always seemed mostly sitting on thrones to me. And really, is it so different outside? I seem to remember, when Thule ran quick and bright, life still consisted mostly of waiting, moment by year, for fortune to turn my way. I lived a long time but it all seemed more or less the same. If I couldn't do it one year, likely I wouldn't do it the next. At least digging is consistent, and rewards effort more or less immediately. Isn't it mostly like that everywhere: motionless, frozen, sad? Save that out there you move so fast that you don't even know the value of a crooked arm, and what it means to struggle a decade and more to achieve a little red flower twined up in a vine."

I started to explain about the Abir, how what you managed one year could be upended by the next, the thrill of it, the waiting, the not knowing. But Fortunatus spoke first, his wings drooping in the dim, stale air.

"It's all inverted, outside Thule," he said, as if afraid to agree or disagree with the shovel-keeper. "There, the elements stay separate, but people's thoughts and dreams and fears are thick and syrupy, a congealed ether, and everyone digs in their spoon, coming up with a mouthful that they can call their own. There, everyone lives in the open air, but their hearts are shared, kept in the street for anyone to see. To turn in a barrel every several centuries, and mix together. It's not better. It's not worse. It's harrowing, but so is Thule. And we only look fast. Some of us are slow, terribly slow, and move in our own mist, and forget, sometimes, which is a relief, but not other times, which is no relief at all."

But John could not hear Knyz or Fortunatus. He could not let them speak.

"The church," he said. "Who built the church? Give me your shovel, sir, and I will make my own way to it."

"Didymus Tau'ma built it. I presume that was a long time ago now—oh, la, centuries and centuries. We told him he didn't need to fool with boards and nails. Just break off a bit of the palace and bury it. It might take a couple of seasons to get it right, but eventually you'll have a nice little spread. Stubborn as a pit Tau'ma was, though, and he put up his own wood and wealth for it, even for the cross. And when it was done, he opened its big doors up to all of Thule and said: *Today is Sunday, which is the Sabbath.* I still don't know what a Sunday is, but he opened the doors and no one came, except to peek in and see what he'd been messing with all those months. But he smiled. He smiled a lot, Tau'ma."

"He means Thomas," John said to no one in particular, barely able to speak. "Didymus is Thomas. He was here, and he built churches."

"And no one came," I pointed out, but he did not hear it.

"You mean Thomas," he said doggedly.

"One day," Knyz said matter-of-factly, digging into another drift of elemental sludge and hefting, "he'll come back."

"Thomas is dead."

"Oh, la, yes, but he'll come back all the same. And change the world again, like Gog and Magog did."

"Christ," John said worriedly. "You mean Christ will come back, and change the world. In the Resurrection."

"I never met a man named Christ." Knyz shrugged his woolly shoulders. "But I met Thomas, and he gave me a ginger pie."

"Thomas told you he would return, that he would come back from the dead?"

"Who can remember? He said it, or someone else. No matter. So much digging to do before he comes, la!"

John threw up his hands. "That's heresy!" he cried helplessly. "We await *Christ's* return! When the dead shall rise and the world shall be remade in the likeness of paradise!"

Knyz dug on placidly. The rest of us tried fervently to be somewhere else while John drew nearer to tears. "That sounds lovely," Knyz said in a conciliatory fashion. "If you're hungry while you wait, I can make a fair mist-pie, with some mist-tea, even a good roast mist."

"Who is the queen you spoke of?" I said quietly, and John peered off in the direction of the chapel he could not reach, could not touch. "The world has gone by while Thule stood still. We do not remember a queen of this city."

"I met her when I was a small beast, la," smiled Knyz. "Great big hands, the biggest you ever saw. She could have squeezed me into milk and a scrap of fur if she'd had a please to. She knew just everything—when Magog first stumbled towards us she saw his shadow fall on the boulevards. She spent weeks practicing sitting still, so she'd be ready."

John begged for the shovel. I tried to put my hand on his shoulder, to hold him back, but he just kept babbling for it, grasping for it, and if we'd let him stay he'd have dug forever, I think, for the promise of a church at the other end of his digging. He dug furiously, sweat pouring off of him and drifting away, to become part of the mist.

"No," Knyz kept saying, becoming more and more confused. "It's mine. It's all I have. If I didn't have it, the fog would stop me, too. No, no."

But John would not stop. He wanted the church, any church. More important than anything, that church. I stood behind him and it stood before him and he crawled like a child and never looked at me once.

We did nothing. We stood aside and let John break himself against the fog. With children, sometimes that is all you can do.

"Did he die here?" the priest asked finally, helplessly, his fists wet and ugly, clenched at his sides. "Is he buried here? God showed me this place, God led me here. He must be here."

"He left us living—we kept his church. You don't tear down churches. Oh, la, it's just not done. He went back home with his wife, who sent word when he died. I think we must have disappointed him somehow."

"Saint Thomas did *not* have a *wife*," spat John, incredulous.

"If you say." Knyz seemed quite done with our priest. Goats and fauns have a highly developed sense of propriety, and John had trampled all over it.

"We could take you with us," I said to the faun. "Out into the world."

"Oh, la, blemmye, there's worlds within worlds. If I left, who would dig?"

"You said there were others."

"But I can't be sure of them. And all my progress would be lost. I appreciate the conversation more than you know—the quickest thing I've done in ages. But no, la, I live here. I see why you wouldn't want to stay, but the queen needs me, and so does the city. Me and my shovel, and that's all anyone can want. To be needed."

We flew up the slow, clingy walls of the bubble, out of the misty well. John wept. I looked into the brume—and saw an arched window come briefly into view, and a dark-haired woman inside it, staring down at hands as huge as wings.

THE SCARLET NURSERY:

I n those heavy days that came rolling toward us like thunder, the al-Qasr bustled and hummed. The queen planned her great work, and ordered a great bronze barrel made, so big the smiths brought it in shards, to be assembled in one of the judgment rooms, which on warm spring days served as ballrooms, when the green shoots yawned and dancing seemed happier than the law. Chamomile blossoms garlanded the great statues that stood watch outside the door: two great serpents carved in sard and ebony, their tails twisting, their mouths open, and in each mouth a golden apple with a ruby embedded in its skin like a bruise. When the sun burned hot and no one desired work, I often saw Houd practicing his slingshot against those apples. He was never very good. I had confidence that the apples were safe.

The children felt the excitement, but they did not know why anyone was excited. This is an apt summary of all of childhood, I think. One feels, and does not understand. They were getting big—Lamis was such a beauty, her orange eyes like gourd-skin, healthy and bright, and how she loved her books, and how I loved her. Ikram could break a young tree in two with her massive hands and had had pygmy designs tattooed around her biceps. She was so strong I wondered if we ought not to send her away to study with the giants in their gargantuan city, just to give her a challenge. And Houd was Houd, but more himself than ever. He brooded; he would be tall.

One day, when the bronze thing in the ballroom was but

half-built, Houd finally managed to dislodge one of the golden apples from the sardian serpent's mouth, and an ivory fang with it. He whooped with joy, and did a little dance, and the color in his cheeks shot up. The apple dashed against the porphyry courtyard, and he marveled that it contained machinery, a tiny pumping bellow, delicate wheels. The girls pressed in to stare at it, to try to guess at its purpose, before turning to me. They were drifting, and I knew it, wanting to stretch the time between discovery and explanation, stretch it like sap, to prolong the pleasure of the mystery. But the apple eluded them, and they came running to find me as I was having my private luncheon: the song of the green kingfishers in the peach tree that afternoon, when the clouds brushed by one another, and the moon had begun to come up, as it sometimes does on summer days, hanging in the sky all pale and gauzy, like a ghost of itself.

Houd, Who Wanted Me to Be Proud of Him for Breaking the Apple: Butterfly! Look what I have done!

Ikram, Who Wished She Had Been the One to Break It: Don't be boastful! Anyone could have done it.

Lamis, Who Felt Deep Shame, That a Thing Should Be Broken, and She Had Not Stopped It: Make it better, Butterfly. Make it well.

I told them that to make it well I would have to tell their mother, and she would have to send a messenger to Chandai, where the great goldsmith Gahmuret lives, and he would have to rouse his daughter Gahmureen, who was a finer goldsmith even than he, though the weight of her genius was such that she had to sleep one full year to save up the vigor to create one perfect work. And Gahmureen would have to wash her face, and drink very strong tea with cinnamon in it, and try to forget her dreams, and then sit at her workbench and stare at this thoroughly broken apple until her mind could contain it, all its workings and meanings, and only then would she be able to fix it, but at the price of whatever wonderful invention she might have fashioned that year, if it were not for Houd becoming quite a good shot.

Lamis, Who Was Beginning to Cry: Oh, please, can you not fix it yourself! You know everything!

Ikram, Who Was Beginning to Be Very Cross With Her Brother: See what you did!

Houd, Who Was Beginning to Doubt My Tales: But what is it? What does it do up there in the snake's mouth?

And perhaps they were finally old enough to know that we live too long. They knew their mother would live forever, and so would they and so would I—and they presumed that meant that we would all live forever as we were then, in the nursery with its thick pillows and red walls, and me right there to explain away every distressing thing, and their mother to rule, and never cease. They believed it because they were happy there—if they had been miserable, they would already have known what the apples are for.

Children, I said to them, my darlingest, do you have ambitions?

Lamis, Who Did Not Know the Word: Did Rastno bring me one?

Ikram, Who Thought of Little Else: I should like to be queen after mother is finished with it.

Houd, Who Thought the Chief Attribute of Ambitions is That They Were Secret, Reluctantly: I should like to be a soldier. But I don't really care.

Of course there are many soldiers already, and a full queen with strong hands. What do you suppose queens do when someone else wants to be queen, and she is still as potent as ever? Or the soldiers who never need cease being soldiers, who have Fountain-water in their veins, who stay young, strong, who need never give it up if they do not wish to?

Now they understood it. I saw it in the children's uncertain, widening eyes.

Death is the mother of ambition, and we are all orphans here. Everyone wants, everyone strives, but we trip over infinitude. If a monarch lives forever, how shall anything ever change? How shall any brilliant creature rise? If the monarch tends toward the despot, how shall we free ourselves?

I leaned in close to the children, so that I could not be overheard, but they would not mistake me.

How do you think your mother became queen?

The meta-collinara discovered the Fountain themselves, as they drew further and further away from the busy settlements of those unlike them, those loud, boisterous, hungry, keen. The swan-headed folk were gentle, and wished nothing but to dwell together and twine their necks, to count their eggs and eat silence. When they found that crevice we all now know so well, they showed us the way and left one of their own there to administer the water—a great sacrifice, for her to be so left behind, while the rest drew further and further away, telling no one the name of their new city. And so the history of Pentexore diverted from the one begun in the Ship of Bones, when they still feared death, and had so little time.

Suddenly, the world possessed an abundance of time. And because we are neither pure nor perfect, we treated it viciously.

Once, some time after the Fountain but before Abir was born (yes, such a cosmos existed, that did not contain her!) there lived a king and a queen in the al-Qasr. What I mean to say is, one man who was king, and one woman who wished he were not. The king, Senebaut, was a vartula-man and so possessed instead of your charming orange eyes, a ring of many-colored eyes around his brow. The aspirant queen, Giraud, was a cyclops maid, with only one eye in her forehead, but that an unusually clear and bright one, which saw far off for many leagues.

Now, ruling Pentexore had for sometime been a brutal business—for if a monarch is merely stabbed or dropped from a great height, she may be buried and, if her tree does not sprout bearing only hair or fingernails, continue to rule as well or poorly as she ever did. To truly eradicate one's predecessor, the body needed to be done away with entirely, obliterated. And perhaps, if she had possessed a more violent nature, Giraud might have been willing to cut Senebaut into as many pieces as she could and confine them in one of the long silver vessels that line the great hall—what did you think they contained? Not spice, nor gold.

Don't cry. History is like this, sometimes.

But even had she liked to cut folk into meat, a vartula-man is never easily caught out, seeing as he does both before and behind. Giraud would find another way.

Houd, Who Felt Sick, Though He Would Not Show Me: Was Senebaut a bad king? Did he arrest people? Did he keep his wives in the cellar?

You might think so, but he was no better or worse than any king. He wanted things his own way—which is the primary trait of a king. He disliked both porridge and economic philosophy. But he threw many festivals, and asked only enough taxes to build a bridge over the Physon, and employed several chroniclers, sculptors, and painters to fashion what they pleased with no requirement that they exalt him in particular.

Giraud was a prodigy of government—ever since she was small she had lorded over the other cyclopes, and with great cleverness and subtlety made certain that they played only the games she enjoyed—though she did not insist on winning, for she had a practical disposition. When she lost, she sank into contemplation for days, until she could pinpoint exactly how the losing occurred. As she grew, she set suitors impossible tasks, such as fetching rings from the peaks of mountains and standing guard for a cycle of the moon without sleep. She did not ask these things because she wanted them done, no, but because she was interested in the exercise of power, in whether they would attempt her tasks, in whether she had power enough over them to compel it. Her single eye burned with purpose, and she became so deft at the leveraging of her own strength that she exhausted all opportunities to test herself save one—and Senebaut alone stood in her way.

It was only that she wanted to be queen. Sometimes we want things, and we cannot quite say why, except that somehow we were made to want them. She was not the first to decide to kill a king—all those silver vessels speak to such considerations.

Without natural death to put a flourish at the end of a reign, it was common as cake, and not just for kings, but any profession a creature longed after. True, a country may support many more blacksmiths than kings—however, there is a limit to the number of possible blacksmiths, and sooner or later someone would think of those silver vessels, and one passing afternoon a sooty face would be replaced by another in the Pavilion, looking fair pleased with itself, and that would be that.

Now, my little cygnets, I exhorted them, before I tell you how the vartula-man was brought low, tell me what death is. Speak up, don't be bashful.

Ikram, Who Had Read About Such Things: Grandmother died. Nobody else, though.

Lamis, Who Was Badly Frightened: I don't know! I don't want it! Make it stop!

Houd, Whose Curiosity Flushed His Cheeks: People go away and unless they get planted they never come back. I don't know where they go. I haven't figured that out yet. Somewhere where they can't talk anymore, or be seen, and maybe they live there like normal and maybe they don't, I don't know.

No one can know. I have listened to many stories and I think we are all more frightened of death because we can avoid it. A mortal girl, if she is uncareful and manages to die early, might lose fifty years or so. Less. We lose time without counting, without end.

And so Senebaut lost.

For Giraud was patient. In a space of rich black mud she planted every noxious thing she could find: hooded serpents and mushrooms and spiders with green spots on their bellies, poppies with black pollen, rice gone sour and prickled with colorful rot. She bent her will to these trees as she had to everything else. She tended them with tears to coax their bitterness, with blood to swell their cruelty. And by and by, a tree rose up in her orchard full of odd, blackish, custardy fruits that not only killed the moths she kept for this purpose, but dissolved their little bodies to a bit of wet dust.

The immortal can afford to wait. Giraud was very beautiful, her single eye fringed with dark lashes, her wit quick, and she had never accepted a suitor. She presented herself as a prospect to the king, with her warm kiss said to him: *I will be queen when you are dead.*

Children, she married him, and every night when he kissed her she told him this, and he laughed, and so did she, for royal folk have a peculiar sense of humor, and for many years they were happy.

Lamis, Who Believed She Would Never Marry: Why would he marry her if she wanted to kill him?

We are more frightened of death than mortals, and also more enamored of it. Perhaps he didn't believe her. Perhaps he thought wifehood would mollify her. Perhaps he looked into her one eye with all his own, and saw the beckoning of the dark. But she bore a child to him, and then another, so that she could be certain no one would deny her the throne when he had gone, and then one night, she lay down beside him, her long hair covering his skin, and gave him a rich tea, full of her own soft fruits. Perhaps he even knew it, as he drank, perhaps he held her close as his flesh went to dust. But he did drink, and she became queen, and ruled well and kindly enough in her time—no worse than Senebaut, no better. She, too, liked things her own way. Kings change not because the country needs them to, but because a body wants to be king. Ambition is the source of all change.

As soon as she was fitted for the crown, the new queen went into Chandai where Gahmuret lived, and asked him to keep her safe from poisons of all kinds, for Giraud was never a fool. Gahmuret sat at his workbench for one year, considering how this should be done. In the end, he could not do it. He scried the stars himself and determined that he and his wife ought to conceive a child, and this child might grow to encompass the task the queen set. And so Gahmureen was born some time later, and born asleep. Her parents cared for her as she slept on and on, growing and dreaming and growing again. When she turned sixteen, Gahmureen woke with a start and commenced to build two great serpent-statues, each with an apple in its mouth, and in each apple a carbuncle that would go black in the presence of noxious poisons, and in the apple skin an alarm that would screech and hiss if the carbuncle darkened. Giraud rewarded the inventor's daughter with a rich bed, piled with down and silk, for her cleverness, and there she sleeps today, in Chandai, where we would have to wake her now, to repair what Houd had broken.

And so went the exchange of kings and queens, one bartered for another, right up until today, with a bronze contraption growing bigger by the day down in the Pavilion.

[It began, finally, here, too, in the margins of Imtithal's text, long curls of pale green slime, coiling like lace, encroaching, stretching toward the text as if to tease me, as if to say: *If I wish I can take it all. Even these sweet little stories, even these.* My heart saw some allegory in this, the corrupt world dissolving pure mind, the invisible demons of air that delight disintegration of these books, the angels of our better nature, racing to preserve purity, wholeness.

Faster, Hiob, faster.]

THE WORD IN THE QUINCE:

Chapter the Seventh: in Which Our Companions Discover a Certain Tower and Its Ruins and Feel Very Fondly Towards It, and in Which a Priest Struggles with the Convergence of Heart and Flesh.

Between Thule and the ruins lay an endless wood—at least it seemed endless, and all the worse for my dreams, which had gone dark and wordless of late. I dreamed of Hagia, and sometimes she had a head, and sometimes a child, and everything so washed with light I was blinded, and sunk into darkness with only her hands on me, only her breath, to let me know I still lived on the Earth and had not been transfigured into Heaven. The heat in my dreams moved on me like deep water. I told no one of any of it, and when I think now on all that has passed I know we were all lost in our own dreams, but then I thought myself specially plagued. I often thought myself special in those early years—I cannot be blamed, I don't think. Everyone was grotesque, save me, everyone knew the lore of the land, save me. Everyone served some false god, or none. But the digging man had renewed my faith; Thomas came here, Thomas died here, and I would find his grave, and pray, and he would tell me what to do. That's what saints are for—to guide us, who are lost on Earth.

Did I lust after her? I did. I confessed my sins to the stars every night, but my desire was not lifted from me. Then, it hurt me like a blade, not that I should swell and need, but that I should be unable to turn away from it, no matter how deformed the object. I should have been stronger. Now, I believe I wanted her at first because her aspect was most clearly demonic. Grisalba, I needed only look away from her tail to think her a mild mortal woman; the gentleness of Hajji excused her monstrous ears, and the male leonines I could love, for God made men for companionship and we find it easy among our own. After all, Daniel walked among lions, and was well. Qaspiel, figured like an angel, caused me no distress at all. But I could not ignore her body, and how like a thing of hell in the margins of a book of virtue she appeared, and how little gentleness dwelt in her spirit, all feminine virtues replaced with boldness, knowingness, and a laugh like a roar. But as Hell strikes fear, so also fills the air with temptation, and she tempted me sorely. For that I tried again not to speak to her, nor look, and treated her unaccountably cruel. But once love is released in a field of red silk flowers, one cannot crush any of it back into the ribs, and deny it ever broke free.

And her mouth moved in her belly like my dream of St. Thomas, and I could not tell what that meant, but it unnerved me and provoked me all at once.

In the night, when all slept, I reached out my hand to her, and felt the warmth of her naked back, and if she knew my touch she did not turn, but I fought myself, and God knows my travail.

I tried not to. That is all Heaven may ask of a man.

I tried also not to know her intimacy with the red lion Hadulph. I could not begin to imagine how they might manage concourse, but they were joined at the heart, and the lion did not need to deny her as I did. In some strange fashion their connection brought to me the truth of Pentexore. For a woman to lie beneath a lion and exult in soft murmurs, in secret pleasures, would rest somewhere beyond obscene and into the realms of madness. I would have thought nothing of locking away any Christian woman who performed such an act of devilry.

But Hadulph spoke, he reasoned, he had moods, he preferred mangoes to bitter-melons, and Hagia to nearly everyone else. If in all ways the lion comported himself as a man, the laws concerning his mating could not be the same, could they? For the lions in Christendom snarl and chase and have no soul, no nature at all beyond the savage. And if that most basic law could be laid aside, that the angelic nature of man should never mix with the vicious bestial, what else might be permitted?

But in the endless wood beyond Thule, I could not allow myself those thoughts. Not yet. Not when Hadulph and Hajji rejoined us on the other side of the great chasm, not when the forest closed in, each tree heavy with silk cloth, spooling down in bright orange, gold, green, already woven, and no worm in sight. Not with Thomas somewhere ahead, somewhere secret, waiting only for me to persevere.

We came upon the ruins near dawn, for the silk forest emanated a perfume that filled us with vigor and wakefulness, and we walked through the night with the moon casting fluttering shadows through the draping, shimmering cloth. I wondered idly what lady had buried her dresses here, to birth such a wood. Hadulph nosed Hagia with affection, and I wished that he would speak again of his mother, or that we might stumble upon her somehow, so that she could absolve me of Hagia entirely, tell me it was not my fault: *Love is hungry, love is severe.* Qaspiel broke out singing, with no words at all, but like a bird, like a trumpeting swan, with much honking and chirruping and clicking that nonetheless seemed a pleasing song, though melancholy, in the silvery evening.

"Why did you come, Qaspiel?" I asked that night, after it had finished its nightingale song. "What do you hope to achieve? Thomas is of no account to you."

"Do you think because I do not mate, because I fly and gestated within a plant, that I am so different? I hope to be loved. I hope that in sharing your road you will be kind to me, and love me, not because you think I am an angel, but because you know I am Qaspiel, and see my heart, and protect me, when it comes to that. Fortunatus wishes to be loved, too, to be loved as his wife and his child loved him, and fill their absence with us, with you. Hadulph wants Hagia to think him brave and fair-minded, that he would stand even with one who insulted her and showed no very great liking for anything our country offers if she asked it. And Hajji—well, she hopes that you will love her for herself alone, and for that reason she learns your Latin and follows you like a hound—you are new, and the only person whose love she might believe. It's all love, John. Even you—if your Thomas loves you and calls you worthy, you will be free, will you not? Free and released and unburdened, and worthy and safe. In the history of the world, no one has done a thing that was not done for love. You must only train yourself to see it—the canny emerald strand that connects a soul to its desire, and all the kinks and snarls in it, that might seem as though they tend toward wealth or power, but mean only: *love me, love me back, love me despite everything.*"

"God is love," I said weakly, and the moon flickered through black branches. I believed then that it was so.

"When you say that, and I say that," said Qaspiel, "I do not think we mean the same thing. You mean it only as a metaphor."

I brooded on that, and the angel walked beside me, the hematite in its hair like black tears.

The wood yielded abruptly to pale sand and wiry green grasses tipped in black blossoms, their exposed roots caked in salt. The dawn showed bony and thin over these and also a great number of broken stones, blue-black against the pearly earth, veined with quartz. An arched doorway, leading to nothing, still stood, and cairns of stones, and not a few bronze shards, crusted in green age, were strewn over the ruins. The stones lay haphazard and crumbling over all the land I could see, no end to them, repeated over and over.

I want to say I felt a profundity there, a sense of… what? The echo of God. But the truth is I felt nothing at all but a mild curiosity and the tingle of my sunburn.

The others, however, went instantly silent and still. I believe no one expected to stumble upon that place, except perhaps Hajji, whom nothing surprised. They began to gather from among their various packs a number of items: some salted yak, some mango blossoms, a flask of water, a scrap of silk from the wood. These they piled up near the doorway, and I saw that many other dried flowers and foodstuffs had been left there, too. When I inquired, there seemed to be some confusion among them as to who would tell me the tale—they encouraged Hajji, but she bared her teeth and gnashed them. Finally, Qaspiel took up the task. The sun beat its bluish skin to grey.

"This is a very holy place, John. Long before any of us were born it was here, long before even the Ship of Bones or the Abir. This was a tower, so high you could not see the top of it, and for generations folk labored to build it—children were born on the heights whose feet never touched earth, who ate seabirds they could shoot from the clouds, and fruit might be passed up hand to hand all the way to the top, the latest and youngest of the great work, and the great workers. They built this tower hoping to reach the nearest of the crystalline spheres, John, which is the Benevolent Silver of the Sphere of the Moon."

"Why? Was the world then so wicked they wished to escape it?"

"You ask this? Who stand before us a relic of a world none of us have seen, extraordinary for that, the fascination of every soul in Nural and more? They wanted to touch the heavens. They yearned for the world to be bigger than it was, for it all to be open and welcoming, for it to welcome them. To touch the great silver belly of the moon and know the smell of the winds there, and know whether there is water, whether some beautiful, rare monsters walk and love and give birth and eat vegetables there. Just to know, John. Just to see."

As Qaspiel spoke I felt the borders of its tale and the borders of my own knowledge kiss and join.

"Some say they scraped the bottom of it and some say they never came close. Some say the tower stood so long that the children born at the top looked nothing like the children born at the bottom—they were small and thin, to breathe the stranger air, and their eyes saw perfectly by darkness, and their ribs grew and their stomachs shrank, for little enough food could reach the top. Their language changed so that no boy repairing the holes in the ancient foundation could understand a syllable of the girls mortaring the newest bricks at the top. Some say the moon rejected them, and some say the tower became a tunnel, connecting the Sphere of the Moon to the Sphere of the Earth and that folk did pass between them, before the great winds between Spheres destroyed the tower. Some say sabotage brought it down, from above or below, that the whole nation lived within the tower, and great-grandmothers had never seen their great-grandchildren, and this grew intolerable, or the folk at the top envied the bounty of the earth. Some say the moon offered nothing of interest, and they all went home disappointed and dismantled it all. Some say they never ought to have tried, that the Spheres are not to be bridged. Some say we ought to try again, now that we are better at architecture, and have winged folk to carry it along faster. But however it occurred, the tower fell. A great number of folk died, falling."

"This place was called Babel, John," said Hagia softly. I felt my belly drop out from me then, my heart quicken, and I felt I understood in a flood how their language was so familiar to me. They spoke the language. *The* language, the only true tongue. They were Babelites, only they did not even understand their hubris, to build that tower so high, did not even understand that God had cast their ambitions down. They were naked, and innocent, so innocent I felt their purity might burn me.

"We honor them, who strove so hard, and all before the Fountain which ransomed us from death," Fortunatus said, nosing the boughs of dried blossoms with his beak to arrange them. "I have myself often thought of flying up and up, so high that I might glimpse that silver Sphere—but I would starve before I reached it, I would tire, and I am not so brave as they, who had only a few years to lose."

I sat down heavily on the broad sands. A stone lay near me; I spread my palm on its warm surface, so old I could not begin to imagine its quarry. How I wished I could show this to Kostas, to my fellow priests—to Nikos, the linguist, who would delight in it, to Anastorus, the flagellant, who would be horrified. I wanted then only to share it with someone for whom it was not familiar and known, someone to share my wonder. To laugh with, for there is nothing else to do when confronted, at the end of the world, with the ruins of Babel.

That day, I felt as though I walked on the Sphere of the Moon, and the folk of that place simply stared at me, saying: *Why do you gawk? Nothing could be more usual.*

But for all their familiarity with it, no one seemed to want to leave. Though the morning barely showed through the orange clouds like birds along the horizon, everyone dallied, touched the stones, sifted the sand through their fingers. I saw Hajji press her lips to the doorway arch and shut her eyes in a rictus of reverence. Hadulph rolled on his back, his paws in the air, growling deep in his chest. Qaspiel walked through the remnants of the tower, its steps like a dance, scratching sweeping patterns in the sand, smiling to itself, its blue teeth gleaming. I watched them all, and I felt my separateness like a body. I knew this place, too, but I could not bring myself to tell them the truth of it, to interrupt their familial connection to those dark, dark stones—the canny emerald strands, as Qaspiel put it, that tied them here. I could not interrupt this joy with a story about God's wrath.

You see how they took me, sin by tiny sin.

But they were so happy in the ruins.

Hagia set out a picnic, and we all ate dates and silk-berries from the cloth wood; they were rough on the tongue but tangy and sweet. We ate yet the last of Hajji's dried yak. The panoti made small ululating noises at the sky, as if calling the Sphere of the Moon to herself. Hadulph snoozed, with his eyes open as I grasped now how he always slept, and Fortunatus leaned against him, flank to flank.

"You understand, don't you?" Hagia said to me as the day drew down and without speaking they all agreed to sleep there, with those tall shadows growing long. "This is home. The whole nation of Pentexore lived here once. So it's home for all of us."

"No," I said softly, lying next to her, my body tense, for nothing could convince my flesh she meant any virtuous thing. "It's Eden."

"You told Fortunatus that word. You said it was where men sinned. But I am not a man, nor a woman, so I feel it has nothing to do with me."

"But it does," I said, eager. "I understand now. This is where Eden was, in the beginning of the world. The earth is fertile here as it could never be in Constantinople or any other city of men; there is a magic here we know nothing of, wealth and jewels that you do not even see, so workaday is their glittering to you. Those trees, those silken trees, and the tree of eyes, and the tree of sheep—could the Tree of Knowledge have been anything other than that breed? And you, and all of them—if the Nephilim could have four faces, and the Ophanim live as burning wheels set with eyes, then who is to say you could not exist?"

"I appreciate your permission."

But I did not even hear her. Not her bitter sarcasm, not her warning. "This *is* Eden, Hagia. This is the navel of the world. Somewhere, somewhere here, I promise you, there is a gate of gold, and a sword thrust through it, blackened and burnt, its flames long since gone out. Somewhere there is an apple no one was ever meant to eat. Just because you have never found them does not mean they are not there. This is the country God kept for men, before we fell."

And I kissed her, so full of the joy of it was I. An innocence like desire in me, so big and pale I could not contain it. I lay so that my mouth could clap the mouth in her belly, and my hand found her waist.

"I am not a monster, John," she said gently, and not without affection, I imagined, her words dropping into the darkness between us.

"Didn't you hear me? I know you're not."

"I did hear you. Now you think I am divine, like your Ophanim, and so your God might permit a kiss. That is no different. It is just another way of saying: *this thing is not like me, and so does not deserve what I deserve, nor need what I need.*"

"That's not—"

"I am happy for you, that you have found a way to fit us into your story, John. But you do not fit into ours, and I fear what you will do when you discover that."

And she turned away from me. The stars over her shoulder were so bright and warm that they seemed to grow out of her skin, all that light within her, hidden, secret. She turned away from me, but when the night grew full, and I moved toward her again, the blemmye said nothing, but arched against my desire, and she tasted like sand as I shut my eyes against her skin, moving together, as innocent as an apple, whole, untouched, unseen, not even dreamed of.

THE BOOK OF THE FOUNTAIN:

I had decided not to love him. I felt certain in those days that it was possible to decide this. Somewhere between kisses and promises, there is a small space where such acts of will may be performed, between a field of red silk flowers and the ruins of a tower. I could enjoy him and not love him. I could preen before Grisalba, who hadn't managed it. I decided. There would be no more discussion, nor would I waste my heart worrying over nights secluded away from the others, with a moon too full, shadows too deep.

I hung back, let the priest and Hajji range forward over the broad Babel stones, and I hated a little that I could not have come to that place alone, known it for myself, without having to explain it to a stranger as though I were a book he read in a pleasant old chair. It is possible to close every door that once lay open, to check the locks, to pull down the hatches and stand sentinels. I did all these things. I would not love him—love cannot exist between an animal and an angel. With his kisses still fresh on my shoulders, for he had not yet been able to bear the sight of my front half while he loved me, I knew how the country lay, in his heart.

"I wish that I had visited your mother," I said to Hadulph, astride his back, my cheek against his mane.

"She is not infallible, Hagia. She would say that if you must have him, you must. It is the only way to rid yourself of love. And if you have had him twice, you will have him a third time."

"He is cruel and hard, and he thinks I am an animal."

"You are. So am I. Only he thinks sourly of it. I like being an animal. It means eating and mating and living and light. I don't know what he thinks he is, if not an animal."

"Hadulph, I have done with him. I will only tolerate so much talk of God and my own ugliness. We will go where we are going and I hope to leave him there. He can worship a grave till he dies. I have no more patience for sneering in the daylight and ardor by moon. That is a child's game."

"He is a child. Only forty! Can you imagine? Can you even remember forty? At forty I still had my mother's milk for breakfast! No wonder he is so rude; no wonder he believes uncivilized things."

"I remember forty. Astolfo could still speak; we made love in the sun and he did not avert his eyes from me."

"I do not avert my eyes," growled Hadulph kindly. "But I forget, you have had only one Abir, you are still young yourself. The coming Lottery will be exciting for you—do you think we will still go into the pepper fields together, afterward?"

"I don't know," I said, turning my gaze to the blue sky so deep, and dusted with green leaves flying. "I cannot imagine life on the other side of the Abir. That is the point of it, I suppose. A door the other side of which is unfathomable." My eyes grew heavy; the clouds wisped apart above me, joining again, and drowsily moving apart. "Do you suppose, Hadulph, that the world itself has Abirs? A day when everything spins around and comes out backwards, inside out, mixed up, and when it is all done, nothing is as it was? Do you suppose we could all keep living on the other side of those doors as we had before?"

Well do I remember now, in these shadowy hours I spend in my minaret, the last thing I said before Hadulph's steady, thumping gait sent me entirely into dreams:

"I am only thankful John will have no chit in the barrel, and no poor soul will be saddled with him."

I guessed that we actually walked parallel to the Fountain road, though a long way west of it, since I knew these spiky, fragrant weeds, and the flecks of snow that drifted aimlessly through the bright sun, portending, but not yet threatening a far-off cold. No markets sprang up here, no hyena-woman with a bauble for my penny. No draughts to refresh, no tables draped with fantastic cloth to dress my waist. It was lonely, though six of us walked that other road, that shadow road, leading not to life but to death, to tombs and graves. For many days I had suspected that we drew near the Gates of Alisaunder, near the high mountains that kept those old ghosts back. The map said so—my history lessons said so. I longed to question Hajji about the snowy lands ahead, where the panotii lived, where she must have lived. But I kept my peace.

We saw a glimmer, finally, far ahead, some weeks out of the ruins, which had stretched further than even I could have imagined. A long plain stretched out, full of black sand—not rich nor scorched, but simply colorless, lightless, dark as a sky. On one side of the vale icy mountains rose up sharply, without foothills, as if dropped there by a careless child. And in a cleft, the sunlight shone through such diamonds that rainbow prisms fell on every stone, and on our skin, and on Hajji's ears, and on John's half-bald pate, and on Fortunatus' beak. Qaspiel spread its wings as if to drink the light, and the glittering refractions played a jittery chase over its feathers.

No one had carved or shaped the gems to be pleasant to visiting eyes; no one had smoothed them and chipped them into intricate designs, but only piled them loosely, crudely, and made them fast. Yet if I had not known its purpose, I would have thought the Gates more lovely than anything I had yet seen in my days. Their rough, strange grandeur outshone entirely the city that spread out below them, the lights of candles and fires sparkling already in the young evening that brought us to the mountains, huts and houses, even estates—no camp this, but a city, not so big as Nural, but something like Shirshya, with a well sunk, and a fountain gurgling, and an amphitheater for the summer rites. We, grubbed, hard-traveled outsiders, walked those streets in wonder, while everywhere the rainbows of the diamond Gates danced and darted. Yet these paths were empty—no one greeted us, or asked us our business, offered food or demanded we leave at once. Only three broad streets intersected in the center of the town, and we walked unimpeded up the grandest one—its dirt was most compacted, most often stamped down by feet and wheels. We walked through the quiet to the very threshold of the Gates, and there I climbed down from Hadulph's great back and reached out my hand to touch the adamant door.

The gems burned me; I drew back my hand with a cry.

"Hot, eh?" came a voice behind me, and all of us looked to see an aged, aged peacock, so old his tail drooped and had gone black, splashed with vivid, searing green. His eyes still gleamed, but weariness spoke in his every feather. Those who drink from the Fountain usually stay young—at least as young as they are when they drink their third swallow of that brackish slime. But some few by chance or an ornery nature did not drink until they had already reached a stately age, and these folk grow instead into a kind of regal senescence, still hale, but colored strangely, or their voice goes rough and deep. This bird had done all this and more—his tail so full and heavy it spread behind him like an emperor's robe. And it was by that I knew him, for what did I not know about the old peacock who chronicled the generations of the cannibal tribes so faithfully? The old rooster had not found his way to the Fountain until he was advanced in his avian years, due to a habit for blackbulb nectar, and a lazy disposition.

"That's them you feel," the peacock said, "the pair of them, always leaning on the Gate, hoping it'll fail. Old bastards. Haven't you got anything better to do back there?"

John required explanation. He always did. But I could not bear to repeat the whole long tale of Alisaunder and the building of the Gates, not now. Let Hajji tell him. Let anyone. I couldn't care. I did not come traipsing across half the known world to tell fairy tales to a prudish fool. Not fairy tales, and not history either. He'd be dead in forty years. What did he need to know? How to wrinkle up and go blind. I had confidence in his abilities to manage that without my help.

I wish now I had been the one to tell him. What I would not give to be able to tell him one more thing he did not know, to tell one story after sunset, and hear him disbelieve me.

"Ghayth," I said, and I felt my smile in my belly so wide,

pulling my skin taut. I shouldn't have said it. I should have greeted him as a stranger. But I could not help myself. "Ghayth Below-the-Wall."

The peacock blinked, and cocked his black head to one side. The Gates thrummed with heat, flooding out over the long road behind us.

"Hagia," whispered Hajji desperately, clutching the sides of her long ears tight around her so that the blue veins shone. "Don't. Please don't."

But Ghayth was Ghayth, and he would not deny it. I kept my smile, valiantly—when one has disrupted protocol, it is best to follow it through. The peacock-historian snapped his great tail up; it arrayed in a huge fan around him, the streaks of green and violet snaking like oil through his black feathers.

"A *reader!*" he crowed, his plume bobbing. "A student! You must love my work considerably to speak so out of turn!"

And there it was, thrown down between us. I had thought only of myself, my joy at meeting him. We are not allowed to speak to one another of who we once were, Abirs past. We are now who we are now. We must inhabit it fully, or else what is the point of going through it at all? If I saw my mother on the road, I would have to greet her as a stranger. I knew Ctiste before. I do not know her now. She is not the same person. It is not the same world. Etiquette is all we have.

"I'm sure Hagia has mistaken you for someone else," Fortunatus said quickly.

"No, no, she has it! Come now, I could pretend I take offense, but look where you are! By any measure, this is the edge of the world. On the other side is hell and horror. This is the end of civilized space, so let's have done with civility. Yes, I was Ghayth, and am. The last Abir made me a writer of *fiction*, can you imagine it?" Ghayth unselfconsciouly pecked at the black dust of the street and came up with a twisted yellow worm, which he slurped down. "I have to imagine things that never happened, and then arrange them in a pleasing order, and then write them down! And they have to be connected with themes and metaphors and motifs! Motifs, I tell you! What rot. I miss being Ghayth Below-the-Wall. Now I am Ghayth Who-Makes-Things-Up-

and-Fusses-With-Motifs." He spat the head of the worm. "Give me a history again! Solid, verifiable, respectable! Let me record the ravages of Gog once more! Let me count the ships in a harbor, or how long a certain copper coin has circulated! Do you know my last masterwork featured two young religions, barely out of their own prophets' diapers, one of whom crossed half a continent to slaughter the other, only to get bored halfway there and slaughter a city that had nothing to do with either of them? Come, that's *fancy*, that's *satire*, it's practically a drunkard's ballad! I just made it up! I was bored! I had to write *something!* I can't be blamed! But my public says it's my best yet."

"Pray tell, who is your public, bird?" John said, and I do think he meant to be polite.

"Well, Azenach, of course. That's where you are. If you had a map, it would say Azenach: *Here There Be Cannibals. Also Peacocks. Sleep Elsewhere.* They put on my fictions down in the amphitheater—quite something, they've masks and pulleys and all manner of machines to make things frightening. They're mainly interested in the frightening. They built a whole trebuchet once, for the battle scenes. Painted it green, in my honor. I suppose it's a bit fun. No one ever put on my histories."

"I copied your histories, for all sorts of people," I said, suddenly shy. "Once for the great library, in the al-Qasr."

"And did you spoil my prose, and add vowels, and make the dialogue much prettier than it would have been in life, and leave off whole episodes?"

"I never changed a word."

"Good woman! For that, I'll feed the lot of you—though I can't promise our local dishes will be to your liking."

Out of the dim, dark houses, each of them little more than curtains and poles, resting in the wash of heat off of the diamond Gates, eyes and hands could now be seen, moving slightly, nervous.

"They elected me Welcomer to Foreigners," Ghayth explained. "The Azenach make people anxious."

A small figure toddled up to us, and for a moment I thought the Azenach might be pygmies—but no, it was a child, a little girl shaped much like John, save that her skin was striped as a tiger's, and her teeth gleamed very sharp.

"Don't be afraid," she said solemnly. "We only eat each other."

"Oh, please!" danced Ghayth, hopping from one three-toed foot to another, his tail wavering beautifully in the diamond-light. "Oh, please, let me tell them! A chance to be a historian again! To tell the truth, a long and honest narrative of real things!"

Several others had drifted out, all striped, all silent and wary. "Yes," some said. "Must you?" sighed others.

"I don't like telling stories, anyway," said the girl, who we would learn was called Yat, and who had only eaten a very little bit of anyone in her life. "We already know who we are. What's the point?"

"The point is that *they* don't, so there is a keen pleasure in sharing knowledge. When you've done, they know, and you know, and you can know together, and make quite good jokes a little while later."

"I want to watch," insisted Yat, and so she did, as the rest of us paid close attention, settling onto patient haunches. All except Hajji, who clutched John's hand, and breathed shallowly, and seemed to be trying to make herself as small as possible, which is to say very small indeed. But I would not make the same blunder twice and cause her worse embarrassment. I made a great show of giving her space, crouching nowhere near her or John, hoping she would know I meant her no harm.

Ghayth lifted one foot in a professorial gesture. "The Azenach got shut behind the Gates, when the giants Holbd and Gufdal closed in the wicked twins, Gog and Magog, and doomed the copper-spired city of Simurgh, along with several other tribes."

John looked sharply at the striped child. "Do you mean to say she has seen Gog and Magog with her own eyes?"

Yat laughed. "Stupid! I wasn't born."

Ghayth stared meaningfully, his beady eyes narrowed. "I had forgotten—when you write a book, no one interrupts you. It is extremely irritating. Now! Many were caught in the closing of the Wall, and the Azenach were but one. For some time, they made their lives as best they could on the other side, but their neighbors were dreadful company. If a family managed a house or a barn, Gog would bite it in half, and Magog would gobble the remainder. Being siblings, they share and share alike. A phoenix—split down the middle. A fast-hold of Fommeperi, sister-tribe to the Azenach—equal warriors for each, portioned out precisely. When they blasted the earth and burnt the soil so no tree could ever grow again, even the specks of dirt showed their equality: half blighted by Gog, half by Magog."

"I have to share with my sister," Yat whispered. "Even when she's bad."

Ghayth nipped at her hair affectionately. "Yes, that's certainly exactly the same thing." He pressed his long neck to Yat's cheek. "It is possible to live alongside darkness and still feast, still have children and sing and celebrate the moon. But not beside those two, one of which takes your left side in tithe, the other of which takes your right. And even worse—those caught on the leeward side of the Wall found themselves cut off from the Fountain. Though they could live forever still, they would now watch their children grow old and die, for their progeny could not drink, nor be preserved. Who could bend under that fate, and yield to it?

Now, it so happens that the Azenach are cannibals. I have not mentioned until now because it tends to prejudice the audience against them, when truly, you are in no danger at all. A cannibal eats her own kind—you are none of theirs, not you, blemmye, nor you, panoti, nor gryphon, nor lion, nor anthropteron, nor whatever sort of pet that one is," he said, indicating John with his head. "As well, they only eat the dead. They have a very ornate ritual in which each of the family members devour a portion of the deceased which represents their connection. Students of the poor soul would share out her brain, those who in their youth scrapped with her, or had been protected by her fierce temper and love for the small, would quite solemnly swallow the meat of her muscles. Her children would eat of her womb, her husband of her heart. They have quite a complicated liturgy of anatomy—fear, for example, resides in the stomach, anger in the spleen, grace in the foot. I could keep you here all night explicating the Azenach body, and all its humors. Love makes residence in the heart, naturally, but also the soldierly arts. What seemed most powerful in an Azenach must be eaten after death. You might think this disgusting, but it is really quite obvious: they loved whomever it was that died, and would have her with them always. It is very respectful, I promise. The whole process is left over from pre-Fountain folklore, but still, occasionally an Azenach would perish out of violence or plague, and religious habits are difficult to shake."

Yat smiled, showing all her razor teeth. "I ate my friend Ott's hand when an ox gored him, because when I was scared at night, he held my hand till I fell asleep again. It didn't taste very good, but I didn't feel so sad, after."

"Well, one by one, the young ones on the other side of the Wall grew into old ones, and the Azenach mothers and fathers looked on, horrified, for they had forgotten that bodies perform that stumbling chorus. And when these mortal children perished, their parents planted their remains, when the bodies had been shared out enough to satisfy both grief and faith. Little by little, the children's bodies grew under the earth, their roots and shoots moving toward the heat that spilled so fervently from the other side of the Gate, intensified by the adamant gems there. And one day, a pale, striped sapling sprang up, outside the Wall. Then another, and another. And they sent out trunks and leaves and blossoms and one day the blossoms opened and a whole generation of Azenach leapt out laughing. Of course, having been shared out as the holy meal before burial, some of them had no brains, and didn't laugh but fell down dead like dumb fruit dropped. Some had no wombs, and never had any children of their own. Some had no spleen, having aggrieved many people in their other lives on the far side of the Gate. But those who had fallen dead before they could even draw breath seemed to have enough for the others to share, and they patched themselves up reasonably well, swallowing their siblings' organs into their bodies. They do, well and truly, take the strength of what they eat. On one side of the Wall, it is a metaphor. On the other, it is fact. Only a few of them have no hearts now—their blood seems to move about in a fashion more like sap, and they are pacifists."

"I can hear my grandfather on the other side of the Wall," said

Yat. She twisted her streaked hands. "He misses me."

"They stay here, close to the Wall, even now that new children have been born in the more usual fashion, like Yat, waiting for the day when the Gate will open and they will be one tribe again. But you mustn't believe her," the peacock sighed. "She can't hear her grandfather. Not even sound breeches the Wall. The Azenach on the other side do not even know this colony exists."

"Don't tell lies!" Yat shouted, leaping up. "I can hear him! I can! He says: *Soon, soon*. And the Wall gets hot."

I shivered. I did not think it was her grandfather, either.

"Oh, Yat, my darling, you must stay away from the Gates. No good will come of you listening to whispers leaking through, and your grandfather does not live in that country alone."

"What do you know? You've never eaten anyone at all!" The child stormed off, and Ghayth made his apologies. The older Azenach held her while she wept dramatically. They all glared at us across the black road. Silently, the Azenach began to light the torches along the way, and while they did it, Yat sucked her thumb. Ghayth stretched his short legs.

"It was good, though, to tell a true tale again! You will stay, won't you? Tomorrow the young persons' chorus will perform my *Romaunce of Twelve Infidels and an Exquisite Rhinoceros*. I don't mean to boast, but I think the motifs are quite adequate. I have nearly mastered the art of the denouement."

"No," whispered Hajji. "We have to go."

Ghayth looked at her suddenly, and the little panoti blanched, if such a thing were possible for a creature the color of the snow.

"Don't look at me," she said desperately. "Stop it."

"But you're her," he said wonderingly. "You're *her*."

"Please!" she wailed. "I don't want to be!"

"If your headless friend here saw fit to shred the veil of modesty and drag me out, I don't see why you should get to stay demure," he sniffed. But he turned to me, unable to conceal his pride: "You see, I am getting the flowery speech down to a science. I can do it for fifteen minutes at a stretch."

The panoti disengaged herself from John and crept up to Ghayth. She put her hands on his avian face, where he had large, handsome white circles under his eyes.

"Please," she whispered, and tears filled up her eyes. "Let me be Hajji. Let me stay Hajji."

THE CONFESSIONS OF
HIOB VON LUZERN, 1699

I have tried to re-compose the text as I imagine it to be—that is part of the work of a scribe, to gracefully transmit the document as though no error ever occurred, as though no single letter were in doubt. But if my Brothers could read this as I saw it in that cell with the bold sunlight seeking purchase on the walls, their heart would fall and fail.

The Lord my God knows what those pages said. I will never know. Why did You not send me an angel to dictate the perfect, undiluted tale to me, as You did to Your chosen scribes in the old days? To Paul and Matthew and Mark, to John and Luke? Why did You not simply inhabit me with Your light, if You wanted these things uncovered, known? It seems to me more efficient.

The red-violet rot had begun to steal letters again by the point of Ghayth's sad tale of the cannibals, even whole words. I would not be worth my beer if I could not surmise that between an *Our Lord in Heaven* and *Thy kingdom Come* there must be an *Art in Heaven*, but I confess the tremendous difficulty of constituting a whole narrative when the pages in my hands soften and shift, and I had to guess at Yat's tears, when perhaps the word (of which I have but a *t* and an *s*) may be something else entirely, for who knows if an Azenach weeps?

And yet, in my secret soul, which I did not even share with Alaric, I was struck dumb by the beauty of it, of the corruption itself, how it made these pages seem not only to speak but to bleed, like stigmata, the blood of some terrible divinity seeping up onto my fingers, staining my hands with its own hungry heart.

If the panoti said more, if the troupe ate at the cannibal feast, if they met the child's parents, if they comforted her—it all disappeared into a soft wing of carmine, staining upward from the bottom edge of the sweet-smelling page.

I tried so hard. I tried to make it all run smoothly, so that I could bind Prester John up in a tome and send it to Luzerne as consummate and reasoned as you deserve. But I felt as the sun grew heavier in the day as though I chased a mercurial hart, and every step deeper into the woods was a step further from my desire.

Yet I could not stop. I could not cease. I reached out for its pelt—and grasped nothing.

The green encroached from the corners of Imtithal's book like four winds, blowing away the ephemeral words. Alaric and I tied cloths onto our mouths so that our breath did not further the process, but it proceeded, always, apace. There was much following the passage I copied out here, but it sank away, only a character or two swimming up out of the verdant sea lapping at the page. *A. M. O.* Nothing I could catch or hold. The patterns of the mold began to entrance me, and I fancied I could see their slow advance, each tiny portion of story sloughing away. When Alaric turned to his work, I tasted the corner of my smallest finger, smeared with the stuff. It tasted like spring sap.

THE SCARLET NURSERY:

O n the day Houd went to the Fountain for the second time, I woke early, to wash him while the boy still slept, which is the only time I found it reasonable to wash Houd at all. With the help of Lamis, my dear conspirator, we lifted him bodily out of bed. He slept naked, for he had read that the cametenna warriors of ages long gone slept so, and announced that, like Aleus the Closed Fist, he would greet his dreams shameless and ready. Ikram laughed, and he pinched her viciously, for I do not allow striking with hands such as they own. But it is good for children to feel they have gotten away with something wicked against a sibling, now and then.

In the porphyry tub, we sunk him into a soapy bath, and scrubbed his sleepy skin with rushes fresh-cut, combed the grime from his hair and scented it with rose-apple, rubbed him down with myrrh and amber. He woke as I smoothed the snarls in his hair, but let me believe he still slept. Houd behaved very stoically as I laid out his clothes—all black, as he preferred, though somewhat less sanguine was he about the beads of jasper and long ribbons I tied into his hair. I painted his eyes myself, and gave him coins for his shoes, for luck. His mother would go with him, but I would make him ready, and despite his taciturn nature, I loved the boy, who was no longer really a boy at all and would soon be out of my care entirely. Perhaps I loved him even more fiercely because he turned away my embraces, because he crouched in corners and would not speak, because he was reticent, and dour. Lamis and Ikram's laughter came easy, and we were close as roses on one vine—but how terribly sweet, when the boy who never laughed gave me one faint smile.

Houd, Who Does Not Even Like Jasper: Why must it be three times? I've already been once, that should be enough.

Ikram, Who Will Go Next Year: I think *you* might need four.

Who can explain such things? It is three times because it has always been three times. Perhaps in the old days, a physician lived who could have told you why. I have heard it said that once doctors were common as rose-hips. If a soul fell ill, a dozen surgeons and herbalists would appear like mushrooms after a rainstorm, and each with a phial, or a poultice, or a tincture, or a blade, each with a wonderful cure—and some of them really worked.

Lamis, Who Is Afraid of Blood: They cut you open? To make you better?

What would you do to save yourself, if death stood on the other side of a man with a knife? Be happy, I admonished my darling girl, that you will never have to think of it. Doctors, those strange and terrible beasts, are extinct—I heard of their dark rituals from Didymus Tau'ma, of whom I have spoken before. He often fell ill, and I had to care for him, for no one else could bear the smell of his sicknesses. I did not know what to do, but he showed me how to make a tincture, at least. Oh, certainly, we all know to wash a wound, if someone should stave in their head, or lodge a palm needle in their knee. But Didymus Tau'ma knew of things like *surgery*, wherein a doctor worked upon a body like a blacksmith works upon a sword. And those practitioners are long gone.

Ikram, Who Will Play Surgery With Her Wooden Gryphon for Weeks, With Red Silk for Blood: Where did they go?

And she opens her hands, for Ikram knows there is a story, and I sit in her palm like a stamen in a lotus, and say:

The meta-collinarum cannot bear bluster and noise; they are mild and reclusive, and prefer their own company. Who can say why they boarded the Ship of Bones with the others? Each year they receded like a pale tide, drawing back over the hills, ranging over the mountains, looking for a place where no one else would ever come, where they could commune in secret. Some say this is on account of their swan-nature, for swans are poorly tempered and strongly bonded one to the other. Others say it is because they find it difficult to speak, with their elongated necks, and have a language of signals and signs all their own. I have only seen the Oinokha. I cannot answer this question except to say she spoke to me. Did it pain her? Who am I to know?

An archer among them found the Fountain first—she was called Celet, and even among the collinarum she kept herself solitary, singular. She rarely spoke, except to trumpet the moon-rise with her rough voice. She scrambled over stones and high places, the fur of her boots all caked with snow, and her arrows were wound with mistletoe, and her eye was grim. But for all that she was never an unhappy girl, only the furthest extension of the character of her people. And thus she explored far ahead of her nomadic band—and one day, like any other day, she discovered a crack in a towering stone, all slimed with green and foaming. She felt compelled by that effusion, and crouched down to stare at it, how the thin sunlight moved in its jellied surface, how the edges froze into green specks of ice. She touched it with her finger and tasted it—do you remember when you tasted it for the first time?

Lamis, Who Only Drank First Last Year: I remember. It tasted like the whole earth.

So Celet tasted, and felt a terrible, unstoppable strength move through her. The water of the Fountain is not sweet, but still she bent her head to the rock and drank hungrily, sucking the life of it from the earth, her spine moving with her pulling up the blood of the mountain from the flesh of the rock. She called together her tribe and they came to her broken trebling—the collinarum drank, one by one, and understood in their bones that they were changed. They did not know more than the strength and joy they felt filling them—they did not know to drink three times; they did not know yet that after the third they would never die. But by and by they uncovered these things, as one uncovers the inevitable end to a story. And they knew it should be shared, that though they loved not the company of the lowlanders and all their many folk, they could not keep it for themselves and dwell as immortal sages on the mountain, concealing their secret and watching other generations shrivel like leaves.

By this we may know that the collinarum are perhaps kinder in nature than their aloofness might suggest.

Houd, Who, Though He Looked Very Dashing, Was Still a Child Yet: I would not share, if I found it. Except with my sisters. And my mother. And perhaps you, Butterfly, if you gave me a ginger-cake for it.

We may be grateful Celet was somewhat sweeter than Houd, then. However, when news spread of the miraculous Fountain, many folk were of your opinion. It should only be the beautiful who lived forever, or only the wise, or only the strong. Only the sciopods, or only the blemmyae. The tribe of doctors felt that they would be destroyed by this new medicine—and they called it that, medicine, so that Pentexorans would think it had all along been the province of physicians. The collinarum would not make arguments, except to say they could have kept it for themselves, if not for the pernicious presence of morality in their swan-hearts.

There was nothing for it but to have a war. Many doctors became generals, to defend their livelihoods, and we cannot judge them, for there are many small deaths to suffer in this world, and no one behaves well when faced with a black door. For this reason it was once called the Physicians' War, though now it is simply called the Last War. Celet proved to be a better archer than any could have known, and she crouched down in the tiny rill of the Fountain which you will all remember, how small it is there, how cramped, and no one threw her down to claim victory and suckle at the slime there, not one.

That was the last time, children, that a large number of Pentexorans died, and I have not the memory to count the years between then and now. A thousand—more. Before Alisaunder and Herododos, before even the lions separated into the white and the red. Now, queenmaking is an ugly business, and there are cliffs to fall down and storms to crush bones, but in all your long lives, you will know perhaps a handful of deaths, and you will mourn them horribly, for their rareness. Mourning will be like a draught from the Fountain—awful, throttling, burning you all through your veins—but you will taste it but seldom, and love life better afterward, for you will have been on speaking terms with its opposite. Perhaps our long lives had to begin this way, so that no one would count it cheaply bought.

I cannot imagine how Celet must have wept, to see from her height all that blood, all that death. I cannot imagine so much death: several bodies lying together and none of their eyes shining, none of them speaking, only bleeding into the snow, never to rise again. I can only speak of it as one tells a story one has heard so many times that it has lost all reality—yes, people die. Didymus Tau'ma died, and I watched it. But so many, so many all together—surely it cannot really happen anymore. Surely someone would stop it. But Celet saw it all below her, all those people dying, to live forever, and she clung to the crags in her grief, honking and braying as only swans may.

And so when it was all done, the collinarum held the day with their allies—the roles of soldiers were sealed up and burned, so that no one would know who fought on which side, and no one would later seek revenge if a poor boy's uncle thought that only cyclopes deserved the gift of the Fountain. When it was all done, the country was sick with it, and constructed a road from Nural and the provinces all the way to the great mountain, and called it a memorial, and one by one, the physicians being dead (though one of their trees, now and again, will fruit with an amazing array of bottles and droppers full of liquors of every color) and children being weak and small, each soul in Pentexore walked that long road, and drank that long drink, and all the things began which continue on this day when Houd will go, and sit with the old Oinokha, who has by now forgotten that her name was once Celet, that they once said she could shoot an arrow through the center of the moon and the moon would thank her for it.

Houd, when you go, when she takes you in her arms to bend back your head and nurse you on that green mountain-blood, you must think of all of this. You must remember it. That is the purpose of stories, that no matter where we walk in the world, we walk twice: once in the warm sunshine, and once in the silvery light of every tale we have ever heard, seeing each thing as it is, and also as it was.

That is why your mother brought me from Nimat when you were but babies, all the way down the long roads lined in yellow flowers, along the blue river, all full of stones. So that you would know how to walk twice, and so that your stride would be kind.

THE WORD IN THE QUINCE:

Nimat-Under-the-Snow. Hajji called it that, this old village half-buried in ice, and the others reacted to the name as if it leapt out of her pale mouth and struck them viciously. I did not understand—and they had stopped explaining to me. The diamond Gates had shaken them all profoundly, and I felt as though I had dropped through a hidden hole in the earth, with no guide to explain to me why any of my companions acted as they did.

Qaspiel said: "We cannot say, John. I do not ask you to show me your mysteries. Perhaps if you had answered differently that day in the amphitheater, when Hagia asked you to take the Fountain. But now we are all stuck, and everyone knows what we are not saying, but we still cannot say it." The creature, which I could not stop calling an angel in my heart, flicked its wings as though it wished nothing more than to be away and conversing with clouds. "To live as we do, John, life upon life, a palimpsest of experience, it is like walking twice through the same field—more than twice. An infinitude of walking, and the field is so dear and familiar, but we are always different, and the difference is all we are."

"If it causes you pain, why do you continue this way?"

Fortunatus interrupted us, squinting in the snow. He turned his liquid golden eyes on me. "Why do you continue in your faith, when it means you must deny all the evidence of your senses and suffer for the promise of ever-postponed bliss? Because it is the way you have found to understand the world, to live in it and not despair. You speak of war in your country; we do not have it. You speak of jealousy, of coveting wives and wealth; we know nothing of this but in old, old tales of times we are glad we do not live in. You speak of vicious cruelty on account of whether or not to paint an image of your God; I and all of us find this obscene, and do not begin to understand it. We live forever and we live in peace and it is *fragile*, John. It is so fragile. And when a thing is fragile, it is best left undisturbed."

"In Christ there is also peace," I said, and the angel said nothing.

Several panotii lived in Nimat yet—in all my days I had never seen a village so elderly, so dwindled. Many houses had simply begun to sink into the icy earth. They emerged like moths from the snow-packed doors of their little yurts, and Hajji embraced them, her ears flowing around one after the other. *This one is my thrice-cousin Isoud*, she said of one. *This one is my friend who painted the frescoes in the al-Qasr a hundred years ago, and her name is Mara.* They looked so ephemeral, so small, like snowflakes, hardly coming to Hagia's waist, their ears open and friendly, diaphanous. In the cold I pitied the blemmye, for though she wrapped a wolflet pelt around her shoulders, her sight obliged her to keep her breasts bare, and gooseflesh rose on them as the wind made her eyes water.

I had decided to love her. Somewhere on that awful ascent, scrabbling on the crags, my skin freezing into a shell, I had decided it was better to love her than not to. It is possible to decide this, to take mastery of the heart, before one passes beyond all questions of mastery. Better to make the choice than to be swept away. I could not enter her body and not love her. It was not in me. I had decided it, before we ever reached Nimat. There would be no more discussion, nor any more nights secluded away from the others, until I could decide further what was to be done with the whole of it.

The one called Glepham, whom Hajji introduced as the ivorysmith she liked best, when she was in the market for ivory, which was very rarely, brought us all a hot, thick, goaty milk swimming with lavender seeds. He explained that the panotii had dispersed, slowly, one by one, "like water dripping from a glass, down into the lowlands, into the capital, to find work and warmth and of course each passing Abir spreads them further, but Nimat is still our home, and here we do not turn the Lottery barrel. In all other cities the panotii remember Nimat-their-touchstone, the way you remember which side of the sky the sun comes up in. We are so pleased to have our little sister back in our arms, to wrap our ears around her and share heat."

I could not in any way account for the distress Hajji clearly suffered. She shook; her eyes darted; she tugged her ears tight around herself. She moved as though she expected some terror to crash down upon her at any moment. She smiled, but her smile was an animal's bared teeth, cornered, desperate.

"We came to see him," she kept saying to Glepham, who demurred—one more cup of milk, sister. One more tale of how Mara upset the white lions by letting the beer boil too long and spoiling it all—one more tale of how dearly the white lions love their black, black beer. I thought of Hadulph's mother. I wondered what her name was. I wondered if she lived here. I thought: *Love is not a mountain; it is a wheel. No harsher praxis exists in this world. There are three things that will beggar the heart and make it crawl—faith, hope, and love—and the cruelest of these is love.* I wondered if, tonight, when the red lion slept, he would repeat his mother's mystifying and beautiful inversion of Paul, and if he would miss her. Again, my thoughts came round and round to it: either this is the devil's country or it is God's. They invert everything I know to be true. But whatever they say is proven real by my eyes, my ears, my hands.

And moored in these thoughts I saw her, in the whipping snow, a monolith of white—Hadulph bounded toward the figure, and pressed his nose to hers. I shielded my eyes from the wind. Their growling came soft and wordless.

"Vyala," Glepham nodded happily. "She knew he was coming. She collected many tears to shed when she saw him again."

"John," said Hajji. "Let us go. You will want to see him by moonlight. It is best that way. His humors are up, at night."

"Who do you mean?"

Hajji shook her head, quivering with anxious energy. "They

will stay if you tell them. Or come. It doesn't matter to me."

"Hajji!" I said, half laughing. "Stop it! Who is it you mean?"

"Thomas," she said wretchedly. "You said you wanted to see him. He is here. He is here because here is where I left him."

Hajji led me as if I were her own meek child. Up, up, further even than Nimat, into the thin air and the ice. I shivered; my beard took on icy beads that jangled in the wind. The others stayed with the hot milk and the lavender and Vyala, whom Hagia especially had longed to meet, and whom Hadulph was passing pleased to present. I had never seen the blaze on his scarlet chest puffed so high. In the end I took only Hajji, though more truly Hajji took me. The others would not understand, or I should hardly see the tomb I came so far to find for pausing to explicate the finer points of the history of Christendom. I was not unaware that they had tried to be patient with my ignorance—but I could not bear their disinterest just then. I longed for the presence of God, for the touch of the pale light of the Logos in my soul, the peace that I had lost.

Hajji squeezed through a gap in the high stones hung all with icicles; I followed her with some difficulty, for the country, even Nimat, ran too rich and fertile not to pad my belly considerably.

All of a sudden, the wind died, the snow vanished, the cold steamed to nothing. We stood in a round clearing flowing with deep grass, and a black sky overhead, hung with stars like crystal censers. And with the wind, and the snow, and the cold, my heart lurched and stopped, and I fell to my knees, and could not even cry.

In the center of the clearing a great tree sprawled, its long, dark roots splaying over the earth like skirts, its leaves arrayed in patterns of silver and amber, catching the dim light, wavering slightly in a warm breeze. The trunk of the thing was bigger around than six men might manage to join arms, the bark wrinkled and slick, burls open here and there, where fragrant myrrh oozed, and the smell of it was sweet as the bodies of saints were said to be, in every book I knew.

It had but one fruit, huge, ripe, growing in the place where two of the great branches meet in a crook, framed all around with amber and silver leaves, three-pointed and shadowy beneath. The fruit was a face, the face of a bearded man, his gaze serene and kind, the lines in his face showing care and grief, but acceptance, too, and in his beard I saw birds, tiny as flies, their white wings glittering in the starlight.

"Thomas," I whispered.

"Imtithal," he sighed. And Hajji ran to him, her ears floating wide, and she stood on her tiptoes to press her cheek against his, her face running with tears, and his too, but his tears were perfume and sap. She put her hands to his beard, his eyelids, and they whispered between them so that I could not hear.

"I came seeking the tomb of Saint Thomas the Doubter," I said—or pleaded.

"And you have found it," said the tree.

My face burned—why could Hajji take such intimacies with that awful face? I came for communion, and Hajji had it, and I did not.

"Who is the panoti to you? Why do you call her Imtithal?"

The face looked mild and curious, his dark eyebrows rising. "She is my wife, and that is her name."

Hajji looked across the clearing at me, her eyes huge and deep. "John, you must not speak of this to the others. I could not bear it. Do you promise?"

I nodded, numb, even in that terribly sweet place.

"You know that we change, in each Abir, life to life. It is more sacred than sacred, and the luck of the draw is law. I am far older than Hagia, or Hadulph, or even Qaspiel. The gryphon is a child next to me. And in my first life, I was called Imtithal, and I married, and became a widow. And I cared for three children whom I loved to distraction, and when they had grown, I wrote down all the stories I ever told them, so that I would not forget the children, nor they me. But John, every one of them down in Nimat drinking Glepham's milk and listening to the great white lion—they grew up reading the stories I told to those little ones. We do love our stories in Pentexore, and our histories, and our fictions. They grew up imagining I was their mother, their Butterfly. They all get to keep their names and no one breaks the rules; they cut up their hearts and keep the pieces in a thousand separate boxes—but I had to change mine, just to keep that light from striking in their eyes every time I spoke. Despite the Abir, they cannot stop wanting to be loved, wanting me to love them, and I didn't want to tell stories anymore. I didn't want to love children anymore. I didn't want to be everyone's mother. Thomas died, and the children—" the panoti put her face into her hands and shook once, profoundly. "Sometimes you're in a story, and also telling it, and it is the worst thing, because you can't change the ending, you can only live through it. John, all this time they've barely been able to contain themselves from embracing me and calling me by my name and begging me to sing them to sleep at night. You saw Hagia and Ghayth—she had only to meet someone she loved enough and all customs evaporate. I suspect she wanted me to scold her, like the nurse I was, so she could have a moment under my rule. Only the most tenuous thread of law keeps them from doing it. I am not the only one—do you think Queen Abir, who began all this, is dead? No one dies—or hardly anyone. Everyone keeps going, forever and ever. But you—" she spread her hands beseechingly, "you've never heard of Imtithal. You could love me as Hajji, just as a no one who knew her way through the mountains, you could love me and never ask me to tell you a story in all of your days. You could love me like Didymus did, while he lived, and I could rest."

"Saint Thomas didn't have a wife," I said, only half understanding her.

"Perhaps not," the beautiful tree laughed. "But I did."

"You understand, somewhere," insisted Hajji. "Because you love Tau'ma that way—Thomas. You want to be in his story, to be in the book you read and loved. And he is dead, so there is room in his story. You need him to be a father to you. He could take that burden, and then you could just eat with me, and talk with me, and I could tell you that I knew already about your Christ—knew very much about him. And you would be so pleased. And we would talk about the separation of flesh and spirit and you could feel at home."

"John is your name," the tree said, and it was not exactly a question. His voice was rough and full, as though it sounded in an oak barrel. The birds in his beard rustled. "And you are a Christian, I presume."

"Yes, yes," I breathed, and crept closer—but they did not seem to mind. Hajji, or Imtithal, sat quietly cross-legged at the foot of the great Thomas-banyan. "I have come so far, to find your tomb, for the honor of my teacher Nestorius, whose teachings are now outlawed in Christendom. I thought that if I were worthy, God would show me this secret thing, this lost place, and I could return triumphant, having been blessed."

The face of Saint Thomas considered for a moment. "Do you believe now you are not blessed, that you were not worthy?"

"I…" I felt my face crumble into ugly tears. "I have sinned here," I choked. "I have sinned." I could not say more, my throat closed up my speech.

"Ah, my son, so did I, so did I," the tree chuckled, and his smile was radiant as candles lit in the black—oh, how my heart hurt. "It's not so bad. Poor child, how you torture yourself. You cannot be the master of all. If you have sinned, there is forgiveness. There is always forgiveness. Nothing is as we expect, not in the whole world. I thought I would live beyond death at the right hand of my brother on the sea of glass where the throne of Our Father glides forever—instead I live forever here, in a glen near the stars, and it is not so bad, not so bad. I lived well, I loved a wife, and if not for her I would not know what it was to drink rain with my skin. I do miss my brother—I do miss him."

"You speak metaphorically," I said carefully, a dread growing in me. I could not hear any more inversions of the world. I could not.

"I speak literally, my son. What do you call me—Didymus Thomas, Thomas Judas, Thomas the Twin? Who did you think was my twin?"

"No, no, Christ was born alone, to Mary, in Bethlehem!"

The Thomas-tree pursed his moist lips. "What is it your teacher Nestorius preaches?"

I reeled within myself, pouring over every Scripture I could recall by heart, to refute the tree, and cling to what I knew to be true: the Logos, the light, the mystery of Christ. "That Christ possessed two natures." I whispered faintly, my stomach sinking as I began to understand, though I did not wish to. "The Word and the Flesh, the Logos, the Light of God, and the Human, the man, and these natures dwelt within him, but were not joined as one. They call this heresy, that it denies His divinity, that it makes of Mary but a clay jar and God a poor foster father."

"John, if you listen to me I will tell you how it was, then, with us, before anyone thought to fancy it all up with Greek diagrams. You may believe the word of a tree in the dark, or you may continue splitting Christ down the middle over and over until he ceases to be entirely. I have no stock in it anymore—I am a tree, and I want little but to look at the stars and look forward to my wife's visits—and she is a wife, and I had a wife, just the way you say you have sinned here and did not mean to. I did not mean to have a wife, but God put her in my path, and I do not make it a habit to deny His wishes."

"I will listen," I said faintly. The perfume of the place made me dizzy.

"The simple truth of my name is that I was a twin, that I was born second, after my brother Yeshua. I was born with the caul draped over my face like a maiden's veil, and I was sickly, where Yeshua was strong, and cried loudly as soon as he left our mother—his hands were red and so were his feet, and he squalled and beat the air. I almost did not take my first breath. Our father removed the caul, but I was grey. He struck my backside, but I did not cry. Finally, they lay me next to my twin, and with those little fists he struck his first brother's blow—and I flushed red and wept and breathed and our mother was not relieved, for we were poor and one son would have been enough. She meant me no ill, but if I had died she would have wept her piece and gone on living—little enough bread and oil was there for the three of them. As we grew, she had never enough milk for me, Yeshua was so hungry, so thirsty all the time, as though he were hollow and could never, never be filled. I grew thin, with only a trickle left in Maryam's breast for me. He was always so full, and I was so empty.

But I adored our mother. I followed her everywhere, barely toddling after her—long after Yeshua had learned to run headlong from one end of the street to the other— as she washed and cooked wheat in the great iron pot which had been the better part of her dowry. I kissed her cheek until she smiled whenever I saw her sad, and I drew pictures of her in the dirt while the other boys played. Yet she never looked at me the way she looked at Yeshua, with a kind of awe, and fear, and love, as he grew lean and strong but so terribly hungry, like a wolf's babe.

As boys it was much the same—he charmed our teachers and knew his Torah as though he had written it. The girls in the village went soft and moon-mouthed over him as his curls grew shiny and thick, his skin deep and rose-brown. They ignored me, or did not see me at all, and I could not remember the holy books like he could, no matter how I studied. But for all that, Yeshua doted upon me, and included me in all his games. We slept in one bed, and told each other children's secrets in the thick of the night. I worshipped him, abjectly. When he looked at me, John, when he looked at me it was like the sun had suddenly noticed me in particular, and shone on no one else for a moment. His attention was exquisite as a knife, and when he turned back to his tablets or his nails and wood, it was as though a darkness had fallen in my heart, suddenly, utterly.

For my part, I had a persistent cough, and bony limbs, lanky hair, and my attention was sought by no one but him. But I was not unhappy. I was clever enough—as he grew more beautiful and wise, as people turned to him for advice and company, he left our mother alone more and more, and a space opened for me to show her that I could be a good son, too. That I could be worthy of love. I helped her to keep the house as no boy should—I burned myself with harsh soap so that she could rest, I learned to cook lentils and garlic in that pot. I recited holy writ to her—and found when I opened my mouth to speak to her, the words appeared as they never had in school with all those severe old men staring at me. And bit by bit, she smiled, and even laughed, and finally, held me close, and called me her lovely boy, and kissed my head, and I shook and shook in her arms, but did not cry. Once, when our father did not come home at night, as often happened, for he drank and preferred company other than Maryam's, she told me that before Yeshua and I were born, a strange man came to her and told her she would have a special child, a wonderful child, that she had been chosen out of all other women to have him, and that she was blessed. The man frightened her badly, and when she saw him out of the corner of her eye, she saw red wings, dark and burning, so colossal they could not fit in her little room, and she knew he was an angel sent to her from God.

'But he never mentioned you,' she murmured, and held me close.

You know much of this tale, I know. He was a great man—everyone listened when he spoke, and so did I. He took on students, and we were a family of thirteen, all of us together, so excited by the nearness of God, by the fire that burned in Yeshua, in all his words and deeds. And then came the fishes. And then the wine, and the boy who was dead but lived. And we all fell silent, because when young men dream together they do not really imagine that things like that will start happening. Yeshua was as surprised as anyone, but he did not show it to the others. In the night, at home, he would open and close his hands and shake, for he did not understand what was happening to him.

I understood. My brother was perfect, that was all. Had it ever been any different? Whatever he desired appeared. It was a law of the universe.

Once, I came upon him in a garden full of pomegranate trees, and date trees as well. The air smelled rich and bitter all at once. Yeshua was speaking in low tones to a tall man under the shade of a pomegranate. Red fruit hung all around them. The tall man had very long, very black hair, and upon his shoulders sat a kind of light that was not light. I tried to look at it, but it was like looking at something through the flames of a fire: the air wriggled like oil, and I could not keep my eyes on it, for they burned. Finally my brother finished his business with the man and left the garden by the far gate. I stood where I stood, and the tall man saw me. He looked startled for a moment, then slightly furtive, as though caught out.

'Hello, Thomas,' he said to me, and my ears ached, though he did not speak loudly.

'Hello. What business have you with my brother?'

'Much business,' he said softly. 'And grave.'

I looked the man in the eye, and we held one another's gaze. 'You are an angel,' I said, and I knew it to be true before I said it. An angel bends your bones apart, to make room for its voice inside you.

'Yes.'

'You came for my brother.'

'Yes.'

'You are the same angel that came to my mother?'

'Yes.'

'Because my brother is special.'

'Your brother is the Son of God.'

The sun beat down upon me. I did not doubt it. I doubted nothing of my brother. Not then. 'What about me?' I said softly.

'You were... left over,' the angel sighed. 'The Word of God displaces mass. Something of Him was left over. Which is to say: The Lord God conceived Yeshua. Maryam conceived you.' The angel shrugged apologetically. 'These things are unpredictable.'

'God could not predict it?'

'God enjoys surprises. Incarnation is... complex. It is not a straight path.' The angel paused abruptly and joined his hands together. His fingers were very long. 'You love your brother.'

'Yes.'

'Perhaps that was what was left over. It's all love, Thomas. That's all. Just love, and death, and the striving toward one or the other.' He turned away from me, and I called out:

'If he is a man, but has within him the Word of God, like a bone or a heart... do I?'

The angel smiled, so slightly that I almost thought he frowned. His black eyes blazed like iron. 'I don't know, Thomas. Do you?'

And he left the garden. The rich and bitter smell vanished with him, and I was left alone.

When Yeshua died, I held our mother while she vomited and clawed her cheeks. Her eyes were empty; she had forgotten who she was. We felt as though a great weight had suddenly fallen between all of us, and we all stood staring at the hole it made, we who were now only twelve, twelve and Maryam, which I suppose made thirteen again. Nothing would be the same. He had been the weight, and where he fell he distorted the fabric of the world, before and behind, so that nothing could run smooth again.

And then, one day, his friend Maryam, who shared her name with our mother and whom Yeshua loved dearly, came leading a man into Peter's house. I did not recognize him—he was so thin and sick, with bony limbs and lanky hair, and the light in his eyes had gone out. He looked so much like me there might have been a mirror between us. Only now I was full, and he was empty. I began to tremble. The man put out his hand to steady himself, and I caught him, by instinct, by habit, because he was my brother, and he lived.

I did not believe it. Anything else, but not this. I missed him too much. I could not believe it. God would not give me this; He would not be so kind as to let me know my brother again under the sun. For Yeshua, the gifts of God. Not Thomas.

'Thomas,' Yeshua croaked, weak, for he still bled from his wounds. 'Embrace me, it is your brother, and I love you.'

'No,' I said. I could not believe.

And he took my hands and pressed them to his wounds. He winced, but I felt the blood there, blood, and also a soft kind of light, a light that was not light, and I was weeping, horrible, childlike weeping, huge gulps of air and sobbing as I held my brother to me one last time, and he gripped my shoulder, and kissed my brow.

'But you are so weak,' I said. 'How can you be weak?'

'Incarnation is not a straight path,' he said wryly, and the man I had known to be more full of life than any was helped by twelve men to a table, and there we shared wine and bread, but he ate none, for he had not the strength. But we laughed, and shared old jokes, and I loved him so profoundly that day that I did not notice when he went. I simply turned and he was gone, and his chair stood empty, but his glass stood full."

[And before my eyes it swam and swelled, the moldering amber, the wavering hairs speckling the surface of that pool of corruption, seething in from the spine, from the corners, from the center. It moved faster than I could read, faster than I could copy, and my hands sobbed with agony, trying to outrace it, trying to defeat it. It devoured words just as my eyes grazed them, and I could not breathe, I could not breathe—the book was dying, dying before my eyes, decaying into gold, passages winking out like stars in the dawn. I caught fragments: *from the far side of the great tree spoke suddenly another head, and then another, and three Thomases looked at me with pitying eyes, and Hajji-or-Imtithal kissed them all, one by one, on the lips, with her whole mouth.* And another: *I remember Vyala the pale lion opening her mouth, and how it was red inside her, and as I shuddered, insensate on the long grass, the lion-mother picked me up by the scruff, like a kitten—*

From the moldering page little orange spores puffed up, wetting words down through the next pages, and I turned them as fast as I could, but I was not fast enough, I could not stop it, it was too fast, and John's book was disintegrating in my hands. I chased it down, down, through the pages, so many left, and I was not fast enough. The words shivered away, the fungal rot snapping at their heels until they were little more than epigrams: *you should not believe a thing just because a tree said it.*

A streak of hungry yellow swallowed even that, and set its teeth to the next lines, each letter vanishing as I read it, turning to golden sludge, hot and horrible, staining my fingers:

Hajji-or-Imtithal went on: he told me these stories on our bridal bed, too. I half-believe them. Why not? I know winged men live and walk and speak very seriously, I know children can be born different, without any living father. I know the body can die, and return when a green leaf breaks the soil. None of those things require a God to occur. They happen every day. Why should they not have happened to him? I think you would find it remarkably freeing to leave religion aside. When you believe no one thing, everything can be true.

The gold darkened like dusk. I peeled back wet, sopping pages; I saw: *in the crook of the white lion's paw Hagia slept, headless, serene.* I saw: *I said to her, with her breasts heavy above me, her eyes burning: yes, yes, I will drink from the Fountain. Take me, take me, I will drink.*

The rest dissolved. With a wet sigh it sloughed over my palms and no more remained except this, wriggling, black on the gold, as if the letters moved and breathed and struggled for life:

I wept.

I wept.

I sought God, and crowned myself Hell's one king.

I wept.

The letters bubbled and broke, the legs and ladders of the characters snapping and turning as if caught in a whirlpool. I watched in horror; I watched in awe. Out of the wreckage of the book, the golden miasma, a single bulb formed in the mire and rose up on a stalk. The bud shone deep, gemlike black, and when it opened, I saw, concealed, an amber seed. It wavered on its stem, back and forth, like a serpent in its market basket. I did not make the choice; I was lost, cast far from myself. You could have saved me, Lord, but You let me devour that fruit—I suppose that is what You have always done. I fell upon it, maddened, devouring the bud, the stalk, the slime of the book, slurping it from my fingers, ravenous to have it within me, to keep it for myself, so selfish, so selfish, but I was always a selfish man. I ate it all, all, like Seth and the grains of paradise; my throat worked and I took it all into my belly, all of it, all of it, and oh, my God, it tasted like light, like light, and I lost everything.]

THE CONFESSIONS OF
HIOB VON LUZERN, 1699:

I regret that I, Alaric of Rouen, must take up Hiob's narrative at this point. As I write, ensconced with him in the personal house of the woman in yellow, who will not reveal her name no matter how I have asked, or offered her several ivory beads I obtained upon my journey to Africa some years ago, Brother Hiob lies insensate on a slab of stone, his skin sallow, his breath thin.

The local king, Abbas, has ordered a great number of flowers brought to the slab to garland my friend, though I have explained numerous times that he is not dead. I believe Hiob mentioned Abbas somewhat earlier in his account (please do not blame me personally for the disarray in his notes, I have tried my best to put them together, in an order pleasing to God, but the chaos of it all quite shocked me—though I am afraid what we have to report is disjointed, incredible, and beyond a doubt heretical, even if it were possible to place it all in the correct order and fashion it into anything like a usual book—forgive me. I am only his secretary). The king is uncommonly devoted to the woman in yellow, and when I inquired after her name, he would only call her *Theotokos*, a word I asked him to repeat, for it took me quite aback, as I am certain it will strike anyone reading my poor notes, for it is not a name at all, but a title: *Mother of God*. If Prester John was a committed Nestorian as there seems little doubt now that he must have been, this word seems all the more striking, as it is one Nestorius sought to divest the Virgin of during his tenure as Patriarch of the Eastern Church. The better part of his heresy was to teach that Mary was only the mother of Christ, and not of the divine portion of His nature. It defeats utterly both my powers of reason and translation to understand why Abbas would insist on calling this slip of a girl by that name. I honestly do not believe he knows what the word means—he has no Greek whatsoever—and she answers to it only when he calls her thus. She responds to my using it in no fashion.

But I was speaking of Hiob—his talent for digression has infected me muchly in our travels. I ought to have stopped him, but my shock was so great I could only stare as he devoured the book. I have tried to understand it since—I feel no compunction myself to eat the remaining manuscripts. But Hiob has been a mystery to me since I first met him. How little there seems to be of the man which is not languages and God. I wish but once I had caught him playing at dice. I feel I would have known a great deal more about him, if I could have seen how he threw. However, in the end, his obsession with Prester John was always greater than mine. It is a story, a very charming story, like those tales of girls and spindles and mirrors old women tell. But we do not go searching in earnest for the spindles. I found this mission odd and sad from the beginning, my Brothers, I will not be shy to say it. I came because my friend bade me serve him, and in service I find a path to God, thin, silver, humble.

And yet, and yet. I have touched these very books. I have smelled them, their sharp, over-rich, winey smells. I have seen that woman called Theotokos move in the dark, and there is a weirdness on her I cannot begin to name. I have not seen the tree Hiob reported, but I expect I shall sooner than later, if he does not wake. I have read everything, now, both his copies and my own, everything save the destroyed conclusion of John's book. Do I believe. I think I must. At least that there was a man named John, and he lived among strangers—perhaps even in this same place where the sun comes so very near to the earth.

But in my heart I ask: Does John mean truly that he lived among blemmyae, gryphons, panotii? In my youth, when I read the account of Prester John, I thought these to be allegory. The panotii representing the virtue of listening to the voice of God, the headless blemmyae of the dangers of abandoning reason, the gryphon in their triune nature symbolizing the Trinity, the amyctryae with their enormous mouth testifying to the glutton's path, the great lions to the division of spirit and flesh. I do not see a reason yet to assume these metaphors are not metaphors, but true beasts. Because a thing is written does not make it so. Am I to take it as fact that somewhere a giant tree grows with the head of St. Thomas hanging on it like a cocoa-nut?

That letter, my Brothers, that promised deliverance of Jerusalem is nearly six hundred years old. Surely he would have come by now, if such a man lived. It is the Year of Our Lord 1699, and we are modern men.

Half of my heart says this. Half longs to see the al-Qasr and all her amethyst pillars. Half of it looks at the woman in yellow with her downy skin, and dreads that every single thing in this world might be true.

And what am I to do with the Gospel of the Tree set forth in this manuscript? Shall I send it back to Luzerne to be packed away with other interesting heresies that no one but old Georg in the library ought to see, peering through his eyebrows at it all? John might as well have been talking to a cabbage and reporting the minutes of the meeting. The opinions of vegetables are evidence of nothing. How am I to defend any of this?

And what now? Is this to become my confession as well? How long until he wakes and I may return to my own prayers and works? Like Hagia, I do not enjoy composition.

Hiob spoke to God here—a hubris that beggars reason to contemplate. I cannot do the same. I cannot bring myself to believe I am worthy of such an audience. I write only to inform my Brothers at home what has happened to us here. I will be my Brother's marginalia, his annotator, his loyal secretary to the last.

I clean Hiob as best I can each morning. It is not difficult. I worry—he has not moved his bowels nor voided since he fell into this swoon, and that cannot serve him well. It is as though he is wholly *stopped*. His limbs are twined in chamomile and mango blossoms, and they have tried to rouse him with both that fruit and that tea to no avail. I have read many medical texts, but my practical experience began the moment Hiob decided to eat his book. I tend him; I serve him, as I always have.

As to the books, I have occupied all my time not devoted to the care of Hiob's mortal form in finishing his work. The oxidation of the pages proceeds, though not as viciously as with John's manuscript—there seems to be little law in the progress of the rot. Sometimes I think I will lose Hagia's text entirely, sometimes it does not swell up for hours. For a long time, Imtithal's sweet tales showed the least inclination to corrupt—but now we have passed some invisible door and the green fingers of it dash and pry at each paragraph I transcribe. I will endeavor to organize the final chapters in such a way that you, my Brothers, are spared the confusion and chaos of reading through a scrim of pink and green fungus. There is enough strangeness in this tale.

I am nearly finished. I confess my heart swells with the possibility. When I am done, will he wake? Will we go home? Will he be pleased? Will I have served well?

Will she tell me her name?

THE CRYSTALLINE HEAVEN

In the three Indies our Magnificence rules, and our land extends beyond India, where rests the body of the holy apostle Thomas; it reaches towards the sunrise over the wastes, and it trends toward deserted Babylon near the Tower of Babel. Seventy-two provinces, of which only a few are Christian, serve us. Each has its own king, but all are tributary to us. And they set not by battles, nor quarrels, nor know of deceit.

—The Letter of Prester John,
1165

THE BOOK OF THE FOUNTAIN:

[I could do nothing to preserve the first portion of this chapter, nor much of its middle sections. While Hiob fell into a seizure and then into his peculiar rictus, it shriveled into a purple lump and fell onto the floor with an ugly, wet sound. If I could have saved it, I would have. But my friend was in pain. I begin again as cleanly as I may:]

As I write, it is night in Susa's Shadow. Outside the cross-hatched screen of my thin minaret-room, the stars rest like tiny birds in the arms of the quince trees. Shadows make no sound. The wind off of the great stony river is hot and dry; it wafts of basalt, and old, old leaves. The moon has gotten fat, an orange egg in the sky, filled full with what strange bird? Everything is so quiet—so few of us are left. Soon it will be only me, and then it will be no one. Dried palm fronds blow across the chalcedony courtyard. The al-Qasr sits as empty as it did in those long-gone days when Abibas the Mule-king ruled kindly from his tree in the sciopod forest, and most of Nural seemed to live there, in the open rooms, the long halls, the drifting curtains. How happy I seem to recall it, all of us playing in the palace like children.

My silver pot scrapes—the ink is nearly gone. And yet the flood of it crests in me, all at once, everything happening at once, the weight behind my eyes, the memory of it. I understand Imtithal now—Hajji. I understand Hajji now. The world is a place of suffering, and the root of all suffering is memory. When you live long enough, the mass of memory is greater than any moon, any sun, so bright and awful and scalding in the dark, scalding—

[A wide swath of garnet-colored mucus devoured the text that followed—I saw what I feared to be a second bud coalescing

243

out of the miasma of it, rising up to release whatever perfume befuddled Hiob. I crushed the page beneath my hand and scooped away the pulp until the calligraphy showed clear once more. I could not afford my Brother's ecstasy—I had to hew to my reason.]

—the gilt edge of the bronze barrel, so full of our little stones, our possible lives. The sard and amethyst of the glazed Pavilion glowed that day, polished with silk flowers and oil. The gryphons had hung every spire and pole with citron blossoms and bright custard-apples like rosy lanterns, boughs of mango blossoms and chamomile fragrant as a mother's skin, and bells, bells in among them, tinny and laughing, hidden in the leaves, invisible music. As Fortunatus had been chosen by Abibas, in his last royal act, to conduct the Lottery, the Great Abir, the gryphons were obligated to prepare the stage. But much visible music I saw, too—gourd drums and lyres the size of wine barrels plucked by cametenna with their huge hands. Singers ululated and danced, the dervishes stamping, stamping, stamping their tattooed feet.

I saw my mother there, Ctiste, in her best scarlet trousers and her belt of silver. I saw the cannibal children playing at jumps; I saw Ghayth, letting young astomi pet his tail. I felt Hadulph's warmth at my side, and I saw Qaspiel, too, its hair long for the occasion, and Hajji, Hajji sweet and silent in a swing of roses.

And John, too, standing sheepish by his gryphon, practically clinging to Fortunatus' tail, afraid of what the day might hold, his eyes hollow with sleeplessness. I pitied him. He could not decide what any of it meant. Did it mean his faith stood proven, and all things he knew real? Or that nothing he believed was now true, and all things hopeless?

At least he had grown softer toward me. And I cannot think of how he looked that day, standing by the great gryphon, his hair clean and snowy and thick, all grown back but never the same, his color high, his back straight, not so old as all that, but not so young, and when I looked at him I knew so many stories about him it was like looking twice; I cannot think of how he looked without thinking of him in my arms as I took him to the Fountain, as I fed that green trickle through his lips like a thread. It is all one, the polished wood handle of the turning barrel, the snowy off-season Fountain road, with only a few lanterns swinging up ahead, up the mountain, only a few tensevetes selling restoratives on the pilgrim trail, and no hyenas at all. We walked alone, the six of us, and Fortunatus carried John upon his back, for after Nimat, he could not stand or speak, so deep he dwelt in despair. Hajji told us much, but I found it all confusing and not a little upsetting.

"Does this mean his God is real? Will we never hear the end of it now? Will we have to learn our Latin in earnest?"

Hajji sighed. "I cannot say. It is a story. Stories are both true and untrue. They are both, all the time. Do I believe Thomas had a brother he loved, and that his brother died? Of course. That's all the story is, really. Love, and death."

"Why did the snow cease in that clearing? I have never seen such a thing, in the high reaches."

And the panoti smiled, gently, but with a ruddy pride. "Trees are bigger below ground than above, Hagia. That place is Thomas, all of it—the tree, the grass, the warmth. Even the little birds in his beard. He is very old; he has grown big."

And even in remembering that, I cannot help but see John on the back of the gryphon so many years later, centuries later, dead and cold, and all of us following, down the river with its crashing stones, John, John, always needing us, and Fortunatus always bearing him up. Everything echoes in my vision, back and back, a hundred times. Pulling him up the final steps, rope by rope, hand by hand, and he like a dead thing between us but breathing, me holding him, his eyes glassy, and the apples around the green and foaming Fountain with all its slime and grudge swelling and shriveling, and the wind, the wind terrible, frigid. Me, holding his head back, and the Oinokha, her feathers ruffling, the night stars a corona over her swan's head, staring at him in fear and wonder. And how we both of us scooped the thick, bitter water from the cleft of the mountain, how the Oinokha held open his mouth as I tilted it in, and how for a moment, for a moment, I was the Oinokha for John, the water of life sliding from my body into his.

It is hard to remember how I didn't love him, even then. But

I know I did not. I tended a sick body. And then, later, at the Abir—what could sour me at an Abir, when the world stood so eager and ready to be made again?

And so he would stay with us, and in ten years and ten again who knew what woman or man might take him for his final journeys there, so that he could hold in his hands that life everlasting he so longed to know? And so he would take a chit in the Abir, and luck take him where she would.

It is night, it is night in New Byzantium and the mockingbirds are singing and there is a little wine left in my glass, just the dregs, just the dregs, and that day Hadulph had to explain to him how the Abir worked, like a little boy who didn't even know which way to hold the oil-jar.

"The barrel is full of stones," Hadulph said, as if John were a little boy who didn't know which way to hold the oil-jar. The sun glittered on the skin of the custard-apples hanging low over our heads. "Each stone has flaws in it, and the flaws spell a life. For example, if Fortunatus said: John of Constantinople, adopted gryphon and foundling, come forward, and then you spun the barrel—you must spin it and no one else, it must be your own hand, so if you are not feeling strong have a cup of tea-wine and practice now—and then you spun the barrel and pulled out, say, a smoky quartz with a black flaw, a crack in the center, and a blue flaw, it would mean that you ought to be a shepherd, and marry the creature who draws the other smoky quartz with the blue flaw, and that—lucky you, you are permitted a child. See? Fortunatus has been studying for several years. He knows it all, every flaw, every crack, every stone's meridian. He will make us proud, and afterward, we will introduce ourselves all over again, and buy him fermented eggs until we are new friends, all of us."

John looked dubious. He had said little since the Fountain, though every day he had grown stronger and his old wounds lighter. It was only that he rarely slept, and I knew he struggled still with himself, with his God, and I, I wanted nothing of any of that fight.

The bone trumpets blared and the noon sun illuminated the barrel, placed just so to catch the light. Fortunatus began, from his prodigious memory, to call the names of every soul in Pentexore, all of whom, when assembled, filled the broad Pavilion in the center of Nural, and some hung out from balconies and windows and high towers, to come down when they heard their names. But there were not so many even then that this seemed onerous, to pack us all in one place.

I remember it in flashes, as I remember my first Abir. How Grisalba drew a silver bead striped with diamond and sard, and hooted with delight for it gave her two husbands and a wife, and a silversmith's bench besides. Hadulph drew obsidian flecked with white, and went north to become a tender of the lavender fields, with a crow for a wife—and I laughed, but there was pain in my heart, too, for though they would not manage mating, they would be wed, and he had not drawn me. I remember all of it, how Astolfo looked at me, hollow and hurt, as he walked up and drew his clear crystal, with no flaws at all, and knew he would be a hermit, a holy man without wife or child, and through the ink stains on his face, I saw him weeping and the shame in me was heavy, so heavy, for I had left him, and I could not undo it.

And of course I remember it. There is no forgetting in me. Fortunatus, with only a small quaver, called John forward—of Constantinople, adopted gryphon and foundling. And a great cheer went up, for he was new family then. He smiled bashfully, uncertain, and he looked beautiful in that moment, innocent, young. He spun the barrel strongly, three times round, and thrust his arm within. When he drew it out again he held his fist closed for a long moment, his eyes closed, head tilted toward the sun. His jaw worked; the bells tinkled lazily, and we all held our breath, to see who the stranger would become.

He opened his hand. On his palm sat a bead of lapis, and in it a red smear of carnelian, but also a speck of emerald. He would have a wife. He would have a child.

He would be king.

Silent shock reverberated through the throng. So many mouths hanging open, so many hearts suddenly uncertain. Would the Abir steer us wrong? Was he such the son of luck that he would rule in his first lifetime?

It was my name Fortunatus called next. In a daze I floated to the platform and spun the barrel, all joy sapped for me—I did not even notice it spin. My mind tripped and jangled—what sort of king would John be? I would not become a Christian, I would not. I reached through the dark door of the vessel and felt within, groping, the warm trickle of pebbles sliding over my hand. I chose one, and I swear it was a true Abir, I did not know, I only took a stone which seemed warm and big, no different than when I chose Astolfo, when I chose my scribe-life.

I withdrew my hand. I knew, even without opening it. I cracked my fingers, and there lay a diamond, a deep red flaw within it like a drop of blood.

I would have a husband. And I would be queen.

And I remember it all at once, Astolfo bellowing from below the stage, storming forward, pointing at John, shaking, enraged, unable to speak to accuse him. And I remember Qaspiel, its face so sad I wanted to die there, just to make it stop.

"I think he means to say: *it's not fair*. I think he means to say: *you cheated, John*."

And I remember lying back on the altar that is a throne that was a sacrificial mound before the al-Qasr was the Basilica, lying back with John above me, and how in the morning the world would be changed and when we woke, the throneroom was full of roses and partridges and orthodox hymns, and peacocks lay sleeping in the rafters. Their blue heads like bruises: the pulse of their throats, the witness of their tails.

"I did not cheat," John said, and Astolfo whirled on me, his eyes blazing, pained, all the blame there: I left him, I left him and hadn't I just wanted John all along.

"No, that's not how it was," I said faintly.

And I remember how John sat me on that ivory chair and knelt at my knees, the beauty that all supplicants possess sitting full and shining on his thick features. He closed his kiss over my navel-mouth and his tears were like new wax. "Say it," he whispered.

And I said his prayer. *Rosa, rosae, rosae, rosam, rosā. Rex. Regis. Regi. Regem. Regē. Ave Maria, gratia plena, Dominus tecum.*

Benedicta tu in mulieribus—

"How could I have cheated?" I remember John saying, spreading his hands. "Only today did I discover how the Abir was conducted. It's far too complicated to fix. And you, you mean to say Hagia cheated, too?"

And that was when I knew he had.

I remember that ivory chair in the night; it curls at its ends into arm-rests in the shape of ram's horns, severed from the sea-goat when the first caravan settled in this endless valley, the first enclave of bird and monopod and gryphon and cricket and phoenix and collinara—and blemmye. And they camped on the beach-head and pulled from the sea with their silver spears a fatted kid, and ate the fat of its tail sizzling from the driftwood fire, and in time those first horns were affixed to the long chaise which became a sacrificial plank which became an altar which became a throne which became my pillow and it all happens at once as his weight pressed the small of my back against the cold ivory—

"I don't want it," I said, and thrust the diamond out to Astolfo. "Take it," I said, tears pricking my eyes. "Marry him yourself. Let me draw again. I don't want it. I want to go back to my mother's fields and stretch parchment over hoops and feel her tree of hands on my face. What will it say for this year? No, no, no."

And my mother, so young and lovely, stepped out of the crowd to put her hand, her real and warm hand, to me, to comfort, even though the rules did not quite permit it, the day of the Abir is liminal, and perhaps there is grace hidden there.

"You cannot give away your fate, my girl. Nor your luck."

"Please," John said later, and wept, for he had tried so hard not to, tried not to brush his palm against my eyelid, tried not to run his fingers across the teeth in my belly, tried not to glance at the soft place where my head is not. He had tried to resist his passion to come to that place when he lifted me onto the nacreous chair, and tried not to enter me like a postulant sliding his hands into the reliquary to grip the dry bone. *Virginity confers strength*, I remember he said when we all took our lessons with him and it was all a game. *It is the pearl which purchases paradise.*

"I love you, my daughter," Ctiste said, and her smile cut me.

I had refused my fate—that salved all question of dishonesty. No one could imagine it, anyway. The Abir was the pillar of the world. No one would even conceive the idea of harming it, of making it cheap and false. Then, I did not even quite understand what Qaspiel meant by cheated. How could you cheat the Lottery? I only thought: *Now that he is king, what will happen to us?*

Now, I understand. I know many wicked things, of which this was the first.

Astolfo reached out for me, his miserable jaw working, his mute protest, his silent need. And I might have turned away right then from all that happened later, might have held him and said I was sorry until my throat tore and I could not speak either. But Hajji appeared by me, as if she had always been. She went to him, her little body standing between my sorrow and his rage. She pushed him backward, and he fell like a feather. The panoti climbed into his lap, wrapping her ears around him, and within her embrace I saw him shuddering with tears. Her grace stopped my heart, and I remembered too that night when we had spoken of Imtithal and how he had loved her when he was a boy.

And I think of her closing Astolfo up and it happens together with the summer night when I led John to the edge of the stone river, the Physon, which possesses no water, only boulders, basalt churning against schist. The roar of it, rocks cracking and thundering, drowned out every sound. The priest sat upon his knees and I stood above him, so our faces could touch. I kissed him, I kissed him because he was my husband and my king and my body betrayed me with its want. I kissed him and took my favorite lapis-and-opal ring from my finger, the one my mother had given me, so long ago, in another life. I moved his hand as I would a child's, digging the furrow by moonlight and the river's din, placing the ring in the earth, covering it with moist, warm soil. *This is my paradise,* I said, *bought so much dearer than pearls.*

The cheer went up in the Pavilion, uncertain at first, then stronger—the world must go on, we must have a king, and deceit was a foreigner here. Abibas the Mule-king was brought out by two young centaurs, hanging in his basket, having been uprooted for the occasion. He blessed us. I felt nothing. And when I think of the sound of the crowd I think of the sound of the river, the stone shattering there, and how I took him later, so much later, to show him the thing we had made: a sapling, whose stem was of silver, whose leaves curled deep and blue, lapis dark as eyes, veined in quartz flaws. Tiny fruits of white opal hung glittering from its slender branches, and the moon washed it in christening light. I stroked the jeweled tree, and showed him too my belly, and the other thing we had made—already swelling a little, already growing. He touched the place where my head is not, the soft and pulsing shadowy absence, the skin stretched and taut, and beneath our tree of blue stone he had spilled his seed into me—it seemed safer than to spill it into the ground.

"Say it, John, say it," I said, as the muscles of his neck strained in his cry, and I held his face in my hands, and his tears rolled over my knuckles, and I lay quietly under him, with the river deafening beyond. "Say it."

"I cheated," he whispered, with our child between us. "I palmed the king's chit—Fortunatus helped me. A Christian king, a priest who is also a king—God wanted me to do this."

"How can you know that?"

"I did not fix your gem, only my own. But I prayed, I prayed like a white flame steaming—and God gave you to me."

It is night in Susa's Shadow, and they are all gone, every one of them now, and I could have destroyed him. I could have broken his secret, and they would have eaten him and none of the rest might have befallen us.

That is my sin, and I beg forgiveness.

There are three things that will beggar the heart and make it crawl—faith, hope, and love—and the cruelest of these is love.

THE SCARLET NURSERY:

Near the sciopods' forest (which they call the Foothold) there lies a broad plain, covered in a fine black powder. Each morning, the dawn strikes the earth like an arrow, and the most ornate flowers twist up out of the soil. Colored like molten glass, they coil and creep toward the light, and by noon have grown as tall as a man, each blossom with four large petals like lips open, fiery. Once the noon-moment has passed, they begin to slump and shrivel, and by night have crawled back into the earth to dream, and in the morning will come up again. This repeats, over and over, forever. All my life I was warned not to eat the flowers, that they are fey and unwholesome. Thus, I have always wanted to eat one. I don't need to eat flowers or fruits, but I can, and I am sometimes curious—what is it like to swallow something that way? To feel it's weight inside you? But I am more or less at peace, having not done so.

Nevertheless, once in a long while, when the children had some pressing lesson or were away visiting relatives, writing back to me about the color of plantain soup, and how the cameleopards are very difficult to ride, even for Houd, who could ride anything, I would walk out from Nural and not stop until I had reached the black field. I would watch the flowers come up and down in their mystifying cycle, and I would eat the sound of them falling. I would watch the flowers and think that this is the time I will be brave enough to pull off one of the thick glassy petals and taste it. But then I would recall how some cousin or aunt said that the addiction could never be broken, and no wine could compete for the dizzying of the head. Sometimes I wondered how they could know.

One day, a day of my own, a day to myself, I watched the sun setting behind the drooping blossoms, their leaves grazing the black powder. And on that day a woman sat down next to me, quiet and beautiful, without a word. Did I know she followed me? Of course. I hear everything. But a queen ought to believe she can prowl so silently—it was not for me to belie her.

Abir's gargantuan hands closed gently over her bent knees as she settled into the greyish grass that bordered the field. They covered her body entirely, a shield of fingers.

Abir, Who Was Older Than She Seems: I am grateful for what you have done for my children, Imtithal. They will be grown soon, and better for you, I think. Even Houd.

I, Who Hurt With Love of Them: Do not think so badly of him. He cannot bear it, not really.

Abir, Who Knew: I wanted to speak with you, far from the al-Qasr and the Nursery. I promised to tell you my story, and I believe the time has come—I am certain, for in a few weeks I will not be able to tell it any longer.

I, Who Had Been Paid Enough: I wait. I am good at waiting.

Abir, Whose Hair Was So Black, Whose Eyes Were the Color of Rich Gourds, Who Wore a Dress of a Black Deerskin and Three Jewels: Come, Imtithal. Sit in my lap as you did that day in Nimat. Let me be wrapped in your ears again.

And I settled into her, and I wrapped her in the pale shroud of my body. I looked into her wide, exquisite face, her full lips and her savage eyes, and I tried to remember this moment forever. The flowers shrank down behind us, and she began to speak.

Abir, Who Would Change the World: I was born in Nural.

You have never seen the cametenna birth-hall—I know you have not, for we keep it to ourselves. The males are fragile when they are in heat. Their skin goes clear and delicate, like thin glass, and on the surface of that skin they project—oh, it is beyond beauty—a play of color and light, shapes like frost shivering over their elbows, their chests, but the frost glimmers like prisms, and the chosen greatmother must breathe deeply to control her desire. But in such a state, if a male were even to trip and fall, he would shatter. So when the time comes, they cloister, under rosy domes and draped tents, a luxurious place where the males eat and drink and play upon small jade flutes—for when the heat comes upon them they go mute, all their energy going to their skin, their seed.

I suppose one day Houd will turn to glass, and go into the hall. I cannot begin to imagine him mute.

It takes twelve males to impregnate a greatmother—the process is gentle, and complex, and takes a full year, after which we emerge gravid and birth follows some time later. We do not speak of it to outsiders. But I will tell you, Imtithal—the children call you Butterfly, don't they? I will tell you, the pleasure of it is profound, and so too the great flooding of the heart.

My mother was prolific—she produced six young. But I was the strongest, and the only female. She was a judge in the court of the queen at that time—an astomi called Cai, Kantilal's grand-daughter. My mother's judgment held sound and absolute in Pentexore—but she earned that, with her wisdom, her severity, and also her mercy. At the quarter-moon market she sat at an ivory podium and heard complaints. Cai loved her well; they were great friends, and drank the white lions' beer together when each day's work was done. I hardly knew the queen—Cai moved beyond my circle of brothers and teachers.

I believe, if we are civilized and do not ask after the other's age, that I am younger than you. But you lived in Nimat, among the panotii and the lions, and a peculiar peace has always held sway there. Here, in Nural, in Pentexore, when I was young—it was a vicious place. Two of my brothers killed each other over a racing debt; kings and queens changed like hands of cards. I saw more of this than most, because of my mother. She would bundle me in a long green swath of silk, and I heard her cases, too. Afterward, she would say: *Abir, what would you have decided?* And I would say: *That bad man stole from the other one. The other one should get to steal anything he likes that belongs to the first man,* which is a child's idea of justice. Or she would say: *Abir, would you steal, if your friend had more than you, and you envied her?* And I would say: *Yes, but I would not get caught.* The Fountain made everyone certain they could do anything they liked; they had no fear of death, no shame. They had lived so long that life became boring, and more and more cruel pleasures were needed to make them feel alive. I recall one male pushed another cametenna against a wall while he was in estrus—the male shattered and died. After the mating season had passed, my mother demanded a reason. The male said: *I wanted to see what it would look like.*

People have not changed since I was a girl, not really, but I felt the savage blood of Nural so keenly then, sitting with my mother at her podium, and it frightened me, when a blemmye-man looked at me lasciviously, that perhaps if my mother were not looking, he would take me, for I was not much less pretty then than I am now, and who would stop him? I was small and weak, I could not hurt back. I wanted to hurt back. I was no different.

But children grow up, even when they are afraid. And I went to the Fountain, and my hair grew so long I braided it into ropes, and I watched, and learned. I watched the queen, I confess, more than I ought to have. I watched how she ascertained those who lied to her, those who meant ill, by smelling with her prodigious nose their sweat, their anxious, mean humors. She could even smell their dreams, their ambitions, and when she looked at me, when she breathed, she grew disturbed, and grave. But still I watched her, and wished I had a nose like that.

I was chosen to be a greatmother early, because my mother had birthed so many, because my brothers had died that year, because I was strong and unmarried. I remember the nervous preparations—the baths and endless soaking, to prepare my skin and make it porous. I remember unbraiding my hair until it fell to the floor, and entering the hall, where I could choose males of my liking. And they were all so beautiful, the bold frost on their shoulders, their quiet hope and adoration. I chose, I fell among them, all twelve, and their kind eyes rejoiced, and more I shall not say of this, for it passes the bounds of decorum.

You must understand, when a cametenna is pregnant, she possesses a strength hardly imaginable. All the vigor of her children yet to be and their dozen fathers moves in her, and if she is not careful her feet will rend the floor and her idlest gesture will shatter bones. This is why she cannot give birth in the hall. She would kill her mates, though she never meant to touch them. I carried my three offspring, that you know so well, not being so prolific as my mother. My head swam with the power my body concealed, and closeted with my mother, who knew all this well, I confessed that I had conceived not only young but a gnawing ambition: I wished to be queen. I wished to be safe, and make my children safe. I wished to play a very long game, at the end of which Pentexore would be utterly transformed. Was this myself or the voice of my gravid strength in me?

My mother said: *You know how these things are done. Cai owns a cleverness and wariness few could claim. And it is all uglier than you know.*

And in my mother's reply I heard the necessity of it—for her child she would betray even her friend to death. I do not like that world.

And so I did kill the queen before me. I have heard that you told my children this. I wish they did not know it—but there it is. It was not as hard as I expected. She smelled me coming, but pregnant I was too fast and strong, and I tore her limb from limb in the throneroom as easily as breaking a toy. Her guards watched—she had done the same to the king before her; they could not interfere. The release of the awful strength in my limbs made me shudder—I had held it in check so long. At the end of it her blood drenched me, and at the core of the wreckage of the queen I saw the drop of the Font her flesh clutched so dearly trickle out onto the floor and steam away. It was over. A silver vessel lay empty and waiting, in the hall. I interred her myself—it was only right.

And I birthed my young, and worried that some other ambitious whelp would destroy me when my strength had ebbed, and so departed. I took up my palanquin and my elephants and traveled my country to discover a city where folk did not consider that living forever meant drowning in the worst cruelties they could fashion. Where despair was not the only law. And I found you.

I, Who Had Desired Cruelty, Too, in My Time: Majesty, there are many in Nimat who have no good qualities.

Abir, Who Did Not Believe Me, Not Really: But not in you. And I brought you here, and the rest you know. Save for what I intend. And what I intend is to break immortality over my knee. I had to wait, you see, until my children were grown, so that no one would think me selfish. I would take wealth and power from my own young, too, not just theirs.

You do not understand.

I will remain queen at the next quarter-moon. No one else will be the same. We will have a wonderful Lottery, and in it will go all possible lives, and we will draw from among them. Whatever the Lottery dictates, so we will live, for three centuries, and then change again. I will only remain queen until the second Lottery, to minister and salve, for it will be difficult. But my children will draw lots, and go where they are bidden. And so, I hope, will you. Can you see it? Boredom will cease and there will be pain, terrible pain, when the Lottery separates families and lovers and children and friends. But that pain will take the place in us that lies fallow now—in a thousand years, in two thousand, Pentexore will forget deceit and rough instincts. They will forget, even, that Imtithal the Butterfly was not chosen for a nursemaid by a spinning barrel, and debate how else your fate might have gone. History is an old, confused crone. But she has her lessons, and her mercies.

They will understand that you must let go quarrels—for the Lottery will erase them, regardless. They will understand the essential truth of the Fountain: if we do not love each other, forever is intolerable. We will find a rhythm. We will create a heaven. It will be done, and no other queen need rot in those silver vessels.

I kept my silence. I did not really think it would work. Memory works its way.

Abir, Whose Face Was Illuminated By the Last of the Sun: Do you know the god of the cametenna? She is nameless, faceless, the seven-bodied goddess of luck, who with three hands throws dice, and with four prays to herself. The Lottery will be a devotion to her. I will sacrifice a whole nation to her holy games, and she will bless us, and protect us, and guide us on the correct path.

You will join the Lottery, will you not? You came from so far. If you draw a stone, many others will know it is a thing of virtue.

And she was my queen. My service belonged to her.

As we rose to leave, Queen Abir strode out onto the field of black powder. With a grace I would not have imagined in those massive hands, she bent and plucked a single petal from one of the blooms, small and miserable now, almost shriveled back into the earth. She held out the wrinkled, glowing thing to me. Its pollen smeared her fingers. As though I meant to tell her a story, I climbed up into her palm, knelt, and she placed the petal in my mouth as I closed my eyes and in that moment I was her child, and I trusted her.

The petal tasted, oh, it tasted like light.

THE BOOK OF THE FOUNTAIN:

I admit it was I who showed him the mirror.

I thought nothing of it—only a mirror, and I am not vain. Rastno the Glassblower made it, long ago, when he was but young, and so clever with glass and all burning things. It hung up in the portico before the pillar fell, draped in damask, for its visions were distracting—but for Rastno's sake we did not wish to dishonor his best-beloved child.

Rastno is gone now, wherever phoenix go when they die and cannot find their way to Heliopolis to bury their old ashes. He who reasoned that his glass should be so terribly, ineffably fine, since no flame but his own could make him tremble. And true to this he filled the capital with every wonderful thing that could be made of glass. And mirrors, of course, mirrors of every shape. But the mirror I showed to John was his last work. Rastno went into the flame and did not come out again. Laughing before he sparked his embers, he said that the mirror he fired in his own feathers would be a wonder beyond even the Physon, the churning river of stone.

When they dragged the shard of glass from the charred bones and blowing ashes of his pearl-lined nest, when they cleared from it the blackened ends of Rastno's beak and talons, and scraped the boiled eye-wet and blood from its surface, they found a sheet of silvery glass limned with mercury, so pure that it showed the whole world, wherever anyone wished to look, into any dragon-ridden corner of the planed earth.

It disturbed them all, for no one could understand what they saw, the many four-limbed creatures, the strange cities. The mirror taught only that their land was best, best by a length of ten giants, and they covered the mirror up again—but hung it in the hall all the same, as a funerary rite.

"Why did you not bury his remains, if that is what you do with your dead?" John asked, when I rolled the bronze-set glass from its resting place behind a bolt of salamander-silk. I shuddered.

"Would you love a tree whose trunk was ash, whose foliage was burnt and blistered flesh, black with flames you cannot see, but the tree remembers? What terrible fruit it would bear! Better that he be eaten, as the dervishes are, or given to the river, than to suffer such a planting."

I showed John the mirror—but he was happy in those years, and his belly was fat, and he gripped me gleefully by the hips in the late afternoons and kissed the place where my head is not, opened my legs and said his favorite mass. He hardly even insisted I speak Latin anymore, or take any saltless Eucharist he might fashion, and only cried the name of his Apostle in his sleep. How could I know?

He put off a second journey to the Fountain. Every year, he was too busy. He did not age, or lessen, but I knew it would have to be soon. And every year I would ask: *Why did you do what you did?* And he would not answer me anymore, as though silence would wash the deed clean.

And once I asked: *When I took you to the Fountain, were you truly weak? Or did you let me believe you were, to soften my heart and make certain I would enter you in the Abir?*

He would not answer that either.

John absorbed himself in a great work soon after taking the throne—at least he considered it to be a great work and whatever a king considers to be a great work meets with general enthusiasm. He called all the separate kinds of Pentexore together, and asked that they send a delegation, to tell to him their own stories of how the world was made, what god ruled it, how their bodies had been formed. He meant to fit all of these together with his own faith, to create a great new Gospel that would witness to all he had seen here, that would fit Fortunatus and Hajji and the Tree of St. Thomas and me into Christ's universe.

"What is it you want from us, John?" I asked of him, as he sat at his desk making notes toward an expanded Genesis. "What would satisfy you? I have sunk to my knees as you asked, I have said your Latin, but it is not enough."

"You did it without faith, Hagia," he said.

"Are there magical words you wish me to say? What would a converted Pentexore look like, to you? Can you not just let us be?"

John set down his pen. "It would look like a brilliance of light, Heaven on earth, immortal and also saved by their knowledge of Christ. It would be the City of God spoken of in Revelations. It would be the city on the hill, free of the flotsam and miasma of humanity."

"You are human."

But he did not hear me. "God would look upon it and be even Himself exalted. Pentexore as one would live on her knees, eyes cast to Heaven, the Earthly bride of Christ in the form of a nation—Israel in truth, for no country can be said to have been chosen more than this. Each city will recall the name of a City of Man—Nural will become New Byzantium, Shirshya will be baptized Ephesus Segundus. I will remake the world, more perfect, more pure. Everything will have to be re-written, Hagia. Everything. And at the end of it all, I will be a saint and a king, and God will forgive me my sins, and no man on earth but His own Son will have done more to ransom the world. You cannot possibly understand, Hagia. You cannot know what it will mean to my people, to know that magic exists, and perpetual youth." His eyes flamed with passion and excitement—I hardly knew him. "I have begun a letter, wife. A letter home. To tell them the wonders I have suffered here. Don't worry. I told them that I converted the land, and the cameleopards say the Ave as well as anyone. I told them this was a Christian land, and utterly at peace. I have written it all out, the Rimal, the Physon, all of it. I do not know how I will send it, but I shall." He paused, and gently brushed the place where my head is not with his soft fingers. "I know you don't mean it, and I knew it, I knew when you put out your tongue for your first communion that you had no faith in your heart, but I did not care, because my fingers could touch your tongue, the sweet tongue of your belly, and I would have given a hundred false communions for that tongue. I left that part out of the letter. But they would not understand, they would think you were devils, just as I first did, and I could not bear for a friar to look on my Hagia and spit at her."

And I thought to myself of those things Imtithal wrote, that men would come from Thomas' country and they would be greedy, and they would be cruel, and they would break us between them like bread. But I kept silent, and yes, you may blame me for my silence. I will take the shame of that. No king had ever really harmed us. How could a king do harm? Old as we all were, we were too young to guess. How could I know? How could I know?

And so the people of Pentexore came, handful by handful, to tell John how the world was made. The cametenna orated for seven hours on the pivotal nature of luck, and how its currents and habits could be charted on blue cloth with a kind of holy chalk, and that luck had made everything. Only those with hands large enough to manipulate these currents were the beloved children of that nameless goddess. The gryphon said that a gryphon's heart beat in the center of the world, which was truly an egg balanced on the star-nest of Am, the mother, and one day the Earth would hatch and a wonderful child would be born. The astomi explained very logically that scent was the only true element in the universe, and all the rest illusions sent by Saillot-Mar, the master of falsity, who sought to trick us all into believing the world was real. The amyctryae, led by Astolfo, though true to the Abir I did not behave as though I knew him, said that the stars were teeth in the mouth of Grandhorm, the Utter Jaw, and the world was His tongue, speaking without ceasing until the end of days.

They came, endlessly, even the apes of the high hills, who communicated by signs that the true masters of the world were the bamboo forests that thought and whispered, and they owed nothing but service to them, who fed and sheltered their favorite children. Even the cameleopards, who said: *You are not worthy to hear it.*

And John refused a scribe, even me, but wrote these all down himself, in his cramped, tiny hand. And those who shared their tales, he rewarded with words of his own, which none of us understood. He named them abbots and dukes and marshals and viscounts, counts, marquises, and bishops, deacons, and cardinals. One of the apes he called a proto-pope, one of the gryphons an arch-pope, and once John had gone to rest himself with wine and blackbulb, the delegations traded these words like coins, and mixed them all up entirely. But in John's presence they behaved as though they were very honored by them.

The kingship of John consisted of a wild mating with his blemmye wife and a wild writing of a thing which none of us read. As long as he worked upon it, I reasoned, he could not devise methods of sending that letter, of bringing his world down upon us. But he seemed happy, and when I knew I was with child, I kept it secret for a year and more, to enjoy that quiet thing I knew and he did not. Blemmyae take five years to birth a child—nearly as fascinated with our many ways of reproducing as with our creation stories, John still kept himself mostly ignorant of my own rhythms, and so it came as a surprise. When I finally did tell him, he smiled at first, as a new father should. But later, as he considered all that had passed he grew silent and grave, and did not speak to me for days. At last he broke free of whatever oppressed him, knelt by me and kissed me several times.

"You must understand, Hagia, I never thought to give up my chastity at all. To have a child is witness to my impurity forever." He shut his eyes. "But perhaps that is past, now."

He smiled. And some weeks later, as a present, I showed him the mirror.

Anywhere you like, I said. *Just think about it, and it will show you.*

He stood for a long time, and nothing showed in the dark glass.

Finally, a flame. An orange spark, growing swiftly to a blaze that burned my eyes. A city burned in the mirror, red and black and white, and we heard screaming there. John stood perfectly still, watching a city with domes of dust and crosses of gold and chalcedony flicker by, watching its stony streets run rivulets of blood like the porches of a dozen butchers, watched horses clatter over altars and books burn like phoenix, curling black at the edges and never return. He watched it all burn, impassive. He watched bodies twist on blades, and horrors I cannot begin to record, having seen nothing like it in all my days. I knew that city not at all, but I mourned it, I mourned it, so far away, so far and so lost.

John stood with the drawn damask clutched in his white hand, and watched a sullen orange sun set on the city of dust, and his beard grew even in that moment, his scalp showed pink through his hair, and his spine became a bent scythe, until he was an old man in my sight, and he wept like a nursing mother.

[Hagia's book perishes here. The red-violet mold defeated me, growing and devouring, sending out their lurid tendrils. No bulb rose up; I ate nothing. I felt only a sadness, an emptiness, as though I had been scraped clean by it all, and left with nothing. Though chapters follow, I will never know them. Pages turned instead to sludge and misery and spilled out over the table and onto my lap like a font of blood.]

THE SCARLET NURSERY:

It is years, and they are grown.

I saw one of them in later days, dancing, his muscles straining with sweat, in service to a very lovely lady—the Lottery, infinite humor, had made Houd a dancer. He was very good at it, actually, and I had seen him perform for his mistress, who always wore a black veil. My throat stopped up with tears, seeing his back arch, his great hands move. I was in that life a brewer of milk-beer, and with my arms full of hops I wept openly, my child, my poor, reticent Houd, beautiful and graceful, moving like a lion, his eyes so bright.

He saw me too, and some days later at the quarter-moon, he cornered me behind a huge amethyst pillar, strong and high and violet.

Houd, Who Danced Like a Flame: I miss you, Butterfly.

I demurred. I whispered he could not call me by such old, familiar endearments.

Houd, Who Didn't Care: I will never obey that rule.

I reached up and touched his face. His skin was warm.

Houd, Who Had Grown So Tall: Come to my house tonight. Come. Swear you will.

And he was my child, and I belonged to him, and I promised. When I arrived, in his little house with a thin roof, the others were there too, and I could not speak for the joy of it, and they all held out their hands to me, wanting my weight on them, and I kissed their cheeks and we all laughed, so relieved to be together, though the room was not scarlet, nor silk.

Ikram, Who Would Dive For Sapphires in the Mountains: Oh, Butterfly, it's so hard! I see my mother in the streets and I cannot speak to her.

Lamis, Who Would Dwell as a Lamplighter in the City of Thule: It is like we were never born. And here, with you, it's like we never grew up.

Oh, but the pleasure of meeting in secret, children. Is it not fierce and wonderful? We could not have such delight without the Lottery your mother made.

Houd, Whose Sole Black Stone Voted Against the Whole Business, But Who Yielded in the End: I do not want to speak of it. Comfort me, instead, Butterfly. Tell us about fate, and stories that must come true because they were always true, and that everything that happens has a purpose. That is what I need to hear.

And I sat in his palm, for the first time. The girls laid their hands on the floor and put their heads on my lap. A fire bloomed in the hearth, and they were still so young, and I loved them so.

Fate is a woman, I said to them. In fact, she is three women. Young, like us, so that they will have the courage to be cruel, having no weight of memory to teach temperance. Young, but so old, older than any stone. Their hair is silver, but full and long. Their eyes are black. But when they are at their work they become dogs, wolves, for they are hounds of death, and also hounds of joy. They take the strands of life in their jaws, and sometimes they are careful with their jagged teeth, and sometimes they are not. They gallop around a great monolith, the stone that pierces our Sphere where the meridians meet, that turns the Earth and pins it in place in the world. It is called the Spindle of Necessity, and all round it the wolves of fate run, and run, and run, and the patterns of their winding are the patterns of the world. Nothing can occur without them, but they take no sides.

I could also say there is such a stone, such a place, but the dogs who are women died long ago, and left the strands to fall, and we have been helpless ever since. That in a wolfless world we must find our own way. That is more comforting to me. I want my own way, I want to falter; I want to fail, and I want to be redeemed. All these things I want to spool out from the spindle that is me, not the spindle of the world. But I have heard both tales.

Ikram, Who Would One Day Pass Beyond the Gates of Alisaunder: I want to stay here, with you.

Lamis, Who Would One Day Become a Queen Like Her Mother, Shrouded in Mist: I want to be a child again, and fear nothing.

Houd, Who Would One Day Die in Jerusalem: There, Butterfly, there. Beginning tomorrow I will love you for all the rest of my life.

[There is more, so much more, but it all dissolved into nothing, in a slither of green and pale blue fungus that tears the living page from my hand and left me with nothing, nothing, no end and no answers, only that lonely boy and his need, and no bud for me, either, to follow Hiob into stillness and dreams and escape the disappointment, the loss of it. I had been widowed by these books, and abandoned. The soft weight of the spine cracked as I threw it, useless, against the wall. I wanted to know, curse them. I wanted to know everything.]

ADDENDUM TO THE CONFESSIONS OF
HIOB VON LUZERN, 1699:

Brothers, I send this back to you knowing in no fashion what tomorrow might bring. I send back Marcel and Abelard over the mountains to bear back this manuscript. Hiob felt at ease speaking to God, comfortably, two aged grandfathers exchanging tales. I can speak only to the page. I write knowing in no fashion what tomorrow may bring. For my own part, I will stay. Hiob cannot be moved, and I cannot leave him.

I have asked the woman in yellow to bear me back to the Tree of Books, so that I may attempt this tale again, make it more whole, fill the places the mold took from us. It is my intent to build a small hut there, on that plain, so as to lose no time transporting the manuscripts back here. It is not for love of Prester John I do this, but for love of Hiob, who should wake to illumination.

Oh, but I lie. I also want to know the rest, I also burn to learn what followed, I also find my heart grown bitter with having those books stolen from me too soon by the mere villainies of air and light. How those volumes corrupt in their turn, so that I feel within me tendrils of green, and red, and gold, swarming over my heart, eating me whole. *Take me back,* I said to her, *take me back, I cannot bear it.*

The woman in yellow, Theotokos, I suppose I must call her, looked intently at me for a long while.

"I will consider it," she said finally.

"Abbas will support me. It is not yours to decide."

The woman turned her head to one side, and I believe she almost smiled.

"It is my tree," she said softly. "It belongs to no one but me. Not Abbas, and not you. Go to him if you like. He rules at my pleasure."

And she made a curious gesture, stroking the skin of her neck, the space just above her collarbone, unselfconscious, bare.

And so I wait. I wait for her to convey me back to that place. I wait and think of Hagia, and Imtithal, and the strangeness of women. I wait and think of how the world was made. I make sure Marcel and Abelard are well stocked with eggs and meat and oranges, and send them off into the ashy day. I eat Abbas' chickens, and pray. Oh, how I pray. I pray you will not condemn us, at home, in those familiar halls, with those sweet chestnuts in the garden. Nothing was as we expected. We are but mortal men. We cannot be blamed for the shape and history of the world.

One further thing I must relate, and then Abelard is eager to depart, for he hates this place, and has the patience of a gadfly. But I have no explanation for what I wish to tell, and no knowledge of its meaning or purpose. I can only say, as John might: *It happened, no denying would stop it from having happened.*

Yesterday, as I sat beside Hiob's slab, dizzy with the scent of the flowery garlands, my master opened his mouth. I started, relief flooding me. He would wake, it would be all right. All would be well and all would be well—but he did not wake. His jaw cracked open, and out of his mouth a small, forked branch emerged, its foliage wet and wrinkled like newborn butterflies, its fruit nearly invisible, finer than dust. It grew out of him, slowly, a delicate stripling, studded with leaves like emeralds, glowing gently against his grey, senseless skin.

ACKNOWLEDGMENTS

When addressing the delicate issue of a book's genealogy, one has to begin at the beginning. I owe a great debt of thanks to Deborah Schwartz, my medieval studies professor at Cal Poly, who awakened in this lapsed Classicist a grand love of the medieval world that went far beyond the ersatz RenFaires of my youth and into something altogether stranger and deeper. Though I bear the shame of having failed to complete my graduate program, Dr. Schwartz rekindled my passion for Arthuriana, Chaucer, romances, and through all of that, finally, led me to the Kingdom of Prester John and all the wonders hidden there. Without her I would never have found my way.

Thank you also to my usual cohort: my husband Dmitri, who not only read every draft and loved them until I loved them too, but checked me into a hotel in the wilds of Maine until I finished this beast. To Elizabeth McClellan, who offered a kind beta read and reassured my frazzled soul, to SJ Tucker, my sister in crimes of art, to Tiffin Staib, Amal El-Mohtar, Deborah Castellano, and Evelyn Kriete, without whom I would be lost. To everyone who has helped me stand up, keep moving, keep smiling, never give up, never fail. You are my tribe; you are my blessed kingdom of monsters and angels.

To my agent, Howard Morhaim, I am forever grateful—he is the Dumbledore to all my bedraggled children, finding them magical homes when I despair. To my team of editors and copyeditors, Jeremy Lassen, Juliet Ulman, and Marty Halpern, all of whom taught me a great deal in the course of processing this book into the form you hold in your hands.

Finally, thank you to the anonymous student who once turned in a very bad poem about the priest-king in the East, and caused me to say to an empty office: *Prester John deserves better.*

Night Shade Books Is an Independent Publisher of Quality SF, Fantasy and Horror

"Michael A. Stackpole is incapable of writing a book that isn't imaginative and intelligent." — Stephen R. Donaldson

THE FIRST BOOK OF THE CROWN COLONIES

AT THE Queen's Command

NEW YORK TIMES BESTSELLING AUTHOR

MICHAEL A. STACKPOLE

ISBN: 978-1-59780-200-0, Trade Paperback; $14.99

1763: The Crown Colonies of Mystria are in turmoil, trapped between warring empires and facing insurrection from natives and colonists alike...

Captain Owen Strake, a wounded and battle-weary Redcoat of the Queen's Own Wurms, has come to this untamed land. At the Queen's command, Owen's mission is to survey this vast, uncharted territory, performing reconnaissance of rival Tharyngians and the savage Twilight People of the wilderness.

From *New York Times* bestselling author Michael A. Stackpole (*Rogue Squadron, I, Jedi*) comes *At the Queen's Command*, the first book of The Crown Colonies, a new fantasy series re-imagining the events of the American Revolutionary War.

Night Shade Books Is an Independent Publisher of Quality SF, Fantasy and Horror

"Jon Armstrong is a genius, with an umlaut, to the fifth power."
Michael Chabon - author of *Gentlemen of the Road*

YARN

JON ARMSTRONG

ISBN: 978-1-59780-210-9, Trade Paperback; $14.99

Tane Cedar is the master tailor, the supreme outfitter of the wealthy, the beautiful, and the powerful. When an ex-lover, on the run from the authorities, asks him to create a garment from the dangerous and illegal Xi yarn—a psychedelic opiate—to ease her final hours, Tane's world is torn apart.

Armed with just his yarn pulls, scissors, Mini-Air-Juki handheld sewing machine, and his wits, Tane journeys through the shadowy underworld where he must untangle the deadly mysteries and machinations of decades of deceit.

From the neo-feudalistic slubs, the corn-filled world of Tane's youth, to his apprenticeship among the deadly saleswarriors of Seattlehama, the sex-and-shopping capital of the world, to the horrors of a polluted Antarctica, *Yarn* tells a stylish tale of love, deceit, and memory.

Night Shade Books Is an Independent Publisher of Quality SF, Fantasy and Horror

PUMP SIX

AND OTHER STORIES

PAOLO BACIGALUPI

"Deeply thought provoking, Bacigalupi's collected visions of the future are equal parts cautionary tale, social and political commentary and poignantly poetic, revelatory prose."
—*Publishers Weekly Starred Review*

ISBN 978-1-59780-202-4, Trade Paperback; $14.99

Paolo Bacigalupi's debut collection demonstrates the power and reach of the science fiction short story. Social criticism, political parable, and environmental advocacy lie at the center of Paolo's work. Each of the stories herein is at once a warning and a celebration of the tragic comedy of the human experience.

The eleven stories in *Pump Six* represent the best of Paolo's work, including the Hugo nominee "Yellow Card Man," the Nebula- and Hugo-nominated story "The People of Sand and Slag," and the Sturgeon Award-winning story "The Calorie Man." The title story is original to this collection. With this book, Paolo Bacigalupi takes his place alongside SF short fiction masters Ted Chiang, Kelly Link, and others, as an important young writer that directly and unabashedly tackles today's most important issues.

Catherynne M. Valente is the author of over a dozen books of fiction and poetry, including *Palimpsest*, the Orphan's Tales series, and *The Girl Who Circumnavigated Fairyland in a Ship of Own Making*. She is the winner of the Tiptree Award, the Andre Norton Award, the Lambda Award, the Mythopoeic Award, the Rhysling Award, and the Million Writers Award. She was a finalist for the World Fantasy Award in 2007 and 2009, and the Locus and Hugo awards in 2010. She lives on an island off the coast of Maine with her partner, two dogs, an enormous cat, and an accordion.